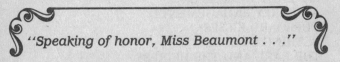
"*Speaking of honor, Miss Beaumont . . .*"

"*No, my lord, I know what you are going to say, and I don't want to hear it. I do not want your words of honor and duty and making things right.*"

He brushed a curl away from her cheek. "*No? What words should I say instead?*"

Words of love, you cloth head, she wanted to shout.

He was staring into her eyes as if the answers to the universe were hidden there. His fingers stroked her knitted brows, her chin, her lips, sending tremors where she did not know tremors could go. "*Perhaps we do not need words after all. . . .*" *His hands had moved to her back, pulling her closer, till their lips came together. . . .*

CHRISTMAS WISHES

Barbara Metzger

FAWCETT CREST · NEW YORK

A Fawcett Crest Book
Published by Ballantine Books
Copyright © 1992 by Barbara Metzger

Library of Congress Catalog Card Number: 92-90598

ISBN 0-449-22078-8

Manufactured in the United States of America

First Edition: November 1992

To the one-year-old Montauk Library with congratulations and best wishes, to the Friends of the
Montauk Library with love, and to Ann, with
thanks.

Chapter One

Juneclaire wished she did not have to spend another Christmas at Stanton Hall. "You would have liked the way Christmas used to be," she told her companion, Pansy. Pansy just grunted and continued her investigation of all the parcels being wrapped and put into baskets for the servants' and tenants' Boxing Day gifts. Bright ribbons, shiny paper, and mounds of presents and treats were spread on two tables and the floor of the rear pantry Miss Juneclaire Beaumont was using to assemble Lady Stanton's largess. Lady Stanton was being very generous this year. She had directed her niece Juneclaire to knit mittens for all the children, to hem handkerchiefs for all the footmen and grooms, and to sew rag dolls for the little girls on the estate. Juneclaire had also been sent to the nearby village of Farley's Grange to purchase new shawls for the tenants' wives and whistles and tops for the boys. All week she had been busy helping Cook bake plum cakes, decorate gingerbread men, and create marzipan angels, after tying colorful ribbons around pots of jam from the berries she had collected all summer and fall. She also made sachets of the lavender she had drying in the stillroom and poured out rose water into little bottles for the

1

maidservants. The orchards provided shiny apples, and Uncle Avery Stanton provided shiny coins. Oh yes, and Aunt Marta Stanton provided a new Bible for each of the servants, whether they could read or not. Last year the gift was a hymnal, the year before a book of sermons. Aunt Marta was very consistent in her Christian charity.

Lady Stanton was so consistent, in fact, that her own niece would receive one of the Bibles and a shiny coin as her Christmas gift and naught else.

It wasn't that she minded being treated worse than the servants, Juneclaire reflected, pausing to share one of the crisp apples with Pansy. Nor did she mind all the work, though that was considerable at this time of year, with helping the maids air the unused rooms for holiday guests and directing the footmen in hanging the greenery after Juneclaire fashioned it into wreaths and garlands. No, she was used to being useful. What she could not and would not get inured to was being used, to being considered a serf with no salary or self-respect. Juneclaire acknowledged that she was a poor relation and that she owed Lord and Lady Stanton her gratitude for the very roof over her head. How could she not accept the fact, when Aunt Marta reminded her daily?

"Still," she told Pansy, pushing a soft brown curl back under her mobcap, "they could have been kinder." Pansy was too busy redistributing a pile of apricot tarts to notice Juneclaire wipe a suddenly damp brown eye with her sleeve. "Here," Juneclaire said, looking over her shoulder, "you'd better not let Aunt Marta see you nibbling on those or we'll be in the briers for sure." She tied a bow on a pair of warm knitted socks and sniffed. "She could at least have let us stir the Christmas pudding and make a wish with everyone else."

Lady Stanton did not believe in such nonsense.

2

She thought such superstitions were heathenish and not at all suitable for a Stanton of Stanton Hall or one of their household. She could not stop the kitchen staff, naturally, not if she wanted a smooth pudding to serve her guests, but she could see that her niece was kept too busy for any pagan rituals. If it were up to Lady Stanton, Christmas would be spent on one's knees, in church. There would be none of this mad jollity, this extravagance of entertaining and gifting. Aunt Marta was religious, proper, strict—and cheap. She wouldn't even distribute Boxing Day gifts if it were not for Lord Stanton and the fact that to discontinue the tradition would disgruntle the dependents and, worse, make her look paltry in the neighborhood. Lady Stanton was very careful of her standing among the local gentry, especially since her own roots did not bear close scrutiny, with their ties to Trade. She had worked hard to earn that "Lady" before her name and intended to enjoy its rewards. If being accepted as the first family in the vicinity meant showing off her generosity once a year, Juneclaire could handle the details. If it meant giving hearth space to her misbegotten waif of a niece, Juneclaire could at least be put to work and molded to Lady Stanton's measure.

Juneclaire kept wrapping bundles, trying to make a happy Christmas for those less fortunate than she was. At least she tried to convince herself that the servants were less fortunate, even though they got an actual wage and could move to another position; the tenants were less well established than Juneclaire, although they worked to better their own lives and had families who cared about them.

"Things were not always this way," she informed her companion. Aunt Marta would have been horrified to see Juneclaire's hands go still while she recalled earlier Christmases, when Maman lifted her up to stir the pudding and make her wish. Papa used to smile at the English ways and tousle her curls. He always knew her wish anyway, and he would laugh. His *petite fleur* only wanted a puppy or a kitten or a pony. Juneclaire received gloves and combs and books and dolls and sweets and, at last, a pony, despite a lack of funds.

Then she and Maman returned to England without Papa, without her pony, to this cold and damp Stanton Hall with its disapproving ancestors frowning down on her from their portraits on the wall. That year she wished that the horrors in Papa's homeland would be over soon and he would send for them. Maman gave her a locket to wear, with a tiny painting of her and Papa in it. Juneclaire touched it now, under her worn brown wool gown.

The next Christmas, when they knew Papa was not coming for them, Juneclaire wished Maman would be stronger in her loss, but she was not, and then Juneclaire was nine years old and alone. For the next ten years she tried not to wish for what could never be.

Juneclaire tried to be grateful for the grudging charity, truly she did, winning the respect of the servants, at least, with her quiet acceptance of her lot. They considered Juneclaire a true lady, sweet and caring, not like some they could mention, with jumped-up airs. Of course, Juneclaire's being a lady set her apart. The staff could take pity on the orphaned chit, and they could be kind to her when Lady Stanton was not looking, but they could not be her friends, not if they wanted to keep their positions. Aunt Marta did not condone familiarity between the classes. For the same reason she did not permit her niece to play with the village children. Juneclaire wasn't good enough to merit a governess or new frocks or a maid to wait on her, but she was too genteel for the locals: her mother was a Stanton. So Juneclaire had no friends.

She did have her cousins, however, if two loud, unruly imps of Satan could be consolation to a gentle female. She was as relieved as everyone else on the estate except Lady Stanton when Rupert and Newton finally went away to school. In earlier days they had made her life an endless hell of creepy things in her bed, slimy things in her slippers, crawly things in her porridge. She was the unwilling plunder when they played pirate, the dragon's victim when they played at knights. They tied her up, locked her in closets, terrorized her in dark attics. And if *her* hair got mussed, *her* pinafore got soiled, she got a lecture from Aunt Marta and no supper. Dearest Rupert, Juneclaire's age, and baby Newton, a year younger, were just high-spirited, according to their fond mother. The Root and the Newt, as their not-so-fond and often-hungry cousin termed them, had no redeeming virtues whatsoever, except that she could listen in on their lessons and ride their ponies when the boys outgrew them.

If Christmas seasons were never joyous for Juneclaire at Stanton Hall, now they were less so when the boys came home for holiday with the only knowledge her scapegrace relatives seemed to have absorbed at Harrow: carnal knowledge.

At age eighteen, Newt was a thin, spotty-faced budding tulip, with yellow pantaloons, high shirt collars, and roving hands. Nineteen-year-old Root was short and stocky, with sausage fingers and damp lips with which Juneclaire was growing altogether too familiar. She'd taken to avoiding dark corridors and to carrying a darning needle slipped through her lace collar as a weapon. Even if Juneclaire were willing—and hell would freeze over first—she thought she'd be without more than her supper if Aunt Marta caught her in one of her darlings' embraces. Root and Newt were so stupid, though, they thought she was just playing hard to get, as they nursed their various pinpricks.

Aunt Marta would not have anything as indecorous as a kissing bough in her house, of course, but the brats had discovered a patch of mistletoe and took great joy in bedeviling Juneclaire in public places, where she could not retaliate. Unaware of her own prettiness, Juneclaire could not understand why they did not share their ardor with a willing housemaid, the way Uncle Avery did. She did not think she could mention this to the randy rattlepates, however, nor could she complain to her aunt, who would only find Juneclaire at fault for her wanton looks. No matter how hard Juneclaire stared at her mirror, she could find nothing siren-like about brown hair, brown eyes, and thick brown eyebrows. Her mouth seemed too full and her nose too short, especially in comparison with her beautiful mother's miniature. And Juneclaire knew for a fact there could be nothing seductive about the shapeless, drab gowns she wore at Aunt Marta's insistence. They were so high-necked and loose-fitting that Root was eighteen before he even discovered she had a bosom. Unfortunately, octopus-armed Newt was not as mutton-headed.

Juneclaire could have gone to Uncle Avery with her problems, she supposed, but he would likely have patted her head and handed her a shilling, the way he used to when he found her in tears. Now she stood taller than the short, portly frame Root had inherited, and she had a fair stock of shillings. She also felt too sorry for her uncle to bring him more difficulties. The poor man hated what he called mingle-mangles, which meant he avoided his lady and her sons every chance he got, contenting himself with his pigs and sheep and cows—and housemaids. To say he was henpecked was a vast understatement. If he were a slice of bread, there'd be no place to spread jam. So Juneclaire made sure her door was locked at night and wished every year would be her last Christmas at Stanton Hall. This year just might be the one.

"What, are you still at this foolish task, you lazy girl? You should have been finished hours ago. I need you to make out the place cards for tomorrow's dinner, Claire." Aunt Marta could not bring herself to give Juneclaire her proper name, considering it too foreign, too affected for one in her niece's position. Lady Stanton unwrapped an apricot tart and held it up to her sharp nose before biting into it. She poked her bony fingers into the various boxes and trays. Lady Stanton had as much meat on her bones as she had human kindness in her heart. "I am placing you between Captain Fancroft and Squire Holmes. You may ask the captain about the war, but remember that no gentleman expects or wishes a lady to be knowledgeable. Whatever you say, do not disagree with him. Squire Holmes is interested in his children and the hunt. You shall *not* express your queer notions of sympathy for the fox. Do you understand, miss?"

"Yes, Aunt Marta. No, I shan't, Aunt Marta," Juneclaire replied from long practice.

"And see that you don't take off your gloves. No need for anyone to see your hands ain't as smooth as a lady's."

"But I *am* a lady, Aunt."

"Hoity-toity, miss. You'll stop putting on airs, too, if you hope to snabble an eligible *parti*."

Juneclaire rather thought she did, even if she wouldn't have used those terms. This year she was being permitted to join Aunt Marta's annual Christmas Eve gathering, in hopes that she would attract some gentleman's eye. There was to be no

7

London Season for Juneclaire, not even a come-out ball in her honor, for Aunt Marta was too nipfarthing and too ashamed of this product of a runaway match between Miss Clara Stanton and her dancing master. Even if Jules Beaumont had been son to a *duc*, he was the third son of an early victim of the Terror, the family wealth confiscated by the upstarts. Juneclaire saw nothing to be embarrassed over in her heritage, even if her parents did not marry until reaching France, and in a Catholic church at that.

Now she raised her chin and said, "I do not think my birth will count against me with a true gentleman, not if he cares for me."

"Poppycock, just see that you don't give them a disgust of you. Holmes needs a mother for his brats, and Fancroft wants an heir while he can still sire one."

"But . . . but aren't there to be any younger men at the party?"

"Not for you there won't be. What did you think, some storybook hero was going to fall in love with your doe eyes? Young men don't offer marriage to dowerless chits with tainted names. They offer *carte blanche*." Aunt Marta checked the hems of the handkerchiefs.

Ah, well, perhaps the captain would be knowledgeable on closer acquaintance, or the squire kindly. She wouldn't mind children, not if it meant a house of her own, away from Stanton Hall, if the gentleman Aunt Marta picked out was nice. She made the mistake of asking.

"Nice? What has that to do with it? You'll take the first one that offers for you or you can go to the poorhouse, for all I care. It's time and enough someone else paid your bills and bought your clothes."

Juneclaire knew the threat of the poorhouse was only that. Aunt Marta would never let the neighborhood see her treat a blood relation in so miserly a fashion, nor would her aunt part with an unpaid servant so easily. No, Fancroft and Holmes must be warm enough in the pocket to offer Lady Stanton handsome settlements for her niece's hand, which meant Juneclaire dared not refuse. And what choice did she have, after all, but to marry a man of her aunt's selection? She never met any strangers, sequestered away at the Hall and traveling no farther than Farley's Grange, and she was ill-equipped for anything but marriage. She was not well-enough educated to go for a governess, she was too shy to go on the stage, and she did not sew quickly enough to be a seamstress. Mostly, she did not have enough patience to continue on as her aunt's lackey.

With the optimism that came with youth and the season of surprises, Miss Beaumont hoped for better than an aging roué or a beleaguered widower. If only Juneclaire could have made her pudding wish, she would have asked for a handsome cavalier, no matter what Aunt Marta said.

At least she had her pretty new gown. White velvet it was, with a high waist and low neck and tiny puff sleeves. Aunt Marta meant her to look like a debutante of the ton: respectable, virginal, à la mode. If all went well, she could be married in the same dress, avoiding additional expense. Juneclaire had spent some of her precious shillings for green ribbon to trim the gown and had woven a crown of holly for her hair. She thought she would do very well, with her mother's pearls and the Norwich silk shawl she knew Uncle Avery meant to give her. Perhaps there would be a young beau who did not need to marry for money or consequence. Aunt Marta didn't know everything, Juneclaire thought with a smile. She didn't know about Uncle Avery's housemaids.

Lady Stanton was checking the names on the

filled baskets, peevishly hurrying Juneclaire along toward her next chore. She removed the bottle of rose water from the package marked Lily; Juneclaire's smile faded. Then Aunt Marta caught sight of Pansy.

"What is that . . . that *creature* doing here?" she shouted, her thin frame going rigid in anger. "I told you yesterday Cook was looking for her in the kitchens! I abhor these unseemly friendships you insist on striking up, Claire, and I won't have it. What if Squire Holmes found out? Captain Fancroft would be revolted, I am sure. I won't have your disobedience, do you hear me?"

Juneclaire was sure the whole kitchen staff heard her, and she blushed with embarrassment. Pansy ran to hide behind Juneclaire as Aunt Marta slammed the door behind her. Lady Stanton stomped off, insisting for the rest of the household who might have missed her earlier screaming that she hadn't raised up a penniless orphan out of the goodness of her heart just to be made a laughing-stock, and where was that bobbing-block of a husband of hers when she needed him to do something about his niece and her willful ways.

"Don't worry, Pansy," Juneclaire whispered, leaving the boxes and baskets, leaving the pantry, but not leaving Pansy in the kitchen.

Now, Juneclaire might have been willing to sacrifice her hopes and dreams on Aunt Marta's altar of greed and meanness, for she was a dutiful girl. She might have put on the prettiest gown she'd ever owned and put herself on display for her aunt's guests, hoping to impress them with Lady Stanton's beneficence. She was even ready to try to charm some overweight old seaman into a declaration to please her aunt. But not Pansy. She would not let Aunt Marta sacrifice Pansy just to puff off her own consequence, just because Pansy was little and lame.

Well, wishing hadn't brought Maman or Papa back, and it would not bring her any handsome and wealthy knight riding to her rescue. Wishing was certainly not going to save Pansy. That Juneclaire had to do herself. So she did. She gathered her few belongings, including the velvet gown and her heaviest cloak, a gray wool that used to be her aunt's. The rabbit lining looked more like rat fur after all these years, but she would need the warmth if she and Pansy were to reach London, where Mrs. Simms, the old housekeeper, resided. Juneclaire hastily estimated that by nightfall she could reach the market village of Strasmere, where not many people would recognize her, especially with the hood of her cloak up. Tomorrow she could find a farmer going to Bramley, the nearest posting stop, and then in a day she would be in London. She counted out her hoard of shillings and nodded. They ought to be enough. Juneclaire wrapped half of them and her mother's pearls in a stocking, which she tucked inside the loose bodice of her gown. The rest she placed in her reticule, along with Mrs. Simms's last letter. She wrapped a white muffler around her neck, knotted off an unfinished pair of mittens, and put them on, not caring that one was shorter than the other. Then she went to the kitchens, where she filled every nook of her carpetbag and every pocket of her cloak with bread and cheese and apples and sliced meats. "For the poorhouse," she told the gaping scullery maid. "So they have a better Christmas, too."

Juneclaire left Stanton Hall without looking back. She did not leave a farewell note. She did not leave her aunt's Christmas dinner.

Unfortunately, Juneclaire's almost instant planning did not take into account Pansy's lameness.

The poor dear couldn't walk far or fast. Miss Beaumont had also not considered that many others would be on the road for the holidays and that there would, indeed, be no rooms at the inn at Strasmere, or the next down the road, or the next. Sheltered as she was, Juneclaire never would have guessed that most innkeepers and their wives would not accept a single woman, traveling without servants, on foot, and in dubious company.

"I run a respectable establishment, I do," she heard over and over. "I'm not having the likes of such a one at *my* inn, I'm not."

Juneclaire raised her determined chin and lowered her thick eyebrows. She was not going back to Stanton Hall, not even if she had to sleep under hedgerows. She would get to London, even if she had to walk the whole way, carrying Pansy.

Chapter Two

*L*ord Merritt Jordan, the Earl of St. Cloud, wished he did not have to spend Christmas at home. He flicked the whip over the leader's left ear as the curricle straightened after a turn that sent the outer wheels two feet in the air. His groom, Foley, took the liberty of long years in service, and a short glimpse of eternity, to speak up. As soon as his insides righted themselves, Foley shouted from his perch behind the driver's seat that he'd rather eat his mincemeat pie than be one. "An' the way you been cursin' about havin' to be somewheres you don't want, I can't figure why you're drivin' like the Devil hisself is behind us, my lord, and catchin' up fast."

St. Cloud frowned, not at the familiarity but at the truth. Damn and blast, he was in no hurry to get to the Priory in Berkshire. He obligingly slowed the pace a fraction. "Now the Devil won't have to run so hard." Why should he, when hell was waiting up ahead?

Foley shook his grizzled head but relaxed a little. Now they were traveling at death-defying speed, not necessarily death-wishing, and there was no one he'd trust with the ribbons more than his master. If Lord St. Cloud didn't have the lightest hands with the reins, aye, and the surest eye toward horseflesh, besides the truest aim with a pistol, the neatest right in the ring and the sharpest skill with the pasteboards of any gentleman in St. James's Street, Foley would eat his hat. If it hadn't blown off a mile outside London. Blister it, if Lord St. Cloud didn't have his black moods like now, he'd well nigh be the best employer in London Town. He was fair and generous, not toplofty, and he didn't truck with women.

Foley had no fondness for the female species; they only distracted a man from the important business in life, like war and wagering. What with their weeping and clinging and flirting and spending every groat of a chap's income, they were more trouble than they were worth, by half. It was a good thing, in Foley's opinion, that Lord St. Cloud was not in the petticoat line. Not that the silly geese wouldn't be littering my lord's doorstep if he smiled on them. With his wealth and title, the debutantes would be pawing each other aside to catch his attention. With his wealth and finely muscled frame the demireps would be clawing one another's eyes out. And with his dark, brooding looks and well-chiseled features, green eyes and cleft chin, every other female from sixteen to sixty would be gnawing on him like a bone, with or without his incredible wealth. If he smiled at them.

Luckily for Foley's misogynistic peace of mind, Lord St. Cloud seldom smiled at anyone, and at women least of all. The groom spit over the downwind side of the careening carriage. Give him his horses anytime. Many years ago, when Foley was a jockey, a waitress at the Green Knight had run off with a linen draper's assistant; the shop boy's hands were clean, she said, and he didn't smell of the stable. That's why Foley frowned if a pretty gal

14

looked his way. Foley never understood about his master's dour expression and dark humors.

"I don't see what's got you in such a takin'," he muttered now, hanging on for dear life as the earl dropped his hands for the grays to pass a mail coach. "After all, it's Christmas and you're goin' home."

Foley couldn't see St. Cloud's sneer from his position at the earl's back, even if the groom's eyes weren't shut as they missed the coach by inches. Home, hah! Merritt Jordan had felt more at home on the French prison ship. At least there he'd had friends among the other captives. He'd only had to worry about disease, vermin, and hunger—not his relatives. Spending any holiday at St. Cloud Priory at Ayn-Jerome outside Thackford, much less Christmas and his birthday, was more like doing penance for being born.

They would all be there, all the vultures. His mother would see to that, filling the moldering old pile with relations, guests, and hangers-on, just so she did not have to face him alone. And they'd all want something of him, as always: money, favors, compliance with *their* standards for *his* behavior. Cousin Niles would have his usual sheaf of tailors' bills and gambling debts to be paid, and Cousin Elsbeth would still be whining for a London Season. Lord Harmon Wilmott, their father and St. Cloud's uncle, would shake his jowls and issue another lecture on St. Cloud's duties and responsibilities. St. Cloud was the last of the Jordan line, Uncle Harmon would intone; he owed his ancestors a continuance. Mother's brother undoubtedly meant that the earl should marry Elsbeth, saving Lord Harmon the expense and aggravation and keeping the wealth in the family, the Wilmott family, that was.

St. Cloud clenched his fists, and the horses took exception. When he had them back under his perfect control and Foley had quit muttering, he returned to his musings of what lay ahead. Grandmother, blind as a bat for the last five years, would be nagging at him that she wanted to see her great-grandchildren, and soon. And every female in the county who could scrape up an acquaintance would be calling, with hopes of becoming the next Countess St. Cloud, by come-hither hook or by compromising-situation crook. He dare not walk in his own shrubbery without an escort or sit at ease in his own library unless the door was locked. Hell and damnation, he thought, not for the first time. The Priory already had enough Lady St. Clouds, and those two did not even speak to each other, not without his grandmother, the dowager, shouting, or Lady Fanny, his mother and current countess until he married, weeping.

The closer his carriage got to the Priory, the more St. Cloud understood how a winded deer felt surrounded by wolves. But he was not defenseless, he reminded himself. He was no longer a child who had to abide by adult rules. He was a grown man, twenty-nine years of age, and Uncle Harmon was no longer his trustee or warder. St. Cloud had made that plain four years ago, the day he came into his majority, after waiting a young lifetime of oppression.

Merritt Jordan had, like most of his class, been raised by wet nurses, nannies, and nursemaids. He seldom saw his parents, his mother being too highstrung for the duties of motherhood and his father not being interested. Then came his father's "accident," as they called it, and subsequent death two years later, when St. Cloud was seven years old. Lady Fanny's nerves deteriorated to such an extent that she could not bear to have her son near her. He was too noisy, too active. He might break something.

Her father took over the management of the estate since there were no male Jordan relatives. Lord Wilmott and Grandmother had such rows about raising the new tenth earl that Lady Fanny took to her bed for a year. Lord Wilmott moved his own family from Motthaven next door into the Priory, and the elder Lady St. Cloud moved to the dower house. Uncle Harmon took over the guardianship when he ascended to his father's baronetcy and later brought his own motherless children to reside under the Jordan banner—and checkbook.

Niles and later Elsbeth could run wild over the estate; St. Cloud had to be groomed for his future dignities. Niles could go off to school at thirteen; St. Cloud at the same age was too delicate to jeopardize among the other sons of the upper ten thousand. Of course his life was precious to the Wilmotts. Without St. Cloud they would have to live on their own neglected property, within their own modest means, for the earldom reverted back to the Crown.

On the one hand, he was wrapped in cotton wool, given the fattest, most placid ponies to ride, kept away from guns and swords, swaddled like an infant prone to croup. On the other hand, he was force-fed a rigorous education by one sanctimonious, sadistic tutor after another. The last was a young curate, Mr. Forbush, who licked his lips when he birched the young earl at every excuse. Lady Fanny cried and did nothing. She was as in awe of her overbearing brother as she had been of her dictatorial father and her grim husband. Uncle Harmon saw nothing wrong with beating the impertinence out of a young boy who questioned his trustee's cutting in the home woods, raising the tenants' rents, or selling off the Thoroughbred stud farm. He approved of Mr. Forbush to such an extent that when St. Cloud finally went to university, Uncle Harmon kept the curate on as the family's spiritual adviser. The hypocrite rained hellfire and brimstone down on the household every Sunday in the old Priory's chapel of St. Jerome of the Clouds. Lady Fanny was confirmed in her belief that she would burn in purgatory, and Uncle Harmon was convinced his self-righteous sacrifices on his nephew's behalf would be rewarded in the afterlife.

The earl enjoyed the partial freedom of university life. He excelled at his studies, but he also found outlets for the years of anger and neglect in athletic pursuits, honing his whip-tight muscles and deadly skills. None of the other lads was foolish enough to think St. Cloud was merely competing for fun. Fun did not seem to exist in the young peer's vocabulary.

St. Cloud's dream, when he came down from university, was to join the army like his deceased uncle George Jordan, whose name was never mentioned. The dowager ranted, Lady Fanny wept, Mr. Forbush prayed. And Uncle Harmon refused. Merritt Jordan was still the last St. Cloud. No Corsican upstart was going to capsize Wilmott's gravy boat.

Defeated, St. Cloud threw himself into Town life like a sailor on shore after months at sea. He followed his frivolous cousin Niles into gaming dens and bawdy houses. He surpassed him in reckless wagers and hey-go-mad stunts. He ran up debts and ran with lightskirts. He skirted the law with innumerable duels and became known as Satan St. Cloud, a deadly rakehell who took his pleasures seriously. Except that he found no pleasure in such an existence, beyond aggravating Uncle Harmon.

On his twenty-fifth birthday, St. Cloud waited until Mr. Forbush had given his Christmas sermon, not about the Holy Child and Peace on Earth, but about the sins of the fathers, blasphemy, adultery, murder. Forbush stared at St. Cloud and licked his lips.

One step outside the chapel doors the curate found himself in an iron-hard grip, being dragged to the gatehouse, where the Earl of St. Cloud celebrated Christmas his own way, beating a man of the cloth to within an inch of his life, then tossing him over the gate like a sack of refuse.

St. Cloud strode back to the house and his astounded relatives with a look on his face that could have been a grimace on anyone else's. London bucks would have recognized it as the St. Cloud smile and fled. The earl notified Uncle Harmon that his services were no longer required; a bailiff had been hired. With a green-eyed look that could stop molten lava in its course, St. Cloud informed him and Niles that the London solicitors were already advised to direct Wilmott bills to Motthaven, not the Priory. He told his mother that if she did not put off her blacks and cease the weeping after nearly twenty years, she could very well go live with Lady St. Cloud in the dower house.

Having turned the Priory nicely on its ear, the earl returned to London to purchase his own commission. Prinny himself refused the request, unless and until St. Cloud had assured the succession. He almost went to marry the first Covent Garden doxie he could find, out of spite, but not even Satan St. Cloud could go through with such an affront to his ancestors. Besides, in the nine months it would take to beget a son, Bonny could be defeated. Or the child might be a girl.

Instead the earl took the offered position of liaison between the War Office and the quartermaster general. The Regent asked him to accept, to see why the troops were not properly outfitted, why ammunition did not reach Wellesley's men in time. A request from the Regent was as good as a command, so St. Cloud became a paper merchant, by damn! He saw enough graft and corruption to disgust even a politician and ended by using some of his own blunt to expedite orders. Three months later he convinced his superior that the only way to see where deliveries were running afoul was in person—St. Cloud's person.

With every intention of joining up with some regiment or other in Spain, St. Cloud boarded a convoy ship for the Peninsula. The ship was attacked and sunk. The earl was wounded and captured and imprisoned on a French barque, without ever touching Spanish soil. Whitehall was not best pleased to have to trade four French officers of high rank for his release, and St. Cloud was furious that part of his parole—negotiated by Uncle Harmon, indubitably—was his word as a gentleman not to take up arms against his captors again.

No longer in good odor at the War Office, St. Cloud took his seat in the Lords and did what he could there for the war effort, for the returning veterans. Fusty political pettifoggery satisfied him as little as bumbling bureaucracy, so he resumed his Town life, but with some new moderation. Merritt Jordan had nothing left to prove and only himself to aggravate with outrageous behavior, like now, when the headache he had from too much drink and too little sleep was pounding in his temples with each beat of the horses' hooves. He should have known better than to start the journey so late. Hell, he thought, neatly turning the grays into the courtyard of the Rose and the Crown with inches to spare between them and an overladen departing carriage, he should have made some excuse to avoid the Priory altogether. He usually did.

While the grays were being changed for his lordship's own matched chestnuts, sent ahead three days ago, St. Cloud was ushered into the inn's best private parlor, also reserved. Over a steaming mug of the landlord's renowned spiced punch, St. Cloud mused that no matter how much he struggled, some bonds never came undone. When Uncle Harmon tried to inflict his opinions on his nephew, St. Cloud could stare him into silence, without even hinting at irregularities in the trust's bookkeeping. St. Cloud could control the wilder excesses of his basket-scrambling cousin Niles with pocketbook governance, and he could challenge any man whose loose tongue overcame his instincts for self-preservation enough to probe the St. Cloud family history. But he could not deal with his womenfolk at all.

He could not frown them into submission, for Grandmother was blind and Mother always had her eyes covered with a damp cloth or a lace-edged handkerchief, albeit not a black-bordered one any longer. He could not affect their behavior through the purse strings either, since both widows' jointures were generous, and he could certainly not still their querulous demands with threats of physical violence. All he could do was stay away.

For two groats he'd have spent the holidays in London, where his latest mistress would have found some way of enlivening his birthday. Instead he was on the road to Berkshire to face the ghosts of his past, literally.

Tapping in the wainscoting, wailing through the chimneys, disappearing foodstuffs—the Priory ghosts were walking the halls. Murdered monks, squirrels in the secret passages, or bats in Lady Fanny's belfry, his mother's letters had gone from her usual vaporish complaints to hysterical gibberish about divine retribution. And company coming.

St. Cloud tossed back another cup of punch and called Foley out of the taproom. At least he did not have to travel in state, cooped in a stuffy coach for endless hours. His bags and valet had gone on ahead yesterday, so he could have the pleasure of tooling the curricle and his priceless cattle through the cold, barren, winter-wrapped countryside. The dreary scenery matched his mood, and Foley knew better than to complain about the speed again, until the chestnuts showed off their high spirits by nearly wrapping the curricle around a signpost.

"I thought you meant the beasts to make it through the next stages an' on to the Priory without a change," Foley shouted over the wind. "They'll be blown way 'fore that, at this rate."

"I think the horses have more heart than you do, old man," St. Cloud replied. "They'll do. I intend to slow down before long to give them a rest anyway, but you want to get to a warm bed tonight, don't you?"

"Aye, and I'm thinkin' there'll be some eggnog and spice cake waiting. So I'd as lief get there in one piece, if it's all the same to you, my lord."

Eggnog and spice cake and Christmas carolers. Marriageable women, skittish women, swooning women. Ghosts and ghouls and noises in the night. "Bloody hell."

The expletive may have been for Foley's impudence, or it may have been for St. Cloud's black thoughts, or perhaps for the tree fallen across the roadway. Foley did not know. He got down to assess the situation as soon as the chestnuts came to a halt, and St. Cloud reached into his greatcoat pocket. Too late. Two men rode out of the screening bushes, and one of them already held his pistol on the defenseless groom.

"Stand and deliver."

Chapter Three

"*B*loody hell."

"Nothing to get riled over, Yer Highness," the man with the gun called out from Foley's side. He was big and broad and had a scarf pulled up over his mouth and a slouch hat pulled down low over his eyes. "Just raise yer hands up slow, like, and everything will be aces."

The other highwayman had dismounted and was holding the chestnuts' bridles. He was also bundled past recognition, but he was smaller, slighter, and as nervous as the horses he was trying to calm. He did not have a weapon in sight, so St. Cloud weighed the odds.

"None of that, Yer Highness," the first man said, catching the earl's tentative movement. He used the butt end of his pistol on Foley's head, then turned the barrel on St. Cloud.

The other robber jumped. "What'd you go and do that for, Charlie? You never said nothing about—"

"Shut your mouth, boy. Do you want to make him an introduction? Can't you see the toff is a real out-and-outer? He was going to go for the gun sooner or later, and much help you'd 'a' been. I couldn't keep both of 'em covered, now, could I?"

"But you shouldn't've hit him so hard. What if he's dead?"

"If he is dead, Charlie," the earl said in a voice that was like cold steel, "your life is not worth a ha'penny."

"Fine words for a gent what's got his arms up in the air," Charlie blustered, but he dismounted and nudged Foley with his toe until the little man groaned. "There, now can we finish this argle-bargle and get to business? You toss the pistol out first, real slow so I don't get twitch-fingered. And remember, I ain't tenderhearted like my green friend here."

St. Cloud's wallet was next, then his gold fob, quizzing glass, silver flask, and emerald stickpin.

"And the ring, too, Yer Highness," Charlie said, searching Foley's pockets for the groom's purse but never taking his eyes, or the gun, off the earl.

"It's a signet ring with my family crest on it. No fence would give a brass farthing for the thing, for they could never resell it; if you're ever found with it, it's your death warrant for sure."

"Let it be, Charlie," the youngster begged. "We have enough."

"Chicken gizzard," Charlie grumbled, leading his horse closer to the curricle to pick up the booty from where St. Cloud had thrown it to the ground. A quick shake of the earl's leather purse had him agreeing and getting back on his horse. "Reckon it's a good day's work, and it is the season for givin', ain't it? Stand back, boy."

The youth let go of the horses, but before St. Cloud could lower his hands and find the ribbons, Charlie fired his pistol right over the chestnuts' backs. "Merry Christmas, Yer Highness," he shouted after the rocketing curricle.

* * *

The thieves were long gone by the time St. Cloud could catch up the reins and slow the frenzied animals, then turn them back to find Foley. The groom was limping toward him along the verge, holding a none-too-clean kerchief to a gash on the side of his head. St. Cloud jumped down and hurried to him, leaving the chestnuts standing with their heads lowered. There was no fear of their spooking anymore this day.

"How bad does it hurt, Foley?" he asked, pulling off his own neck cloth to make a bandage. "Can you hold on to the next inn or should I come back for you with a wagon?"

"Don't fatch so, m'lord, I'll do. 'Tain't my head what's botherin' me as much as my pride anyways. The chestnuts could've been hurt in that panic run. And you, too," he added as an afterthought, seeing the twitch in the earl's lips. "To think I was taken in by that old trick like a regular Johnny Raw, why, I'm slumguzzled for sure."

St. Cloud helped the older man back up to the curricle, wishing he had his flask, at least. "Whatever that is, don't blame yourself. I shouldn't have been wool-gathering either, but who would have thought there'd be bridle culls on this side road in Berkshire?"

"Amateurs, they was, you could tell."

"Yes, I was able to convince them to leave my ring, when any flat knows the thing can be melted down for the gold."

The groom spit through his teeth in disgust. "An' only one gun between them."

"It was enough," the earl answered, trying to keep the chestnuts to the least bumpy portion of the road. "And now they have mine." He was trying to recall how soon they could expect to come upon the next inn. He'd lost track of their position in the headlong rush and in truth hadn't been paying proper attention before then. There had to be something closer ahead than the Rose and the Crown was behind, even a hedge tavern. He didn't like Foley's color.

The groom was barely conscious when St. Cloud turned into the yard of a place whose weathered signboard proclaimed it the Fighting Cock. Dilapidated, in need of paint, and with one sullen stable hand to come to their assistance, this inn was a far cry from the Rose and the Crown. There was a vast difference in their style of arrival, too. Now the horses were lathered and plodding, the curricle was scraped and spattered, the earl was disheveled, and his groom was bloody and sagging on the seat. And there was no pocketful of coins to grease the wheels of hospitality.

Their reception was commensurate with their appearance. The earl had to rub down the horses himself while waiting for the doctor. He had to leave his signet ring as pledge for the surgeon's bill and the laudanum he prescribed as well as for Foley's bed and baiting the horses. The innkeeper offered to throw in some stew as part of the bargain, but St. Cloud was too furious to eat. There were no horses to be hired, not on tick, and no room for the earl, not on Christmas Eve.

"You can't mean to set out so late," Foley complained from his rude palette behind the kitchen stairs. "And without me." He tried to sit up.

The earl pushed him back down. "Stubble it, you old hen. I'm not your only chick. There are a few hours of daylight left, and we're not that far from St. Cloud. Anyway, it looks to be a clear night ahead. I'll send a carriage back for you at first light."

"But the chestnuts, m'lord, they're tired."

"They've had their rest, and I'll travel slowly. Besides, I wouldn't leave my cattle in this cesspit."

Foley grinned as the laudanum pushed his eyes closed. "Aye, but you'd leave me."

St. Cloud tucked the thin blanket around his man. "No choice," he told him. "Lady St. Cloud is frantic enough as is. If my bags arrive and I don't appear as promised, she'll send out the militia. Blast all females and families."

"And footpads and fools."

"And clutch-fisted innkeepers."

St. Cloud was still furious an hour later. Two hours later, when he got down again to lighten the load as the chestnuts strained up yet another hill, he was furious, footsore, and hungry.

Some other traveler must have had trouble with the incline, he observed, spotting a small pile of books by the side of the road. The books were neatly stacked on a rock, off the damp ground and in full view, as though waiting to be picked up. St. Cloud did not think they were left for anyone in particular, for night was coming on, this country byway was practically deserted, and the books were neither wrapped nor tied. No, the chap must simply have grown weary of carrying the heavy volumes. The earl picked them up, thinking that if he came upon his fellow traveler, he could offer a ride and restore his belongings.

Oddly enough, the books were all religious in nature. Who would bother to carry a hymnal, a Bible, and a book of sermons, only to discard them on Christmas Eve? A heretic making a quiet statement? A distraught mourner abandoning his faith? With nothing better to occupy his mind but his own sour thoughts as he paced beside the horses, St. Cloud idly thumbed through the pages. More curious yet, the Bible was written in French, with no inscriptions or dedications. What, then? A spy shedding excess baggage as he fled the authorities?

27

No, a fugitive would have hidden his trail, not left the evidence for the next passerby to find. Furthermore, the French pedestrian could not be a spy; St. Cloud had had his fill of adventure for the day.

The earl chided himself for his flights of fancy, using some poor émigré bastard to take his mind off his own empty pockets and empty stomach.

That poor émigré bastard had food. Midway up the next hill St. Cloud discovered an earthenware jug on an upturned log, with crumbs beneath it that the forest creatures hadn't discovered yet. "Damn," he cursed. The jug was empty, naturally. All that was left was a whiff of cider, just enough to make St. Cloud's mouth water. He stowed the jug under the floorboard, next to the books.

So the Frenchman was too poor for wine, and he was not far ahead. He could read, bilingually, and he was countryman enough not to leave an empty bottle where it could injure a horse and rider. St. Cloud hoped to catch up with him soon and hoped the fellow had something more to eat, to trade for a ride.

The earl stayed afoot, looking for signs of his would-be companion. If he had been mounted or traveling faster, he would have missed the next bundle, a paper-wrapped parcel carefully placed in the crook of a tree.

The earl looked around then, feeling foolish. He shrugged his broad shoulders and untied the string holding the soft package closed. Then he felt even more foolish for the previous observations he'd considered astute. Either the Frenchman was going to have a cold and lonely holiday after abandoning his *chère amie*'s Christmas gift, or the Frenchman was a female. She would come just about to his chin, St. Cloud estimated, shaking out the white velvet, with a delicately rounded figure indeed, he knowledgeably extrapolated. The gown was not up to London standards, though an obviously expensive piece of goods, in good taste and the latest fashion.

Not even St. Cloud's fertile imagination could figure a scenario for a young woman—the gown was white, after all—strewing her possessions about the countryside on Christmas Eve. If this was some local ritual, it was a dashed dangerous one, with shadows lengthening and highwaymen on the prowl.

He rewrapped the parcel and took it to the curricle, where the chestnuts were cropping grass. This time he climbed up and set the pair to a faster pace. The sooner he had some answers, the better—for his own peace of mind and for the woman's sake.

Nothing prepared him for the answers he found around the next bend. Hell, the answers only led to more questions.

The woman trudging ahead was covered head to toe in a gray hooded cape. She carried a tapestry carpetbag over one elbow and an infant slung over her shoulder! What in the world would a mother and child be doing out alone miles from nowhere?

Then she turned to face the approaching carriage as he pulled rein alongside of her, and all rational thought fled from his mind. She was exquisite, with a soft, gentle look to her. Thick eyebrows were furrowed to mix a touch of uncertainty with innocence in her big brown eyes. The babe's head was covered by a blue blanket, reminding him of nothing so much as a Raphael masterpiece. He expected a donkey to trot out of the bushes at any moment to complete the tableau.

Instead the woman noticed her dress parcel on the seat beside him and smiled. "Oh, you found my gown. I was hoping someone would, who could use it." She was well spoken and her voice was low, with no French accent or country inflection.

"Had you tired of it, then, ma'am?" He lifted the books from beneath his feet. "Or these?"

She smiled again, a quicksilver thing, like sun peeking from behind clouds. "You must know it was no such thing, sir. I simply had not realized when I set out how few wagons I would meet along the road, nor how heavy Pansy would seem after a few miles."

"You have been out on the road by yourself for more than a few miles? I would say that is remarkably poor planning indeed," he said in an angry tone. "Almost criminally cork-brained, in fact, considering, ah, Pansy."

Juneclaire took a step back, wondering at this stranger's hostility and wondering what else he thought she could have done about Pansy. As her heavy brows lowered in displeasure, she informed him, "We are not so far from Bramley now, sir, so I shall be on my way."

Bramley was at least two hours away, by carriage, and in the opposite direction from the Priory. St. Cloud cursed under his breath at the idiocy of what he saw before him and at what he was about to do. There was no decision, really. Not even the most stone-hearted care-for-naught could leave a fragile, gently bred mother and her baby on the road alone, afoot, in the dark, on Christmas Eve. Not if he was any kind of gentleman. "I am headed to Bramley myself, ma'am. May I offer you a ride?"

Juneclaire had been hoping for that very thing, but now she was hesitant. The man's accents were those of a gentleman, but he was scowling and speaking as if he thought she enjoyed her difficult situation. Did he think she would have left herself open to insult from every passing sheepherder on a whim? She was not reassured by his travel-stained appearance either. His greatcoat was caked with dust, and his cravat was missing altogether. The carriage was none too neat, and the horses were spent. A gentleman down on his luck, Juneclaire decided, no one she should know. Which was too bad, she regretted, since the dark-haired stranger might be very attractive if only he would smile. She bobbed a shallow curtsy with Pansy still in her arms and said, "Thank you for your kind offer, but it would not be proper for me to accept."

"Not proper? How can you consider propriety at this late date? And even if you were some innocent miss who had to protect her good name at all costs, how could you put such thoughts ahead of her welfare?" He nodded toward the blanketed bundle in her arms.

Now that was unjust! Juneclaire turned her back on him and set off down the road.

St. Cloud cursed the caper-witted female, then drove the chestnuts up to her. He started to get down, but he saw the woman shrink back and glance furtively to either side, as if seeking a way to run. He sat down, hard, his green eyes narrowed. "You're afraid of me," he stated matter-of-factly.

Juneclaire bit her lip. "You are angry."

"I am always angry, ma'am. Now I am enraged. I have been set on and robbed, my groom injured. I have been treated worse than a horse trader at a miserable inn, and my feet hurt. I am tired and hungry and dirty. Soon I will be cold. If that's not enough to try the patience of a saint, which I am not, I come upon a woman in circumstances no female should be forced to endure. *That* makes me furious."

"You are mad for my sake?" Juneclaire asked quietly, disbelievingly. No one had ever taken her part in anything before.

"I have been trained since birth to recognize damsels in distress, ma'am. The books never tell you they are so reluctant to be rescued, nor that they might be more afraid of the knight errant than the dragon. Truly, I only wish to spare you the dangers and discomforts of the road."

He was not looking nearly so fierce, Juneclaire thought, and the holdup could account for his bedraggled appearance. She realized that although his voice bespoke education and refinement, he could still be a plausible villain, but the very idea of highwaymen in the vicinity sent a shiver down her spine.

He saw her tremble and held out his hand. "Come, ma'am. At the rate you were going you would have no possessions whatsoever by the time you reached Bramley. And I don't eat babies, I promise."

She looked down at Pansy and smiled, then took a step closer to the carriage. She had the feeling that her stern-faced savior would not take no for an answer anyway.

"There, why don't you hand the baby up first."

She flashed him a quick grin that was more naughty schoolgirl than dignified matron and lifted Pansy to his waiting arms. The earl had a hard time tearing his eyes off the enchanting sight of her dimples and transferring his gaze to the unfamiliar burden.

"I've never held a—"

Christmas pig.

Chapter Four

St. Cloud threw his head back and laughed. Then he looked at Pansy on the seat beside him, a bristly black-and-white Berkshire pig with stand-up ears, little pink eyes, and a pink snout wriggling up at him. He recalled his promise not to eat her and laughed till tears ran down his eyes.

Juneclaire clambered up and took Pansy in her lap, laughing, too. She was right—he was attractive when he smiled. Actually, he was the most stunningly good-looking man she had ever seen, but since she hardly saw any men except for the farm workers, the vicar, and her uncle, she thought her judgment was suspect. The smile took years off his age and made his green eyes sparkle. He no longer wore that hooded, forbidding scowl, and Juneclaire settled back on her seat, contentment easing her tired muscles.

St. Cloud patted Pansy on the head before giving the horses the office to start. "Thank you for the joke. That was the most fun I've had in years."

"You should laugh more," Juneclaire said, then followed the startling familiarity with an explanation of sorts. "She really is a fine pig, you know, and a very good friend. I've had her ever since Ophelia stepped on her by mistake."

"Ophelia?" His lip quirked. "Never tell me that's the sow? Then the boar must be Hamlet?"

"Of course. It wasn't fair that Pansy should be the runt and lamed, too, so McCade—he's Uncle Avery's head pig man—gave her to me to feed and raise."

"She seems, ah, well behaved, for a pig."

"Oh, she is. And smart and clean, too. I bathe her in buttermilk to keep her hair soft, and then she licks it up for a snack."

"How efficient," he teased, knowing full well what was coming next, with a tenderhearted girl and a tender-meated piglet.

"Yes, well, you can see then how I could not hand Pansy over to the butcher just so Aunt Marta could impress her fine London guests. She wanted a boar's head, the way she thinks things used to be done, but McCade wouldn't part with Hamlet, of course."

"Of course," he solemnly agreed, his eyes on the road so she could not tell if he was bamming her again.

"Then Aunt Marta settled on a suckling pig, with an apple in its mouth, but there were no new litters. It isn't Pansy's fault she's so small, but Aunt wouldn't listen. All she cares about is putting on a show for the toplofty London titles visiting in the neighborhood, without spending a fortune. The peers only come for the party anyway. Those snobs will never accept her in the highest circles no matter what she does, in spite of Uncle Avery's title. Aunt Marta's father was in Trade," she confided.

St. Cloud was suddenly sobered, the habitual frown again marring his fine features. His passenger wasn't a mother, a matron, or a married lady. She wasn't a seamstress or a serving girl. By the Devil's drawers, she was a cursed highborn virgin, a runaway, and a pig thief! Oh Lord, what had he got himself into now? Perhaps if he knew the family, he could just sneak her back with no one the wiser.

"I'm sure your family must be worried about you, Miss ... ?"

She must have read his intent, for she sat up straighter. "No, they are not. They never did before. And it's Juneclaire. One word."

"Very well, Miss Oneword, I am Merritt Jordan, at your service." He was not about to put notions in her head by mentioning his title. He couldn't bear to see that typical calculating gleam come over her guileless brown eyes. Besides, she seemed to have a low-enough opinion of the shallow Quality already. Heaven knew what she would think of Satan St. Cloud. For some reason her thoughts mattered.

Juneclaire was studying him, fitting his name to the strong planes of his face, the cleft in his chin. "I suppose your friends call you Merry?" she asked doubtfully.

Friends, relatives, acquaintances, everyone called him St. Cloud and had since he was seven. "Only my uncle George used to call me by a pet name. 'Merry Easter, Merry,' he used to say. 'Merry Christmas, Merry.' That's my birthday," he told her, not examining how easily he revealed personal details to this chance-met waif. He doubted if anyone outside his immediate family knew his birthday or cared. And he never mentioned George to anyone, ever.

"How wonderful for you! I suppose Christmas is your favorite day of the year, then."

"Hardly. That's the day Uncle George died."

"Oh, I'm sorry. I didn't know." Juneclaire was upset, thinking sorrow turned his lips down.

"Of course not, how could you? And no, the rest of my doting family does not call me anything half-charming," he went on. He heard the bitterness in

35

his own voice and saw regret in her serious little face. Dash it, the chit felt sorry for him!

The earl quickly turned back to the horses to hide his scowl, but Juneclaire huddled deeper in her cloak, squeezing Pansy to her so hard the piglet squealed in protest. She did not understand this man at all, and his uncertain temper unnerved her.

"I told you I don't bite," he said gruffly, then added, "I would be honored if you called me Merry, if you like. If your chaperon"—a nod toward Pansy—"permits this breach of etiquette. I think the circumstances are such that formal rules need not apply." There, she was smiling again. St. Cloud released the breath he didn't know he'd been holding.

"Thank you. My family calls me Claire, or Clarry. I hate both of those," she confided in return.

"Then I shall never use either," he vowed, again enraged at the way the girl's family seemed to hold this rare treasure in so little esteem, so careless of her feelings and well-being. If she was his . . . sister, he'd be out scouring the countryside. For sure he would have found her before some stranger with who-knew-what on his mind could offer a ride. Or worse. The earl masked his outrage at her poor treatment as best he could, with so little practice at hiding his ill humor. He'd quickly realized his little innocent could be startled by the slightest hint of anger, like some wary forest creature. He made a conscious effort to ease the set muscles of his face into an unfamiliar smile. "I shall call you Junco, then, for a gray-and-white snow bird in the Colonies." He reached over to touch the gray cloak and the white muffler she had wound around her neck. His gloved hand briefly grazed her cheek. "It's not quite the *rara avis* I think you are, but a brave and cheery little fellow. Do you mind?"

Juneclaire shook her head. Then, to hide the color

she knew was rushing to her face at his words, at his touch, she bent to the carpetbag at her feet. "Would you like something to eat, Merry? I have some bread and cheese and—"

"I thought you'd never ask!"

Later, after a silence broken only by the steady beat of the horses' hooves and Pansy's vocal table manners, the now content earl asked, "You do have friends waiting for you in Bramley, don't you?"

He had a hard time holding on to his temper and his new resolve not to look like thunderclouds when she gaily answered, "Why, no, I am just going to meet the coach to London there. I was hoping to make the afternoon mail, but now I shall have to wait for tomorrow morning."

St. Cloud ground his teeth in an effort not to curse. "Tomorrow is Christmas; no coaches will run."

"Oh, dear, I hadn't thought of that."

"I warrant there are a lot of things you hadn't thought of, miss. Do you have enough brass for a respectable hotel? For sure I cannot help you there. The thieves barely left me the lint in my pockets."

Juneclaire suddenly found a need to inspect behind Pansy's ears. The piglet complained loudly, which hid Juneclaire's whispered "No."

"Did you say no? You ran away without enough blunt to hire a carriage or put up at an inn? Of all the cork-brained, mutton-headed ideas, why, I—"

Juneclaire was pressed against the railing at the edge of her seat. St. Cloud took a deep breath and unclenched his jaw. "Forgive me, Junco. I am just concerned for you."

Concerned? He looked ready to strangle her! "The money doesn't matter. I do have enough for my London coach fare and a night on the road, Mr. Jordan, and perhaps an inn in Bramley, although not the finest. But the inns are all filled with holiday travelers, and they don't seem to want unescorted females at any price. Or pigs."

There went St. Cloud's plan to drop her off with some respectable party in Bramley and proceed on his way before anybody recognized him. "Just what had you intended to do, then, if I might ask?"

She didn't like the sarcasm and raised her straight little nose in the air like a duchess. "I intend to sleep under a hedgerow as I did last night, for your information. It's not what I would like, but don't worry, Pansy and I shall manage."

Don't worry? Tell the Thames to stop flowing! Didn't the chit know what kind of villains roamed the roads? Thieves, beggars, gypsies—if she was lucky. Didn't she understand that she was ruined anyway? One night away from home was enough to shred her reputation. One hour in his company had the same effect, and that's how well she managed.

He could make up some Banbury tale about being brother and sister and pray no one recognized him, the chestnuts, or the crest on the side of his curricle. That close to St. Cloud? Hell, he may as well pray the pretty bird-wit turned into a bird in fact and flew off. And her damned pig with her. St. Cloud could hire her a coach and four and send her on her way, except that the banks would be closed, and tomorrow, too! What a coil. For twopence he would take her home, beat some sense into her relations, and be back on his way before midnight. He would, if the chestnuts weren't spent and she did not look so appealing, with her brown curls tumbling around her hood and a crumb on her chin.

"How old are you anyway, little one?" He wondered if he could throw her back, like a too-small fish.

"Not so little. I am nineteen, old enough to be out on my own."

"So ancient." She looked younger, he thought, with that untouched look. She did not have the brittle smile or the coy simper of a London belle years younger. "If you are such a mature age, how is it that you are still unwed? Are the men around here blind?"

"I do not go out in Society, so I do not know many men. But thank you for the compliment, if such it was."

Gads, she couldn't even flirt, and she was going to make it to London? "It was, Junco. But are you in mourning that you had no come-out?" he persisted.

Juneclaire picked at the unfinished hem of her mitten. She'd have the thing unraveled if he did not stop asking his probing questions, but she felt she owed him her answers, for his caring. "My parents died many years ago. Aunt is . . . embarrassed. They ran away, you see, and their marriage was irregular by her standards. But I am not quite on the shelf. Aunt Marta is looking for a husband for me, among the widowers and older bachelors."

No, he would not take her back, even if he knew her direction. He noticed that she was careful not to mention an address or a family name. At least the peagoose had some sense. St. Cloud wondered if she would trust him enough to hand over her coach fare so he could hire job horses and drive her to London himself. It meant a long, uncomfortable night, but he'd had worse and she would be safe, he thought. "Who is it you go to visit in London, Junco? You and Pansy?"

"Mrs. Simms, our old housekeeper. I thought she might find me a position in the mansion where she is employed."

Juneclaire had to grab Pansy to keep the pig

from falling off the seat, so the curricle stopped suddenly, and she was sure the words coming from Mr. Jordan's lips were not meant for a lady's ears. She knew he would have that ugly look on his face, but by now she was confident enough that he was not going to turn violent on her. He simply had a volatile temper, no patience, and a colorful vocabulary. Juneclaire had nearly reached the end of her tether, too, however. "I know my plan is caper-witted," she shouted back at him. "But I have no-where else to go. And not just for Pansy's sake. I'd rather go into service—be a scullery maid or such—than be married off willy-nilly to some overweight sea captain or a snuff-drenched squire whose only conversation is about what animal he killed last. I have no choice! I am not a man, who can join the army or take religious orders or read the law. No one will even teach me a trade! All I have is Pansy. What am I supposed to do?"

Two days on the road had taken their toll on Miss Beaumont's courage. A short tirade against this scowling stranger was the best she could manage before tears started to well in her eyes. Silently St. Cloud handed her a fine lawn handkerchief and then clucked the horses into motion.

That tore it, he conceded. There was no choice but to take the chit to St. Cloud Priory, but heaven knew the little pigeon deserved better than the flock of vultures there. He'd get fresh horses at Bramley one way or another and then turn around. The earl did not know how Miss Juneclaire Oneword was going to accept his high-handed decision. Not well, he guessed from her last burst of indignation. He'd face that hurdle once they reached Bramley.

As a matter of fact, where the hell was Bramley? They had turned off the Thackford road miles back at a cross sign and should have reached the town, he thought, although he did not know the way so well from this direction. "Ah, Junco, is this the road to Bramley?"

"How should I know?" she snuffled into his handkerchief. "I've never been here before."

Chapter Five

*T*hey were lost. Juneclaire was glad she could not see her companion's face in the gathering darkness. He was on foot, leading the horses up an uneven dirt track they were hoping led to a farmhouse. So many muffled imprecations came back to her through the cold night, Juneclaire began to wonder if Mr. Jordan had ever been a sailor. He certainly was not a countryman, stubbing his toe on every stone.

"Oh, look," she called out to distract him, "the evening star. Let's make a wish."

"Ouch! Bloody bastard bedrock." She'd distracted him too much. "I wish you to Jericho, Miss Juneclaire—ooph."

The one word he uttered was not even in her mental dictionary, thank goodness. With her breath making clouds in front of her face, Juneclaire stated, "Then I shall have to wish for you. I shall wish for your heart's desire."

"Right now my heart's desire is a hot tub and a warm brandy. If you can produce those, Junco, I shall believe in leprechauns, genies, and brown-eyed goddesses. Otherwise, wishes are for schoolgirls."

She made her wish anyway, not for his bodily

comforts but for his troubled soul. The man might be an aristocrat, but he was not happy. Juneclaire had finally taken a better look at the cut of his coat and the quality of his horses, after she got over being terrorized at his arrogant ill humor. She refused to be embarrassed by her earlier remarks about the nobility, not if he was unabashed at his profanity. He *was* toplofty, refusing to let her go on alone, looking down his distinguished nose at her plans. He was obviously not used to being disagreed with, she thought with chagrin, recalling the row that had ensued when he tried to blame her for getting them lost, as if she should have known to bring a map with her when she left home. He had not demurred when she called him "my lord" either.

No matter, Lord Merritt might have everything in the world he wanted—not at this moment, of course—with no need to make wishes, but Juneclaire thought otherwise. She thought he was so cynical, he'd lost the capacity to believe in miracles. Perhaps he had been disappointed too many times. Juneclaire mightn't have a home or a loving family, a fortune or a settled future, but she still looked for magic. So she made her wish for his inner contentment.

Ice-cold well water for washing and tepid lemonade for drinking were not what Lord Merritt requested, his lowered brows reminded Juneclaire, but she smiled complacently. He was much happier now that they had found this old barn. He even whistled while rubbing down the horses. There were no lights at the farmhouse, but the barn was half filled with workhorses. St. Cloud thought the family must be off visiting for the holiday. He put his chestnuts in a loose box near the end of the row and swept out two other stalls with no signs of recent occupation. There was fresh hay for the horses, straw for their own beds, and a lantern by which to eat the rest of her hoarded food. Pansy was having a wonderful time, rooting around in the corncrib, and Juneclaire was pleased.

"Why are you wearing that Mona Lisa smile, Junco? We are miles from nowhere, with an irate farmer liable to burst in on us at any minute, and our next meal has just eaten more than her fair share of this one."

Juneclaire wasn't worried, since he was scratching behind the little pig's ears while he spoke. "This is a great improvement over sleeping under a bush," she told him, then lowered her eyes. "And I feel safer with you here."

He snorted, or Pansy did. "I daresay I am more protection than the porker, but not much. Some hero I have been. In one day I have gotten myself robbed and lost. I have no money, no pistol, no map, and I am eating your food."

"And you shouted at me."

"That, too. You should be demanding my head on a platter instead of feeding my pride. Any proper hero would have found you a proper bed."

Juneclaire settled into the straw and began to take her hair down. "But you found me just what I wanted. I have always dreamed of staying up all night in a barn on Christmas Eve to see if the animals really do speak at midnight, as the old tales say."

"Do you believe they will?"

She did not notice the way his eyes watched her, green glitters in the lantern's light. "Goodness," she said after removing the mouthful of hairpins to her pocket, "I have no idea and won't until I see for myself. Aunt Marta would never let me, of course. She was petrified that I might find myself

44

alone with the grooms and stableboys. Aunt Marta is a terrible snob, you see."

"I daresay she would be relieved that you are alone with a wellborn rake," he noted dryly.

Juneclaire paused in her efforts to brush her hair out of the thick braids that had been wound into a bun at her neck. "Are you really a rake?"

St. Cloud leaned back in the straw, a reed in his mouth. He watched the way the lantern cast golden highlights through her soft brown hair, way past her shoulders, covering her . . . cloak. He sat up. "I suppose I was, once. Now? Maybe it depends on one's definition. Are you afraid for your virtue?"

She looked like a startled fawn, those brown eyes wide open, thick brows arched high. The thought had never occurred to her. "Should I be?"

The earl had given over thinking of Juneclaire as Madonna-like hours ago. Now he was rearranging his impression of this hobbledehoy waif. The translucent beauty and the purity were still there, but Miss Juneclaire was no child. She was a damned desirable woman. He could think of few things he'd rather do than run his hands through those silky masses or feel her soft lips smile with pleasure under his kisses or—

"No," he answered curtly, getting up to snuff out the lantern. "I don't seduce innocents."

"Oh." Juneclaire could not keep the wistfulness out of her voice. She'd never even met a rake before and was hardly likely to again. She sighed and thought she heard a chuckle from his makeshift bed in the neighboring stall. She must be wrong. Her stone-faced savior was not much given to light humor. "Merry?"

"Yes?"

"Don't you find me attractive?"

That was a definite chuckle, followed by his own sigh. "Very, minx, but I find I am still somewhat

45

of a gentleman. You are under my care, and that means you are safe, even from me. Especially from me. So stop fishing for compliments and go to sleep, Junco. It's been a long day and you must be tired. I am."

He rolled over in the straw. Juneclaire pulled Pansy closer for warmth but did not shut her eyes. She could see starlight through the chinks in the barn's roof. Every now and again one of the horses would stamp its foot.

"Merry?"

He turned around again, bumping his elbow on the wooden partition. "Blast. Woman, do not try my patience."

"But, Merry, I do not wish to sleep. Then I will never know about the animals. Won't you talk to me a bit so I stay awake?"

He grumbled, but she could tell he sat up. "What do you wish to talk about?"

"I don't know. . . . What do you do all day? Usually, I mean, when you are not traveling about the countryside saving silly girls?"

So he told her about his clubs and his wagers, Gentleman Jackson's and Manton's, the House and the War Office, agricultural lectures and investment counselors. He told her about the opera and the theater and balls, thinking that's what a rural young miss might care about. None of it whatsoever seemed interesting to him: neither the telling nor the living. Juneclaire, however, seemed to be swallowing his tales as eagerly as Pansy relished the windfall apples stored in another unused stall.

Juneclaire was thinking that she was right: he was indeed a man of means. His lordship's life was full and glamorous, dedicated to his own pleasure. He was as far above her as the stars overhead. She never felt her lowly status so much as when he asked what she did all day and she had to tell him about going to church and visiting the sick, helping Cook and directing the housemaids, mending and polishing and tending the flower gardens.

St. Cloud thought again of seeing her relations drawn and quartered for turning their own flesh and blood into a drudge. They hadn't managed to ruin her spirit, though, for he could detect the pleasure she derived from her roses and her sugarplums, the pride she took in seeing her aunt's house run well. Juneclaire was a real lady, and a rakehell such as he was not fit to touch her hem.

That did not keep the earl from moving his pile of straw to her side of the partition, though, so they could talk more easily. Juneclaire scrunched over to give him more room. St. Cloud did not want to talk about tomorrow, when he would have to force unpleasant decisions on her, and Juneclaire did not want to discuss the future, when this enchanted interlude would be only a memory to savor. So they talked about the past, the happier times before his father was injured and her father was killed, before his mother turned him over to tutors and hers slipped away. They talked of Christmases past.

"When we were in France, the whole family gathered in the kitchen to stir the Christmas pudding. Did yours?" she wanted to know.

"The children, sometimes. I doubt my mother even knows the way to the kitchen. What about you? Aunt Marta doesn't sound like one to take her turn after the potboy."

"She thinks it's all pagan superstition," she said regretfully, then added, "but I used to sneak down and have my turn anyway. Cook would call for me last, just before it was done."

"And would she put in the ring and the key and the penny? I cannot remember the other charms that were supposed to bring luck or wealth or whatever."

47

"No, Cook never dared to put the lucky pieces in the pudding she made for the family. I think she made another just for the staff."

"It was rigged in my household anyway. Aunt Florrie always got the little silver horse. She would cry otherwise. Aunt Florrie is not quite right," he explained, wondering if he should also mention his hysterical mother, wayward cousin, devious uncle, blind grandmother. No, he decided. Why chance giving the chit nightmares? And that was without reference to the ghost. He pictured Juneclaire crying out in the night, her hair tumbled over her shoulders, throwing herself into his arms in the straw. He shook his head. Unworthy, St. Cloud. "Oh yes, and once she was permitted at the table, Cousin Elsbeth always managed to receive the piece of pudding with the ring in it. It never helped, for she is twenty and still unwed."

"Then she must not have wished hard enough."

"I suspect it has more to do with her ambitious expectations and her shrewish nature. But I am certain you must have made a wish, fairy child that you are. What did you wish for?" He thought she'd confess to seeking a visit to London, fancy clothes and balls, like Elsbeth.

Suddenly shy, Juneclaire answered, "Just the usual schoolgirl fancies, I suppose." She was not about to tell him that her wish was going to be for a handsome cavalier to rescue her from the corpulent captain or the smelly squire. That had already come true, without her even making the wish! "I know," she declared, changing the subject, "let's make our Christmas wishes anyway. No, not for a hot meal or anything silly like that, but something special, something important. It's supposed to come true by Twelfth Night if you are deserving, so your wish must be for something worth being good."

"Do you mean only the righteous can have their

wishes answered? I thought those were prayers," he teased.

Juneclaire considered. "Being good never hurts."

Oh, doesn't it? he wondered, pondering the ache in his loins to think of the dark-haired beauty not two feet away from him and two lifetimes apart. "You go first."

"I suppose I should wish for an end to the war and peace for everyone."

"No, no. That's being too good. Take it as a given and wish for something personal. After all, it's your one and only Christmas wish, practically in a manger. It's bound to come true, little bird." He reached over and found her hand.

"Do you know what I wish, then? I wish for a place of my very own, where I am wanted and welcome and no one can send me away or make me ashamed to be there."

He squeezed her hand, there in the dark. "I think . . . Yes, I think I wish for fewer people dependent on me, fewer responsibilities, and not having to listen to them tell me what's right for me. Then I mightn't feel so inclined to do the opposite."

They were quiet for a moment, lost in their own thoughts. Then Juneclaire started to hum a Christmas carol, and Merry joined in. They went through all the old songs they knew, English and French. His fine baritone held the tune better than her uncertain soprano, but she knew more of the words. They might have done better the other way around, but the horses and the pig did not complain.

Despite Juneclaire's determination to stay awake, her eyelids were too heavy to hold open when they ran out of songs. She had put in two long, hard days, even for a country girl used to physical exertion and fresh air. They drifted into sleep nestled in the straw, their hands entwined, the pig between them.

Chapter Six

*V*oices! It was true! Animals really could—A hand was clapped over Juneclaire's mouth before she could sit up and exclaim over the wonder of it all. The lantern was lighted, so she could see Merry's face inches from her own, scowling at her. He shook his head no. She nodded and he took his hand away but stayed so close, Juneclaire could feel his breath on her cheek. There were miracles and then there were—

"I tell you, Charlie, old man Blaine will have our hides for using his horses."

"Shut up, boy. Who's to tell him? He'll come back tomorrow an' be none the wiser if you bed 'em down proper. Left you in charge, didn't he? 'Sides, it wouldn't do to take my own cob out, now would it? I swan, you got less brains'n a duck, Ned Corbett. Riddles is back in the livery over to Bramley for all the world and his brother to see. For aught anyone knows I'm tucked up tight, and you been here watching the Blaine place all day and night just like you ought to be."

"That last carriage was too close to here, Charlie. Magistrate'll be here in the morning asking questions."

"Not on Christmas Day, he won't. Lord Cantwell

likes his stuffed goose too well. And if he does, you didn't hear nothing anyway. 'Sides, that last coach was a bonus, you might say, for a good day's work. Who'd expect some widder lady to wear all her diamonds to midnight service? Finish up with them horses, boy. I want to divide up the take and be gone."

"I still don't like it. I wish you hadn't gone and hit that groom this morning. He dies and we could hang, Charlie."

"Stop worritin' at it, Ned. We could already hang for highway robbery, boy. What do you think, they hang you twice?"

"And you never said nothing about pulling a gun on no swell."

"What did you expect, boy? His nibs was going to hand over the blunt if we asked him pretty please? You're acting like a bloody schoolmarm."

"I never wanted to go anyways, Charlie. My ma finds out, she'll die."

"You're forgetting why you agreed to help me in the first place. You needed money for medicine, 'member, else she'll die. Sounds like she's going to cock up her toes anyway, may as well go in style."

"You leave my ma out of this, you makebate! She always said you'd end on the gallows, and she was right."

Juneclaire could hear the sound of a scuffle. She moved to poke her head over the wood to see, but St. Cloud quickly held her down with his body across her chest. All she could hear was heavy breathing. No, that was hers.

"Let that be a lesson, boy. No one messes with Charlie Parrett. You just cost yourself an extra yellow boy I was going to throw in for your ma. You'll think twice about giving me lip next time."

"There ain't going to be no next time, Charlie. I ain't going out with you again."

There came the sound of a heavy slap. "You ain't with me, boy, then you're against me. I'd never know when you'd give my name over to Cantwell for the reward money. O' course, the second they take me up, I'll shout your name so loud, your ma will hear even in heaven."

"I wouldn't cry rope on you, Charlie. I just don't want to do it again."

"You already been on the high toby, Ned, so there's no backing down. You don't come with me, I'll have to leave town and this easy-picking territory. Afore I go, naturally, I'd be sure to send a message to Cantwell, asking him where you got the ready for your ma's doctorin'. Now stop your sniveling and take your money, you poor, tender little dewdrop. Why, you're nothing but a whining pansy."

So Pansy went out to investigate. She slipped past St. Cloud while he was still lying across Juneclaire. Juneclaire held him and her breath.

"What's that?"

"What do you think it is, you looby, the lord-high sheriff hisself come to arrest you? It's a bloody pig."

"Farmer Blaine doesn't keep pigs."

The next sound Juneclaire heard was the cocking of a pistol.

After that, a blur. St. Cloud hurtled out of the stall with a shout, and Charlie swung the pistol around. The earl was on the bigger man before the thief could take aim. Ned jumped up, but Juneclaire hit him on the back of the neck with a bucket. The two older men fought for possession of the weapon, one hand each on the gun, St. Cloud's other hand going for Charlie's throat, Charlie's trying to gouge at St. Cloud's eyes. Juneclaire was ready to brain Charlie Parrett with her bucket when she had a clear shot. Ned started for the pitchfork near the door but tripped over Pansy and went down. June-claire hit him over the head again. When she looked up, his lordship and Parrett were rolling on the ground, the pistol between them.

They rolled into the upright where the lantern hung, sending the light flying. Now they struggled in the dark, with harsh panting noises and grunts the only sounds, till Juneclaire heard the crinkly rustle of loose straw catching on fire. Then Ned was rushing by her, stamping at the burgeoning flames. The horses started to kick at the walls of their stalls, and Pansy was squealing. Juneclaire found the other bucket, the one she'd washed with, and tossed the water on the fire. Then she took her cloak off and threw it over the sparks and started stomping up and down on it while Ned scraped the unlit straw away with his hands, leaving just bare dirt that could not burn. Then the pistol went off.

Juneclaire froze in place. Not Merry, she prayed, not even thinking of her own devilish situation if the enigmatic gentleman was hurt. There came the scrape of flint and a tiny glow. Whatever was keeping her knees locked upright, whether bravery, fear, or stupidity, gave out when she saw who lit another lantern. She sank to the ground on top of her wet, charred cloak and hugged Pansy so hard, the pig squealed loudly enough to wake the dead, but not Charlie Parrett.

Ned dashed for the door, to be stopped by an iron-hard clasp on his wrist. The boy made retching sounds, and St. Cloud shoved him toward one of the buckets.

"I guess I should have let him go," he said in disgust, watching Juneclaire hand the boy a handkerchief—St. Cloud's own. "Are you all right, Junco?"

"Yes, I think so. The fire is out. And you, my lord?"

"All in one piece, at least." He gingerly explored a bruise on his chin, which, from its feel, would add a less-than-festive touch to his appearance by the morning. Juneclaire thought he looked more human with his hair all mussed and his face dirty. He certainly was more endearing, though she could not go toward him to wipe away the smudges or push the dark curls back off his forehead. Not with Charlie at his feet.

"Is he . . . ?"

"Quite. We've saved the county the price of a trial." St. Cloud dragged the limp figure into one of the empty stalls, out of sight. He came back to poke through the pile of loot. His silver flask went into his greatcoat pocket, along with his fob, gold quizzing glass, and stickpin. He kept his pistol in easy reach and his eye on Ned while he counted out coins and bills. "Of course, this leaves us with a tad of a predicament, my dear, especially since I am sure you wish to be involved with investigations and your name to be brought out at inquests as little as I do. It could be much simpler, really. You know, a falling-out among thieves . . ."

"Merry, you wouldn't, just to save yourself some trouble!"

"Please, my lord, my ma—"

St. Cloud gave the youngster a look that sent Ned back to the bucket. "We heard all about your mother, sirrah. How proud she'd be to see her baby now," St. Cloud said with a sneer. "How much her health would improve to see you hang."

"But, Merry, he's just a boy!" Juneclaire pleaded.

"Just a boy who terrorizes the countryside, robbing and injuring innocent travelers. What about justice, Juneclaire?"

"But it was Charlie who hit your groom. And Ned said he wasn't going to do it again, and he did help put out the fire. And we can give the money back

54

now. What's the justice in hanging a boy who looks after his mother the best way he can? Someone should have been helping them before, the parish or landlord. Then this wouldn't have happened."

St. Cloud had a dark inkling who was the title holder for these miles around St. Cloud Priory, in the vicinity of Bramley. It was only an inkling, mind, so he thought he'd keep it to himself while Miss Juneclaire waxed eloquent. Ned must have appreciated her defensive oratory as well, for he looked up and said, "Thank you, ma'am. It's Miss Beaumont, from Stanton Hall, ain't it? My aunt keeps house for the vicar at Strasmere, and we visited once before Ma took sick. She mentioned a Miss Juneclaire Beaumont, who decorated the church and taught Sunday school to the children."

So much for squeaking though this coil without trumpeting their identities to the countryside, the earl thought, angrily stuffing what he determined his share of the thieves' haul into his wallet. He checked to make sure his pistol was loaded.

"No!" Juneclaire screeched, rushing to put her hand on his sleeve, having correctly interpreted the earl's aggravation if not his intent. "He won't tell anyone I was here, will you, Ned?"

"No, ma'am. Never. I'll do anything you say, my lord."

St. Cloud patted her hand, taking a moment to think. "Very well, Junco, you've won your case. Ned, you'll take Farmer Blaine's horses out again, with a lantern and your friend Charlie. You'll ride to Lord Cantwell's house to head him off from coming here. Tell him you were asleep . . . where? The loft over the cow barn? Fine. You heard a shot, went to investigate, and found this suspicious character dead in the stable, the horses in a lather, a sack of jewels and gold next to him. You don't know anything else, did not see anyone run off, but suspect it was as we mentioned, an argument over the split. The other chap must have shabbed off when the shot woke the house. You had no pistol, so you couldn't give chase.

"That should keep Cantwell happy, with the money returned." The earl fixed Ned with a penetrating stare. "And be assured, bantling, I know exactly how much is left in that sack to be returned to the victims."

"You don't have to worry, my lord, I wouldn't touch a groat. Not now."

"Very well, I believe you. How long should that take?"

"No time at all. Bramley's right over the next rise, around the bend."

St. Cloud called curses down on the vagaries of fate while he searched in his pockets for a pad and pencil. "When you are finished with the magistrate, you will have to ride back to the Fighting Cock. I am sure you can get there and back before morning riding cross-country, even in the dark."

Ned nodded, while St. Cloud tore a page from his book. "The note is for my groom. You needn't see him, just give it to the innkeeper and redeem my signet with the purse I will give you. If you are back here with my ring, say, an hour past dawn, we can forget the whole bumblebroth. If not, young Ned, I will go straight to Lord Cantwell. And you can bet your bootstraps that Uncle Hebert will take my word over yours."

Ned was nodding, swearing on his mother's head that he'd do everything his lordship ordered, as fast as the horses could fly. He'd try to hold back dawn for an hour, too, if his lordship wanted.

"But what *about* his mother?" Juneclaire wanted to know. "They'll be in the same mess."

"I'll see that the mother is taken care of," St. Cloud promised, "if I see the son in the morning."

Juneclaire was satisfied. Her knight's armor wasn't tarnished.

"Oh, by the by, Ned, there is no need to mention me or the lady in any context whatsoever. If, however, someone is looking for her by name, you may inform him or her that Miss Beaumont's fiancé was escorting her to his family home for the holidays when there was a carriage accident."

Juneclaire's contentment shattered into rubble. Her knight's armor must have been made of cheesecloth instead of chain mail, that he received such a grievous blow to the head to addle his wits.

Ned knew there had been no female in the curricle that morning, but he also knew he was lucky to get out of the barn with his skin on. This devil could best Charlie, who was bigger and a dirtier fighter, and he had a look that could freeze a fellow's blood right in his veins. If the swell wanted him to swear, Ned would say his lordship was marrying the pig!

The earl helped the boy take the body out and tie it to one of the horses. Juneclaire tried not to look. She draped her cloak across one of the partitions in hopes it would be dry by morning. Then she started shivering.

When St. Cloud came back, Juneclaire found it the most natural thing in the world that he should hold his arms open and she should walk into them. He wrapped his greatcoat around her, rubbed her back, and feathered kisses on the top of her head until the trembling stopped.

"I'll never be a disbeliever again, Junco," he murmured into her hair, sending shivers through her again, but not from the cold this time. "And you must have been very, very good to compensate for my wickedness, to get our wishes answered so quickly."

"I don't understand." She didn't understand any of the feelings she was feeling either.

"Your wish, Miss Beaumont, for a place of your own. It's cold and dreary, but I'm sure you can change that in jig time with one of your smiles. They work for me, you know."

Juneclaire looked up at him in such muddled confusion, he had to kiss the tip of her nose, which was cold, so he held her closer still. "My house, goose. Your house when we marry."

She pulled back as far as his arms would let her, perhaps a quarter of an inch. "Oh, pooh, you don't have to marry me. I know you were being honorable and all that for Ned's benefit, but he'll never talk. You put the fear of God into him."

"God would be more forgiving if he doesn't get back. And I was not being honorable just for Ned. I am a gentleman, as I keep reminding you. The boy won't talk soon, but someone might see us in the morning, and sooner or later he'd mention your name. You have to be a respectable married lady by then."

"But you cannot want to marry me."

"To be honest, I haven't wanted to marry anyone, but why not you? You are kind and brave and loyal, and handy with a bucket. You're beautiful and you make me smile. What more could I ask? You'll be getting the worst of the bargain, but I need you to make my wish come true."

"All those responsibilities and people dragging at you?"

"Exactly. One of my responsibilities is to produce an heir, and now you'll keep me safe from all the matchmaking mamas and predatory females."

"Silly."

No one had ever called the Earl of St. Cloud silly before. No female had ever fit so perfectly next to his heart before. No matter what he told Juneclaire, he'd known their fates were sealed from the moment she stepped into his carriage and proved to be a lady. The matrimonial noose had been tightening around his neck with every mile until he could barely draw in his last gasps of freedom. Now the idea did not seem so bad, as he whispered reassurances in her ear until she fell asleep in his arms, his greatcoat spread over both of them. The pig whiffled in the corncrib.

Chapter Seven

𝒯he earl awoke to the sound of church bells. The sun was well up, but St. Cloud did not want to disturb Juneclaire by searching out his fob watch. She still slept next to him under the greatcoat, not even the top of her head showing. St. Cloud shut his eyes again to savor the feeling. He almost never woke with a woman in his arms, never caring to stay the night with any of his paramours. Now he thought he might enjoy starting the days this way. Not with unfulfilled desires, naturally, but a special license would take care of that problem. He expected the other, the feeling of comfort and joy, just like the old carol they sang last night, to last for the next fifty or sixty years. God rest ye merry gentlemen.

Time didn't matter anyway. St. Cloud was already long overdue at the Priory, and Juneclaire had no coach to catch in Bramley, even if they were running. And the boy had returned. He could hear Ned whistling about his tasks and jingling harness. Tactful lad.

St. Cloud wondered what Juneclaire would be like in the mornings. Some women, he knew, were querulous if roused early. Not even the earl dared approach the dowager Lady St. Cloud until Grandmother had her fortifying chocolate. Others, like his cousin Elsbeth, were vain of their looks until safely in their dressers' hands, and his mother had to lie abed all afternoon if forced to bestir herself before noon. Junco was not temperamental, conceited, or missish. St. Cloud could not wait to find her reaction to being kissed awake like Sleeping Beauty. He himself woke up amorous.

He raised the coat to stroke her smooth cheek—and his hands touched hair more bristly than his own side-whiskers. His eyes jerked open to stare into little red-rimmed beady ones, with absurdly long white eyelashes.

St. Cloud jumped up. Pansy jumped up. St. Cloud shouted: "What the hell!" And the pig raced off with a piercing whee that sounded like the gates of hell swinging shut.

"Stop that, you confounded animal," the earl ordered. "You weren't hurt, so quit overplaying your part, you ham. Your mistress must be out talking with Ned, so you're wasting your time trying to get sympathy." St. Cloud felt he was the one who deserved pitying, denied the pleasure of waking his bride-to-be. On his way out of the barn he tossed Pansy an apple saved from Juneclaire's hoard the night before. "There, and don't tell anyone I tried to kiss a pig good morning!"

Juneclaire wasn't polishing tack with Ned. She must be using the convenience, or be out by the pump, washing. This would be the last time in her life she'd use icy water or sleep on the ground, St. Cloud vowed.

Ned jumped off the upturned barrel and touched his cap. Then he fumbled in his pocket and withdrew St. Cloud's ring. "Here, my lord. I was back by first light, I swear, but you didn't say nothing 'bout waking you up."

The earl could see that the curricle was clean and

shining in the wintry sun. The boy must have been back for hours, working outside in the cold. "Thank you," he acknowledged, nodding toward the equipage, and Ned blushed with pride. He was no more than twelve or thirteen, St. Cloud saw now by light of day, though tall for his age. He shouldn't have been out riding the roads all night, damn it, but he shouldn't have been mixed up with highwaymen either.

"Did you have any trouble?" the earl asked.

"Nary a bit. That widder lady went back toward Bramley, and the innkeeper sent her to Lord Cantwell at High Oaks to report the robbery. She was still kicking up a dust over to the manor. Magistrate was having to give her hospitality for the night, it seems, 'cause she was too afrighted to go back on the roads and had no money for the inn. He was right pleased to see me with the widder's purse and sparklers, I can tell you that."

"And what did he say about Charlie?"

"He said good riddance to bad rubbish, is what. Charlie'd been poaching up at High Oaks for as long as I can remember, only Cantwell's man could never catch him. His lordship being magistrate and all, he had to have proof. Charlie Parrett was too smart for that."

"If he was so smart, he should have stuck to poaching instead of going on the high toby."

Ned scuffed his worn boots in the dirt. "I reckon. Anyways, Charlie was right about his lordship and his Christmas dinner. Magistrate said he'd come out tomorrow to look over the place. No hurry today, with Charlie dead and the killer long gone, he said. And the widder had her money back, so he could stop her caterwauling and send her on her way before she curdled the cream for his pudding. Takes his supper serious, Lord Cantwell does."

"Very well, and if you just volunteer as little information as possible when he does arrive, the whole thing should blow over shortly. You can play dumb, can't you?"

The boy grinned at him. "Seems I've had a heap of practice, my lord."

"Quite. And did you do as well at the Fighting Cock?" He hadn't put his ring on yet, just turned it in his hand. "Did that innkeeper give you any trouble?"

"Nary a bit, once he saw the brass. And I saw your groom, too." Ned looked away. "I wanted to make sure he was, you know, not mangled or nothing. He was sitting in the taproom, happy as a grig, Wilton's daughters making a fuss over him on account of the bandage on his head. Said he slept the day through, then woke up for supper right as rain. He was glad to get your letter, I could tell, and wanted particular to know the horses was safe."

"Trust Foley to care more for the chestnuts than for me."

"Prime 'uns they are for true. I brushed them down quietlike this morning while you were sleeping. But he asked about you, too. Said he didn't recognize me a bit, so I was thinking I was home free, till he wanted to know why I wasn't wearing livery, and if I wasn't from the Priory, where'd I meet up with you and where'd you get the blunt to pay his shot and hire him a carriage. I didn't know what you wanted me to say, him being your man and all, so I did what you said just now and played dumb. He thinks I'm stupider'n a rock," Ned complained, "what doesn't even know its way home." He paused to look up at the man who towered over him. "Is it true you're St. Cloud? The earl hisself, who owns half the county?"

St. Cloud cursed. He wished Foley's head had

been hit just a mite harder. "I am the earl, yes, but nowhere near as wealthy as all that."

The boy whistled through his teeth. "St. Cloud hisself," he marveled. "And I brushed your horses. Wait till I tell Ma."

"You'll tell her nothing of the sort," the earl ordered, but knew the boy would burst if he didn't tell his mother, so tacked on, "until I am long gone. You'll have to figure a way to tell her without mentioning the robbery. A carriage accident, I think, and you helped. That way you can explain about the money for her doctor." He flipped the boy two gold coins. "But don't mention the lady with me."

Ned looked confused. "The lady?"

"Excellent, boy. You'll have that rock perfect yet. Now tell me, did you send Miss Beaumont to the farmhouse to freshen up? We should be on the road soon, lest Cantwell decide to do his civic duty between meals after all."

Ned was shaking his head no, and St. Cloud suddenly felt an emptiness in the pit of his stomach that had nothing to do with hunger. "She's not at the house?" He raced around the barn to the well, Ned and Pansy on his heels. St. Cloud spun back and grabbed the boy's thin shoulders. "Tell me you gave her directions to a stream or something where she's gone."

White-faced, Ned shook his head again. "She . . . she wasn't here when I came back, sir. I thought you knew."

The earl ran back to the barn to search the stalls in case she woke up and realized the impropriety of sleeping next to him. Maybe he snored. Maybe . . .

Her things were gone, except for Pansy and the blue blanket. And a page from his notepad, stuck on a nail in the stall where they'd slept. St. Cloud sank down on a bale of hay while he read.

Dear Merry, Happy birthday and Merry Christmas. You are an honorable man, and under other circumstances I would be proud and happy to be your wife. Circumstances were such that I feel I can call you Merry, instead of Lord Jordan or whatever your title, but I cannot marry you. I cannot take advantage of your nobility and generosity and am therefore leaving. I have nothing to leave you for a Christmas gift or to thank you for your kindness, except that I might help grant your Christmas wish after all. Now you shall have one less responsibility, one fewer persons hanging on your sleeve.

For your birthday I am giving you Pansy. I cannot travel well with her, and she would not be happy in London, but that is not why I am leaving her with you. She is a very smart pig, and I know you will care for her, but mostly she will make you smile. I defy any man to be a sobersides with a pig as a companion. She likes sticky buns and having her ears scratched, but I expect you already know those things.

I have borrowed five shillings, so you do not need to worry about my reaching London. I shall return them to you in care of the postmaster at Bramley as soon as I am able. I regret taking them without your permission, but you would have argued about my decision to leave, and I could not bear to see you angry again. I shall remember you sleeping instead. Thank you for your kindness and best wishes to you. Sincerely, Juneclaire Beaumont.

St. Cloud cursed and threw his ring across the barn, the ring he was going to give her as proof that *her* Christmas wish was coming true. Pansy chased it, chuffing at the new game, nosing in the straw until she found it.

"Botheration," he raged. "The blasted animal will likely eat the damn thing and choke. Then Junco will have my head for sure." As he traded the last apple for his ring, St. Cloud realized he was thinking of Miss Beaumont in the future, not the past. Never the past, gone and forgotten. He was going after her.

He wiped his slimy, gritty ring on his sleeve—the once elegant greatcoat was ready for the dustbin after these two days anyway—then put it on his own finger, until he found Juneclaire and could place it on hers. After he strangled the chit.

"Fiend seize it, she must have been gone for hours! She could be halfway to London by now if Bramley is as close as you said." The boy nodded from the doorway, miserably aware that he should have awakened the gentleman ages ago. He wiped his nose on his shirtsleeve, to his lordship's further disgust. The earl stomped back to the stall where his pistol and his flask lay.

"After all my efforts to keep her out of this scandalbroth," he growled, "she has to go make mice feet of her reputation. The Devil only knows what she'll say about Charlie Parrett or you."

Ned was inching along the railing in the barn, not sure whether to flee his lordship's wrath or stay to take the pig home after the furious gent butchered it. Ma'd be right pleased to have fresh ham for Christmas dinner and bacon for Easter. Mention of Charlie Parrett stopped him in his tracks. "Me? You think she'll go to the magistrate and turn me in?" His voice was so high, it cracked. "But she didn't want to last night."

"No, brat, she won't peach on you on purpose. She's got bottom. But if she comes from this way, the good citizens in Bramley are bound to ask if she saw anything. And how is she going to explain being on her own? And if I go after her, there are certain to be more questions."

"Naw, no one'd dare quiz a fine swell like you." Ned didn't mention that most of the villagers would run inside and slam their doors rather than ask such a fierce-looking, arrogant nobleman what he was doing in their midst.

St. Cloud was pacing the length of the barn, the piglet trundling after. He was talking more to himself than to Ned, who was filling buckets for the horses. "But if they don't talk to me, I'll never find out where she went. And if I don't give some answers, they'll make them up. I know village life; it's the same as London gossip. No, I'll have to hope no one recognizes me."

"What about your uncle Hebert, the magistrate? He has to know you."

"Prosy old puff-guts always hated me, too. He's not even a real relation, just by marriage, his sister to my uncle. The dastard's bound to ask a lot of questions."

"Like what happened to your face."

"I haven't even seen how bad it looks." The boy's grimace told him. "A carriage accident."

"And where did you sleep?"

"Under a hedge."

"And what were you doing Bramley way, when everyone knows the Priory is clear west and north?"

St. Cloud started leading out the chestnuts, and Ned ran to help. "I was meeting Miss Beaumont to escort her to my home. And if anyone asks where is my groom or her maid and how did I mislay a female in my care, I'll tell them it's none of their deuced business. Especially not Hebert Cantwell's."

Ned whistled, impressed in spite of himself. "Guess it's no wonder they call you Satan St. Cloud, telling all those bouncers, and on the Lord's birthday, too! But they're going to wonder all the same, a top-of-the-trees gentleman like yourself all mussed up and Charlie Parrett laid out dead. What'll you say if anyone asks if you killed him?"

"The truth, brat, that he was such a bungler, he shot himself with his own pistol."

Chapter Eight

*J*uneclaire was on her way out of Bramley before St. Cloud was aware she was gone.

How silly he was, she had thought on the short walk toward the village earlier that morning, as soon as the cock crowed in predawn light. How silly and how sweet, to think about saving her from gossip. But ruination was only for ladies of the ton, not poor females. Indigent misses could not afford to worry overmuch about their good names, not when they had to consider their next meal. As for Juneclaire, she had no name to speak of, so how could she lose it? Her aunt already considered her no better than she should be because of her parents' marriage. She made it plain no respectable man would have Juneclaire to wive without good reason.

Merry, Lord Jordan, though, with all his talk of heirs and London, was Quality. He was of the ton, and he respected Juneclaire enough to offer marriage when he need not at all. He thought she was good enough to bear his own name, bear his children. No one else's opinion mattered.

He said she was beautiful and brave. The thought kept her warm on the way to Bramley. She was not feeling very courageous, once wagons and carriages started passing her, local people on their way to church dressed in all their finery, staring at the outsider. She was truly alone now, without even Pansy to talk to, to watch out for. Her own solitary state seemed much magnified without the little animal, now that she was coming among strangers. Merry would look after Pansy, she assured herself, before she fell into a fit of the dismals with missing her companion. The pig, not the man, she tried to convince herself. He was a real gentleman—the man, not the pig—so Pansy would be safe. Juneclaire did not think he'd bring that formidable temper of his to bear versus an innocent creature. Not that his ill humors were a sham, she admitted, but they seemed more an ingrained habit than from genuine meanness. He was kind. He had been mostly gentle with her and more than fair with Ned. He was concerned about his groom and worried that his people were fretting at his late arrival. He was a good man. He wasn't appreciated by his relatives either, which was just about the only thing he and Juneclaire had in common, besides a night in the barn. Her mind had come full circle. That was enough to dream about, not enough to marry on.

"Do you need a lift into town, miss? Bells are starting to toll." An old couple in an antique tilbury had pulled up alongside her while she was wool-gathering. "I be Sam Grey," the man said, "and this be my Alice."

Alice took in the odd condition of Juneclaire's cloak, as well as the quality of its cut and fabric. Juneclaire felt those old eyes missed nothing, not her tapestry bag, the muddied half boots, or the mismatched mittens. Juneclaire bobbed a curtsy, lest these good people think her manners as ramshackle as her appearance, and smiled. "A happy day to you, sir, ma'am. I am Juneclaire Beaumont, and I would be delighted to accept your kind offer."

Alice smiled back at Juneclaire's pretty behavior and moved over on the seat. Her black dress crinkled as she moved, so starched it was. She had a new green bow on her black ruched bonnet, and Sam wore a sprig of holly in his lapel. "Can't think what folks is about," he groused now, clucking the equally ancient horse into motion, such as it was, "passing a little gel like you up on the way to church, and this being a holy day and all."

"You know what it is, Sam, what with highway robberies and shootings, folks think they can't trust anyone. Little Bramley has never seen the like. Our Johnny brought the news this morning, Miss Beaumont. Such goings-on."

Juneclaire only had to nod and exclaim "How terrible" a few times while Sam and Alice speculated on the unmourned demise of Charlie Parrett. Sam spit over the side of the carriage. "Should end any of this bobbery about a gang of footpads in the neighborhood. Charlie Parrett was ringleader, mark me, and you'll see no more lawbreaking roundabouts, and a sight more rabbits and grouse on Lord Cantwell's estate, to boot." He laughed and coughed and spit again.

Alice patted his hand, then turned to Juneclaire. "A nice young lady like yourself hadn't ought to be alone on the roads during such uncertain times."

There was no censure in Alice's remark, just a great deal of curiosity. Juneclaire knew her face would turn red if she tried to lie to this shrewd little woman, and her tongue would twist itself in knots. It always did, so she told the truth. "I have no choice, for I had to help a friend in need, and my own situation was intolerable, so I am going to London to seek a position. I have coach fare and a bit extra."

Sam spit again but Alice *tsk*ed. She didn't know about any friend, but she could imagine what kind of trouble bedeviled such a pretty gal. "Well, you won't find the men are any different in London, Miss Beaumont. I can tell you, for Sam and I were in service at one of the great houses for years, we were, till the master pensioned us off and we came here. I suppose you have references and appointments and friends to stay with till you are settled?"

Juneclaire stared at her mittens, wishing the right one could grow an inch up the cuff. "No, ma'am, just the address of our old housekeeper. I was hoping she might—"

"Without references? You must have come down with the last rain, Miss Beaumont. And if Bramley sounds bad, with talk of highwaymen and poachers and murderers, you should see London. There's cutpurses on every corner, and that's not the worst of it. Why, a pretty girl like you would get swallowed up the second your foot touched pavement. There are folks there who meet the coaches looking for just such ones as yourself. They offer the little country girls jobs and rooms and rides—and do you know where the girls end up?"

Juneclaire didn't, but she could guess. Aunt Marta had preached about the fleshpots of the city often enough. Feeling slightly ill, Juneclaire thanked Mrs. Grey for her warning. "Now I shall know better how to go on."

"You've never been in service, have you, dearie?" Alice guessed, shaking her head.

"Not that I ever got paid for, no. But I cannot go back. Pansy—"

While Juneclaire was realizing that she no longer had to worry about Pansy's future, Mrs. Grey was bemoaning a world where gently bred females—and she did not hesitate to declare Miss Beaumont a lady—had to leave home and hearth to see their virtue intact. Alice didn't doubt this Pansy had been seduced and abandoned by some rakish lordling or other, and Miss Beaumont was next.

"Don't fret, missy, I'll talk to Mrs. Vicar Broome right after service. She knows everything that's going on in the parish, so she'll find you a ride toward Springdale. That's the next closer coaching stop to London, and folks in Bramley have lots of relatives there. Someone's bound to be going off for Christmas dinner. And we'll fix you up with some kind of letter of introduction. I still have lots of friends in London, though I wish there was another way."

During Reverend Broome's reading of the Nativity, Juneclaire thought about another way. Would she rather be a servant in someone else's household or a drudge in her aunt's? Servants got paid pittances, barely enough to repay Merry's loan, and that was assuming she found a position at all. Back with the Stantons, though, she did have a room of her own, the use of Uncle's library, all the food she wanted to eat—and no strangers whispering about her in church.

She knew she was an object of speculation, but she would have been horrified to hear her tale so embroidered. By the time Mrs. Broome had pressed a hot roll and a shilling into her hand, Juneclaire was escaping a ravening monster and ravishment. Pity the man who pursued Miss Beaumont to the hitherto peaceful little village.

Juneclaire was bustled toward Mr. Josiah Coglin, who was waiting with his wife and daughters for their coach to be brought round from the inn. The owner of the mercantile and his family were bound for Springdale, where Mr. Coglin's brother ran a similar enterprise. Mr. Coglin was all sympathy to Juneclaire's plight, quickly whispered into his ear by the efficient Mrs. Broome. Of course, the vicar's wife would never be indelicately explicit, but Mr. Coglin got the idea. So did Mrs. Mavis Coglin, who thought the drab little chit with heavy eyebrows must have invited any insults, since her looks had nothing to recommend her. Mrs. Coglin saw no reason to chance such a questionable miss with her own blond-haired, blue-eyed angels, or her husband. Miss Beaumont could ride on the seat with the driver and footman, she declared, lest the ladies' skirts get crushed. Further, if the chit wished to go into service, she'd better learn her place.

Juneclaire clutched her carpetbag in one hand—no one offered to take it for her—and waved goodbye to the Greys and Mrs. Broome with the other. Once the Coglin ladies were settled inside, the grinning footman took his seat, nearer to Juneclaire than she could like. She was already pressed against the coachman on her other side, and that man's watery eyes were more on her than the horses.

Could Stanton Hall be worse than this?

They stopped at an inn about an hour later when the younger Miss Coglin complained of queasiness. The footman, whose name Juneclaire had learned was Scully, hopped down smartly to lower the steps. All the while he was handing out the ladies and Mr. Coglin, he kept his leer on Juneclaire, hoping to catch a glimpse of ankle when she clambered down from the box without assistance. Mrs. Coglin turned her back on Juneclaire with a flick of her ermine tippet and demanded a private parlor, instantly. Mr. Josiah Coglin looked back at Juneclaire with a shrug of regret, either for his wife's manners or for missing a pretty sight.

Juneclaire brought her satchel, thinking she might take the opportunity to freshen up, but the innkeeper's harried wife was quick to direct her toward the kitchens, where the help ate.

"I am not a servant," Juneclaire stated. "Not yet,

at any rate." And she vowed never to accept employment with such jumped-up mushrooms. She took a seat at a window table in the common room so she could see when the carriage was ready to leave. Mrs. Coglin might just forget her guest the same way she forgot to invite her to share the early nuncheon her strident voice was demanding.

When Juneclaire managed to get the attention of the serving girl, she asked for tea and a quick snack. The maid, who looked none too clean and none too happy to be waiting on a solitary female who looked as if she hadn't a feather to fly with, took her not-so-sweet time before plunking down a tepid pot of tea, a watery egg, dry toast, and a rasher of bacon. Bacon! To keep the tears from her eyes, Juneclaire looked about the room at the other travelers. To her right was a large, noisy family whose children never stayed in their seats long enough to count. One small girl toddled over to Juneclaire, so she gave her the bacon, receiving back a runny-nosed, gummy grin. To her left snored two sheepherders, judging from their smell, with their heads on the table. Across the way was a party of loud young men still on the go from last night's wassail or this morning's ale.

One of the men was looking at her the same way Scully had looked at her, and she felt dirty again. She left a coin on the table and went to find a place to wash.

The innkeeper's wife met her in the hall and thrust a tray into her hands. "Here, you may as well be useful. Bring this in to your mistress." She jerked her head toward an oak-paneled door and bustled back toward the kitchen before Juneclaire could repeat, "But I am not a servant."

The tray had a steaming pot of tea, lovely biscuits, and golden currant buns. Juneclaire sighed.

She tapped lightly on the door, balancing the heavy tray in one unaccustomed hand, and went in.

"Put it there," Mrs. Coglin directed, again not offering to share the room or the food with Miss Beaumont. She didn't say "Thank you" either. Even Aunt Marta, the worst snob Juneclaire had ever known prior to this, always said "Thank you." She might pay her staff nipfarthing wages and treat them as interchangeable mannequins, but she always said "Please" and "Thank you."

Juneclaire demonstrated her own manners and breeding in inquiring as to the health of the younger Miss Coglin. That beribboned miss did not answer, too busy cramming biscuits into her rosebud mouth as fast as her dimpled fingers could snatch them away from her sister. Juneclaire turned to go, declining to curtsy.

"You can take this with you," Mrs. Coglin instructed, indicating yet another tray. This one held a single glass and a bottle of some reddish restorative cordial. Juneclaire thought of refusing, of giving her oft-repeated line like a bad drama, but then she thought of the miles to Springdale. She took up the tray.

Scully was coming out of the kitchens, wiping his mouth, when he spotted Juneclaire in the dark hallway with her hands full. Before she could begin to guess his intent, he grabbed hold of her and was slobbering damp kisses on her neck and cheek as she struggled to avoid his mouth on hers.

"Come on, pet, it's Christmas. Give a fellow a kiss now."

It was all of a piece that such a self-inflated shopkeeper as Mrs. Coglin would have a loose screw for a footman. Juneclaire didn't have a darning needle about her person, so she pushed at him, but he was too strong. Or the ale he'd been drinking was.

"What's the matter, lovey? Who're you saving it

for? That last gent couldn't've been any good if he
sent you on the road. Scully'll show you a better
time."

What Scully showed her was that he was bigger,
so she'd better be quicker. Scully was Mrs. Coglin's
servant; let *him* carry the blessed restorative, drip
by sticky, sugary, reddish drip. Down his face, down
his shirt, down his ardor.

Now she couldn't go on with the Coglins.

Juneclaire fetched her bag and left the inn just
as that noisy family was departing. A gaunt woman
with an infant in her arms was trying to herd her
brood onto the back of an open wagon half filled
with boxes and bundles and two chickens in a crate.
The father chewed on the stem of his pipe and patted the workhorses hitched in front while he waited.
The patient beasts' noses were pointed west, toward Strasmere, toward Stanton Hall.

"Pardon, sir, but could I ride along with you for
a bit? I can pay my way, and I won't mind sitting
in the back with the children."

Juneclaire was going home. Uncle Avery would
never let her be thrown on the dole, and Aunt
Marta would just have to take her back. It might
be too optimistic to hope Lady Stanton would appreciate her niece more, now that she had a day or
two of running the Hall by herself, but no matter.
Juneclaire was good at it. What she wasn't good at,
it seemed, was facing the world on her own. She
wasn't quite that brave, no matter what Merry
thought.

Despite what she saw as a grievous flaw in her
character, and a disappointment to Merry if he
should find out, Juneclaire was determined not to
be cowed by her relations. She would *not* marry a
fusty old man of her aunt's selection, not after turning down the most handsome, most intriguing rake
in England. She would *not* be harassed by her cous-

ins, not after routing Scully, and not after spending a night safe and unafraid in the arms of a true gentleman.

Juneclaire pulled the little runny-nosed moppet toward her and curled up on the hard wooden wagon bed, her satchel under her head as a pillow. She'd just rest after her adventures, and she would *not* cry.

Chapter Nine

*S*t. Cloud thought he'd leave the pig. Then he thought of trying to convince Miss Beaumont that he was a worthy candidate for her hand without that blasted pig in his. There was no way he could look into those soulful brown eyes and tell her that he'd found Pansy a good home. Not when he was bound to recall Ned's thin frame and hungry, hopeful expression every time the boy glanced at the porker.

Then the earl had to consider that he couldn't spring the horses without seeing if pigs really could fly. Those little trotters weren't meant for clinging to a swaying bench going sixteen miles an hour, nor was St. Cloud willing to dawdle. Neither could he manage the chestnuts, fresh as they were, with one hand.

Rope, that's what he needed. Ned almost lost his front teeth, grinning at the impatient nobleman, but he did fetch a coil of hemp. St. Cloud made a harness of sorts, looping the rope under Pansy's legs, across her belly, and over her chest, around her neck, meeting in a sailor's knot on her back. The other end was snubbed to the arm rail, over Pansy's vociferous protests. The shoat was even more unhappy when, not three yards from the barn door, she slid off the seat to dangle inches from the wheels, all four feet kicking in the air. The volume of noise coming from the baby swine was far out of proportion to her size and was only equalled by St. Cloud's curses.

"Is there a crate around, boy?" he demanded of Ned, who was thrilled to be enlarging his vocabulary. Ned shook his head, then learned a few more new words.

St. Cloud gave up. He unbuttoned his greatcoat and stuffed the piglet into his waistcoat. Pansy stopped complaining immediately. The earl rebuttoned all but two middle buttons of the outer garment so Pansy could stick her snout out and breathe. No one in London would believe this.

No one in Bramley would either.

It had surely been an eventful Christmas morn in the little village: that widow screeching about highwaymen, then Charlie Parrett riding in face-down, and a slip of a thing running off to London to save herself from a fate worse than death, now this bedlamite. The fellows brimming with Christmas cheer in the inn's taproom couldn't decide if the raggedy chap with the thunderous look was Charlie's killer and confederate, a rapist, or just a raving maniac. Then the hostler who led the horses away reported a well-known crest on the curricle. Worse yet, he was Satan St. Cloud.

Now, coincidences were one thing, but not one of the men gathered at the bar doubted for an instant that all the day's unlikely events circled around this nasty-looking nobleman like steel bits near a magnet. From his reputation and the ugly bruise on his face, they assumed he'd helped Charlie Parrett to the big poaching preserve in purgatory. From his reputation and his query about a missing young lady, they knew he was bent on having his way with the chit. Not in Bramley, he wouldn't, not when jobs were scarce and prices were high, with him closing down the old quarry and shutting down the wood mill, and half the farmers paying him rent without ever getting to speak their piece about repairs or crops. They dealt with his uncle or his agents, and that wasn't half-right. St. Cloud sure wasn't going to be helped in his hellraking, not when many of the local families sent their girls to the Priory to be maids and such. Not even rounds for the bar loosened tongues.

They drank his ale and watched out of the corners of their eyes when he poured his mug into a saucer and fed it to the pig. His reputation or not, none of them could figure out about the pig. None of the locals had any truck with the gentry anyway; queerer than Dick's hatband, all of 'em.

St. Cloud ordered breakfast for two and carried his mug and the pig's dish over to a table to wait, to think about his next move. On the way, he saw himself in the cracked mirror over the bar—and shuddered. Black hair sticking at all angles, purple bruises on his cheek and chin, no cravat whatsoever, and two days' growth of dark beard—it was no wonder the sots at the bar wouldn't give him the time of day. They most likely thought he'd steal it from them! In London the earl shaved morning and evening, bathed at least as often if he was riding or boxing or fencing, and changed his clothes from buckskins to pantaloons to formal knee breeches without a second thought. His valet, Todd, was liable to go off in an apoplexy if he saw the earl in such a state. Then he'd quit.

The citizens of Bramley might be more forthcoming if he didn't look like Dick Turpin, and he'd feel better, too, the earl decided after a satisfying breakfast of beefsteak and kidney pie, potatoes, hot muffins, and coffee. Pansy did not care for the cof-

fee, so he drank hers also. Then he addressed the
landlord about a room to wash and shave in. Money
still opened some doors, he was relieved to note,
although he was forced to rent the room for a day
and night, payment in advance. No amount of
money was going to see Pansy up the innkeeper's
stairs, so St. Cloud tied her to his chair and tossed
a coin to the barkeep to keep her ale flowing.

There wasn't much he could do about the bruise.
Todd would have some concoction to cover it up, but
he was at the Priory, likely steaming imaginary
wrinkles out of St. Cloud's evening attire. And
there was no hope for the caped greatcoat. It would
have to be burned. St. Cloud could wash, at least,
and didn't cut himself too badly with the borrowed
razor. The serving wench who brought the hot water managed to find a cravat somewhere, likely
some other guest's room, he didn't doubt from the
way she quickly tucked his coin down her bodice.
There, now he felt presentable again.

The maid must have thought so, too, for she
stayed to admire the earl's broad shoulders and cleft
chin.

"I don't suppose you know anything about a
young woman wearing a gray cloak, do you?" he
asked her, thinking she might be interested in talking.

That's not what Betty was interested in at all.
She shook her head. Foolish chit, refusing the likes
of this top drawer. So what if he looked like storm
clouds, he was generous, wasn't he? A girl could do
worse. "Why don't you stay the night and I'll ask
around? Maybe I'll find something out, or maybe
you'll forget about looking. The room's paid for
anyways."

The earl smiled at her, if you could call a cold
half sneer by that name, and walked by her without commenting. Something in his bleak look made

Betty call after him, "I heard she came through town early, but she never came by the inn that I saw. You might try the church."

St. Cloud didn't know if the suggestion was for the sake of his immortal soul, his manhood, or his quest for Juneclaire, but he had nowhere else to try.

He gathered up a sleeping pig, a sack of potato peelings and yesterday's muffins, and proceeded to the church.

The second Christmas service was in progress; maybe Juneclaire was inside praying. He eagerly stepped over the threshold, then halted. Not even the Earl of St. Cloud would bring a pig to church. Pansy barely roused when he tied her to the hitching rail outside, between a dappled mare drowsing over a feed bag and a fat, shaggy pony harnessed to a cart decorated with greenery and red ribbons. St. Cloud scattered a few muffins near the piglet just in case she woke up hungry—she always woke up hungry; in case she woke up, period—and fed one to the pony. Then he went into the little church and took a seat near the rear.

Now Merritt Jordan was not one for practicing religion on a regular basis, but never since his school days had he sat on bare wooden pews with the reprobates and recalcitrants avoiding the preacher's eye. He scowled, and his neighbors on the bench scooted over. That was one benefit of two days in the same clothes, he told himself, and sharing them half that time with a pig. Now he was free to stare at the backs of the worshipers ahead of him, those too well bred to turn around to look at the latecomer.

There was Cantwell in the first pew, the one with the carved aisle piece. St. Cloud wagered old Hebert's fat behind wasn't on any hard bench. He'd have soft cushions for himself and his family while the rest of the congregation, his people, wriggled and writhed in discomfort. Cantwell's wife was the broad-beamed lady beside him with the stuffed white bird mounted on her bonnet. What kind of hypocrite killed a dove for Christmas? he thought maliciously, flicking his gaze over the rest of Cantwell's party: two washed-out blond misses, a sandy-haired youth.

The earl studied each rear view in the church. There were five ladies with gray mantles, but two had gray hair, one had black, another was suckling an infant under the cloak, and the last one's head barely reached over the pew in front. Of the brunets, in case Junco had removed her cloak, only one was of the right height and slimness, with erect posture and neatly coiled braids. He stared at the woman's back, willing her to turn around. She did and gave him a wink from one of her crossed eyes.

The minister was stumbling over "the Lord coming among us this day," and the choir was singing the final hymn. St. Cloud turned his back to study the stained-glass windows as the parishioners filed out after the recessional. When the foot shuffling and whispers had passed, the earl turned and approached the doorway, where the vicar was shaking the last hands.

"A word with you, Reverend, if you don't mind? I'll only take a minute of your time."

Mr. Broome nodded, pushing the spectacles back up his nose. He led the way back down the church aisle and out a side door to a covered walk leading to the manse.

When they were seated in the vicar's office, the earl declined a politely offered sherry, knowing the reverend must be wishing him to the Devil, with his Christmas dinner growing cold.

"To be brief, sir, I was told you might have information about a young woman passing through here this morning."

Mr. Broome polished his glasses. The earl ground his teeth. When the spectacles were wiped to the gray-haired man's satisfaction, he looked up at his caller and asked, "And who might you be?"

The earl was trying his damnedest to hold his temper in check. "Merritt Jordan," he replied, thinking to keep his unsavory St. Cloud reputation as far away from Juneclaire as possible.

The vicar blinked, then blinked again. Yes, he had that look of his father and uncle before him. Broome had grown up with the Jordans. But the young earl was said to be an intelligent man, among other things. How could he suppose that a vicar who got his living from the family would not instantly recognize his patron's name? Didn't Reverend Broome pray for St. Cloud's reform and redemption every night?

"Ah, what might you want with the young lady, if I might ask?"

St. Cloud bit back a curse. He was not in the habit of explaining his actions to anyone, yet he knew he wasn't going to hear a word until he reassured the old dodderer. "Nothing havey-cavey, I swear. I intend to marry the girl."

Thank you, Lord. The vicar raised his head with a smile. "Do you, now?"

"As soon as I find her, damn it. Excuse me, vicar. You can perform the ceremony yourself to see it's all on the square, if you just tell me where Miss Beaumont is."

Positively beaming now, Mr. Broome rose and poured out a glass of the unwanted sherry. "I'll just go speak with Mrs. Broome for a moment. She's the one who saw the young lady off, you know. She wasn't happy about such a sweet young thing out on her own, going to London, so she'll be pleased as punch to make your acquaintance. I'll just be a second, my lord."

He was more than a second, and his wife was not pleased to be called out of her kitchen with her hair coming undone and her cheeks flushed from the oven fires. Red-faced, the vicar returned, while angry whispers sounded in the hall.

"I'm afraid my good wife is, ah, concerned. Not that I doubt your sincerity, mind, but, ah . . ."

"Get on with it, man. I don't have a special license in my pocket to prove my intentions are honorable, blast it. Do you want me to swear on your Bible?"

"I think you have sworn enough, actually, my lord," the vicar gently reproved, making the earl feel about six years old.

He apologized, then sipped the sherry to restore his patience. "What, then?"

"It has to do with a friend of Miss Beaumont's. Pansy, I believe."

Sherry spewed down St. Cloud's new cravat. "Pansy? Your wife is worried about Pansy? Is everyone demented? Pansy is under my care, sleeping off a drunk right now."

The vicar shook his head sadly. His wife was correct, poor Pansy's ruin was complete, and his lordship showed no remorse. "I am sorry, my lord, in that case I cannot—"

"Wait, let me get her. You'll see for yourself, and Mrs. Broome, too."

Mrs. Broome was wringing her hands when the earl returned and dumped a tipsy piglet on her polished wood floors. Pansy tried to gain her feet, scrabbling against the shiny surface. Then she gave up, collapsed in a heap, and passed wind.

"Meet Pansy," St. Cloud announced. "You should have let sleeping hogs lie."

Chapter Ten

"*W*hat do you mean, I'll have no trouble recognizing the Coglins' coach because Miss Beaumont is riding on top with the driver?" No matter that he intended to take her up in his own open carriage, without footman or tiger. How dare anyone else treat Juneclaire so roughly! He jumped up and stalked to the fireplace.

"But, my lord," the vicar's wife tried to explain, fearing for her prized collection of china shepherdesses on the mantel, "Miss Beaumont had no maid or escort, and her clothes . . . Well, Mrs. Coglin did not see her for a lady."

"Anyone with two eyes in their head can see she's a lady! Hell and damnation, what kind of bobbing-block puts a female up on the box in the middle of winter?" He grabbed up a paperweight from Vicar Broome's desk.

Mrs. Broome was wringing her hands again. She didn't know whether to worry most about her bric-a-brac, the goose roasting in the kitchen, likely burning without her, or the lace curtains, which the pig was now tasting. She didn't want to offend his lordship, of course, but he was not a comfortable guest. "Mr. Coglin is the wealthiest shopkeeper in town, so his wife tends to get a bit above herself."

"Very charitably put, my love," her husband noted, his eyes twinkling. His lordship's anger warmed Reverend Broome's heart, it did, showing just the right amount of pride and protectiveness. This wasn't some hole-in-corner affair; the earl really cared for the girl. The vicar sighed when Lord St. Cloud gave his graphic opinion of coxcomb caper-merchants and their encroaching, overblown wives. Not all of his prayers for the earl's salvation had been answered, then. No matter, Mr. Broome was a patient man; he did not expect miracles.

Mrs. Broome was scarlet-faced, having snatched her beloved snow globe from the earl's hands before he could punctuate his comments about toplofty tradesmen by smashing it onto the desk. "No matter where she's riding, my lord, if you miss the coach along the road, you'll find the family at Coglin's dry-goods store in Springdale. You'll want to catch up with them before Miss Beaumont parts company with them, so perhaps you should hurry. Please?"

St. Cloud considered asking if he could leave Pansy with them for a while but reconsidered when the pig started nibbling on the carpet fringe. He did beg Mrs. Broome for a large hatbox, which she was only too happy to fetch if it would see him on his way with the blessed pig.

While he waited, the earl wrote a check against his London bank, made out to Mr. Broome. He did not fill in an amount. "Here, vicar, buy some cushions for the back pews. I promise you'll have better attendance on Sundays."

Who said prayers weren't answered?

Mavis Coglin loved to visit her sister-in-law, Joan, in Springdale. Joan and her family had rooms over the store on the main street, a cook-housekeeper, and a shabby landaulet. Mavis possessed a fine clapboard house overlooking the village green in Bramley, employed four domestics, and had a traveling carriage plus a chaise for local calls and such.

"No, Joan, dear, don't apologize," Mavis oozed. "We don't mind being cramped in this little parlor, do we, Mr. Coglin? And I am sure whatever your Mrs. Burke prepares is adequate, though how she had the time with all her other duties . . . So I had my own cook fix some of her specialities. Scully is bringing them up from the coach now. That's the traveling coach, of course. You won't mind if Scully helps serve, will you? I know your dear little girls are used to passing dishes and such, but truly, Joan, it's not quite the thing." Mavis was having a grand time, especially when someone knocked on the shop door right in the middle of dinner.

"You see, Joan, dear, how inconvenient it is to live near the store? Every Tom, Dick, and Harry is forever ringing your bell when a button falls off or a ribbon goes missing. Isn't that so, Mr. Coglin? Why don't you let Scully get the door, Joan? He'll send the inconsiderate fellow to the roundabout fast enough. So much more the thing, don't you know, than sending one of the children. I never answer the door myself, of course, except when Lady Cantwell calls. Dear Lady C. needed to confer with me about flowers for the church altar."

"Here now, mister, the shop is closed. Just because you went and spilled some wine on your neck cloth ain't no reason to ruin gentlefolk's Christmas dinner. I got splashed some myself and I'm still serving. And it ain't going to stop me from celebrating tonight neither, when the folks is home in bed."

St. Cloud wasn't listening, not to Scully anyway.

He was hearing the sounds of the family upstairs and trying to pick out Juneclaire's soft voice.

Scully put his hand on the earl's shoulder to set him on his way. "G'wan, now, pal. Come back tomorrow."

Scully's hand was removed by an iron vise around his wrist. "You forget yourself, *pal.* I am here to see Mr. Josiah Coglin, and you shall stand out of my way."

"It's worth my job, an' I let you go up," Scully whined, his fingers growing numb from the continued pressure.

"And it's worth your life if you do not." Eyes as cold as green ice bore into Scully, convincing him. He gulped and nodded. "Here," the earl ordered, thrusting a large hatbox into the footman's arms, "guard this. And if you value your neck, don't let it out."

Don't let what out? Scully sank down on the floor between the glove counter and the lace table, staring at the hatbox. He pushed the box across the aisle with his foot and rubbed his wrist. The fellow had the Devil's own strength.

Scully did not give a thought to his employers' safety upstairs, too concerned with his own skin and what was making noises in the dread box. Weren't no bonnet, that was for sure, with moans and grunts coming from it. The greasy hairs on the back of Scully's neck slowly rose, leaving a chill right down his spine. B'gad, the thing could be a goblin or some such creature from hell, ready to drink his blood if it got out. Scully had to know.

Fellow said don't let it out, not don't look. Scully edged closer on hands and knees to where he could peer in one of the holes poked through the lid. He took a deep breath and put his eye to the opening. A red-rimmed eye with no white showing looked back. Scully was out the door before his heart remembered to start beating again. He ran around the corner, jumped into the traveling carriage, and slammed the door. He wasn't going back upstairs till that warlock left and, no matter what the limb of Satan ordered, he wasn't staying downstairs with no soul-snatching hell fiend, not in a pig's eye.

"Sirs, ladies, forgive me for intruding, but could you tell me where I might find Miss Juneclaire Beaumont? You brought her here from Bramley."

Nearly all the Coglins had their mouths hanging open. Mavis closed hers with a snap and demanded that the impertinent fellow remove himself at once, before she called for her footman.

"Your man already greeted me at the door. Please, ma'am, Miss Beaumont? Then I shall be more than happy to leave you to enjoy your meal in peace."

Mavis sniffed. "I am sure I do not know what became of the baggage. She left the inn where we stopped for refreshment without so much as a by-your-leave."

"She just left? Surely you asked her where she was going, with whom?"

"I never had the chance, sirrah. The wanton went off without a word to anyone. No one saw her leave. And you can be sure I asked, for I meant to make the jade pay for my footman's new uniform, if the stains did not come out."

A muscle twitched in St. Cloud's jaw. "How did Miss Beaumont come to be responsible for your footman's uniform?"

"She threw a bottle of wine at poor Scully. Fine return for our Christian charity, I say. Now you can leave us decent people to our meal."

"A moment more, ma'am, so I understand perfectly. You let an innocent young lady set off by herself from an inn in the middle of nowhere?"

Mavis wiped her mouth delicately with her napkin. "I told you, I made inquiries. And there was no proof that she is, indeed, a lady. In fact, the innkeeper mentioned some young bucks passing through. Perhaps she took up with them."

"Ma'am," St. Cloud ground out through narrowed lips, "were you a gentleman, I would call you out. Were you a lady, I'd see every door in London closed to you. Miss Beaumont has more ladylike grace in her little finger than you possess in your whole overdressed, overweight, overreaching self."

"Josiah, throw him out," Mavis screeched, her face swollen and splotched. "Do you hear the way this ruffian is speaking to me? Do something, I say!"

Josiah Coglin figured the intruder to be five inches taller than himself, fifteen years younger, and in fitter condition by half. Jupiter, the most exercise Josiah got was carrying the cash envelope to the bank. Besides, the fellow was right. So Josiah did something; he passed around the mashed turnips. His brother snickered, and Joan hid her satisfaction in her napkin. The children still watched, wide-eyed.

Mavis saw no one was coming to her rescue and the rudesby was still glaring at her. "Pish-tosh," she blustered, "fine words coming from a fine jackanapes with rag manners and rags on his back. What do you know about gentlemen and ladies? Bounders like you come into the shop all the time, looking for a piece of gimcrack frippery to turn the girls' heads. For all we know, you're the doxie's fancy man. I know your kind."

St. Cloud's gaze could have withered the silk blossoms at Mavis Coglin's heaving breast if they were not already dead. "No, ma'am," he said on his way to the stairs, "you don't know my kind at all. Not many earls buy their own shoe buttons or silver polish."

* * *

Scully was still cowering in the coach when St. Cloud found him. The earl banged open the door and plucked the footman out like a pickle from a barrel. He held Scully by the collar, feet off the ground. "Why did Miss Beaumont throw the wine at you?" he demanded.

Scully was saying every prayer he ever heard, including the last rites. The earl shook him. "Why?"

"N-nothing, gov, I swear. She just come over violentlike."

Juneclaire, who pleaded mercy for a young robber? St. Cloud tightened his grip and shook the weasel again. "You must have done something to insult her. What?"

"A k-kiss, that's all."

That's all? St. Cloud broke the dastard's nose and darkened both his daylights, that's all. Scully was relieved the devil hadn't sent the demon in the box after him.

Damn! St. Cloud took a swallow from his flask while he tried to think through the fog of anger clouding his mind. He absently poured some of the brandy onto a roll for the pig nuzzling at his sleeve.

She could be anywhere! She could be halfway to London or asleep under a hedge. She could have taken a ride with anyone passing by that inn or been taken by the young blades for sport. Not even the brandy warmed the chill in his gut at the thought.

He needed more people to help search. He needed more money to pay them. The earl decided to drive home and organize the armies of servants at the Priory. He'd have them combing the countryside, searching every coach and cart. He'd get rid of the pig, thankfully, and saddle his stallion so he could

93

cover more territory. He'd get to London, hire Bow Street runners, and knock on every door in London asking if a Mrs. Simms was housekeeper.

Just let her be safe until he found her.

St. Cloud stuffed the pig back in her box and whipped up the horses, wondering at his determination to locate a chit he'd only known a day or so. It wasn't just pride, he told himself, because she had refused him, and not just how he hated to be thwarted. He wanted her, but this was more than lust, more than the thrill of the chase. He had to find her to fill that empty space where his dreams had been. He had planned on showing her the Priory, her future home; he'd pictured her in the portrait gallery, the orangery, the morning room. He could practically see her there. Now he'd be looking around the corners, staring in the mirrors, waiting for her to appear like Mother's ghost. He had to find her.

But he didn't find her, not even when his curricle overtook the lumbering old wagon full of noisy children. He didn't notice the sleeping woman among the bundles and boxes and babies and crated chickens. He kept on driving.

Chapter Eleven

Matthew Mulvilhill shoved his brother Mark into their sister Anne, who started bawling, which woke Baby Sarah, wailing in their mother's arms. Their father, John Mulvilhill, reached behind him to clout the nearest young Mulvilhill without taking his eyes off the horses. Lucas, minding his own business, was carving his name in the planked wagon with his new pocketknife. The knife slipped, ruining his perfect L, and Lucas said a word not found in the Bible. He hopped up to get out of his father's reach and tripped over little Mary, who was cuddled next to Juneclaire, who awoke to shrieks and kicks and a suspicious damp spot on her much-abused cloak.

Christmas carols held the children's attention for perhaps a mile, at the horses' phlegmatic gait. Somewhere in the middle of a wassail song Juneclaire noticed that in addition to the general bumpiness of the wagon now that they'd turned off the larger road, and the seeming inability of the children to sit in one place for the count of ten, one of the bundles was moving.

" 'Heigh-ho, nobody—' What in the world is in that sack?"

"Kittens. We're taking them to Granny's."

"In a sack?"

"Sure, you puts a rock in with 'em and they go down fast."

"A rock? You're going to drown the kittens?"

"Pa says we have too many cats; they'll eat the chickens, else."

"But . . . but it's Christmas!"

"That's why we gots to take 'em to Granny's. Our pond is froze, but she's near a good running stream. Pa says I can toss 'em in."

"No, it's my turn!"

"I can throw the farrest!"

"Pa!"

Juneclaire had no idea where she was. She was alone on a wood-bordered dirt track with no habitation in sight. She had only Mrs. Broome's roll by way of food in her satchel, two precious shillings less in her purse, and a sackful of kittens in her hands. And it was starting to snow.

She would *not* cry. The kittens would, and did, a pitiful mewing that hurried her to a log under a tree whose branches offered some protection. When she opened the sack, four pairs of bluish eyes blinked up at her. Another pair of eyes would never open again, no matter how hard she tried to blow life into the tiny mouth.

She didn't have time to cry. The other scrawny babies wouldn't eat the roll; it was too hard. They were too cold, too thin, too weak from hunger—and she couldn't just leave the dead one there for the badgers and crows. She made room in her carpet-bag and folded the sack on top of her belongings, then carefully lifted the kittens in. There were two gray-striped ones, a patchwork brindle, and an all-black kitten who tried to suck on her finger. She unwrapped her warm scarf and draped it over the top of the satchel, one corner turned back for air.

Crying was for children. Juneclaire cleared leaves away from a spot between two jutting roots of the tree. She laid the dead kitten on the ground, then covered it with the leaves, sticks, and whatever stones she could find. Then she placed her French Bible, the hymnal, and the volume of sermons on top of the makeshift grave and set out down the country lane, wiping her eyes. For the second time in two days she left her books on the side of the road; she couldn't begin to count how many new heartaches she carried with her. But those weren't tears, they were snowflakes.

If Juneclaire were alone, she would keep walking. She'd eat her solitary roll and walk until she found a likely cottage or tidy farmstead to seek directions or hire a cart ride back to Bramley. Sam and Alice Grey would put her up for the night, she thought, or Vicar and Mrs. Broome. She'd walk all through the night if she had to, if she were alone, rather than approach the derelict thatch-roof hovel and its broken-doored barn. This place seemed too poor for a horse or a scrap of food for the kittens or a warm fire. Goodness, the hut looked so poor, the people couldn't afford to give directions!

Maybe it was deserted, Juneclaire thought cheerfully as her brisk steps took her nearer. Maybe it was the haunt of one such as Charlie Parrett. Her feet dragged.

Then a dog started to bark. It was a big, mud-colored mongrel with a hairier strip down its back, charging out of the old barn.

"Good doggy," Juneclaire called. The dog came nearer, stiff-legged, snarling, sniffing the air. "Nice doggy," she said. The cur's ridge hairs were standing up, its teeth showing. Not a nice doggy at all.

The beast was barking and snarling in earnest now, darting up to snap at the air perilously close to her ankles. Juneclaire was going to throw her satchel at it, until she remembered the kittens. The kittens! She raised the bag over her head, shouting, "Go away, you miserable mutt! You're not going to eat my kittens, not on Christmas Day!"

The outcome was still pending when a sharp whistle pierced the air. The dog dropped to its belly as if poleaxed, though it still kept a yellow-eyed gaze on Juneclaire, daring her to take one more step. An old man hobbled out of the barn. Sam Grey was old; this man was old enough to be Sam's father. He was old enough to be Noah's father. He was bent, bald, and toothless, with skin like autumn leaves. But he controlled the big dog with a simple "Down, Jack. Good boy."

"Thank you," Juneclaire said. "I'll just be—"

"Don't know what's come over old Jack." He paused to think about it. "Usually it's just cats what get him so riled."

"It's my fault, then, for that's what I've got in my bag. I'd better get on my way. Good afternoon to you." She started to back away, keeping her eye on the big dog.

The old man was peering at her from under unruly white brows. His blue eyes were clear enough, though. He took a wheezing breath and said, "Hold, missy. What's a mite like you doing out here?"

With a simple hand gesture from his master, Jack was on his feet, rumbling low in his throat. Juneclaire stopped her retreat. "I . . . I was going to London to seek a position, but I decided not," she told him, thinning the story to its bare bones. She saw no reason to mention a pig, a nobleman, a highway robber, or Scully. "Only, the family that was carrying me back had all these children, and they were going to drown the little kittens. I couldn't let them, so I got off with the cats. Only, I don't quite know

98

where I am, and the kittens need something to eat, and yours was the first place I came to."

He nodded slowly, like a rusted hinge. No words came from his sunken mouth, so Juneclaire nervously went on, "I am heading west of Strasmere, but I have friends in Bramley. I just met them today, actually, but they are nice people. They'll help me. And . . . and I can pay my way."

Still there was no response. He couldn't have frozen in that position, could he, with the dog on guard? Juneclaire imagined them all turning into snow sculptures, the whole tableau waiting for the spring thaw. "F-forgive my manners." She bobbed an awkward curtsy. "I am Miss Juneclaire Beaumont, from Stanton Hall, near Farley's Grange."

The old man bent at the waist, and Juneclaire almost rushed forward to catch him, except the dog stood between them. "I'm Little Yerby," the ancient announced once he'd straightened and paused to catch his breath. "My father was Big Yerby. He's gone, but the name stuck. Even my Aggie calls me Little." There was another halt for breathing. "She's gone off to our daughter's lying-in with the donkey, else I'd ride you to town." He scratched his bald head. "Guess you better come in, then. Coming on to snow. My old bones've been warning me for days." He turned toward the house.

"But what about Jack and the kittens?"

"Jack does what I tell him."

Juneclaire hoped so, as she followed him toward the mean cottage, only she hadn't heard him tell Jack anything.

There were two rooms inside the dwelling, both neat as a pin. Fresh rushes covered the packed-dirt floor, and calico curtains fluttered at the windows. Vegetables and herbs hung from the rafters, and a warm fire burned in the open hearth. Juneclaire observed that Little Yerby's clothes were clean and neatly mended, as he took a copper kettle off the hob. He poured some of the hot water into an earthenware pot for tea and added a little to a saucer of milk for the kittens. Juneclaire crumpled the roll into the warm mixture and put it and the kittens, on their sack, near the fireplace.

With a mug of hot tea in her hand, Juneclaire was more than content to sit and watch the kittens attack their meal. "How could anyone think of destroying such sweet and innocent babies?"

"Be worse to let them loose to starve." Little Yerby was in a cane-backed chair, warming his gnarled fingers on the mug more than drinking from it.

"But they wouldn't eat so much."

"Big family like that, they was prob'ly scraping by just to feed their own young'uns."

"But they don't take them out and drown them if there are too many!"

"World's a hard place, missy."

Juneclaire sighed. "I know."

"Next choice is worse." Little Yerby stood up in stages, then turned and gave Juneclaire a toothless grin. "Don't know what my Aggie'll say—'tain't proper with her away and all, me inviting a pretty little thing to spend the night—but there it is. You can bunk near the fire, where my girl used to sleep. There be an old quilt somewheres." He shuffled off to the bedroom and rummaged in a chest. "Here 'tis. If you'll help with the chores, I'll add some vegetables to the stew Aggie left me. Can't chew much more'n that, you know. Still, I saved some dandelion wine for Christmas supper."

He halted at the pantry. "Sorry Aggie ain't here. It's the first Christmas since we married. Sorry my girl married away, too. What was I looking for? Oh yes, the wine. Mind wanders some, you know."

Then he slapped his thigh and doubled over, laughing. "Won't they talk down to the local, Little Yerby and a rare charmer. Aggie'll be tickled pink!"

Juneclaire smiled back. "And I'd be honored to be your guest, Mr. Yerby, and help with the chores."

"Yeah, the chores, near forgot. Not as spry as I used to be. You know anything about cows?"

"No, but I know a lot about pigs." Juneclaire was transferring the kittens to a basket he held out to her so they wouldn't wander too close to the fire.

Little Yerby slapped his leg again. "You ever milked a sow? There, you go on start; I'll put up the stew."

How hard could it be? The cows were all lined up, their heads in the food troughs. A bucket and a stool stood ready by the door. Jack sniffed at her but didn't growl or anything, so Juneclaire carried the equipment to the first animal in the line. She put the stool down, then shoved the bucket under. She removed her mittens and blew on her hands, then straightened her shoulders, sat down, and reached under the—uh-oh.

"Guess old Fred is tickled pink, too." But not as pink as Juneclaire's cheeks as she cautiously backed away.

The cows were easier. Juneclaire only got half as much on her as she got in the bucket, till she got the knack of the thing. Little Yerby skimmed off a ladle of cream and stored the rest of the milk while Juneclaire rinsed the buckets at the well.

After supper Little Yerby nodded over his pipe, and Juneclaire sat on her cloak by the fire with the kittens playing in her lap, their bellies round and full. Then Jack scratched at the door.

"Oh, dear, does he usually come in at night?"

"Just for an hour or two afore he settles down with the cows. He can stay out, though. You know, Aggie always wanted a cat. Said Jack was my dog, not her'n. Cat'd keep mice out of the pantry and the root cellar, too."

"And you have the milk for it, till the kitten can hunt on its own. But what about Jack?"

He knocked the pipe into the fireplace. "Never tried an infant before."

Juneclaire gathered the kittens on their sack. "He wouldn't . . . ?"

"Jack does what I tell him," Little Yerby answered, opening the door. "Down, Jack. Stay."

The dog lay rigid, tense, and ready to spring, the hackles at his back erect, his muzzle creased to show huge white teeth. Little Yerby nodded, and Juneclaire put the kittens down, about a foot from his nose, and held her breath.

There was a puddle of saliva under Jack's mouth by the time the kittens noticed him. He didn't move, but he growled. One kit dug its sharp claws into Juneclaire's skirts and tried to climb, one disappeared into the rafters, and another found the other room and hid under the bed. The last kitten, though, one of the gray-striped ones, arched its back and hissed. Jack raised pleading eyes to Little Yerby, who shook his head no. The kitten reached out a tiny paw and batted at Jack's nose.

"Look at that," the old man said. "Just like David and Goliath."

Juneclaire was ready to snatch the idiot cat out of harm's way, but Little Yerby told her to let them be. Jack nudged the kitten's foot, toppling the wee thing, which meowed loudly. Jack opened his mouth—and licked the kitten. Juneclaire gasped. David, as the hero was instantly christened, be it he or be it she, circled around and curled up to sleep next to the big dog's chest, between Jack's feet.

Juneclaire rounded up the other kittens and soothed them in their basket, with the familiar sack. She did not want to offend the old man's hospitality but had to renew her offer: "You have been so kind, Mr. Yerby, and I was no help with the chores at all to speak of, and David won't be feeding on Mrs. Yerby's mice for a while still, so will you not accept my shilling for his feed?"

"Nay, less, you'll be needing it more. Howbeit you can do something worth more than gold, missy. I couldn't get to church today without the donkey, not on these old legs, and I never did learn me my letters." He handed her a worn book. "Would you read me the story?"

So Juneclaire sat on the stool by the fire that Christmas night while the old man leaned back in his chair, one knobby hand resting on his dog's head, the other stroking a sleeping kitten.

" 'And it came to pass in those days,' " she began, " 'that there went out a decree from Caesar Augustus, that all the world should be taxed.' "

Chapter Twelve

*H*ome for the holidays. Oh, joy.

St. Cloud meant to head directly to the stables to begin to organize the grooms' search. Instead, he saw the gardener's boy race from the gate lodge across the lawns to announce his arrival at the Priory. Oh, blast!

By the time the earl tooled his weary chestnuts through the tree-lined drive, over the bridge at the ornamental lake, past the formal gardens and the maze, a welcoming delegation was waiting in the carriage drive.

His relatives would never be so outré as to demonstrate what might be taken for affection; they'd be waiting in the gold salon having predinner sherry and dissecting his character. St. Cloud Priory kept Town hours, even though Countess Fanny hadn't been to London in years. Instead, they sent servants to wait outside in the snow. There were two grooms and Foley to help with one curricle, three footmen to carry his bags that had been delivered the day before. His valet, Todd, took one look at the earl and about-faced up the steps to order a hot bath. Talbot, the butler, remained at attention in the open doorway and a maid was there to—Hell, St. Cloud couldn't figure why a maid was there at all, shivering. He handed her the hatbox and told her to wait inside.

He waved off the footmen and let the grooms take the chestnuts, with orders to double their rations. He held Foley back. The wiry ex-jockey was pale, with a small bandage still on his head.

"Old man, am I glad to see you. How are you feeling?" the earl asked.

"Fairly, my lord, iffen I can say the same? It's a rare takin' they been in, up to the house, with me no wiser from talkin' to that boy you sent with the blunt. I was that worried about the chestnuts, I was," the older man scolded.

"They've taken no harm, I swear. Listen, Foley, I need a groom to ride to London as soon as possible, through the night if the snow doesn't get worse."

"I'll go saddle Lightning, my lord. You have a message for me to take?"

"You're not going. Find one of the other men, someone you trust."

"You mean a younger man. I'll be handin' in my livery, then."

"Don't get all prickly and puss-faced on me, old man. Not now. You've been hurt, and I need you here."

Talbot coughed from up the stairs, subtly. "Old stone britches should shut the door if he's gettin' cold," Foley pointed out, not so quietly, not so subtly.

"Ignore him. Here is the message your man is to give to my secretary at Jordan House: I want every available footman and groom out in Mayfair, going house to house, looking for a housekeeper named Mrs. Simms. Some of the knockers will be off, but they should be able to ask around for the house-keepers' names."

Foley pulled at the bandage on his head. "I

thought I was the one concussed. Of all the crack-brained starts—"

"Enough, Foley. I am sure there will be more than one lecture waiting for me inside. I do not require yours."

Foley knew the short limits to the earl's patience. "Yes, my lord. And when the men find this here Mrs. Simms, what are they supposed to do with her?"

"Send for me, but give Mrs. Simms ten pounds to hold on to the lady—she'll know who I mean—and keep her safe until I can get there. I also want a man at every posting house that takes coaches coming into Town from Bramley, Springdale, or anywhere closer. They are to look for a lady in a gray, rabbit-lined cloak. She has brown hair and a smile like a Madonna. The man should follow her, find out where she goes, and make bloody hell sure she gets there safe. And send for me. I'll be in London as soon as possible. Is that clear?"

"Clear as pitch. Every man jack in London is to look for a housekeeper or a pretty chit."

"Right. Now go, get someone started while there's still light."

Foley left, shaking his head and muttering. "I take my eyes off the lad for less'n a day and there's a female involved. Should've known."

"Welcome home, my lord," Talbot intoned as he bowed the earl through the door. "Merry Christmas, my lord, and may I offer you the felicitations of the day on behalf of the staff and myself. The coincidence of your natal day with the Nativity brings double cause for joy and celebration." Talbot must have been practicing since yesterday. "The family and guests are in the gold parlor. Shall I announce you?"

"Good lord, no. I'm not fit for company, much less

milady's dinner table. Tell them to go in without me. I'll join them later for tea." He took the hatbox from the blushing maid, who curtsied and fled down the hall. "I have a great many arrangements to make, Talbot. I am sure Todd is seeing to my bath, but could you send up some dinner on a tray? Make that a large dinner. And a basket."

"A basket, my lord?"

"Large. And a decanter of that cognac my father put down. Large, if I have to face the family later."

Before St. Cloud could cross the black-and-white tiles of the huge entry hall to reach the arched stairways, his grandmother's less-than-dulcet tones floated down the hall: "So where is the scapegrace? Been home twenty minutes by my count, two days late, and nary a word for his worried kin. If I hadn't sent my maid out, we'd be sitting here like ninnies not knowing if he was dead or alive. Why, the jackanapes could have expired on the doorstep, and without an heir, mind you."

The dowager's words were punctuated by raps of her cane and, since she couldn't see what she was thumping, muffled oaths and tumbled footstools. "Sad lack of manners you taught the boy, Fanny. No sense of responsibility either, the rakehell. I've been sitting all day in this mausoleum among confounded strangers waiting for the whopstraw to show, instead of being home in my own comfort with my own people. Deuced if I'll stay here all night waiting on his convenience. Be like waiting for your haunt to come, Fanny. I'm going home. Talbot! Munch! Get the carriage! Where's my wrap?"

Before St. Cloud could flee upstairs past Talbot's stiff-spined, measured tread, the dowager's cane rapping started down the hall, followed by the crash of china. Lady Fanny's fluttery "Mother St. Cloud, please" came after. "What about dinner? Oh, I feel ill."

"Not in front of the guests, you ninny." That from Uncle Harmon. "Who's got the vinaigrette? Where's that blasted Talbot? No, Florrie, we won't burn feathers under Fanny's nose. Give Lady Pomeroy back her headpiece, you clunch. Elsbeth, stop batting your eyelashes at the admiral. Get over here and help your aunt."

Welcome home, my lord.

St. Cloud's silent appearance in the gold salon put an end to all the commotion except the dowager's flailing cane and demands for her carriage. "I am here, Grandmother, so you can stop enacting us a Cheltenham tragedy and upsetting Lady Fanny. I simply did not wish to present myself in all my dirt."

The dowager sniffed when he kissed her powdered and rouged cheek. "I can tell why. So what fustian are you going to give us for being two days late and near missing your own birthday party?"

"Why, Grandmother, you should know me better than that; I haven't seen fit to explain my actions since my youth. Surely you don't expect a rakeshame to make excuses?"

The dowager cackled and banged her cane down on Talbot's foot. The butler did not disgrace his calling by more than a wince, St. Cloud observed, as the earl turned to kiss his mother's brow, removing a lavender-soaked handkerchief to do so. "I am sorry if I interfered in your plans, my lady. You should know better than to fret over me."

"Dear boy, how could I not? My condition . . ."

St. Cloud was already shaking hands with his cousin, ignoring the younger Wilmott's smug looks. Niles was wearing white satin knee breeches, a white satin coat, and a white waistcoat picked out with red-and-green embroidered holly. None of it paid for, most likely. St. Cloud took great care to pat Niles on the shoulder in greeting, leaving a smudge. His cousin Elsbeth presented the tips of her fingers for his salute, her nose wrinkled. "That's more than travel dust, St. Cloud."

Uncle Harmon Wilmott did not put his hand out or step closer. He nodded curtly, frowning. "I think you could show more remorse for turning the house upside down and upsetting your mother's delicate nerves."

"Do you, Uncle?" The earl spoke slowly, deliberately, watching the color rise in the baronet's pouchy face.

Lady Fanny was quick to step into the silence, although she found interchanges between her son and her brother particularly wearing. "Yes, dearest, I was quite overset to think something must have happened to you, and there was the bother of redoing the seating plan, you know. I don't see what I would have done without Harmon's support. It's been that way for years, of course, and we mustn't let Harmon think we're ungrateful, dear."

St. Cloud bowed in his uncle's direction but did not add to his mother's words. She held a gray filmy scarf to her cheek. "You really should have been here," she reproved. "Harmon had to light the Yule log in your place. You know the head of the household holds that honor."

"I am certain Uncle Harmon found no difficulty in usurping my . . . honors." He turned to greet others of the company while his mother searched for her hartshorn.

Lord, even Sydelle Pomeroy was dressed—or undressed—to the nines. Red silk with nothing under it, unless he missed his guess.

"I knew you wouldn't forsake us, my lord," she breathed, making his appearance a compliment to her undeniable beauty.

" 'Us,' my lady? How could I forsake you when I did not know you would be here?" The sultry widow had been after St. Cloud's title as long as Cousin Niles had been after her fortune. Lady Pomeroy had been Uncle Harmon's wife's godchild and milked the tenuous relationship for all the invitations she could. She and Niles made a fine pair: cold, calculating, and conceited.

Damn, he wished they were all gone! Then St. Cloud remembered Junco—he hadn't thought of her for at least five minutes—and her wishes. An evil kind of grin came over his face, lips half quirked, eyes slightly narrowed. Only Niles recognized the St. Cloud smile for what it was and left off denigrating the earl's shabby manners. St. Cloud stepped back to the hall and returned with the hat-box.

Aunt Florrie clapped her hands together. "Oh, goody! You brought us a present!"

"My gifts to you must still be with my baggage upstairs, Aunt Florrie. This was a present given to me, which I was going to take upstairs, if I had been permitted. Since you've all made me feel so welcome, I'll share it with you."

He tipped Pansy out to the floor, and the piglet headed straight for the scent of biscuits, in ladies' hands, on low tables, and under gentlemen's pumps, where crumbs were ground into the Aubusson carpet. So Juneclaire was right, St. Cloud acknowledged. Christmas wishes come true. The room was almost clear in no time, the indomitable Talbot having the presence of mind to announce dinner. Juneclaire was right about another thing: a man with a pig really did have more opportunity to smile. St. Cloud was positively beaming.

None of those remaining in the parlor seemed to share his good humor, except for Florrie, who had tied a napkin around Pansy's neck and was helping her sip from the hastily discarded sherry glasses. The dowager was shouting to know what was going on, and how could everyone have gone into dinner without her taking precedence. Niles was snickering at more evidence of his cousin's gaucherie, and Lady Fanny had collapsed back on the sofa.

"Come, Mother, they cannot start without you." The earl half lifted his mother into Niles's arms. "Uncle Harmon, I am sure I can leave you to escort Lady St. Cloud into dinner."

Lord Wilmott was seething, his jowls quivering. "How dare you, sir, shame your mother by setting an animal loose in her drawing room? How could you bring such disgrace to this house?"

St. Cloud took out his quizzing glass, blessing Charlie Parrett for treating it kindly, and surveyed the overturned furniture, the broken glassware, and, finally, the livid baronet. "Odd," he drawled. "I thought this was my house." He bowed. "My ladies, I shall see you after dinner."

Chapter Thirteen

"*H*ogwash," St. Cloud told his cousin Niles. "The man works for me. If Todd can't look after one little pig for an evening, he's not worth his wages."

The efficient, even-tempered, and elegant gentleman's gentleman was worth a fortune, which was about what it took to convince Todd to play swineherd for a few hours. St. Cloud had no intention of discussing his domestic arrangements with Niles, however, not even to rid the coxcomb of that supercilious grin.

Todd had wrought miracles. The pig was fed, walked, and bedded down in St. Cloud's dressing room, with promises that Pansy would be installed in the stables tomorrow. And St. Cloud was combed, brushed, and polished to a fare-thee-well, from glossy black curls to glossy black footwear. His cheeks were as smooth as a baby's bottom, and the bruise on his face was almost unnoticeable. With his muscle-molding white Persian knee smalls, wide-shouldered black coat of Bath superfine and stark white linen enlivened only by an emerald stickpin the color of his eyes, he made Niles look like a man-milliner and the squire's sturdy sons look like bumpkins.

Most of the guests reassembled in the gold salon

chose to treat the pig incident as a fine joke, reinforcing St. Cloud's belief that an earl with upwards of forty thousand a year had a great deal of social latitude, and that Society was a jackass. It also appeared to St. Cloud that the joke became funnier the more females a man had to marry off. The admiral, with his three platter-faced chits, thought it was hilarious. He joined the squire, with one daughter and two nieces, in proposing toasts to the earl's birthday. Everyone joined in, in high good humor, especially once the lambs' wool punch was served round twice, except Mr. Hilloughby, his mother's current tame cleric, who stuck to tea, and Uncle Harmon, who was in high dudgeon.

Lady Pomeroy sat at the pianoforte, having arranged the candelabrum to best highlight her mature décolletage while shadowing the tiny signs of passing youth. She skillfully picked out carols, seemingly by heart, but purred a request for the earl to turn her pages for her.

Uncle Harmon frowned when St. Cloud acquiesced, taking a seat on the bench so near Sydelle that a draft couldn't have come between them. Lord Wilmott wanted the earl for Elsbeth, Lady Sydelle and her inheritance for the spendthrift Niles. The older man grew perfectly bilious at the thought of his goddaughter and his nephew making a match of it, melding their fortunes while his own expensive progeny got short shrift. Being well aware of his uncle's ambitions, and dyspepsia, the earl moved closer to the alluring widow.

The reverend decided it was time for one last Christmas invocation, for faith, hope, and chastity, and a benediction for the Christ child.

"Speaking of children, St. Cloud, when are you going to provide some for this old pile?" The dowager did not wait for Hilloughby's amen. She couldn't see the blushes of the younger girls, invited for his consideration, St. Cloud made no doubt, and wouldn't have cared anyway. "It's time and past you married and got yourself an heir. I want grandchildren!" She thumped her cane down, hard, on one of the squire's chits' gowns. The girl ran crying from the room, trailing a flounce. "What's that ninnyhammer Fanny crying about now?" the dowager demanded.

St. Cloud removed the cane from her fingers. "You don't need this while you are having tea, and that was not Lady Fanny, Grandmother, but an innocent miss you have embarrassed with your wayward cane and wicked tongue."

"Humph. If all the young gels are such niminy-piminy, milk-and-water chits, it's no wonder you haven't taken leg shackles. But I can't wait forever, you know. This place has been in the Jordan family for centuries, boy, and it's your job to see it stays there."

He sipped slowly from his cup. "I am no longer a boy, Grandmother."

"And I wouldn't ask a boy to do a man's job!"

Lady Fanny tried to play peacemaker again, handing round a plate of sugarplums. "I am sure St. Cloud knows his responsibilities to the name, Mother St. Cloud."

"And to his family," Uncle Harmon put in, as blatant as a battleship. He dragged Elsbeth away from one of the squire's sons and thrust her onto the sofa next to her cousin.

Elsbeth was her usual sulky self, in a pet this evening because she was not the center of male adulation. She and Aunt Fanny had invited the plainest girls in the country for St. Cloud's perusal, knowing Elsbeth would shine in contrast. Now he and every other man in the room, including the squire's gapeseed sons and her own brother, were panting after that fast Sydelle Pomeroy. Even Mr.

114

Hilloughby's collar got too tight when the widow walked past him, as slow and slinky as sin. Elsbeth bet the widow's skirts were dampened. Red silk, while Elsbeth sat as demure as a debutante in pink chiffon! It wasn't to be borne. Worst of all were the calf's eyes St. Cloud was making at the older woman, when everyone in the room knew he was as good as promised to Elsbeth. Papa said he was only sowing more wild oats, that he'd only offer a lightskirt like Sydelle a slip on the shoulder. Well, Elsbeth was tired of cooling her heels in Berkshire while St. Cloud was kicking his up in London.

"Yes, cousin," she lisped. "Just when are you going to drop the handkerchief?"

He dropped a bombshell, not a handkerchief. "I already have."

The admiral called for another toast. He'd wasted an evening, but the punch was good.

"No, sir, it's not official yet. I haven't had a chance to seek her family's permission, but I expect her here within a few days."

"Oh, dearest, how wonderful! Who are her people? Shall we like her?" The countess's various shawls and draperies dipped in the tea, in her excitement.

"Her name is Juneclaire, and I'm sure you'll love her, Mother. And, no, you do not know the family. They are from Farley's Grange." He pushed the tray back farther.

"Nobody who's anybody lives in Farley's Grange, boy. When do we get to meet her?"

"As soon as I can arrange, Grandmother, and her grandfather was from the *ancien régime*, not that it matters a halfpenny."

"Foreigners," the dowager muttered, secretly delighted he'd chosen anyone but that Pomeroy high flier or Harmon's brat.

"You must give me her address, dearest, so I can extend a formal invitation."

St. Cloud took a deep breath. Thinking it was better to get over rough ground quickly, he flatly announced, "I have no idea where she is."

His mother dropped her vinaigrette bottle. "You aren't bringing one of those independent London bluestockings here, are you? I couldn't bear to live with another pushy fe—" She held her gauze scarf to her mouth and looked away from the dowager.

St. Cloud patted her hand. "No such thing, Juneclaire's sweet and gentle. You'll see."

"When you find her, cuz?" Niles taunted. He was also delighted, recalculating his odds of winning the Pomeroy's hand. "How did you happen to mislay the bride-to-be?"

"There was a bit of a mix-up with the coaches. That's why I was detained," he said with a bow in his still-speechless uncle's direction. "I am not sure precisely which carriage took her up when the one she was traveling in had a spill." The spill may have been all over Scully, the footman, but St. Cloud was sticking to the truth as closely as possible. He had no idea what he would say if anyone thought to ask how he met the young lady, much less when. "There's nothing improper about it," he lied now, for the squire's wife and the rest of the neighborhood who would have the story by noon tomorrow. "She may have returned home or be staying with the vicar and his wife at Bramley. She might even have gone with her housekeeper on to London. I'll send the footmen out tomorrow to make inquiries, and I'll ride to London myself."

"But you can't send the staff away tomorrow, dearest; it's Boxing Day. All of the servants have the day off for their own feast and celebration. And you have to be here when the tenants come calling for the wassail."

"For their gifts, you mean. Damn."

"Oh, but Mr. Talbot takes care of the staff gifts, and your secretary in London remembered the check for the church alms box. And the bailiff delivers the boxes for most of the Priory tenants. They come just to see you and wish you joy of the season."

"Like feudal times, cuz, you know, lord of the manor and all that. *Noblesse oblige.*"

Lady Fanny thought a moment. "I suppose Harmon could stand in for you."

St. Cloud put his teacup down with a thud. "That's all right, Mother. As you say, they are my people, and I shall be here."

The countess looked toward her brother to make sure Harmon saw what a good boy St. Cloud was. "Besides, dearest, you cannot go up to London, not with our New Year's ball next week. You couldn't have forgotten?"

St. Cloud bit the inside of his mouth. How could he, when she'd written to remind him seven times in the past month? The Priory hadn't made much of Christmas since his father's accident and Uncle George's death, but the dowager insisted that Lady Fanny had to entertain the county somehow over the holiday season, to repay all the invitations she received and to uphold the St. Cloud name. They had settled on a New Year's masquerade ball when they were out of blacks years ago, and the tradition took. Lady Fanny still wore half mourning, and she still piled all of the details for the ball on Talbot, the housekeeper, the bailiff, and her son. He hated the whole affair. "Now there I should appreciate Uncle Harmon's management. It's time Cousin Elsbeth learns how to manage a party, too. I make no promises after tomorrow, Mother."

"But you did promise to see about the ghost, son. I haven't slept easy in my bed in weeks, and that cannot be good for my health, on top of all the work for the ball. And then there was the upset about your tardy arrival and now the excitement of your betrothal. I really must have my rest. Of course I cannot be comfortable in my room. . . ."

"Blast it, Fanny, I told you I had the steward go over the whole east wing, and the fellow found nothing. The ghost is all in your head." Lord Wilmott finally found his voice with the realization that there could be no wedding without a bride. Let the boy go haring off to London while Harmon made his own investigation. There was some hugger-mugger here, and he was determined to get to the bottom of it and get rid of this upstart nobody. Elsbeth still had a chance.

For once in her life Fanny held firm, even against her brother's wrath. "No, Harmon, it's a St. Cloud ghost and perhaps only St. Clouds can see it, although the servants have heard it crying through the chimneys. And there was *no* wind that night, so you can take a damper, Harmon."

"Brava, Fanny," the dowager said approvingly. "You can't keep the boy tied to you with your megrims or your mutton-headed mismanagement. Now you'll try things that go bump in the night!"

Fanny held the cloth to her eyes, and St. Cloud was tempted to take the cane to the dowager and his uncle. Yes, Lady Fanny was vaporish; did anyone think she was going to change now? "I thought you'd heard noises in the Dower House, too, Grandmother."

"I'm getting old, boy, not senile. You worry about finding the gel, St. Cloud; Hilloughby can say an extra prayer to get rid of the ghost. That's about all he's good for anyway." The dowager had almost given up hope that the cleric—or anybody—would offer for Fanny and get the peagoose and her Wilmott relatives out of the Priory once and for all.

The New Year's ball had been her idea at first, to get Fanny socializing again in hopes of marrying the wigeon off. No one wanted her, more's the pity.

With the St. Cloud fireworks seemingly over for the night, the dinner guests took their leave. There was no reason to stay later, with the earl as good as a tenant for life and snow falling. If the snow hadn't been falling, Lady Sydelle might have ordered her carriage and headed for London. As it was, she was in such a snit, she forgot to slink on her way down the hall, after excusing herself to the family still in the gold salon. She stomped down the hall and up the stairs with such determination that she split the back seam of her too-tight dress. There was a crash below in the hallway. Talbot was not made of stone, after all, and neither was the Limoges teapot.

With only family left, Aunt Florrie wanted her Christmas gift, since she wasn't getting to keep the pig and Harmon took the sugarplums away. They all moved to the smaller parlor, where a wooden candle pyramid had been set up on one of the tables and lighted, St. Cloud's gifts on a red cloth beneath. Harmon did not hold with bringing a tree into the house, even if Queen Charlotte was trying to foist her Teutonic notions of *tannenbaum* on the London gentry. Fanny thought a tree with candles, apples, garlands, and cookies sounded lovely. Maybe next year, she thought, when there was a new countess.

She gave her son a pair of slippers with the family crest embroidered on them by her maid. He gave her a pearl-and-diamond brooch selected by his secretary. The dowager gave him her late husband's gold watch, which, besides being mentioned in the entail, was the same watch she gave St. Cloud every year. Every year he had it returned to her bed stand, knowing she hated to be without it. The earl gave her an ebony cane with a carved handle.

"What is it, boy? A snake?"

"No, you old fire breather, it's a dragon."

He gave Aunt Florrie a music box with a bear in a tutu twirling around on top, and she gave him a rock.

Elsbeth presented the earl with some monogrammed handkerchiefs. Her maid did not sew as well as Lady Fanny's. She went into raptures over the gold filigree fan that caught his eye one day as just the kind of gaudy trumpery she might enjoy.

St. Cloud next delighted his other cousin by saying he'd write out the Christmas gift as soon as Niles presented the reckoning, so Niles gave him the snuffbox in his pocket.

He and Uncle Harmon exchanged nods.

"You know, Papa," Elsbeth said, practicing her attitudes over the fan, "now that I am not to marry my cousin, can I finally have a Season in Town? I know Aunt Fanny doesn't go to London, but perhaps St. Cloud's wife can present me. Is she good ton, cousin?"

"Don't be a gudgeon," her brother told her, still in an expansive mood. "If she were a gap-toothed hunchback from the Outer Hebrides, St. Cloud's countess would still be good ton."

"Why? Aunt Fanny isn't."

Chapter Fourteen

𝒯he horses were straining in the traces, hurtling into the night. Foley rode silently beside him. No, it was Todd—No, someone else, watching him try to manage the runaway team. He couldn't do it. They were out of control. Then the carriage shaft started creaking, crunching, cracking under the stress of the wild ride. They'd be thrown, or dashed under the horses' hooves, and the passenger just watched. Then St. Cloud felt the wind and waited. His legs must be broken; he couldn't move them. The horses! Someone, help! The passenger laughed and laughed and—

St. Cloud jerked awake, gasping. He could feel the sweat on his bare chest and hear the echoes of distant laughter. The velvet bed curtains were open—and Pansy was sprawled across his legs. "Damn." There was no way the pig could get up on the huge canopied bed herself. St. Cloud even used the low stool. If this was Todd's revenge for having to nursemaid a pig, St. Cloud would have his head come morning. Boxing Day indeed. He'd give the fellow a box on the ears for this night's work. Then again, this was more like Cousin Niles's style of bobbery, foolish since the check was not yet signed. St. Cloud wouldn't even put such a prank past Sydelle, a woman scorned and all that. He sighed. Either way, he was awake.

"Are you hungry, pig? Silly question, you're always hungry. Let's go." St. Cloud lighted his candle and found his robe and new slippers. He also found where Pansy'd eaten her way out of the wicker basket. "At least that explains the crunching noises I heard."

He piled two plates with leftovers from the kitchen and led the pig into his library, where he restarted the fire and settled back on the worn leather chair. Then he heard the noise, a tapping almost like Grandmother's cane, although more regular. That must be Lady Fanny's specter, he thought, getting up to stand closer to the fireplace, where the sound was loudest. There must be a squirrel in one of the disused chimneys, tapping to open a nut or something. Maybe an owl. The noise would carry through all the grates in the place, echoing eerily enough, he supposed, to spook his susceptible parent. He didn't know why Uncle Harmon or the steward hadn't just sent for the sweeps. He'd do it tomorrow.

No, damn it, tomorrow the servants did not work, and he would be busy shaking hands and listening to speeches. Blast. All he wanted to do was get on his fastest horse and ride to find Juneclaire. He wandered toward the window, a glass of brandy in his hand. The snow was still falling, though lightly. Lord, let her be safe and warm.

He was up at dawn, before most of the household except for Cook, who took one look at her kitchen and started screeching about Priory phantoms and the walking dead. Breakfast was going to be late that morning. St. Cloud and the pig strolled through melting snow toward the stables, where Pansy, at least, could find apples and oats. The earl found his man Foley up and ready to be sent on the hunt. Word had come down from the house last night that the missing female was no less than the future Lady St. Cloud. Foley would ride to hell and back to see his lordship settled, even if he couldn't abide females personally.

"O'course I'm sure I can ride. I had my rest, didn't I? And no, us stable men don't put up with tomfoolery like them at the house, not doing their jobs 'cause it's a holiday. Horses still has to be fed, don't they? And we may as well exercise 'em on the way to somewheres as around a ring. Your message'll be in London by now, my lord, so where else do you want us to look?"

The earl wanted someone to watch the departing coaches at Springdale and at Bramley, but he wanted Foley himself to head toward Farley's Grange by way of Strasmere, making inquiries along the way. "Ask if anyone has seen her, but if not, keep going toward Stanton Hall. Snoop around there if you can, and find out what they're saying about the Stantons' niece. The servants must have some idea of what's going on. I want you there because I know you won't add any more to the gossip than there already is. Try not to use her name when you ask along the way, too. We've got to keep this as quiet as possible."

Sure, then only *half* the county would know the Earl of St. Cloud had misplaced his fiancée.

Little Yerby made Juneclaire wait an hour for the snow to finish melting so her shoes wouldn't get wet and ruined. Then he sent her off with three well-fed kittens, a jar of milk, a loaf of bread he could spare because Aggie was coming home soon, and hope.

There was a family of gentlefolk not a mile down the road, Little Yerby told her, with a sickly little girl. "Mayhap they need someone to teach the young'un her letters, if she lives that long." He took a pull on his pipe, then coughed. "Else Mrs. Langbridge might want another lady round about. There's no family that anyone sees. Mister's a solicitor in Bramley. Tell them Little Yerby sent you."

While St. Cloud prepared to greet his household staff and hand out their vails under Talbot's supervision, Juneclaire prepared for her first interview. She shook Little Yerby's flooring off her cloak, rebraided her hair, and kissed the old man good-bye.

Mrs. Langbridge met her at the door and tried to press a shilling into Juneclaire's hand. "Oh, you're not here for Boxing Day? Of course not. You're not a—Oh, I am sorry. There's just so much to do. Why did you say you had come?"

"Mr. Little Yerby sent me, ma'am, to ask after your little girl and to see if you might need a governess for her."

"My poor Cynthia." Mrs. Langbridge wiped her eyes with an already tear-dampened cloth.

"She hasn't . . . ?"

"Oh, no, she is just distraught over the move." Mrs. Langbridge waved a hand at trunks and bags waiting in the hallway. "She does not want to leave her friends, and her papa, of course, but the doctor thinks a healthier climate might . . . So we are going to Italy tomorrow, Cynthia, Nanny, a maid, and I. Mr. Langbridge cannot travel with us just yet, you see, so things are all at sixes and sevens, with packing and trying to leave the house in order, and Cynthia will fret so, which cannot be at all good for her. Do forgive me, Miss . . . ?"

"Beaumont, ma'am, and you must be wishing me to Jericho. I can see you do not need a governess and you do not need a stranger to keep you from your preparations. Please forgive me for the intrusion and accept my wishes for a safe journey and a swift recovery for your little girl."

"No, Miss Beaumont, please forgive my manners, after you were kind enough to call, and I haven't even offered you tea." She tried to brush away another tear. "I am sorry, my mind is in pieces, what with leaving my Tom and Cynthia so inconsolable."

"Mrs. Langbridge, you seem exhausted. Would you like me to sit with Cynthia for a bit while you catch your breath? It will be no bother, I assure you, for I am in no hurry to go home and only need get as far as Bramley this afternoon."

"Would you, Miss Beaumont? How kind. I should like to spend some time with Tom before he has to go visit a client. Some old hag called him out today, of all days! He is getting ready now and could drive you to Bramley when he leaves."

Juneclaire was removing her cloak. "That would be perfect. And could I make another forward suggestion? Don't you think that Cynthia would be happier about the trip if she could take a friend of her own along?"

"A friend? But we cannot . . ."

Juneclaire reached into her satchel and pulled out a kitten. "Why not?"

"I'll name her Holly," the little girl announced, "so we both remember an English Christmas. Do you think they have holly in Italy, Miss Beaumont?"

"I have no idea, Cynthia. You shall just have to go and see, won't you? Perhaps you shall write and tell me, so I'll know for the future." Juneclaire was pleased to see the hectic flush leave Cynthia's cheeks, although the spots of color remained, betraying her illness. The child was calm now and had taken her medicine without complaint, too rapt in watching the three kittens tumbling on her bed covers. She chose the black kitten "because Papa says everyone in Italy wears black. But, Miss Beaumont, what if Holly isn't a girl? Can a boy cat be called Holly?"

"I don't see why not. Do you know Mr. Little Yerby?"

"Of course, everyone knows Little. He brings the milk twice a week, and sometimes he lets me ride his donkey."

"Well, Mr. Little has one of Holly's brothers or sisters, and he is going to call the kitten David, no matter what."

"Oh, but if Little says his cat's a boy, then that's what it is. The animals always do what he says."

While Juneclaire was spending the morning entertaining a sick child, St. Cloud was standing on the steps of the Priory's porch, drinking wassail toasts with his tenants. By noon he was drunk as a lord, and so was the pig at his side, dressed in a ribbon-and-lace collar Aunt Florrie had stayed up all night sewing. None of his other relatives had made a showing yet, and none of his minions had reported back from the search. Two more hours of this, St. Cloud promised himself, and then he could ride to Bramley, if he could sit a horse.

Juneclaire stayed to watch Cynthia fall asleep for her nap with a smile on her thin face, and then she took luncheon with the Langbridges, at their insistence, although she did not want to intrude on one of their last moments together. They were all praise for her handling of their peevish child. "Oh, no, I cannot take any of the credit." Juneclaire laughed. "Once I showed her the kittens she was a perfect darling."

Mr. Thomas Langbridge was a pleasant-looking, sandy-haired gentleman with a worried frown. "I wish a kitten could work such magic on the client I have an appointment with this afternoon. I feel sorry for the old grande dame truly, because she is blind and has lost most of her family, but I wish she would not choose to change her dashed will every time her rackety grandson sneezes."

"And today of all days," his wife complained.

"Not even you, my dear, can accuse Lady St. Cloud of purposely selecting the day before your journey. She had no way of knowing. We must be thankful she waited past Christmas to send for me. And she keeps country hours at the Dower House, at any rate, so dinner will be early if I stay, and you know I must if she invites me, if I wish to retain her as my wealthiest client. I never understood why she did not take her business to any of the solicitors in Ayn-Jerome or even Thackford."

"Most likely she turned them off in her previous tantrums." Mrs. Langbridge was rearranging the food on her plate. Juneclaire had no such loss of appetite and busied herself with the turbot in oyster sauce.

"More likely she trusted my uncle. Try to show a little compassion for the old countess, my dear, even if she is a crusty beldam."

While he enjoyed his mutton, Mr. Langbridge's solicitor's mind was busy chewing a different bone. Somewhere over the vanilla flan he presented his idea: "You know, Miss Beaumont, you might well apply for a position with Lady St. Cloud if you are seeking employment. We would take you on in a minute for Cynthia if the situation were different. You are patient and kind, refined and intelligent. That's just what the old bat—ah, lady needs. I admit to having concerns about her, alone in the Dower House with just her old retainers looking after her. You and your kittens wrought such a miracle with Cynthia, I'd be happy to recommend you for the dowager's companion."

Juneclaire smiled and thanked him. "But I'm afraid you haven't painted a very pretty picture of your employer. I think I should rather face my own family's ill humors than someone else's."

"You can think about it on the way to Bramley. I am stopping by my office there to fetch copies of papers she wants to emend. You could drive out with me, and if you find you don't suit or she is not interested, I shall simply bring you back to town on my return trip."

While Juneclaire once more deliberated over her future on the way to Bramley, the Earl of St. Cloud was riding in the opposite direction, out of the little village. Vicar Broome was aghast to think that Miss Beaumont had not reached Springdale, but he was helpless to provide the earl with any other information. Poor fellow, he thought, the younger man was so smitten, he hadn't even stayed to have a sip of Madeira. Mr. Broome sipped it himself, in celebration of the handsome donation the lovesick earl had made to start up the poor box after the day's distribution. Reverend Broome wiped his spectacles and contemplated his own venality. Should he have reminded the mooncalf of his generous gift just the day before?

He wiped them again, then took them off altogether when the young lady in the rabbit-lined cloak walked into his study. "Miss, ah, Beaumont?" he mumbled, wishing his wife were there. He might know what to do with finances; affairs of the heart were Mrs. Broome's venue. While he was deliberating whether to send a boy after the earl— but who in town could ride at that neck-or-nothing

pace?—or after Mrs. Broome, Juneclaire was
thrusting a striped kitten into his arms.

"Because you and your wife have been so kind to
me," she said, looking so sweet and innocent, he
couldn't tell her how cats made him sneeze. And
itch. And weep at the eyes.

"How happy I am to see you, Miss Beaumont.
There was a gentleman here asking for you. We
were all concerned for your welfare."

"A gentleman? Not a portly, middle-aged man
who wears a bagwig? That would be my uncle Avery, and I never suspected he would make the least
push to find me."

"No, this gentleman was not, ah, portly. He gave
his name as Mr. Jordan."

"Oh, Merry!" Then she blushed. Her face was almost as red as the vicar's was becoming from stroking the cat.

"Oh, dear, Mr., ah, Jordan did not insult you in
any way, did he? That is, your blushes and . . ." He
blew his nose. Oh, how he wished Mrs. Broome did
not have to visit the almshouse this afternoon!

"Mr. Jordan? Never! You mustn't think such a
thing. He is a true gentleman."

Well, that relieved Mr. Broome's mind, if not his
nose. "Have you decided not to go to London, then,
Miss Beaumont?" he asked, changing the subject.
"Mrs. Broome will be pleased." More pleased than
she was going to be about the cat. "May I tell her
your, ah, alternate plans, then, so she does not
worry."

"Thank her for her concern, sir, but I am not sure
what I will do."

The vicar could feel a rash starting on his neck
and the check for the poor box itching in his pocket.
"My child, have you ever heard of St. Cloud Priory?"

Juneclaire looked startled. "Why, Mr. Lang-

bridge just mentioned it, that I might find a position with the dowager countess there. After what
he said about her, though . . ."

"Perfect!" Broome wouldn't even have to consult
his conscience about pitchforking this lovely young
innocent into the arms of a hardened libertine. The
old harridan would make sure nothing untoward
took place, and if the young earl was as sincere as
he seemed, Vicar Broome would be calling the
banns next week, if his throat didn't close right up
with cat hair.

Now the minister might believe in the efficacy of
prayer, but he also believed in giving his prayers a
helping hand, or a shove in the right direction. "I'll
write a reference myself. I know the dowager has
the reputation of being a holy terror, but I've seen
worse reputations proved false, this very afternoon.
She's just old and lonely. She needs you. The Lord
must have sent you to Langbridge for just that purpose."

He was almost pleading. He was actually crying.
Juneclaire was so touched, she said she would re-
consider.

Then the reverend clinched her decision. He
begged for divine forgiveness and lied through his
teeth: "She likes cats."

So while the Earl of St. Cloud was racing past
uninformative Springdale and heading for London,
where he would knock on back doors himself if need
be and haunt the coaching inns, Juneclaire was
headed toward his own haunted house to knock on
his own grandmother's door.

Chapter Fifteen

*N*o one answered the knock. Juneclaire thought they should leave.

"No, old Pennington must have the gout again. We'll just give him a few minutes to get here. He's Lady St. Cloud's butler, and he's older than dirt. So's her abigail, Nutley, who's too deaf to hear the door anyway. Mrs. Pennington is the cook-housekeeper and she, ah, tipples."

Juneclaire was positive they should leave. She set her carpetbag down on the steps of the gray stone house. "Goodness, no wonder you didn't tell me this before we got here. Why ever doesn't Lady St. Cloud retire them if they are so far beyond their work?"

"I asked the dowager once and almost had my head bitten off. They're like family, it seems, and have nowhere else they'd rather go. Help comes from the main house—you can't see it from here, but the Priory is just beyond those trees. They do the cleaning and such, so Lady St. Cloud's retainers' positions are more nearly pensions."

"Is there no one in the household younger than Methuselah? It cannot be very comfortable or even safe for the old lady."

Mr. Langbridge knocked again, harder. "There's

a young maid, Sally Munch, and a footman. They are walking out, according to the dowager, and I am afraid they are walking out more often than they are working indoors. They're most likely off on holiday this afternoon anyway. But you mustn't think no one cares about the old lady's welfare. The earl has tried to get her to move to the Priory countless times, I understand, but the dowager and the present countess, the earl's mother, have never gotten on. Well, there is no point waiting out here any longer," he said, which Juneclaire was relieved to hear until he concluded, "We may as well go on in. I know the dowager is expecting me."

The solicitor guided Juneclaire to a bench along the wall of the long entry hall. The furnishings were old-fashioned but elegant, obviously expensive and scrupulously clean, from what she could see in the near dark. The dowager might be blind, but surely her staff needed more light than this? And there were no flowers or plants, not a holiday decoration of any kind. If *she* were here, Juneclaire speculated, there would be garlands of fresh-smelling greens, bowls of dried lavender or crushed rose petals, and clove-studded apples. Surely the dowager could smell what she could not see. She'd light all the sconces, too, Juneclaire mused, so the place felt warmer. Yes, she could be useful here.

When Mr. Langbridge came out of a room down the hall, he seemed even more worried than before. "She's agreed to see you," he said. "Alone. I beg you to try to please her, Miss Beaumont, for I'm afraid the dowager grows more addled in her wits every time I see her. She sent for me today because the Angel of Death visited her last night, she claims, so she knows her time is near. I fear for her, indeed I do."

"I heard that, you jobbernoll, you," came an angry voice from down the hall, accented by the pounding of a cane. "Don't you know a person's hearing gets better when they lose their sight? And I ain't dicked in the nob, you paper-skulled paper pusher. Now are you going to send the female in, or are you going to sit in my hallway gossiping about me all day?"

The old lady was still muttering when Juneclaire went into the room and curtsied, even knowing the small, white-haired woman didn't see her. The dowager sat perfectly erect, not the least bit frail or withered. Juneclaire touched her on the hand and said, "How do you do, my lady? I am Miss Beaumont. Thank you for meeting me."

"Humph" was all the response she got back. "Thinks I need a keeper, does he?"

"No, ma'am, just a companion."

"What for? To jaw me dead? Not much else for a companion to do around here. I can't play cards or go for a ride. Can't even do my needlework."

"But I could read to you, and I could drive you about if there's a cart. And I could teach you to knit. Once you get the hang of it, you don't need to watch the needles."

"Humph. Knitting ain't genteel. Ladies do fancy work, miss."

"Yes, but there are many people who need scarves and mittens more than they need another altar cloth in the church. I should think a lady might consider that, too."

"There's some sense in what you say, but you ain't going to be preaching to me about the poor, are you?"

Juneclaire laughed, a pleasing sound to the old lady's ears. "Not if I don't wish to join their ranks, it seems. But I am sure you think just as you ought, my lady."

"You're not one of those Methody Reformers, are you? I don't want any holier-than-thou reverencer

133

sneering behind my back. Frank language ain't going to shock you, is it, Miss Beaumont?"

"My cousins cured me of that ages ago, my lady."

"Ages? How old are you, anyway? Langbridge said you were just a girl. I don't want any shriveled up prunes-and-prisms spinsters around me either. Let me touch your face, girl."

Juneclaire knelt so the old woman could touch her soft cheek, her straight nose, and heavy brows, the thick braids of her hair and the smile on her mouth.

"I am nineteen, my lady, and I haven't put on my caps yet." She laughed again. "In fact, I had a very attractive offer from a gentleman just recently."

Juneclaire jumped aside as Lady St. Cloud thumped her cane down. "What kind of offer, miss? I won't have any hanky-panky around here. It's bad enough with the lower orders sneaking off to the bushes and the pantry and the basement at all hours."

The laughter was gone from Juneclaire's voice. "You insult me, my lady, and also the gentleman. It was a very fine, very proper offer of marriage."

"Pish tosh, miss. If it was such a fine offer, why didn't you take it? You can't tell me you'd rather look after an old crone than have a house and husband of your own. Coming it too brown, my girl."

Juneclaire sighed. "I had to refuse, Lady St. Cloud. He offered out of honor, you see, not out of love. I couldn't hold such a fine gentleman to an empty marriage. It wouldn't be right." She sighed again.

"But you wanted to, didn't you, girl?" the old woman shrewdly interpreted.

"Oh yes, Merry was everything I ever thought a man should be."

Merry? The cane dropped from Lady St. Cloud's

hand. "Miss Beaumont, what did you say your first name was?"

"Juneclaire," she answered hesitantly. What new quiz was this?

"And how many gals named Juneclaire do you think are running around Berkshire right now?"

"Why, none others, I should think. I was named after my mother, Claire, and my father, Jules. Why do you ask?"

The old lady didn't answer. She just laughed and laughed. "Turned him down, did you? Oh, how I am going to enjoy this!" She laughed some more, till Juneclaire began to worry about her sanity after all, especially when the dowager recovered and suddenly asked, "You ain't afraid of ghosts, are you?"

So confused was Juneclaire that she blurted out, "They cannot be more frightening than you."

The dowager laughed some more, then reached out to pat Juneclaire's hand. "You'll do, girl, you'll do."

"Does that mean I am hired, my lady?"

"Hired? I suppose it does, for now. Go send in that young solicitor of mine. I want to discuss your, ah, wages with him."

"Thank you, my lady. I'll try to please, I swear it. There's just one other thing, though. Do you really like cats?"

"Cats? Pesky creatures. Can't abide the beasts, always underfoot or carrying around dead things."

"Oh. I'm sorry, truly I am, for I should have liked to stay. But I have this kitten, you see, that no one wanted, and I cannot just abandon it with no home. So I'll have to—"

"I'll learn to love it."

When Mr. Langbridge came back out for her on her bench in the hall, he looked at Juneclaire as if she'd grown another head. Nevertheless, he silently beckoned her back to her ladyship's parlor.

"I have invited Langbridge to take potluck, Miss Beaumont. Are you too tired from your travels, or do you join us?"

"I, um . . . Oh, dear, I know this is not the proper way to start in my new position, my lady, but did you know that Mr. Langbridge's daughter was ill?"

"Of course I did. Asked first thing."

"Yes, but she needs to go to a warmer climate, and Mrs. Langbridge is traveling to Italy with her tomorrow."

"That's well and good, I wish them Godspeed, but what is that to—Oh, I see. We won't keep you then, Langbridge. I expect you to stay next week when you bring those papers back for my signature. I daresay you'll be glad for the company then. And as for you, miss, I suppose you think just as you ought. Just remember, I find it deuced uncomfortable being wrong." The dowager spoke with a smile, though, so Juneclaire went cheerfully off to get ready for her first dinner in her new home.

The three old retainers were in various somnolent stages in the kitchen. Juneclaire introduced herself and explained her new position to Pennington, the only one whose eyes opened at Juneclaire's entry. The butler instantly recognized her for a lady and slowly lowered his bandaged foot to the floor so he could rise and make her a proper bow. Juneclaire had to help him back to his seat. He shouted the news loudly enough to wake his wife from her post-tea, predinner stupor and for Nutley, the abigail, to hear. If Juneclaire worried her ladyship's longtime servants were going to be jealous of an upstart, she was soon dissuaded from that notion. The three were relieved someone else was going to help look after their mistress and thrilled someone else was going to be the butt of her temper. Mrs.

Pennington vowed to fix a special dinner, and Nutley asked if miss needed help with her unpacking. What Juneclaire needed was a hot bath, but none of the servants looked fit enough to walk up the stairs, much less carry a tub and tins of water.

"Never you fear, miss," Mrs. Pennington said, wobbling to the door, "by the time we get a room aired and your things put away, young Sally Munch'll be back with her beau. They never stay away through supper."

Her room adjoining the dowager's was twice as big as the one Juneclaire had slept in most of her life. Did she just leave Stanton Hall a few days ago? It seemed a lifetime. There was a fire in the grate and lavender sachets in the drawers for her few belongings and a thick carpet for her feet. The kitten was being fussed over in the kitchen, and she was being fussed over here. Nutley insisted on brushing out her hair and taking her second-best gown to be pressed. The abigail had not even commented on the meager contents of her carpetbag.

As Nutley remarked to Lady St. Cloud as she helped her mistress change for dinner, "Young miss is Quality, anyone can see that, and if she had deep pockets, she wouldn't be going for a companion, now, would she?" Nutley did not hear the dowager's comments any more than the dowager could see Juneclaire's appearance. Mistress and maid were as one, though, in agreeing that Miss Beaumont was, on first meeting, a jewel.

The jewel was going to look far more brilliant without all the dust. Juneclaire looked at her bath when it came as a starving man looks at a slab of beef. Aunt Marta would call such sybaritic pleasure sinful, so Juneclaire would not think about Aunt Marta now. The morning was time enough to send her aunt a note that she was well. Juneclaire leaned back in the suds. She was very well indeed.

* * *

After dinner Juneclaire read the previous week's mail to the dowager and laughed at her stories about the people mentioned in her friends' *on-dits*. For a woman who did not do the Season, Lady St. Cloud used to keep abreast of the latest gossip with a vast network of correspondence. She was hoping her grandson did not return to steal the girl away before Miss Beaumont got halfway through the letters. Well, he could take the girl, but he wasn't getting the cat.

At first she was worried. "It's not going to trip me up, is it? Wouldn't do to fall at my age, you know."

"Cats are very good about things like that, my lady. And you do have your cane to sweep in front of you. You'll have to be more gentle with it, of course, not knowing the kitten's location. Here, hold it."

Silk and a sandpaper tongue and the rumble of tiny thunder that went on and on. It was love at first touch.

"What does he look like?"

Juneclaire wasn't quite sure what to say. This was the fourth kitten, the one no one wanted. "Well, his eyes were blue, but I think they are going to be yellow. He has a little gold on his chest and a black spot over one eye, and white feet, except for the back right one. That's kind of brownish. And there's a faint gray stripe down his back. He's a bit of this and a patch of that. But he has the sweetest personality!"

"Patches. I like that. Will that do for a name, do you think?"

Juneclaire laughed. "That cat is lucky to have a home; a name is icing on the cake."

"Lucky, then. No, what do the Irish call those

patches of lucky clover? Shamrocks! You did say he had green eyes?"

"Well . . ."

The dowager countess listened while Juneclaire played a few ragged carols. "I'm sorry, my lady. I never had many lessons; my aunt thought them a waste for a female with no prospects. I have no excuses for my poor voice, so I shan't subject you to that. Would you rather I read to you?"

"Perhaps tomorrow. This has already been a most pleasant evening, Miss Beaumont. I don't want to use all my treats in one day, like a child who cries when Christmas is past."

"But there are twelve days of Christmas, my lady," Juneclaire said with a smile in her voice. "What would you like to do now? Do you retire early?"

"What I would *like* to do is play cards." Lady St. Cloud reached for her cane to punctuate her vexation. She remembered the kitten asleep in her lap just in time.

Juneclaire thought a minute, and then her face cleared. "I'll be right back," she told the dowager, then ran off to find Nutley and shout until she had what she wanted. Out of breath but smiling, she came back with her prize, a sewing needle.

"What is it, girl? What are you giggling about?"

"Something else my scapegrace cousins taught me. Here, feel this." She held out a card. "The corner."

"Why, why, you're marking the cards! That's cheating!"

"Not if we both know the marks, it's not. I don't think we'll get so proficient that the dealer will have such an advantage, do you?"

"Miss Beaumont, I think I am going to learn to love you like a daughter. Or a granddaughter."

Chapter Sixteen

*Th*e dowager was having a nightmare. "Don't lie to me, Death. I know who you are and I'm not ready yet, I tell you. I have to make sure St. Cloud is settled before he's ruined for good and all. You'll see, the girl will be the making of the rogue."

Juneclaire heard the old lady's strident voice in the room next door. She had to recall which side held the bed stand before she fumbled for candle and flint in the unfamiliar room.

"You can't take me yet," the dowager was shouting. "He's already made mice feet of the thing. No, I don't want to hear any more of your wicked falsehoods about my sons. Go."

Trust Lady St. Cloud to tell the Devil to go to Hell, Juneclaire thought as she tied a wrapper Nutley had laid out for her over her own flannel nightdress. She hurried to the dowager's room and scratched on the door. When she got no answer, Juneclaire turned the knob and pushed the door open, shielding her candle. The dowager was fast asleep in a large bed. She was snoring gently, and she wore a satisfied smile on her face, having bested the Angel of Death for one more night.

Resisting the urge to peer in the corners or look under the bed, Juneclaire checked to make sure the silver bell was within the dowager's reach in case she needed to call for her companion during the night. Then Juneclaire went back toward her own room. Before she got to the doorway, though, she felt a prickle of sensation at the bottom of her spine. Someone was watching her. She whipped around, almost putting her candle out, but the steady sleep noises were still coming from the dowager's slightly open mouth.

It's just all the talk of death, Juneclaire chided herself, that and Sally Munch's chatter about the Priory ghosts stirring again. The slain monks were walking the ancient halls, Sally had declared as she slid the warming pan between Juneclaire's sheets . . . or something worse.

The young maid's imagination was as overheated as the rest of the little flirt, Juneclaire firmly told herself, blowing out the candle and getting between the long-cold sheets.

Then she heard a tapping noise, like the dowager's cane but not quite. She had that same feeling of being observed. "There are no such things as ghosts," she declared out loud. Then she shouted, "Begone," figuring that if it worked for the dowager, it was worth a try, just in case. She thought she heard a chuckle, but she could not be sure, not with the covers pulled over her head.

The dowager never rose before eleven, but Juneclaire was up with the birds, so she looked around for other occupations to keep her busy. She helped Penny make bread and hid whatever bottles of wine she could find. She fetched the silver tea service, epergne, and sconces for Pennington, where he was polishing at the kitchen table, his leg propped on a stool. And she dragged Sally Munch and the footman out of an unused bedroom where they were checking the bedsprings, to help her gather greens.

The footman cut the holly and pine branches Juneclaire indicated, while she fashioned a wreath out of some vines. Sally, naturally, knew just where they could find some mistletoe. As they worked, Juneclaire tried not to listen to the servants' gossip about the doings at the Priory, some possibly scandalous goings-on between the master, a recognized rake, and his latest flirt. Bets were on in the servants' hall, it seemed, that a betrothal was all a hum, St. Cloud was never going to give up his profligate ways. The stable had it that the master was dead-set on the female, whoever and wherever she was. Juneclaire did not feel she could reprimand the maid for her chatter, but she found the whole conversation distasteful.

"It's worse than that, miss. What did he do yesterday but hare off in the middle of the tenants' visits. Castaway, they say he was. Left in a great rush without saying when he'd be back or nothing. Then what happens but stablemen start walking in the halls at night, with pistols. By hisself's orders, they say. Why, mistress was near swooning, they say. Then comes this morning. Molly, who comes to clean at the Dower House, says a whole herd of workmen arrived at dawn, on Lord St. Cloud's instructions, they say, to check for loose boards and such, banging on the walls. If that weren't bad enough to set the house on its ears, an army of sweeps comes looking for owls and squirrels and bats in the chimneys. So there can't be no fires!"

"And there are guests? I can see where that would upset even the most serene household."

"Which that one's not. Why, that cousin—"

Juneclaire did not wish to hear any more details of life at the Priory. She quickly asked the footman to carry a message to the sweeps to come check the

Dower House flues if they got a chance. "I thought there must be woodpeckers, myself."

"Oh, no, miss. That be the ghost."

Juneclaire read the newspapers to the dowager before luncheon and answered some letters from her dictation. She thought about writing to her relatives. Later.

After luncheon the dowager announced it was time for her nap. "And I want you to go outside and get some exercise. Can't be healthy for a young thing like you to be cooped up inside with a parcel of old biddies, working so hard."

"What work?" Juneclaire laughed. "This has been the easiest day of my life."

"Doesn't say much for the rest of your life, but I'll hold my tongue on that. Can you ride?" Lady St. Cloud asked abruptly.

"Yes, but I did not bring my habit." Juneclaire knew the dowager was well aware of the fact. Nutley must have enumerated Juneclaire's scant wardrobe to her mistress the first day, thus the night robe. Juneclaire had two day dresses, the blue one she had on and the heavier gray one she'd worn on the road. She had the almost fashionable rose muslin castoff from Aunt Marta that she wore to dinner last night and, of course, her unworn white velvet gown. At least the dowager did not have to look at her companion in the same gowns day after day. She wasn't going to get as weary of them as Juneclaire was going to. Juneclaire supposed she could ask her uncle to send on her clothes when she wrote to him, but the gowns she had left behind were all faded and threadbare, and her habit was so thin in the saddle, one more gallop might have her petticoat showing. Perhaps when she got paid, Juneclaire would purchase a dress length or two. But wages had not been discussed, nor a possible day

off for her to do any shopping. Since her employer
was being almost pleasant, Juneclaire hated to
bring up such awkward topics. Instead, she added,
"I do like to walk."

"Humph. Walking's for peasants, girl, unless
you're on the strut in Hyde Park or such. Nutley
can alter one of my old habits for you. Certes, I
don't need them anymore."

"If you wanted to ride, we could—"

"No, I'm not going to trot in a circle at the end
of a lead line, by Jupiter. It used to be neck-or-
nothing with me, and I ain't going to change now."

"Oh, then you weren't always . . . ?"

"Blind. No, I used to see fine; just saw too much,
the specialists said. Too many birthdays, mostly.
Now I'm too stiff to get on a horse and too old to
chance breaking a bone anyway. So those habits
are just taking space in the clothespress."

"But I couldn't—"

"Have to. There's no one else who can exercise
my mare for me. Flame never held anything but a
sidesaddle, don't you know. Prettiest little filly in
the whole county, she was. Now go on, get. I need my
rest if I'm to learn this knitting of yours tonight. Oh,
and don't ride toward the Priory. No reason for you
to face those spiteful cats up there without me. My
daughter-in-law's relations, they are, and a worse
pack of dirty dishes you'll never find."

"You haven't met the Root and the Newt."

"But they're just boys, you said. Fanny's niece is
a spoiled hoyden, and that other one is no better
than she should be. The nevvy is a basket scram-
bler. You watch out for him, girl."

Juneclaire laughed. "I thank you, ma'am, but I'm
not likely to tempt a man of that ilk. I don't have
a fortune and I'm no dasher, as my cousins say."

The dowager had Nutley's opinion that miss
would be a real diamond, with some careful dress-

144

ing and a new hairstyle, should brunets come back in style. She also had the fact that one of England's premier bachelors had offered for the chit. "You be careful, that's all. When my grandson gets back is soon enough for you to meet the rest of the jackals. Now go."

"Yes, my lady." She curtsied, even though the dowager couldn't see.

"Why, that old—" She bit her lip, even if Nutley couldn't hear. A brown velvet habit was already altered, likely from measurements of her other day dress. The dowager had meant to have her way, no matter Juneclaire's feelings. "Thank you, Nutley," she shouted, giving the abigail a quick hug as she flew down the stairs in her eagerness for her ride. They were used to sending to the Priory for the rare times the dowager went out, Pennington explained while she filled her pockets with apples and sugar cubes (and hid another bottle of cooking sherry that was not destined for dinner). A carriage arrived every Sunday to carry the dowager to chapel at the Priory, he said, and a boy came every day to attend the small stable that served the Dower House.

He wasn't there now, so Juneclaire took down a gleaming ladies' saddle herself and went to lead the mare out of her stall. She did not have the heart to put the saddle on Flame's back. If ever the mare had a flame at all, it had sputtered and gone out before Juneclaire was born. Flame had barely enough teeth to crunch the apple, after Juneclaire found a knife to slice it, and barely enough energy to put one foot in front of the other.

"Still, you cannot be happy in this dark barn all day, and the dowager said we were both to get some exercise, so come along."

So Juneclaire, with the skirts of the most elegant riding habit she had ever worn trailing in the mud and the dust, ambled alongside the geriatric equine on the path where she'd been gathering holly that morning.

When Lady St. Cloud sent Juneclaire out for an airing, she hadn't been thinking of the chaos at the Priory. Lady Fanny was busy having spasms, Lord Wilmott was growing more bilious with each hammer blow, as if the search for defects were a personal affront to his care of the earl's property, and Florrie was in the attics, in the workmen's way, finding pig-size baby clothes. Things were in such a state there that even a ride to the Dower House appealed to the younger members of the house party, since it promised the diversion of investigating the new companion. On being informed by Pennington—after a wait that had Lady Sydelle rapping her crop against her leather boots—that the dowager countess was resting and miss was riding through the holly path, they decided to ride after her. Niles wanted to wager the unfortunate creature wouldn't last a week; neither his sister nor Lady Pomeroy took the bet.

"I bet she is a perfect antidote," Elsbeth declared, "for even the poorest female can find a male to support her if she has any looks and is not fussy. I'd rather be married to a coal heaver than be Lady St. Cloud's galley slave."

"You mightn't have either choice, with that wasp tongue," the Widow Pomeroy snapped at the younger girl, having married a dirty old man whose dirty fortune came from coal mines, although that fact was not well known among the ton.

Leaping to his intended's—his intentions, not hers—aid before Elsbeth could unleash even more venom, Niles taunted, "I don't notice you making any grand match, sister, now that your plans for St. Cloud are scotched."

"Unlike others I could mention, I am waiting for

a love match. Not all females sell themselves for security, you know."

"And not all females are so totty-headed. I bet even the cipherous companion would jump at an offer to escape the drudgery."

"An honorable offer, of course," the widow agreed. "But are you willing to back your wager on another kind of offer? Companions are notoriously virtuous. I'll bet my diamond pendant against—*do* you have anything worth wagering, Niles?—that this Miss Beaumont will accept something less."

"Do you mean you're betting that Miles can seduce the dowager's companion? Why . . . why, that's evil."

"And so entertaining. We have to do something to enliven the days till the New Year's ball, don't we? Niles, do you take me up?"

Niles was reflecting that the woman he wished to make his wife could show a little more interest in his fidelity to her. Not that he intended to remain faithful once the wedding vows were exchanged and the marriage settlements signed, but he hoped for some sign of jealousy, possessiveness even, before the fact. If there was to be a fact. "Sight unseen?" he asked. "I'm afraid I need longer odds, my sweet Sydelle. What say that if I succeed, I also succeed with you, my pet? My honorable offer, naturally."

"Naturally. And if you lose?"

"You can't do this, Niles, not the dowager's own servant. St. Cloud will kill you." Elsbeth was horrified, but not as horrified as Juneclaire, on the other side of the boxwood hedges where Flame was nibbling at the last grasses. And Elsbeth, it seemed, was more concerned with danger to her brother than any damage that might be done to the poor downtrodden companion! Juneclaire could not hear Lady Sydelle's answer as the group rode away.

The dowager was right. These people were scum. They were beautiful, Juneclaire's peeks through the branches told her that, but they were cold and cruel. They were as exquisite as swans, and just as vicious close up. Lady Sydelle wore a scarlet habit with a tiny veiled hat perched coquettishly on her guinea gold locks, and her horse had specks of blood on its flanks from her spur. Juneclaire had never seen a man dressed as elegantly as Mr. Wilmott, or heard one speak so casually of ruining an innocent female. She almost wept to think of Merry and his precious offer. These three did not have enough honor among them to be worthy to shine Merry's boots.

If they were representative of Lord St. Cloud's friends and relatives, Juneclaire wanted even less to do with the Priory than before. She'd had no great esteem for the libertine earl since Mr. Langbridge related the man's scandalous reputation, and that opinion was lowered a notch when she saw his grandmother's condition. He kept her in, if not outright penury, then straightened circumstances, unprotected and locked away where he never had to see her. His very behavior gave the poor woman nightmares; his associates would put even that rough-tongued lady to the blush. The earl did not seem to care what havoc he wreaked on his mother's delicate health either, or on his staff, from what she'd seen. Juneclaire, for one, wished he'd never get back from his latest mad jaunt, undertaken when he was in his cups. She pitied the poor girl he was going to marry and hoped he never found her.

Chapter Seventeen

$\mathcal{S}$t. Cloud returned two days later. Even before his horse was led away, the dowager knew he was home via the servants' grapevine. She calculated how long before Fanny or his man Todd filled St. Cloud's ears with gossip, sending him posthaste to her doorstep demanding an explanation. She sent Juneclaire out early for her ride, saying that her old bones felt snow coming on. Miss Beaumont had better exercise the mare early, she claimed, lest Flame get too rambunctious from standing around all day.

Her grandson arrived not ten minutes later and managed to hold his patience in check for at least five minutes more.

"Grandmother," he said in an affected drawl after the formal greetings, "there seems to be a small creature stalking the tassel of my new Hessians."

Lady St. Cloud was sure he'd have his quizzing glass out, the fribble. "Adorable, ain't he?"

The earl did indeed have his glass out, but he was swinging it on its ribbon to the delight of one of the least prepossessing representatives of the feline species he'd ever seen. "Adorable is not quite the word I would have chosen, my lady. But, pray tell, how does it come about that you have a cat, no, any animal, in the house? You surely never approved of such a thing during my lifetime."

Oh, how the dowager wished she could see his face! "I've changed my mind, St. Cloud, since my new companion insisted."

Aha! The new companion! St. Cloud was on his feet and pacing. His forceful appearance was marred, had the dowager only seen it, by the scrap-cat chasing after him, intent on those dangling tassels. "Insisted, is it? The Dowager Countess St. Cloud taking orders from some encroaching female? They were right: you are not fit to be living alone!"

"I am not living alone, you nodcock. That's what the girl is for. And if any of those sponge-mongers up at the Priory dared to suggest I am missing a few spokes in my wheel, I'll have their guts for garters, see if I won't."

The earl picked up the kitten and dropped it, with his quizzing glass on its ribbon, into the dowager's lap before his boots were irreparably scored with needle claws. He cleared his throat. "We were speaking of the companion, ma'am."

"No, St. Cloud, you were. I was speaking of the hangers-on and dirty dishes you permit to reside under your roof. Your grandfather, the earl, would be spinning in his grave."

"He'd be coming back to haunt me if I left you here with some strange female whose name nobody remembers! They can't tell me where she came from or why. For all I know, she's here to stab you in your bed and steal the silver. You don't understand about unscrupulous people, Grandmother, how they prey on the"—he was going to say old and infirm, thought better of it—"unsuspecting. She could cozen you into changing your will or—"

"Already have."

"What?! I'll see the bitch in gaol first!" He struck his fist on the mantel.

"You'll sit down, boy, and mind your tongue in my parlor. You're giving me a headache."

The earl sat, took a deep breath, and tried again. "My apologies, Grandmother. But I have tried for years to hire you a companion, a respectable female to bear you company and look out for your welfare, since you refuse to move to the Priory. I found women from the best of families, with unimpeachable references. Young women, old women, women I personally knew, by Jupiter! And you refused to meet any of them. Dash it, I would have hired one of the royal ladies-in-waiting if I thought you'd have her. But you, madam, without a word to anyone, take on a perfect stranger. Is it any wonder I am overset?"

The dowager hadn't enjoyed a conversation so much in years. She should have been an inquisitor. "You always were pigheaded, boy. Do you think no one else knows what's best for themselves? You're a fine one to speak, clunch. I have found myself the perfect companion, and we suit to a cow's thumb. Which is a lot more than I can say for you and your misbegotten engagement."

The dowager stroked the cat during the following silence. When St. Cloud finally spoke, she could hear the sorrow in his voice. "There is no engagement, Grandmother. That's the other thing I came to the Dower House to tell you. I haven't said anything to the others yet, but I couldn't find her. I left messages, deuce take it, I left enough bribes to finance Prinny's new pavilion. I found her old housekeeper in London, who didn't know what I was talking about. I promised Mother I'd get back to help with the blasted ball, but my staying in Town wouldn't have made a difference. There's nothing, Grandmother, she's gone."

Not even the dowager could enjoy torturing a broken man, even if he was her only grandson and a cow-handed chawbacon to boot. "About my companion . . ."

"You were right, Grandmother, it's none of my business. If you are pleased, then I am pleased."

"She was not entirely without references, you know. In fact, Langbridge, my man of business, brought her out to me . . . from Bramley."

"From . . . ?"

"With Reverend Broome's commendation. He mentioned something about church pews Mr. Langbridge couldn't quite—"

St. Cloud was gone. Then he was back. "Where the bloody hell is she?"

"Why, I believe she is taking Flame cross-country. There is nothing like a good gallop to put roses in a girl's cheeks."

This time he kissed her hand in farewell but said, "You know, my lady, you are lucky that only the good die young."

If the dowager thought to send him helter-skelter over the Priory's acreage, she sorely misjudged her grandson, and Flame. He left his own horse in the small stable and followed the only path that led away from it. If the old nag could make it farther than the second clearing, he'd eat his hat, which he'd left on the dowager's hall table in his rush out the door.

He did not see them on the path, but then he heard a familiar off-key carol. The angel choir in heaven couldn't have sounded sweeter to his ears. He followed the song through a break in the hedges, and there she was, leading the blasted horse like a dog on a leash. She was wearing the same tatty gray cloak—Juneclaire didn't bother with the long-skirted habit for Flame's daily constitutionals—and her nose was red from the cold. She was beautiful.

"Hallo, Junco," he called.

"Merry!"

Neither knew how the ground was covered, but she was in his arms, or almost, looking up into his face. He was looking as handsome as Juneclaire remembered, certainly neater, in fawn breeches and a bottle green jacket, but his eyes looked tired, and the planes of his face seemed harsher. He'd forgotten how to smile, again. He held her shoulders and said, "Wretched female, I don't know whether to shake you or kiss you."

"Do I get a choice?" was all she could think to say. She felt her face go red at her own ungoverned tongue, but he pulled her closer, then yelped.

"What the deuces?"

"Oh, I am sorry. It's a needle I've taken to carrying around with me." Niles Wilmott had not wasted much time making good on his boasts to Lady Pomeroy. He'd tracked her down yesterday while she was out with Flame. First he plied her with heavy-handed compliments, then barely disguised hints of a financial arrangement. Finally he tried physical enticements, as if she could ever be attracted to a snake in gentleman's clothing. Overdressed clothing at that. Forewarned was forearmed, however, and Niles would not be approaching her again soon. She hoped he died of blood poisoning. Merry raised one eyebrow, meanwhile, waiting for further explanation, so she said, "It's in case I ran into that dastard from the Priory again."

She instantly knew she'd made an error, for the hands on her shoulders tightened till she'd have bruises there. "What dastard? Who insulted you, Juneclaire? I'll—"

"Oh hush, silly. I'm fine. Everyone has been so

nice to me. Well, almost everyone. I have so much to tell you, but you tell me first, instead of glowering at me so. What are you doing here and why are you in such a taking?"

"I am upset, goose, for I have been looking for you for days now, nights, too, in Bramley and Springdale and London and everywhere in between, and you've been right here. If I don't strangle you, it's just because I am too tired. You have led me a fine chase, girl."

"But why, Merry? We are friends, nothing more. I told you you were not responsible for me."

"Nothing more? After a night in a barn? That made you my responsibility, Miss Beaumont." That sounded too severe, even to the earl's ears, and hope made him add, "I cared."

Her hand touched the dent in his chin for an instant, and then she looked away, suddenly shy. "But . . . but how did you find me here?"

"I didn't. I came home to lick my wounds, and there you were."

"Home? You live here, at the Priory?" He nodded. "You're not one of the earl's disreputable friends, are you?"

"Worse," he told her.

Juneclaire felt a hollowness in her stomach. "A relative?"

"Worse still."

She'd known he was an aristocrat. That assurance and, yes, arrogance of his just had to be matched to a title, but the Earl of St. Cloud? If Flame had an ounce of speed left in her, Juneclaire would jump on the mare's back and ride who-knows-where. Merry—the earl—could walk faster than Flame at her quickest, though. Juneclaire did the only thing possible. She kicked him in the shin with her heavy wooden-soled walking shoe. "You liar!"

The earl was wondering why he'd bothered to

save his Hessians from the cat. "I am sorry about being the earl, Junco, sometimes sorrier than you can imagine, but I didn't lie. I am Merritt Jordan."

Juneclaire was limping away, at Flame's speed. "I am sorry, too, my lord, for the earl is not a person I wish to know."

"I did not lie to you about my reputation, Juneclaire, and I shall not lie now and say that it is undeserved. I am no longer that reckless, rebellious boy, however." He took Flame's lead out of Juneclaire's hand and walked beside her. "Besides, you can help me mend it."

Juneclaire ignored that last. "You're not caring about your mother, from all I hear. Aunt Marta says you can judge a man's worth by how he treats his mama."

"That sounds like what a mother of sons would say. My mother has never been comfortable with me, Juneclaire, and I gave up trying years ago. It would take the patience of a saint to put up with her vapors, and I never lied about that. And didn't Aunt Marta tell you not to listen to gossip?"

"Well, you aren't kind to your grandmother either, and that is not hearsay. I can see for myself that you keep her on a tight budget. Those old servants, this one pitiful excuse for a horse. If all this"—she waved one mittened hand around—"is yours, that is unforgivable."

He took that mittened hand in his gloved one and continued walking back to the stable. Juneclaire didn't remove her hand. "Now who told you that faradiddle about my holding the dowager's purse strings? Grandmother is one of the wealthiest women in the county in her own right. She could hire an army and operate a racing stable if she wanted. Have you tried to get her to do anything she *didn't* want? She lives the way she does out of her choice, not mine."

Juneclaire was thinking of some of the other things she'd heard to the earl's disfavor when she remembered another item altogether. She pulled her hand away from his so fast, he was left holding her mitten, the odd, not-quite-finished one. "They say—and it is not gossip, for even Lady St. Cloud mentioned it—that you are engaged."

"Yes."

"Yes? That is all you can say, yes? You can hold my hand"—and make her heart beat faster, although she did not say that—"when everyone is waiting for you to bring your betrothed home as soon as you fi—oh."

"Yes." He kept walking but glanced at her out of the corner of his eye. She was biting on her lower lip and kicking at rocks, and her brows were lowered. He wanted to take her in his arms more than anything, needles and kicks and all. "I told them we were engaged."

She came to a standstill. "Were you disguised then, too? You must have been to say such a thing when you knew it wasn't true."

"I am not a drunkard, Juneclaire. You don't have to worry about that, at least. I said we were betrothed because it's right that we marry after you were so compromised."

"But no one knew that I was compromised at all, and it was my fault for being where I had no business being!"

"They'll find out. And I also said it because I wanted it to be true." There, he'd confessed.

Instead of being won over, Juneclaire stamped her foot. "Well, you're not Little Yerby to make it so because you say it, and I am not Jack!"

"I should hope not, dear heart, whoever Little Yerby and Jack are. Will you come for a walk with me?" They were back at the stable, and he handed Flame's lead to the stable boy.

"But the dowager . . ."

"Knows all about it. Come." He stuffed her unresisting hand back in the mitten and held it firmly, going in the opposite direction. "Are you warm enough?"

She just nodded, lost in her own thoughts. After a bit she said, with not much of a quiver in her voice, that she could not marry an earl.

"Why, my love, are you holding out for a duke? I understand there are few on the marriage market this year, and those are well into their dotage. You'd do much better with a young earl."

"How can you tease? I am a nobody, with no dowry and no connections. And . . . and my parents ran off to France to marry. I know I told you that, but it's worse. They . . . they didn't say their vows until they got to Calais, a week later!"

"Shocking, Junco, shocking. Someday, when I am not trying to convince you to join your name with mine, I shall describe my own parents' marriage. Suffice it to say that Lady Fanny has not been to London in over twenty years for fear of being cut. I have tried to convince her that the past is long forgotten, but Uncle Harmon cautions her otherwise. It is not in his interest to see her remarry, or even move to Town, for then he would have no place here. He knows I will not have him set one foot over the doorsill of Jordan House in London. Juneclaire, if I do not hold you responsible for your parents' sins, can you forgive me mine?"

She nodded, but her mind was only half attending. The other half was gazing in awe at the edifice sprawled across her horizon.

"I promised you a house of your own, remember? I, ah, never said it was small. Do you hate it? It's even worse inside. We don't have to live here, you know. There's London and the stud in Ireland, and I have a hunting box in Leicester. We could buy a cottage somewhere, damn it. Juneclaire, say something."

Something? "I want to go home." The Priory was surely the biggest building Juneclaire had seen since leaving France, where she'd visited some of the cathedrals with her parents. It was possibly the ugliest building she'd ever seen. Gray stone, tan brick, an Elizabethan wing and a modern wing, crenellated towers on one side, Roman columns supporting a two-story porch built right on top of the old Priory itself. One wing ended in the original chapel, another in a vast ballroom built in Henry's times. She could not see the conservatory from here, Merry—Lord St. Cloud—told her, but it formed the central wing.

Juneclaire had to laugh. He was teasing, of course.

"No, Junco, I am not bamming you. I need you."

"The dowager needs me."

"We'll share. I need you to convince her to move up here, where she'll be looked after better. There's a private suite all ready for her. I need you to keep peace between the countesses and referee the cricket matches between the Priory phantoms and the Angel of Death."

"Woodpeckers."

"You heard it, too? See, your calm good sense is just what they need. What I need. Please, Junco, at least consider my proposal. Say you'll come to dinner tonight, you and Grandmother, of course. The relatives mostly grow worse on closer acquaintance, but I swear no one shall insult you."

"I have nothing to wear to such a grand house."

"I believe you are turning craven on me, Junco. Is this the fearless amazon who attacked a bandit with a water bucket? Who fended off an amorous footman with a wine bottle? Who wears a blasted porcupine quill in her lapel? I happen to know you have a beautiful gown, a white velvet gown. I should love to buy you rubies to go with it, or emeralds. I should like to touch the softness of it, against your skin. But I can be patient. Not very, as you know. Come tonight, Junco, come get to know us and give us a chance. Give me a chance."

Chapter Eighteen

St. Cloud sent over red rosebuds from the hothouses. Nutley wove them through the wreath of holly Juneclaire wore as a headpiece, with her hair pulled up and back, tiny curls framing her face and a long sweep of brown waves trailing over one shoulder. The abigail pinned another of the roses to the green ribbon that sashed under the high waist, helped Miss Beaumont fasten her mother's pearls around her neck, and declared the young lady a diamond of the first water. The groom, draping the borrowed black velvet mantle with red satin lining over Juneclaire's pale shoulders, stared wide-eyed and open-mouthed. Sally Munch gasped.

"Well, tell me, girl, tell me," the dowager demanded, banging her cane down once she knew Shamrock was tucked in the kitchen with Penny. "Will she do?"

Sally swore she was bang up to the mark, and Pennington, holding the door, added that miss was top of the trees, if my lady excused the cant. Juneclaire wanted to sink with embarrassment. "Really, ma'am, there is no need to make such a fuss."

"There's all the need in the world, miss, and you know it. Facing that pack of barracudas, you'll want all your defenses up, and a gel's best defense is looking her best."

Juneclaire was surely doing that, she acknowledged. She'd never felt so elegant, so pampered, or so unsure of herself. "Will they like me?" she asked, as the footman and Sally helped the dowager into an elegant carriage.

"What's that to the point?" the dowager replied as soon as the coach started moving. "Hell, they all hate me, and I've never lost a night's sleep over it. Besides, if you're worrying about St. Cloud, don't. He likes you enough to chase all over England after you, and he never cared what anyone else thought, especially not that parcel of flats. Oh, Fanny's just a flibbertigibbet, I suppose, afraid of her own shadow and that brother of hers, but the others are—Well, you'll see for yourself."

A very proper butler announced them to those assembled in the gold parlor: "Lady Georgette Jordan, Dowager Countess St. Cloud. Miss Juneclaire Beaumont."

They walked in to a sea of stunned faces. Then St. Cloud came forward and took Juneclaire's trembling hand. He squeezed it and winked. "Oh yes," he addressed the company at large, "I forgot to mention that Grandmother's new companion was my Juneclaire. With all the skimble-skamble over carriages and directions and such, she cleverly came ahead on her own to wait for me here, under the dowager's aegis, of course. Didn't you, my pet?"

His pet was wanting to box his ears, even if he was overwhelmingly attractive in his formal clothes! The devil had very nicely sidestepped awkward questions but also added to the impression that they were affianced. Juneclaire couldn't cause a scene, not when he was leading her to the two women on the sofa. One of them was weeping into her handkerchief. His mother hates me already,

Juneclaire thought in despair. But he was bowing to the other woman.

"I am so glad," Lady Fanny trilled after introductions were made, and Juneclaire thought she meant it.

The other woman was moaning by now, and Juneclaire could not understand how everyone else in the room was ignoring her, even turning their backs.

"Aunt Florrie," St. Cloud was calling, "what's wrong? Aren't you happy I found Juneclaire and she is safe?"

"She'll want her pig back," Florrie wailed.

Juneclaire blinked, then said, "Oh, have you been taking care of Pansy? Isn't she a fine pig? I did give her to Mer—the earl, however, so I shan't be claiming her back. Did you know that we have a new kitten staying at the Dower House? Perhaps the dowager will invite you to tea so you can meet Shamrock."

Florrie was gone, skipping toward the dowager, who sat alone in a high-backed chair. It would be the first conversation between those two unlikely friends. Lady Fanny smiled her thanks and St. Cloud patted her hand, still firmly held on his arm, as he led her away.

"Why haven't you told your mother that we are not engaged?" she hissed at him, trying to maintain her smile.

"What, and cause another *crise de nerfs*? I thought you wanted me to be more careful of her sensibilities?"

They were in front of the other two females in the room, and during the introductions, Juneclaire had to pretend she did not know their identities. Miss Elsbeth Wilmott's gaze was clearly speculative, then superior when she compared her own blond curls, lace overskirt, three tiers of ruffles and

162

rhinestones to Miss Beaumont's rustic simplicity. The country drab would never have a fitting place in society, Elsbeth's curling lip seemed to say. If this sour-faced young woman was the girl Merry might have married, Juneclaire reflected, he was better out of it.

The other woman looked right through Juneclaire, judging her and finding her unworthy of notice. Lady Sydelle Pomeroy directed all of her attention on the earl, having decided that a nonesuch like St. Cloud would tire of the little nobody in weeks. Juneclaire was thinking much the same, observing the older woman's gold locks and nile blue gown, what there was of it. More bosom was showing out of Lady Pomeroy's bodice than Juneclaire had in hers. The woman made her feel like a gauche schoolgirl, and she was happy when someone placed a glass of sherry in her hand.

Then they were facing Niles, the toad. His face was as white as his high shirt collars, and he was tossing back sherries as if they were Blue Ruin. Juneclaire smiled as she held out her hand for his salute, forcing him to extend his own bandaged paw, which he was desperately trying to conceal from the earl. Trying to seduce a paid companion was one thing; attempting to have his way with his cousin's wife-to-be was another. He swallowed audibly. St. Cloud was such a deuced good shot. And had such a deuced short temper. Juneclaire took great satisfaction in letting him squirm a bit, then she inclined her head and said, "How do you do?"

"Magnificent, my lady," St. Cloud whispered in her ear after Niles scuttled away. "And I apologize. That performance was surely worthy of a duchess. I also apologize for my cousin," the earl added, having missed none of the byplay. "He'll never bother you again."

Niles, meanwhile, had attached himself to Lady

Pomeroy's side. He needed a wealthy wife more than ever.

"What about our bet, Niles?" Sydelle asked, not bothering to lower her voice.

"What, are you dicked in the nob? Even if I succeeded, I'd not live long enough to enjoy my winnings. Besides, the fellow just paid all my debts."

The last two people in the room were the live-in curate, who welcomed her kindly, and St. Cloud's uncle Harmon, who uttered his greeting in form. Juneclaire did not have to be a mind reader to sense his disapproval. He wanted his daughter to be countess, she had that from the dowager, and he had an overweening sense of pride. If Juneclaire did not know she was unfit to be Lady St. Cloud, Lord Wilmott's slack-jowled sneer would have told her.

"Don't let Uncle Harmon bother you," the earl told her as they went in to dinner together, forgoing precedence. "He has digestive problems. An overabundance of spleen."

Someone, the earl most likely, had been very careful of the seating arrangements. Juneclaire sat on the earl's left, across from the dowager, with Mr. Hilloughby on her other side. The table was vast enough that she did not have to converse with any of the Wilmotts during the four courses and several removes, although she felt all their eyes upon her, waiting to see if she reached for the wrong fork or spoke with her mouth full. Aunt Marta would have scolded her for less.

Dinner was fairly pleasant, at her end at least, with the dowager quizzing the earl about her London acquaintances. They were quick to include Juneclaire, providing histories and reciting anecdotes that had her laughing. Juneclaire was glad to see the old lady happy and pleased to note how gracefully the earl made sure her food was cut and directions tactfully whispered.

Mr. Hilloughby was pleased to relate the history of the Priory chapel when she turned to him, and begged to show Juneclaire the fine rose window, at her convenience, of course. Then the dowager started recounting bits of her own London Seasons, which had Juneclaire in whoops. She *had* had a bit more wine with dinner than she was used to, on top of the sherry.

She needed it, to get her through the after-dinner gathering in the drawing room, before the men joined the ladies.

The dowager was drowsing near the fire, and Aunt Florrie was counting chair legs, "just to be sure." Countess Fanny had taken up her Bible and seemed to be praying; her lips were moving, at any rate, so Juneclaire did not want to intrude. That left her at the mercy of the two blond beauties.

"Did we hear you were from Strasmere? I suppose you know the baron, then, and his lady. So charming, don't you think?"

"Wherever did you find such a clever seamstress, my dear? So daring to set new styles, isn't it?"

"You are nineteen? Then you must have had your come-out. I do not recall seeing you in London. So many debutantes, you know."

St. Cloud would have seemed like an angel of mercy if he weren't scowling so. He took Juneclaire's arm to lead her away, but not before Lady Pomeroy asked if their newest member couldn't entertain them with a song and some music.

"*All* ladies can play, of course, and I am sure the company is bored with my poor offerings."

They'd be more than bored if Juneclaire sat at the pianoforte, she thought with just a tinge of hysteria, not wanting to shame Merry. She was saved this time by the dowager, who, rousing from her nap, declared that not all who could play well were ladies. "I wish more young gels knew their limits, instead of foisting their meager accomplishments on poor dolts with nothing better to do. Besides, Miss Beaumont has other talents, like teaching a blind woman how to play cards. I'll take you all on at whist, with her help. And my own deck."

Sydelle excused herself with a headache, rather than waste her time talking to Elsbeth or Lady Fanny. The men were all commandeered for the dowager's game, except the curate, who was aiding Fanny at her devotions. He didn't count anyway.

Juneclaire sat behind the dowager, whispering the discards. St. Cloud was partnering his grandmother, straight across from them, and Juneclaire could see his brows lift when he felt the rough edges of the pinpricks. Niles smiled; marked cards were nothing new to him.

Lord Wilmott, however, was furious. He threw his hand down and jumped to his feet. "This is an outrage! These cards have been tampered with." He glared at Juneclaire. "We don't consider cardsharping a drawing-room accomplishment in our circles, miss."

Juneclaire felt the roast pheasant she'd enjoyed at dinner try to take wing. She couldn't look at Merry. It was the dowager who spoke first, though. "Of course the cards are marked, you popinjay. What did you think, I was reading my hands through Miss Beaumont's eye? And where was the advantage, Harmon? If I remember correctly, you had the deal."

Lord Wilmott sat down, red-faced and muttering. Juneclaire released her breath. Then St. Cloud spoke, every inch the earl. "I believe you owe the ladies an apology, sir. Lady St. Cloud has ever been the best whist player of my acquaintance; she has no need to cheat to beat you. And Miss Beaumont is many things, including a guest in this house, may I remind you, but she is not a Captain Sharp. I did not like your comments."

Lord Wilmott mumbled his apologies and took up his hand, ungracefully. His antipathy toward St. Cloud was barely concealed and was magnified when the earl suggested Lord Wilmott apply to Lady Fanny for a physic, if his stomach was in such an uproar it disordered his senses. The dowager cackled and Niles smirked. Lord Wilmott glared most at the outside witness to his humiliation, Juneclaire. Worse, in his eyes, he and Niles were sadly trounced. He excused himself before the tea tray was brought in.

Soon after, Juneclaire noticed that the dowager was looking peaked, exhausted by her triumph. "We should be going, my lord," she told the earl.

He walked with her toward the other side of the room, where the gold drapes were drawn against the night. "I, ah, took the liberty of having the dowager's and your things moved over to the Priory during dinner." He wisely stepped back.

"You what? Why, you arrogant, overbearing—"

"Now don't cut up stiff, Junco; you know it's best for the dowager."

"I know it suits your plans, my lord, and I know you like having your own way."

"Why, there have to be *some* advantages to having a title," he teased.

She was not amused. "I resent being forced to go along with your whims, willy-nilly."

"This, my little bird, is not a whim. I am trying to show you that. Since you are already up in the boughs, I may as well admit to the other decision I took on myself. I had my man Foley tell your people that you were safe here, with me."

Juneclaire had written three letters to her family, then ripped them up, not knowing what to say.

She should be thankful, she supposed, that Merry had undertaken an unpleasant task, but Aunt Marta was not likely to consider her safe, not if she knew the earl's reputation, and not if he kept stroking the inside of Juneclaire's elbow, where her gloves ended. And certainly not if she knew how Juneclaire wanted to succumb to the gleam in Merry's green, green eyes. "Oh, dear."

Chapter Nineteen

*H*e was arrogant and overbearing and quite, quite wonderful! He led her himself to the family wing to a white-and-rose room with Chinese wallpaper. Pansy was waiting there, wearing a baby's bonnet, but clean and shiny and noisily ecstatic to see Juneclaire. Shamrock was curled in a basket by the fireplace, and a freckle-faced young maid sat sewing, ready to help her to bed. The dowager was installed in the suite next door, he explained, with Nutley and Sally Munch each assigned a bedchamber off the dressing room. Nutley was pleased so many more servants would be listening for the dowager's calls, and Sally was thrilled to have all the Priory footmen to practice her wiles upon. The Penningtons, St. Cloud continued, wanted to stay on as caretakers at the Dower House, where they were comfortable, rather than be interlopers in the Priory staff hierarchy. He was sending young Ned and his mother, who was feeling much better with the proper medicine, to help look after the house and the old couple. That should keep everybody out of trouble, the earl said. Then he kissed her hand good night, in view of the new maid, and thanked her for coming, as if she'd had a choice!

He thought of everything, Juneclaire had to admit. Her own three gowns hung in the wardrobe, with the brown habit and two simple gowns she and Sally and Nutley had managed to make over from the dowager's castoffs, and two other new dresses. These, her new maid Parker happily informed her, had been run up by the Priory's own resident seamstress that afternoon, with more to come since miss's trunks had so unfortunately gone astray in the carriage mishap.

There were powders and oils and hot towels, hothouse flowers and a stack of books on the bed stand, a dish of biscuits if she or Pansy got hungry during the night. What more could a poor orphan runaway want? Plenty.

Merry was kind. He cared for her. He wanted her and needed her, he said, and she believed him. He never mentioned love. Juneclaire could barely think in his presence, her blood pounded so loudly in her head. She thought he was the most splendid man in the world, if a trifle imperious and temper-prone. She thought she could make him happy, since the mere thought of him made her smile. She also thought she was halfway in love with him from the night at the barn, and the other half was a heartbeat away. But she was, indeed, a poor orphan runaway, and she would never burden him with such a wife, only to have him regret his good intentions later. Unless he loved her . . .

Merry asked for time to change her mind. Perhaps in time she could change his from just wanting to marry her to not wanting to live without her. It was possible. She thought she'd ask Mrs. Pennington to save her a wishbone when she visited them tomorrow. She went to sleep, smiling.

Tap, tap. Tap, tap. There it was again, Juneclaire thought in a muzzy fog. All those workmen and they never found the woodpeckers. Merry would be angry. She snuggled deeper in the covers.

Tap, crunch. Tap, crunch. Woodpeckers riding on rats? Merry would be very angry. Juneclaire turned over.

Tap, crunch, sigh. On remorseful rats? That was too much. She fumbled for the flint. Someone handed it to her, and she automatically said "Thank you" before lighting her candle.

Either there was a ghost in her room, or Juneclaire'd had too much wine. She opted for the wine. No self-respecting ghost ever looked like this. He had salt-and-pepper hair, a full gray beard and mustache, a brocaded coat from the last century—camphor-scented to prove it—that couldn't button across a wide paunch, and a peg leg.

Oh, good, Juneclaire thought, still half-asleep, that explains the tapping. The empty plate of biscuits by her bed explained the crunching. Well, they were gone, so the ghost could leave and she could go back to sleep. She bent to blow out the candle, and the ghost sighed again, a mournful, graveyard sigh indeed. It occurred to Juneclaire that she should scream. She opened her mouth, but the ghost stopped her by saying, "So you're Merry's bride."

Merry? Only one person ever called him Merry, he'd said. "Uncle George?"

"Aye." He pulled a chair closer to her bed and fed the last biscuit to the pig when Pansy came to investigate. Then he sighed again, scratching behind Pansy's big ears poking through the baby bonnet, as though it were the most natural thing for a pig—or a ghost—to be in a lady's bedchamber at three in the morning. Juneclaire swore she would never take a sip of wine again.

Then she got a whiff of her guest, past the camphor. He'd been partaking of the grape, too, it seemed. "Um, Uncle George, how did you get in here?" Her door was locked; she didn't trust that Niles. The specter waved vaguely at the wardrobe against the far side of the room. Juneclaire nodded. That made sense. Ghosts didn't need to use doors. "Can you tell me why you've come, what it is that you want?" She was thinking in terms of revenge, or a better burial, typical ghostly reasons for haunting their ancestral homes.

"Someone to talk to, I guess." He sighed again. Life, or half life, was hard. "Fanny gets down on her hands and knees and starts praying every time I try to talk to her, when she doesn't swoon. I don't know how many more visits from me Mother's heart can take, what with her sure I'm Death come to carry her off. And Merry nearly ran me through with his sword tonight, thinking I was some nightmare from his French prison days. I tried old Pennington, but he drank down his wife's last bottle of rum and passed out next to her. Now he's taken to wearing garlic around his neck."

"Is that what it is? I noticed something. . . ."

"Don't want to go near the old fellow, and I can't ever rouse Nutley. I swear the woman sleeps like one of the dead."

He should know, but "She's deaf," Juneclaire told him.

"Oh. None of the other servants have been around long enough, so you see, there's no one to talk to. They all think I'm dead."

"Aren't you?"

"I don't think so. Are ghosts hungry?"

"How should I know? You're the first one I've met." Shamrock was now twining himself around the apparition's leg, and Pansy was wearing her idiotic grin of a hog in heaven. Juneclaire shrugged and slipped out of bed. She gingerly reached out her hand and touched his arm with the tips of her fingers. Solid. She poked her own arm to make sure.

Solid, and awake. Unless she was dreaming about pinching herself to see if she was dreaming. She sat back down on the bed. "Uncle George? That is, may I call you Uncle George?" He nodded, with another sigh. "Why don't you just come back tomorrow, in the daylight, and have Talbot announce you?"

"I wish it were that easy, lass. I wish it were. I can tell you've a wise head on your shoulders, and I'd explain all about it, if only I weren't so devilishly sharp set. I'd go down to the kitchens, but Merry's got a guard posted there with a pistol. One along the corridor here, too."

"Someone's been stealing food and things and frightening the servants, to say nothing of poor Lady Fanny. You should be ashamed, sir."

"I am, child. Very ashamed. And very hungry."

So Juneclaire went to find the kitchens, with Uncle George's directions tumbling about in her head. She was in the east wing; the kitchens were two stories down, halfway along the central transverse in what was the old Priory's refectory. She went in her bare feet so as not to wake anybody, especially the guard who was asleep at the end of the corridor. A hunting rifle was propped alongside his chair, barrel pointing up. Juneclaire shielded her candle and tiptoed past. So did Pansy.

The kitchen guard was awake, playing patience and sipping an ale. He thought nothing odd about a barefoot houseguest in her white flannel nightgown helping herself to another dinner. Hell, he thought, everyone knew the gentry was peculiar. Once you got over the pig in the baby bonnet, the rest didn't make a halfpenny's difference.

Juneclaire found a hamper to fill, as if she and Pansy were going on a picnic, then covered the whole with a napkin so the guard couldn't tell how much food she was taking, she hoped. She could barely carry the basket as it was, with the candle in her other hand.

"I'd help you, miss, but it'd mean my job, were I to leave my post." The guard was back at his game.

"But you will tell them in the morning that I took the leftovers, won't you? I don't want anyone to think there were burglars or . . . ghosts."

"I'll be sure to mention it, lest they think I was eating more myself than Napoleon's army during the whole Russian campaign."

Juneclaire blushed but held her head high and retraced her steps. She thought she did, anyway. Somehow she found herself in the servants' quarters, built out of the old monks' cells. She turned around quickly and let Pansy lead the way, trusting the pig's unerring nose to get them . . . back to the kitchen. The guard sent her on her way in the other direction, shaking his head.

Her feet were cold, the basket was heavy, and Juneclaire was sure she must have dreamed the whole thing. She tiptoed carefully past the sleeping hall watchman but was not quite as careful about Pansy, who stopped to investigate. Her pink leathery nose whiffled into the watchman's dangling hand to check for crumbs. The guard jumped up and shouted and his chair fell back, crashing. The pig ran away, screaming, and the leaning gun went off, blowing a porcelain bust of Galileo into cosmic dust indeed.

The first door to fly open was Lady Fanny's. Right in front of her was a figure swathed in white cloth, surrounded by swirls of otherworldly clouds. Juneclaire moaned. The countess collapsed onto the floor at her feet, out cold.

The dowager was shouting to know what was going on and demanding to be taken home to the Dower House, where a body wasn't likely to be shot in her bed. Sally Munch poked her head out of the door, fireplace poker in hand.

Then St. Cloud was there, carrying his mother back to her room, calling for her woman, shouting the dowager back to bed, dismissing the guard and the twenty or thirty other servants in various stages of undress who appeared from nowhere. And looking at Juneclaire in sorrow.

She held up the basket and pulled out a roll. "I . . . I wanted it for the pig."

Elsbeth giggled until a glare from St. Cloud had her scurrying away. He jerked his head to be rid of Niles, too. But Uncle Harmon stayed, spluttering about harum-scarum chits and animals who should be in the stable or—with a dark look at Pansy—on the table. The look he gave Juneclaire was no better. "Milkmaids," he huffed, pulling his nightcap back down around his ears and stomping off to the other wing.

St. Cloud clenched his jaw and said he had to check on his grandmother. He would see Miss Beaumont in the morning. He tightened the sash on his paisley robe and bowed.

Juneclaire didn't doubt he was wishing the sash was around her neck. She fled to her own room and threw herself on the bed. Uncle George was gone, naturally. No one would believe her anyway, and now she had lost Merry's esteem.

His family hated her. They thought her a gape-seed, an unmannered bumpkin born in a cabbage patch. And they were right. She *had* been a milkmaid, just that one time for Little Yerby, true, but she was no fine lady like Sydelle and Elsbeth. She couldn't play or sing or flirt or fill a gown so well. Her friends were farmers and servants and barnyard animals, not lords and ladies and London luminaries.

And Merry was disappointed. She could see it in

175

his angry face. He did not need another hysterical female in his household, or one who caused more ruckus and row than all the others combined—and on her first night there! Juneclaire sobbed into her pillow; the cat and the pig were already damp with her tears. She did not belong here, she thought, and she would have to leave before she disgraced Merry further. There was no way he could learn to love a milkmaid, and there was no way she could make a proper countess. You couldn't make a silk purse out of a sow's ear.

Chapter Twenty

𝒯he food was gone in the morning. Juneclaire had put it on the desk, out of Pansy's reach, and the maids had not been in yet to light the fire, so Uncle George must have come back. Juneclaire wished he'd woken her up for a chat, for if he thought being dead was hard, he should try being Miss Beaumont. She was not *really* Merry's fiancée, she no longer had duties as the dowager's companion, and everyone, snooty relatives and well-trained servants, was treating her with polite condescension. They hated her. There was a hideous sculpture of some martyr being devoured by a lion in the niche where Galileo used to be. Lady Fanny most likely directed the maids to find the ugliest piece in the house, in hopes Juneclaire would relieve them of it next.

Breakfast was a disaster. Juneclaire and Aunt Florrie were the only women there. That court card Niles made oinking noises at her, while eating rasher after rasher of bacon. Lord Harmon barely concealed his disgust behind the newspapers, and Mr. Hilloughby kept his eyes firmly on his kippers. Merry pretended nothing had happened.

With his black curls damp from combing and his cravat loosely tied, Merry looked so handsome,

Juneclaire had a hard time swallowing her toast past the lump in her throat. His brows seemed permanently puckered and his lips never turned up, but he was courteous, caring—and cold. He was too busy to show her around this morning, he apologized, what with the New Year's Eve ball just tomorrow night, and no, thank you, he said, there was nothing she could do to help; she was a guest. The weather was too inclement, at any rate, for her to accompany him on his rounds. He had arranged for Mr. Hilloughby to show her the chapel this morning and for Aunt Florrie to take Juneclaire to the attics to pick a costume in the afternoon. This was from the man who wanted her to spend time getting to know him, to see if they would suit. He had obviously decided.

Juneclaire was set to ask the dowager for a carriage ride back to Stanton Hall as soon as Lady St. Cloud awoke. That way Merry could have no worries about her safety, no embarrassing responsibilities toward her. Before she left, though, she was curious about one thing: "My lord, what happened to Uncle George?"

Niles dropped his coffee cup, and Mr. Hilloughby took a coughing fit. The footmen's eyes were all on the carved ceiling. Juneclaire barely registered all this. She was pinned in St. Cloud's stare like a mounted butterfly. She'd never seen him so angry, not even last night, when he walked barefoot over Galileo's remains, not even when Charlie Parrett had him in a death grip. Still, she would not look away. Let him think she was an unschooled hobbledehoyden. Let him think there was a breeze in her cockloft. He would *not* think she was a coward, unless he heard her knees knocking together.

He finally broke the silence by pronouncing, "We do not speak of George Jordan in this house," in the same tones he might have used to intone the eleventh commandment.

Then Aunt Florrie chirped, "We don't mention making water either."

Juneclaire would not stoop to questioning the servants, who were so in dread of the master's temper that they'd take the turnspit dog's place sooner than go against his wishes. She could not chance upsetting the dowager or Lady Fanny with her queries, and she was not about to ask Mr. Hilloughby, not after St. Cloud's edict.

She did, however, manage to check the family Bible in the old chapel, after dutifully admiring the age and architecture of the place. The stained-glass windows did not glow, not on such a dreary day outside, and the stone floors kept the sanctuary bitterly cold. Worse, Mr. Hilloughby was a historical scholar. While he described the life and last days of the original St. Jerome of the Clouds in excruciating detail, Juneclaire read through generations of Jordans. Uncle George was crossed out.

The dowager refused to hear of Juneclaire's leaving.

"That's a shabby return for my taking you on, girl, leaving me alone with the hyenas. No, I won't hear of it." She stabbed her cane halfway through the Turkey runner in her sitting room. "You will be happy here, and that's final."

The earl had inherited more than a title and wealth, it seemed.

Juneclaire was surprised at how well Florrie knew her way around the vast attics. She understood the earl's aunt was frequently lost in the Priory's warren of corridors, chambers, and alcoves. Aunt Florrie knew just what she wanted for

Juneclaire, too, and knew right where it was, give or take a trunk or three or four. The St. Clouds must never have thrown anything out.

"Here, this will be perfect for you, dearie," Aunt Florrie said, holding up a wide-skirted shepherdess dress, complete with apron, crooked staff, and stuffed, fleece-covered lamb. "It's the best of all the costumes."

Juneclaire's heart was not in preparing for a masquerade. It was downstairs, brooding. She didn't care what she wore. She didn't care if she attended, even if she'd never been to a real ball in her life, much less a masked one. Aunt Marta would convert to Hindi before she let such wickedness occur under her roof. Nonetheless, the outfit seemed to mean a great deal to the older woman, so Juneclaire said, "Perhaps you should be the shepherdess, Aunt Florrie, and I could be something else." She looked around. "Queen Elizabeth, maybe, or Anne Boleyn." She felt like Anne Boleyn, after all.

"Oh, no, you have to be the shepherdess. It will be wonderful, you'll see." She was cutting apart the stuffed lamb with embroidery scissors from her pocket. "Besides, I am going to be Yellow. Last year I was Rain, but Harmon became angry when the floors got wet."

The dowager decided to have dinner on a tray in her room. Juneclaire suspected the old lady was feigning weariness for her sake, so she did not have to face the company again, but she leaped at the excuse.

"It's no such thing, missy. I saw them Christmas and last night, and I'll have to do the pretty for the ball tomorrow. That's three times in one week, and with that bunch of counter jumpers, three times a year is enough. Of course, you're free to go down if you want."

"Oh, no, I promised to teach you to knit cables, and you promised to teach me vingt-et-un. And Lord St. Cloud sent up Miss Austen's new novel and Scott's ballads. I need to try on my costume for tomorrow and—"

"Cut line, girl. I'm glad for the company."

The dowager approved the theme of Juneclaire's costume. "Innocent and sweet, in case there's any talk. But pretty and feminine, too, if I remember correctly. Just the ticket. My costume? I'm going as a crotchety old lady, what else? No one'll recognize me, and that's only fair, for I sure as Harry won't recognize them!"

Juneclaire kept back all the uneaten food from dinner and asked for more to be sent up, for the pig. She let Parker help her into her night rail and brush out her long hair, and then she dismissed the maid for the night. She got into bed with a Gothic tale from the Minerva Press and waited for Uncle George.

The heroine was locked in a deserted tower. The steps were crumbly, the candle was low, small things chittered nearby. Everywhere she turned, spiderwebs stuck in her hair. Drafts blew through the cracked windows, and the door . . . slowly . . . creaked . . . open.

And there was Uncle George, stepping out of Juneclaire's wardrobe. Tonight he wore doublet and hose.

While he was eating, she told him her troubles. "They all think I'm a clodpoll, except for Merry. He thinks I'm a nightmare. The dowager won't let me go, and the rest of them will make fun of me if I stay. Tomorrow night at the ball they'll have all their friends to laugh and sneer at poor St. Cloud's goat girl. Elsbeth and Lady Pomeroy will be gor-

geous, and I'll forget the dance steps. I've only practiced with my cousins, you know."

George waved a chicken leg. "Your problem,
puss, is lack of confidence. Don't worry, I'll take
care of it."

"You? How can you take care of it when you don't
even exist?"

He sighed, feeding Pansy the cooked carrots.
"Never could abide cooked carrots. Do you think a
ghost cares what it eats? As a matter of fact, why
would a ghost eat at all? I thought we settled that
last night."

"Yes, but they won't talk about you, and they've
struck your name out of the records. If you're not
dead, why don't you just come back?"

"I promised I'd explain, but it's hard. You see, if
I'm not dead, then I'm a murderer."

"A murderer?" she shrieked, louder than she intended, and suddenly there was a pounding at her
door.

"Juneclaire, are you all right? Open the door."

St. Cloud would kick it open if he had to, she
knew. She looked helplessly toward Uncle George,
who shrugged and picked up another chicken leg.
She unlocked the door and opened it a crack. "I am
fine, my lord."

He was glaring at her again. "I thought I heard
voices." He thought he heard a man's voice. He
tried to look past her into the room.

She did not think this was a good time to mention
Uncle George again. "I was, ah, reading."

"Out loud?"

"I was practicing, you know, for when I read to
the dowager."

"And you are all right? Not frightened by those
silly stories of the Priory ghosts?"

"Oh, no. Not at all. Are you?"

He snorted. "Hardly. I'll just be going, then. Good night, Miss Beaumont."

"Good night, Lord St. Cloud."

Juneclaire was almost as unhappy as the night before, until she started to hear screams and screeches from the far corridor, where the Wilmotts were installed. She tied on her robe and found her slippers and ran with St. Cloud and some of the servants to the east wing. Niles and Harmon Wilmott were already in the hall, trying to comfort Elsbeth, who was sobbing, and Lady Sydelle, who was raving hysterically about goblins, ghosts, and going home. Elsbeth had her hair tied in papers, and Lady Pomeroy had some yellow concoction spread all over her face. Juneclaire smiled. Uncle George was taking care of things for her.

The Earl of St. Cloud sat in his library, his head in his hands. Half a bottle of cognac hadn't helped. He was still in a deuce of a coil. He was fond of his Aunt Florrie, but he did not want his children to be like her. Juneclaire was touched, dicked in the nob, attics to let. Or else she was playing some deep game he did not know about. How could she look like such an angel and be so jingle-brained, if not downright evil? Nothing she said rang true anymore. He did not know what to think, except that she was turning his life and his household upside down.

And yet he was so attracted to her that just the memory of the chit in her virginal white nightgown, with her brown hair tumbling around her shoulders, set his juices flowing. Then he remembered how he was ready to commit mayhem at the thought of someone in the room with her. He was jealous of the blasted ghost! Botheration, he was jealous of the damn pig that got to spend the night with her. Life with Juneclaire would be hell.

But how could he cry off the engagement? A gentleman did not. And he was the one who had insisted, who had announced their betrothal to his family. He was obliged to marry her now, aside from the night in the barn. Blast her and the dashed pig. They had him by the shoat hairs.

Chapter Twenty-one

Juneclaire was walking the pig before breakfast when she heard the commotion. She followed the noise around the ballroom wing to find St. Cloud and a group of servants with axes, ladders, and hammers. They were searching for ways an intruder could have entered the house, Sally Munch explained to her, from her place at the fringes of the workers. Lord St. Cloud was directing the removal of climbing vines and overhanging branches. He walked ahead of the group, checking the loose ground under the windows for signs of recent disturbance. He paused to study an area under a balcony where a great many footsteps showed in the dirt. The workers gathered round, wondering if the master was going to order them to chop down the balcony.

Sally Munch was hanging back, so Juneclaire had a fairly good idea to whom at least half the prints belonged. Pansy snuffled around, then went straight to the new footman, the one with the shoulders of a prize fighter. Sally blushed, but the earl merely requested that Miss Beaumont kindly remove the pig from the field of investigation.

Juneclaire stepped closer and looked down. Thinking out loud, she said, "Those can't be his

footprints anyway. Uncle George has a peg leg."
She clapped her hand over her mouth. "Oh."

With one frigid glance the earl sent the workers
off. Juneclaire shivered. Her words would be spread
throughout the mansion along with the coffee cups
and chocolate. She had to go explain to the dowager
before Lady St. Cloud heard from that prattlebox
Sally. Before she took one step, a steel-gripped hand
clasped her wrist like a manacle, and she was silently pulled away from the house. That is, St.
Cloud was silent, frowning fiercely down at the
ground. Juneclaire protested, struggled, and ran to
keep up lest he drag her face-down in the dirt if she
fell.

He did not stop until they reached a high stone
wall and a gate. St. Cloud released her hand, with
a look daring Juneclaire to try to escape. She was
too busy catching her breath and wondering where
they were. He found the key under a loose stone
and unlatched the gate, then pulled her through.
They were in a small cemetery, and Juneclaire had
a moment's fright that he meant to murder her and
leave her body there. How awful to think her last
sight of him was to be that terrible scowl. He wasn't
even looking at her, though, continuing his long,
angry strides toward the far corner.

"There," he said, stopping finally in front of a
small grave site. "Uncle George."

Pansy was happily rooting in the leaves and stuff
that had fallen on Uncle George's marker. Juneclaire pushed her aside and read the dates.

"He has been dead these four and twenty years,"
St. Cloud said. "My fifth birthday."

"There must have been a mistake."

A muscle flexed in the earl's jaw. "The only
mistake, madam, was in my thinking you a sane,
sensible type of female. You are upsetting my

household with these idiotic ravings, and you will cease at once."

Juneclaire stood up. "I see. Uncle George is dead; therefore I am seeing ghosts, talking to spirits, feeding phantoms."

"There are no such things as ghosts. You are either hallucinating or else you are the victim of some unscrupulous charlatan, preying on your weakness."

"Unless, of course, I am in league with this fiendish scheme to . . . what? To send your mother into a decline, to rout your houseguests, and terrorize your servants. Thank you, my lord."

He watched the pig. "I never said that."

"No, but you thought it. Did it never occur to you, my lord, that you could be wrong for once? That someone, dead or alive, could act contrary to your wishes?"

"I saw him, dash it! I saw his body when they brought him in!"

"Tell me," she said quietly, holding out her hand.

St. Cloud took it, thinking he would air the dirty linen and then she would be gone. That was best for all. He looked around till he spotted a bench under a stand of bare-branched lilacs. "Come. It is not a short story." He did not sit down next to her but propped one Hessian-clad leg on the stone seat. He stared into the distance, into the past.

"The Wilmotts lived on the neighboring estate, Motthaven; they were minor gentry but, then as now, perpetually overextended. Uncle George and Mother were childhood sweethearts. The second son of an earl should have been a good enough match for his daughter, but Lord Wilmott wanted more, and Robert, the oldest son and heir, seemed interested. George was reckless, drinking, gambling, all the usual vices, so Wilmott had an excuse. He refused his permission. The two tried to elope but were brought back by Wilmott, his son Harmon, and Robert. Uncle George was shipped out to the army, more dead than alive, I understand. And Mother . . . Mother married Robert Jordan, the heir to St. Cloud and soon to be the earl.

"They were happy enough, I suppose. I seldom saw them, for they spent most of their time in London or traveling. Uncle George never visited." St. Cloud started pacing, kicking up leaves.

"Then he was gravely injured, and the army sent him home to St. Cloud. He was here over eight months, recuperating, and I got to know him well. He was full of stories and games to delight a little boy, when he felt well enough. We were nearly inseparable, they say. He was bored and I was . . . lonely. Then came Christmas and my birthday. My parents came here, with a large house party. And . . . something happened between the brothers."

Juneclaire knew he was not telling the whole story, but she did not interrupt.

"There was a confrontation, in view of the entire company, where Uncle George threatened to kill his brother. The two of them stormed out of the house, and Uncle George was never seen alive again."

"What happened? Did he kill your father?"

"My . . . father? No, but not from lack of trying, I fear. When neither came back that night, search parties were sent out in the morning. They found my father at the old quarry, grievously wounded and at death's door. They found George's body the next day, at the bottom of the quarry. I saw them bring him home. No one intended a small boy to be there, of course, but I was. It was a sight I shall never forget." He cleared his throat and went on: "The earl had a ball lodged against his spine, pneumonia, and severe loss of blood. They feared for his life. Still, he managed to declare the disaster an accident. Lord Wilmott was magistrate and so proclaimed it, rather than let the county know the brothers had been fighting over his daughter, my mother. As if that could stop the gossip," he added bitterly.

"The earl partially recovered. He never walked again and was angry and pain-racked for two more years until he finally succumbed to an inflammation of the lungs. He never permitted George's name to be mentioned. Mother never recovered her spirits and never dared face the ton, beyond the narrow Berkshire society."

"Then George isn't a murderer at all?"

"Wasn't. Legally, no, for his shot did not actually kill my father. Morally? He is dead and better so for what he did to my parents' lives. Leave him rest, Juneclaire, let my family's skeleton stay in the closet. Stop upsetting my mother."

But Juneclaire was not listening. She was wondering how to get word to Uncle George.

First she had to explain to the dowager.

"It really is George with a peg leg and not someone hammering nails in my coffin? That's a relief. You're sure it's George and not some other spook come back to life? I wouldn't want to see my late husband anytime soon."

"He won't eat cooked carrots."

"That's George. He tried to tell me, but I was too foolish to listen, I suppose. The boy never had a particle of sense anyway, always falling into one scrape or another. You tell him to stop playing off his tricks and get back here. Now go on, girl, I need to be alone to think about this."

Juneclaire locked her door so the servants would not think her more addled than ever, and then she tried calling Uncle George. She whispered his name in all the corners of her room and under her bed. She tried her best to find a secret door in the back of her wardrobe, dislodging everything and pounding on the bare wood. If there was a false wall, like in the Minerva Press books, it must catch from the other side. Finally she took to calling, "Uncle George" up the chimney and down the floor grates, unaware, of course, that the sound echoed throughout the family wing.

Countess Fanny was prostrate, too unnerved to attend her own pre-ball dinner. Her frightened abigail let Juneclaire talk to her for a minute.

"No," the countess cried, "he has to be dead, or he'd have forgiven me by now. I said I would wait, and I did not. Now he's come back to haunt me."

Juneclaire wanted to kill the wretch herself, if he wasn't already dead, of course. She was no more kindly disposed to George's nephew either, especially when St. Cloud directed the footmen not to serve Juneclaire anymore wine with dinner. Her only satisfaction was seeing Elsbeth's pasty face and the black shadows under Sydelle's eyes.

Juneclaire was a success at her first ball. So was Pansy. The shepherdess costume was becoming, with the apron tied at her narrow waist, the short, ruffled petticoats allowing the merest glimpse of well-turned ankle, and the low bodice not as innocent as her flower-decked hair. Pansy, a ham in sheep's clothing, trotted alongside, to the delight of the company.

Since the ball was a masquerade, none of the sixty or so guests was announced, but everyone knew who she was. They had all come to inspect the female who rumor claimed had snabbled St. Cloud. The men were quick to sign the pretty gal's dance card, and the ladies were pleased to find her a well-behaved chit. With the dowager's approval, Miss Beaumont could be no less.

Precedence also went by the wayside. St. Cloud asked her to stand up for the first dance, instead of partnering the highest-ranking lady. He was dressed as Sir Philippe d'Guerdon, the sword-for-hire knight who first won the Priory of St. Jerome of the Clouds for the Crown. The Frenchman was wily enough not to wreck the place during the siege and wise enough to ask for it as his reward. He anglicized his name to Jordan and founded his own dynasty. His ancestors stayed wise and wily, increasing their holdings, filling their coffers, staying on the right side of whatever war or rebellion occurred. They prospered until this night, when the last Jordan stood in the guise of the first, bowing to the lady who would continue the line, God and Juneclaire willing. And if St. Cloud could get his heart and his head to come to the sticking point.

She was so damned beautiful, innocent and appealing at the same time, how could he doubt her? She greeted his neighbors as if she were truly glad to meet the stuffy old matrons, the giggly young girls, the spotted youths, and the snuff-covered squires. He was proud to lead her into the dance, he told himself, proud they all thought she was his.

His bow was as courtly as only a knight wearing a chain mesh tunic and scarlet tights could make it, and the broadsword at his side threatened only once to trip him up in the dance. Juneclaire thought this moment might be worth the rest of her lifetime listening to Aunt Marta's scolds. She smiled, and the sideline watchers shook their heads that another green girl had fallen for the elusive earl. Then he smiled, and they all sighed. St. Cloud was cotched at last.

Aware of their recent awkwardness, St. Cloud tried to reestablish some of the closeness he had felt with Juneclaire at first. "I suppose you have a New Year's wish all picked out, Junco. Does it have to be a secret?"

"New Year's is for resolutions, sir knight, not wishes, didn't you know? Instead of depending on luck and happenstance, resolutions depend on one-self."

"May a humble knight not wish for a favor from a pretty maid?"

She showed her dimples. "A man may wish all he wants, but a man resolved to have a thing works to make his own wishes come true. And a lady's favor is a paltry thing for a whole year's resolution."

"I believe that depends on the lady. But what is your resolve, Miss Beaumont?"

Juneclaire knew better than to interpret his words as a desire to win her heart; he was just a practiced rake. She also knew better than to admit her real resolution, which was to reunite Uncle George with his family. Instead she said, "I think I shall try not to be so impetuous. I've been in too many hobbles as is."

He gave her another of those rare smiles, so she impetuously went on: "And you, sir, should resolve to laugh more. Uncle George says you were a cheerful little imp of a lad."

Juneclaire found herself by the dowager's side before the music had quite finished. She excused herself to check on Pansy in the refreshment room with Aunt Florrie, who had changed her persona, not her costume, to Sunshine.

When she returned to the ballroom, St. Cloud was dancing with Sydelle Pomeroy, Cleopatra in a black wig and a cloth-of-gold gown held up by little more than asp venom. She had a bracelet on her upper arm and half of Egypt's kohl supply on her eyelids. And a crocodile smile on her lips. Niles was glaring from the sidelines, an unhappily togaed Marc Antony, the cost of persuading Sydelle to stay for the ball. His bare shoulders and hairy shins were sorely missing their buckram wadding and sawdust pads, all Juneclaire's fault, naturally.

"Dash it, puss, if you keep setting his back up like that, it's no wonder he turns to that high flier."

Juneclaire turned. Father Time was standing beside her, long beard, flowing robes, scythe in one hand, hourglass in the other. "Uncle George, I've been looking all over for you! Where have you been?"

"Hush, missy. Not now."

Her next partner was approaching, Sir Walter Raleigh with spindle-shanked legs. "But when? I have news."

"The library. Twelve o'clock. They'll all be busy with the unmasking. Sh."

Juneclaire had to let him go off to the refreshment room.

"Deuced fine costume, that," Sir Walter commented. "Even has the ancient's shuffle down perfect."

She danced with a cowled monk, Robin Hood, Henry the Eighth, and a Red Indian in face paint, feathers, and satin knee breeches. She watched the French knight dance with Elsbeth's wood nymph, a Columbine, and Diana the Huntress, complete with arrows that fell out of her quiver during the Roger de Coverly.

She also watched Father Time say a few words to the dowager, but mostly he stood near the windows, watching Lady Fanny where she held court on a divan. St. Cloud strolled over in his direction once, chain mail being devilishly warm to dance in, and Juneclaire held her breath.

St. Cloud thought it was too bad that the rules of a masquerade didn't permit him to quiz the guests, for he'd dearly like to know the identity of the fat joker in the fake beard. St. Cloud had first noticed Father Time because of Juneclaire's intense interest in him, but then the fellow kept eyeing the St. Cloud ladies. St. Cloud included Juneclaire in that small group, for he was determined to announce the engagement at the unmasking if she was willing. Everyone was expecting it, from the sly looks and innuendos he was receiving, and Juneclaire's name would be bandied about if there was no public notice. In the meantime, Father Time was as close as a clam, and St. Cloud had to partner the admiral's youngest daughter. He didn't know what she was supposed to be, but she looked like a lamp shade. No one else had asked her to dance this evening and, as host in his own home, swearing to be a reformed character, he knew his duty.

He knew his duty at twelve o'clock, too, when Juneclaire was not in the ballroom for the unmasking. He couldn't very well make the announcement without her, and he could not even kiss her happy New Year, damn it, when the infuriating chit had shabbed off on him. Again. Plainly his duty was to find her and hold a pillow over that beautiful face. He started looking for her as quietly as he could, considering he clanked with every step.

Juneclaire was in the library, explaining to Uncle George that he wasn't a murderer at all, but he was buried in the family cemetery.

"Must have been my man Hawkins. He was supposed to ride for the doctor. I never could figure what happened to him." Uncle George was sitting at the earl's desk, eating lobster patties and drinking champagne.

"But aren't you happy? You can come back now. Vicar Broome over at Bramley remembers you; he said so when he was sending me here. He can help you reestablish your identity if Lady Fanny won't. You can come home!"

Uncle George took another bite. "Old Boomer Broome still wears the collar, eh? Well, he can help with my soul, but that's not enough, I'm thinking, to keep my body from getting to hell via a hempen ladder. You see, I wasn't quite honest with you, poppet. Not that I didn't think I'd killed Robert. When Hawkins didn't send me word, I was sure I had, and I fled the country. And after that, nothing seemed to matter, so . . ."

Juneclaire's heart sank. "How bad?"

"Bad, puss. Did you ever hear of Captain Cleft, the pirate?"

"No."

"Good."

"Surely there's something we can do. Merry would know who to—"

"No, I won't hand the boy any more shame." He was up and using the scythe as a cane to limp toward the door. "Come on now, you're missing the ball. All those young fellows will be looking for the second-prettiest girl here."

"Who is the first?" she asked, dreading lest he name Sydelle.

"Why, Fanny, of course. I wonder if there are any macaroons?"

They were nearly to the supper room when Juneclaire begged him to consider consulting a lawyer. "Lady St. Cloud's man Langbridge is very kind. I'm sure he'd help. Please say you'll try. Otherwise I'll—"

She never got to say what she'd do, for just then St. Cloud spotted them. He was furious that Juneclaire had deserted him, and for a pillow-stuffed humbug at that! He was even more furious when Father Time limped into the refreshment room and his flowing robe billowed up to reveal a peg leg.

This was the bastard who was haunting St. Cloud's house!

With a mighty bellow St. Cloud drew the broadsword from its sheath at his side. The bloody thing was so heavy, he needed both hands to hold the point up. Guests scattered, women screamed. Father Time saw Nemesis coming and reached out with his scythe. He swept the punch bowl to the floor, then the tub of raspberry ices, shipped out from Gunther's specially. Then he fled back to the library, while the French knight picked his way through the sticky mess past one happy pig in sherbet. When St. Cloud reached the library, followed by half the company, the old man was gone. Disappeared, vanished.

"Good show, St. Cloud," the admiral called out. "Out with the old year, eh? Happy New Year!"

Chapter Twenty-two

"*It's* not Uncle George, I tell you!" The teacups were rattling again. St. Cloud wondered if he'd ever know another peaceful breakfast, with coffee and kippers—and no conversation. Why couldn't Juneclaire be like other women and sleep till noon? Why did she have to look so delicious in peach muslin, with a Kashmir shawl over her shoulders?

"He likes macaroons and hates carrots, just like the dowager said he would," she insisted.

"Juneclaire, *I* like macaroons and hate carrots. That does not make me Uncle George any more than it makes your impostor."

"But he knows the secret passages and the priests' holes. Not even you know them."

"I told you, my father died before he passed on the information. He was afraid Niles and I would get lost in the tunnels."

"He knew you'd bedevil the housemaids, more likely," Lord Wilmott interrupted. "You were an undisciplined cub even then. I say this is outrageous. George Jordan, indeed! The fellow is gone and good riddance."

Juneclaire stuck doggedly to her argument. "But he would know the trick to getting into the hidden compartments. His father would have told him, my lord."

"Any number of servants could have known, even this Hawkins person he mentioned. Maybe that's who he is, some old employee come to blackmail the family or something. It won't wash; the dirty linen's been hung in public so long and so often, it's not worth a brass farthing. I told you I would have my man in London look into the matter of Hawkins."

"You won't find him; he's in the graveyard."

"Damn it, Juneclaire, you only have some actor's word for that!"

"But I wasn't seeing ghosts, was I? There really was a man with a peg leg?" He had to agree. "Then why can I not be right now? I'm not crazy, Merry. Why do you have to be right always, just because you are St. Cloud?"

Uncle Harmon's gorge was rising. "Why are you even listening to this rag-mannered fishwife, St. Cloud? George Jordan disgraced this family, miss, and it has taken over twenty years to rebuild our standing. Twenty years before *you* got here to stir things up."

Now St. Cloud pushed his plate away. "You forget yourself, Uncle," he said quietly. "Miss Beaumont is entitled to her opinions, and I respect her for expressing them. She and I may or may not quarrel over the coffee cups for the next twenty years. That is our decision. Where you break your fast is yours . . . for now."

Juneclaire was not sure if he meant they may or may not be married, or they may or may not argue, but she was content. He had stood up to his family for her.

Harmon Wilmott was not content. He knew better than to disparage the drab female who was ruining all his plans, but the thought of another uncle coming back from the beyond, this one with a more valid claim to St. Cloud's largess, stuck in his craw. Drooping jowls quivering in outrage, he declared, "George Jordan is better off dead. The man was a coward and a ne'er-do-well."

Before Juneclaire could say that Uncle George seemed to have done well enough on the high seas, St. Cloud stood up and tossed his napkin on the table. He may as well have thrown the gauntlet. "Uncle George was a soldier, a decorated hero. No one shall say else. If you are finished crumbling your muffin, Miss Beaumont, perhaps you would accompany me this morning."

He took her to the attics again, leading her gently this time, pointing out various ancestors' portraits along the way, telling her some of the history of the place. What he wanted her to see was in the lumber room with the broken bed frames and rickety tables. The earl pulled a gilt chair with only one armrest over toward the window and wiped the seat with his handkerchief for her. Then he pulled a painting out from behind a warped chest of drawers and turned it so Juneclaire could see.

Two young men looked back at her. Boys, really, they were cut from the same cloth as Merry. Both had black hair, worn long and tied in back as was the style, and both had green eyes. The seated one had Merry's serious look, as if he already knew the weight of his duties. The other, younger lad was smiling. He had Merry's chin. Captain Cleft.

"This is not the man I chased last night," St. Cloud said. "I knew Uncle George. I knew him well."

"But that was over twenty years ago, you clunch, and you were just a child. People change, especially when they lead hard lives. You said yourself the body they brought back was mangled. It could have been Hawkins, Merry. It could."

He sat on a stool next to her chair and looked out the window. "I said I will send to London, have my man-at-law look into the matter. But—"

"But you are not happy at the possibility. You'd prefer to think that I am a gullible nodcock and some plump old graybeard has fallen down your chimney and into the wainscoting by accident."

He took her hand. "I am sorry for thinking you were foxed or purposely trying to cause trouble. And I swear I'll try to keep an open mind." He laughed at himself, bringing her fingers to his lips. "How is that for a resolution? Is it too late? I've already admitted I was wrong about you. But, Junco, there is more to the story than you know. My mother is weak, you know that. And she went through hell for the man, not once but twice. I cannot ask her to face him again."

"It has to be her decision, doesn't it?" She returned the pressure of his fingers, trying to give him strength and comfort.

"Then where is he? If he is George, why doesn't he walk through the front door and shake my hand like an honorable man? Why didn't he come forth and say what happened that night at the quarry? You said you convinced him he wasn't a murderer."

This was not the time to tell Merry his uncle was a pirate. Then again, she thought more cheerfully, if he could accept that, he could accept a penniless nobody in the family, too. "I, ah ... believe he's working on that now. You St. Cloud men seem to have a surfeit of pride, you know. He has his own sense of honor."

St. Cloud stood and drew her up beside him, still holding her hand. "Speaking of honor, Miss Beaumont," he started.

She pulled her hand back. "No, my lord, I know what you are going to say and I don't want to hear

200

it. I do not want your words of honor and duty and making things right."

He brushed a curl away from her cheek, but his hand stayed to touch the soft skin there. "No? I thought marriage proposals were supposed to start that way. I am supposed to ask for the honor of your hand, and you are supposed to thank me for the honor of the offer. That's what I've always heard, anyway. I only did it that once before, you know, in the barn. But here, I've turned over a new leaf for the new year. I'll admit I could be wrong again. What words should I say instead?"

Words of love, you cloth-head, she wanted to shout. But she only whispered, "If I have to tell you, I do not want to hear them."

He was staring into her deep brown eyes as if the answers to the universe were hidden there. His fingers stroked her knitted brows, her chin, her lips, sending tremors where she did not know tremors could go. "Ah, my sweet, perhaps we do not need words after all." He bent his head. She raised hers and closed her eyes. His breath was warm on her lips. His hands had moved to her back, pulling her closer till their bodies were touching, the lean strength of his against the soft curves of hers. His breath came faster as their lips came to—

"Pardon, my lord, but there are two young persons come to see you and Miss Beaumont."

"Good grief," Juneclaire said, "what are you two doing here?"

Rupert and Newton Stanton were staring around his lordship's library as though they'd never seen so many books in one place. For all the attention they spent to their schooling, likely they had not. Root was wearing a spotted Belcher neck cloth in imitation of the Four-Horse Club, and Newt was dressed in the height of absurdity in yellow pantaloons and shirt collars so high and so starched, his ears were in danger.

After Juneclaire's introduction St. Cloud surveyed them through his quizzing glass like particularly unappealing specimens of insects suddenly come among his books. "Indeed, to what do we owe the unexpected pleasure?" he drawled.

Root squirmed and Newt felt his collar shrink. They knew Satan St. Cloud's reputation. Then again, it was his reputation that sent them here.

"Actually, Mama sent us," Root confessed. He was the eldest. He knew his duty. Hadn't Mama spent two days drumming it into him? "She got your note, saying Clarry was here under your protection."

Newt giggled nervously. "There's protection and there's protection," he continued, trying to sound worldly. Compared to St. Cloud he was as urbane as a newly hatched chick. "So Mama sent us to check."

Juneclaire was embarrassed for her family. "You gudgeons, you are insulting the earl," she hissed.

Root stood firm. "Reputation, you know. His. Yours."

"Well, of all the—"

"Excuse me, Miss Beaumont, I am not quite clear on the purpose of our guests."

Juneclaire knew from that sardonic tone that St. Cloud was very angry. "It's my fault, my lord. I should have written to Aunt Marta myself, to reassure her of my well-being. I'll just take my cousins to the kitchens, shall I, and get them a bite to eat for their return trip and send them—"

"I say, Clarry, we just got here!"

"Mama's not going to be happy, 'less she knows for sure there's nothing—"

"Miss Beaumont," the earl interrupted, in a

quiet, smooth voice, "prefers to be called June-claire."

The boys nodded. "Yes, sir" and "Yes, my lord." Their tutors would have been shocked to see such instant obedience. Even Juneclaire was impressed.

"Now, Master Newton, Master Rupert, you shall answer me this: Did your esteemed parent really send two unlicked cubs to ask my intentions toward her niece?"

Juneclaire giggled, thinking of his intentions not ten minutes past. He sent her a quelling look. Both boys found the design in the carpet fascinating. Put like that, Mama'd sent them to their doom. And the earl was not finished. "Did she treat her responsibilities so negligently that she did not inquire into Miss Beaumont's health, how she came to be here, or her future plans, but only the state of her virtue? Did she think so ill of Miss Beaumont to think that she might consider *carte blanche*? That does not speak well of her upbringing at your mother's hands. Finally, did you, men-about-town that you are, think that I would bring my *chérie amour* here to my ancestral home to meet my mother and grandmother?"

"That's enough, my lord. Let them be. They're only boys; they meant no insult."

"No? I wonder what they were supposed to do if they found you dishonored, call me out?"

Newt was quick to pipe up, "Oh, no, my lord, we were only supposed to tell Cla—Juneclaire not to come home again, ever. But if things were all right and tight, we were to invite you back to Stanton Hall."

"Hell will freeze over before I—" Then he noticed Juneclaire's scarlet mortification. "I am sorry, my dear, that you had to be witness to this." To the boys, he said, "You may tell your parents that Miss Beaumont is respectably established."

Root did not think such a bang-up Corinthian would shoot a fellow for doing his duty. He knew his mother would have his hide for not. "Don't see no chaperon," he stated. "Don't see no ring."

"If you want to see your next birthday, you'll—"

"With your permission, my lord, I'll introduce my cousins to Lady Fanny and the others in the morning room. Perhaps Mr. Hilloughby, the *curate*, will be there, Root."

The boys were in love, Root with St. Cloud's pastry chef and Newt with Niles Wilmott's hummingbird-embroidered waistcoat. Add to that heady mix tales of ghosts, secret passages, and lurking strangers, to say nothing of being able to tell their friends they were on intimate terms with Satan St. Cloud himself, and the Stanton boys would have sold their mother for a chance to stay at the Priory. Then Elsbeth walked in.

Miss Wilmott had been feeling sorely used, neglected, put upon, and cast in the shade. Her cousin was not going to marry her, and her father was not going to take her to London. Ordinarily two rustics barely her own age would not hold the young beauty's interest, but the Stantons treated Miss Beaumont with the greatest indifference and called Sydelle Pomeroy "ma'am," the same as Aunt Fanny! Elsbeth's Cupid's bow lips smiled at the brothers, and anyone in the room could hear two hearts fall at her feet.

"Please, Clarry—Juneclaire, ask him if we can stay. Worried about you, really, no matter what Mama said."

"And it's snowing. You don't want us to have to ride out there in that, back to dreary old Stanton Hall, not while there's such jolly times here. Please ask him, and we will give Mama any story you want about how you got here."

His brother kicked him. "Not blackmail, cuz. Stick by you anyway."

Juneclaire had taken her cousins apart from the others. Aunt Florrie wanted to count their teeth. Now she had to laugh at their earnest entreaties. "Why don't you ask him yourself?"

Newt stammered, "He's not an ... ah ... easy man, Juneclaire. One look from him and I feel like checking my buttons. And his reputation ain't one to let a fellow rest easy if St. Cloud imagines some insult. Aren't you afraid of him?"

She smiled. "No, he's just a bear with a sore foot sometimes, especially when it comes to things like honor and family." And me, she thought fondly.

Root looked at her with respect for the first time in her memory. "Brave for a girl, Juneclaire. Proud to be kin."

So she walked the earl over to the window to note the heavy snowfall. "I know they're not much," she admitted, "but they are mine. And perhaps you'll be a good influence on them."

"Heaven help them." St. Cloud looked over to where the others sat, the two halflings vying with each other to bring a giddy Elsbeth the choicest tidbits. He smiled. "On the other hand, perhaps Uncle Harmon will have an apoplexy."

It snowed for two days and nights. There were no visits from neighbors, no mail in or out, and no Uncle George. St. Cloud put the Stanton sprigs to work in the library, looking for a hidden latch to the trick door. The proximity to so much learning might have had an effect if Elsbeth hadn't insisted on helping, for lack of anything better to do. Her father suddenly insisted Elsbeth get some fresh air, so all of the young people went on sleigh rides and indulged in snowball fights, even St. Cloud. Then Harmon thought Elsbeth should practice her needlework more, so the mooncalves sat at her feet, sorting yarns and making up absurd poems to her lips, her ears, her flaxen curls. Uncle Harmon was tearing his hair out, and it looked as if Elsbeth was getting to London after all, anything to get her out of the reach of the nimwit brothers.

At night there were card games with the dowager, charades, children's games of jackstraws and lotteries that turned into hilarious shouting matches, caroling round the piano. St. Cloud was enjoying every minute of his uncle's distress and every moment of the lighthearted games. Even if he did not participate, or when he made up a table for the dowager's whist, he watched Juneclaire and listened for her laughter. He imagined other holidays, real children playing at jackstraws and hide-and-seek in the mazelike Priory—their children. He smiled.

The third night he suggested dancing. He wanted to hold her in his arms. Between Root and Newt, the dowager and his own mother, the earl was finding it deuced hard to be alone with Juneclaire. The dowager, Harmon, and Mr. Hilloughby were at the deal table with Talbot, the butler, who had been drafted to make a fourth. Lady Fanny sat with her needlework behind her mother-in-law to call out the shown cards for Lady St. Cloud. This was the closest the two women had sat to each other since the former earl's funeral.

Aunt Florrie was playing the pianoforte, erratically but energetically. Niles danced with Sydelle, St. Cloud finally got to hold Juneclaire, and the Stantons took turns with Miss Wilmott. The other brother turned Aunt Florrie's pages, although she never seemed to be playing the same song as in front of her. Elsbeth begged for a waltz, and Root, the odd man that set, picked up Pansy, who was dressed for the occasion in diamond ear bobs and pearl choker. Everyone was laughing and gay, even Lady Pomeroy, for once, when a shrill scream rent the air.

"What is the meaning of this?" A sharp-featured woman pushed into the room, dragging a portly gentleman in a bagwig behind her past the inexperienced footman who'd been left holding the door. Rupert said, "Mama," and Juneclaire's face lost its pretty flush. Aunt Florrie kept playing.

Aunt Marta took a better look around, dripping snow on the carpet. There was a blind woman playing cards, one of her sons was dancing with a tousled hoyden, the other with a pig wearing jewels. Her niece was in the arms of the worst rake in England—with no ring on her finger! "I demand to know," she screeched, "just what is going on!"

St. Cloud bowed. He pulled Juneclaire closer to him with one hand and used the other to encompass the room. "Obviously an orgy, ma'am," he drawled. "You know, swine, women, and song."

Chapter Twenty-three

"*F*or your information, Lady Stanton, I have never seduced a female in my care, be she house-guest or housemaid." The earl chose not to recall that was before what almost happened in the attics. He had also never struck a female, but that was before meeting Aunt Marta. This was the outside of enough, being taken to task by an evil-minded old skinflint who never prized her niece in the first place and likely only wanted to wrest a healthy marriage settlement out of him. First she'd sent her husband, Avery, for a "man-to-man" talk. Avery got as far as "Nice gal, my niece. Want the best for her," before St. Cloud's frosty stare had him switching to a discussion of crop rotation. Lady Stanton was not so easily intimidated.

"We'll stay till Twelfth Night since the countess invited us; then I am taking Claire home."

"Miss Juneclaire stays as long as she wishes, with the dowager's blessings."

"Humph. We'll see about that. What future does the gal have here, I'd like to know?"

"What future did she have at Stanton Hall? Mother to someone else's brats, or your unpaid servant? She is a valued guest here, better dressed, in more congenial company, and with far fewer de-

mands on her time, Lady Stanton. Is her happiness
worth nothing?"

"Not as much as the banns being called, and I
don't care who you are! Lord Stanton is still her
legal guardian, and *we'll* see where Claire goes and
with whom."

St. Cloud was not worried about the harpy's
threats as much as the idea that she might stay
past Twelfth Night, three very long days away. No,
Avery Stanton was not going to challenge St. Cloud.
Not even that mouse of a man was so foolish. What
concerned the earl more was Juneclaire's feelings.

After luncheon he asked her to visit Lady St.
Cloud with him, knowing full well his grandmother
was napping. Nutley made the perfect chaperon,
sewing in the dowager's sitting room; she was busy
and she was deaf.

Juneclaire sat on a brocade divan near the fireplace with the kitten on her lap playing with—Drat,
so there's where his tassel had disappeared to. She
looked the picture of innocence in a high-waisted
sprigged muslin, a soft glow on her cheeks from the
fire's warmth. He knew she was also a woman of
great spirit and caring. He thought she was even
coming to care for him. He did not want to hurt her,
ever.

"Miss Beaumont, Junco, I, ah . . ." She looked up
at him with those doe eyes, her dark brows raised
in expectation. "Blasted expectations!" he muttered, pacing the width of the room.

"Oh, dear. I suppose Aunt Marta's been filling
your head with her flummery, my lord. Believe me,
I do not expect—"

"Well, you should, and it's not flummery! I should
have offered for you in form days ago. I should have
asked your uncle's permission the minute they
stepped through the door."

"But you did offer. You were everything honorable, and so I told Aunt Marta. There was no need—"

"There was every need, and more every day you spend under my roof even if you are too green to see it. Now it's too late."

"Too late?" Her heart must have stopped because suddenly she could not breathe. Now that he'd seen her family, he realized how impossible an alliance was. Now that she was convinced she had to marry him for whatever reasons he chose to give if she was to be a whole person ever again, he had changed his mind. He was withdrawing his offer.

"Yes, and it's all that dastard George's fault! How can I offer you my name when it may not be an honorable one? How can I discuss marriage settlements when I don't know if I'll have a roof over my head?"

"I don't understand, but none of that matters." She was perilously close to tears. He hated vaporish women.

"Of course it doesn't matter to you, Junco. You'd live in a cow byre with your goats and pigs and sheep—only you'd starve to death because you'd never eat any of them! It matters to me that I can provide for you, that you can take your place in society with your head high, not stay hidden away like my mother."

She swallowed past the lump in her throat. "Uncle George?"

"Uncle George. I didn't tell you the whole, that day in the cemetery. You'll find out soon enough, if the cad has come back. I'm just surprised your aunt hasn't filled your ears with the tale; it's common knowledge." He kept pacing, not looking at her. "George came home from the wars injured, remember? My parents stayed away the whole time, until the holidays. I don't recall if they spoke then. I was in the nursery most of the time, of course, and there were other houseguests. I was brought down for luncheon that day. It was Christmas, you know, and my birthday. You have to realize that I was small for my age, and Uncle George had never been around children before. He said 'Merry Christmas, Merry. Happy fourth birthday.' And everyone laughed, because it was my fifth birthday. And then he must have counted back—I remember him mumbling while I waited for my cake. Suddenly he shouted, 'If he's five, he's mine!' and he lunged at my father, knocking him down. In front of forty *belle monde* busybodies. I have carried a certain unsavory stigma throughout my life, as you can imagine."

"But your—the earl acknowledged you."

"Who knows what he would have done if there had been another son? But he was paralyzed that day, and George was dead. I was the last Jordan. Until now. You, at least, are convinced that I am not. If George is alive, *he* is the earl."

"No," Juneclaire insisted. "You were baptized as Robert's son and reared as Robert's son. And Uncle George would never make that kind of trouble, I know he wouldn't."

"How do you know what he will and will not do? He left my father there to die, Juneclaire."

"No! Hawkins was to have gone for help. Uncle George has as much honor as you do! That's why he hasn't come back, Merry, because his past isn't quite . . . suitable."

Merry stopped pacing. "Pray tell, Miss Beaumont," he drawled in that slow, deadly tone he used to frighten lesser mortals, "precisely how . . . unsuitable is Uncle George's past? Where has he been all these years?"

"At sea."

"It could be worse. Other Jordans have gone into

the navy, although I suppose he signed on as a common seaman."

"Not the navy," Juneclaire croaked.

"Then a merchant marine. Better still. Perhaps he joined the East India company and made his fortune."

"I believe he made his fortune," she said, barely above a whisper. "Have you ever heard of . . . Captain Cleft?"

"Oh, God, we're all ruined. You'll go home with your aunt. Uncle Harmon will have to find Elsbeth a husband before . . . and Mother. Hell and damnation, Mother."

Now it was even more important that they find Uncle George.

Luckily the company made a short evening of it so they could look. The dowager refused to join "those toadeaters" downstairs, and Lady Fanny had taken to her bed under Aunt Marta's aspersions that the countess was not a proper chaperon for a young girl. Uncle Harmon was closeted with vinegar water and digestive biscuits, and Aunt Florrie was busy writing a letter to her dear friend Richard. The Lion-Hearted.

Sydelle had excused herself after dinner. She was leaving in the morning, despite Niles Wilmott's fervent, nay, desperate, pleas. Lady Pomeroy saw no reason to stay. With that battle-ax of an aunt in the house, St. Cloud could never wriggle out of an engagement, and Lady Pomeroy was not cooling her heels until Twelfth Night, just to see a parcel of peasant urchins dress up as Magi and go around begging gifts. She'd had enough of those bucolic entertainments, thank you, and was anxious to get back to London, even if it was thin of company. So *la belle* Pomeroy used her packing as an excuse to avoid the gathering of puerile Stantons and lost-cause St. Clouds.

Root and Newt had escaped their mother's eye to the billiard room, forsaking even Elsbeth, who quickly claimed a headache. Niles took himself off to drown his sorrows with his cousin's excellent brandy, for lack of a better idea, and Mr. Hilloughby declared he had to work on his sermon.

All of which left Juneclaire and St. Cloud all alone in the gold parlor, except for Aunt Marta and Uncle Avery. Aunt Marta did not believe in gambling, so cards were out. Juneclaire did not play well enough to entertain with music. They had no mutual friends and no common interests, and the earl and Aunt Marta each represented what the other most despised. It was not a comfortable gathering, especially in contrast to the past few nights. St. Cloud as host could not retire before his guests, and Aunt Marta would have dyed her hair red and gone on the stage before leaving her niece alone with the earl. Therefore Juneclaire yawned, and yawned again until Lady Stanton decided they would all do better with an early night. She walked Juneclaire right to her door and would have locked her in if she weren't sure that the libertine had copies of all the keys to the house anyway.

Juneclaire would just have to do her hunting without Merry. Under the heavy eyes of Pansy—Aunt Florrie had tried darkening the pig's lashes with bootblack to match Sydelle's—and with the assistance of a curious kitten, Juneclaire removed every single item from her wardrobe. When the closet was absolutely bare, she pulled and twisted, pushed and poked at every shelf, hinge, and hook. There had to be a way to get into the secret passage from her room. Uncle George had done it, at least twice. There were seams in the wood panels on the sides and back, but she could not get any of them to move. Nothing.

She rested her hands on the closet rod that held the hangers while she thought—and the bar turned under her hands. Then she rolled it the other way, away from her, and one of the panels slid back. She found it! Juneclaire poked her head through, hoping to see Uncle George on the other side, but she saw nothing, only darkness past the little circle of her own light. She thought she'd better go get Merry.

As Juneclaire backed out of the opening, though, the cat came to investigate and kept on going. "Oh, no, Shamrock. Here, kitty. Come back, kitty, kitty." Kitty did not come back. Shamrock would be lost forever, and the dowager would be heartbroken. There was nothing for it; Juneclaire had to go after the foolish furball.

She was *not* being impetuous. She made sure she had a fresh candle in her holder and another in her pocket, along with a flint. She put a hatbox in the opening to make sure it did not shut and checked the mechanism on the other side, a kick-wheel device, so she could get back in, in case.

Someone had swept the floor in the secret passage, but not well, and she could see footprints and, yes, the mark of Uncle George's peg leg going in both directions. Shamrock's went in only one. Juneclaire followed, trying to keep count of the doors, the turns, the side passages. She couldn't. She turned to check and no longer saw the light from her own room. For one awful minute she thought she'd be lost forever; maybe curiosity was going to kill more than the cat this night. Maybe Merry would be heartbroken. No, he would be relieved. Then reason reasserted itself: Merry would come after her in the morning and give her one of those dire looks and sarcastic comments. She'd better find Uncle George to lead her back.

She found the cat instead, sitting next to one of the wheel devices, licking its feet. Juneclaire picked the kitten up, hugging it more for her comfort than its. Now she had two choices: she could wander around these corridors looking for her own room for the next eight hours or so, or she could turn this wheel and pray. "Please let the room be unoccupied."

Her prayer was answered. Unfortunately, the answer was no. She found herself and the kitten in her hands in a closet so full of silks and satins and shoes and hats that there was hardly room for her to stand. A light shone through the crack in the door facing into the room, and she could hear voices. She took a deep breath. Hungary water . . . Niles. She decided to assay the dark passage again, with rats and bats and spiders, rather than come face-to-face with that slug in his bedroom.

As she was backing out of the narrow opening in the back of the closet, however, Pansy was coming in. The lonely pig's sharp nose had no trouble finding her mistress in the maze and no trouble detecting the wine and biscuits Niles had in his room. She pushed past Juneclaire, who lost her footing. Juneclaire reached up to save herself and the cat and the fop's expensive wardrobe from a fall, and grabbed onto the hanging bar, which turned, nearly shutting the rear panel on Pansy's curled tail. Pansy went flying forward, pushing open the doors.

Juneclaire followed. What else could she do? If a woman, a pig, and a cat flying out of an armoire astounded Niles and his companion, the sight that met Juneclaire's eyes was only slightly less shocking.

Somewhere in the middle of his second bottle downstairs, Niles had finally had a better idea. Instead of letting the Widow Pomeroy and her voluptuous charms—not the least of which was her ample checkbook—hie off to London in the morning, Niles had one last card up his sleeve. And a cinder in his eye.

Juneclaire's garbled account of the cat, the secret passage, and "I'll just be going now" was lost as the elegant widow, *en dé shabillé*, explained how poor Niles needed her assistance. What Niles needed was more time. The wine stood ready on the low table, the bed stood ready, and his flea-brained sister had dashed well better stand ready to burst in on them at the right moment. This wasn't it, so Niles shoved the damned interfering wench out the door.

Juneclaire leaned against the wall, breathing hard, her eyes closed.

"My, my, what do we have here?"

Her breathing stopped altogether, and her eyes snapped open. Merry, with his abominable quizzing glass, was surveying her disarranged hair, her heaving chest, her flaming cheeks. "Do you know what a good influence you have been, Miss Beaumont? I am still maintaining my New Year's resolution to keep an open mind. I find my affianced bride coming out of my loose screw cousin's bedroom, looking, ah, shall we say, hot and bothered, and I haven't even skinned him alive yet. Aren't you pleased?"

Juneclaire was happy there was a wall holding her up; for sure her trembling knees were not. "We . . . we're not engaged," she quavered.

"True. Then I'll skin him after I murder him."

"No, he didn't . . . I wasn't . . . Don't go in there!"

"Why, did you already do him in with your darning needle? And here I thought you were going to be less impetuous."

"Stop it, you gudgeon, he's not—"

"Juneclaire Beaumont, what are you doing out of your room?" Aunt Marta yelled loudly enough that Uncle Avery peered out of his room across the hall. "And you, St. Cloud, how dare you carry on in this abandoned fashion right under my very nose? I'll—"

They were never to find out what Aunt Marta was going to do because a shriek came from inside Niles's room. The earl pushed past Juneclaire and flung the door open.

When Niles tossed Juneclaire out of his room, he forgot about the pig. Pansy didn't mind, as long as the biscuits were in reach. When they were gone, she went snuffling around, looking for Juneclaire or another friend. Her wanderings took her closer to the fire, where Sydelle was leaning over Niles, dabbing at his eye with a scrap of handkerchief. Pansy whiffled closer, right up Lady Pomeroy's skirt. Hence the shriek. Sydelle fell forward, and Niles, simply doing what came naturally to an immoral, licentious lecher, pulled her down on top of him.

"Congratulations, cousin," St. Cloud said from the doorway. "May I be the first to offer my felicitations."

And Elsbeth, tripping down the hall, said, "For heaven's sake, Niles, if you changed your plan, you should have told me."

Aunt Marta declared, "Well, I never," to which Uncle Avery sadly replied, "Twice, my dear, twice."

Chapter Twenty-four

*Th*e dowager was so pleased with the match that she decided to go downstairs to see Niles and Sydelle off to London. Lady Pomeroy wanted to see the last of St. Cloud Priory, and Niles wanted to see the notice in the papers before Sydelle changed her mind. Juneclaire was walking the dowager down the long hall.

"Tell Talbot to serve champagne," Lady St. Cloud ordered. "That ought to ruffle your aunt's fur, the old hellcat. Maybe she'll take those scamps of hers and leave early."

Aunt Marta disapproved of the couple, among other things. She would not come down. Juneclaire was afraid St. Cloud really was going to send her off with the Stantons, though, so she tried to divert the old woman. "Do you actually think Niles and Sydelle will suit?"

"Like hand in glove. He'll have his glove in her pocket, and she'll have her hand on his—Well, she'll keep him under her thumb. They're both decorative, expensive fribbles, with less morality than alley cats. He'll have his gaming and clubs, she'll have her respectability and a title when Harmon sticks his spoon in the wall, and they'll both go their own ways. Perfect marriage, my dear, perfect."

"I think it sounds perfectly horrible, cold and mercenary."

"Wouldn't do for just everybody, mind, but those two? Besides, it'll get them out of my grandson's house. Now, if I can just remind Harmon that the older Stanton twit will inherit a tidy pig farm one day, and won't he and Elsbeth be happy in Farley's Grange, I might get them out of here also. What are you giggling about, girl? You don't think Harmon's already figuring that Sydelle has that London town house and the right connections to fire Elsbeth off? Trust me, the man's liver mightn't be up to snuff, but his wits ain't gone begging."

She was right. Lord Wilmott had decided that Sydelle needed his chaperonage on the journey to London and Elsbeth's help with the wedding plans. Root's and Newt's hearts were breaking as they stood on the steps waving farewell to their first love, until the earl invited them to help exercise his bloodstock. Lady Fanny waved her handkerchief to the departing coaches, and Aunt Florrie waved a dead halibut.

Juneclaire helped the dowager back inside and made her comfortable in the morning room with the rest of the champagne. "Fine day's work, my girl," the dowager said, lifting her glass to Juneclaire. "Now if we can just see the dust of your relatives, the place will be near livable again."

Juneclaire rearranged some figurines on the mantel. "I . . . I'm afraid I'll be leaving with them, my lady."

"Gammon, you're engaged to my grandson. You belong here."

"No, my lady. I am not really engaged. He just offered because he had to."

"Nonsense, girl. Satan St. Cloud hasn't done anything he hasn't wanted to since he was in short

219

pants. You're good for him, miss. I could hear him laugh when you were dancing and such."

"But Uncle George . . ."

"Faugh, you haven't got your eyes on a man old enough to be your father, have you, girl? He's Fanny's. Always was and always will be, though heaven knows what he or his brother ever saw in the widgeon. Robert wanted her, too, you know. Always jealous, even if he had the title and estate. For the life of me I don't know how I raised two such bobbing-blocks. If you tell me my lobcock of a grandson is making mice feet of his future now, too, I'll take my cane to the both of you, I swear I will. But don't worry, girl, George'll bring him round."

"Then Uncle George is here, and he can tell Merry about—?"

"He said he'd make it right. Soon. Word of a Jordan."

Juneclaire couldn't wait, not if Aunt Marta was going to carry her away after tomorrow night's celebration marking the end of the holy season. It may as well be the end of Juneclaire's life, she thought dismally. Aunt Marta was already guarding her like a rabid sheepdog, not allowing her two minutes alone with Merry, following her to her bedroom and coming back an hour later to make sure Juneclaire was in bed, alone, with her door locked and bolted.

Locks and bolts on the bedroom door meant nothing to Juneclaire, of course, but no one had thought to ask how she came to be in or out of Niles Wilmott's bedroom last night. She had no chance to explain to Merry about the trick of the secret passage until now. It was his house; he should know.

Juneclaire wrapped a warm shawl over her shoulders and turned the bar. It was much harder, with the hangers all back in place, but the back panel finally slid aside. She counted doors until she was behind the master suite, she hoped. She turned the wheel and the door opened, revealing . . . nothing. She was in an empty closet. She mentally recounted doors and rooms, until she realized she must be in the mistress's chamber. The unused bedroom reserved for the countess, Merry's wife. Good. At least now she—and Pansy, of course—wouldn't have to burst out of my lord's closet like blackbirds from a pie. She nudged the wardrobe door open, waiting for protests from unused hinges, but rust must be another one of those things unacceptable in an earl's residence. Edging her way out of the closet, she tiptoed toward the right, where light showed under a connecting door. Juneclaire listened for a minute, in case Merry's valet should be with him. Should she knock? Maybe this wasn't a good idea after all.

As usual, Pansy took matters into her own . . . knuckles. She knew a friend was on the other side of the door, and she knew her friend had something to eat. She grunted, loudly.

"What the bloody—"

Pansy trotted through the now open doorway, but Juneclaire stood where she was. She never thought he'd be naked! Or half-naked, for he did have britches on, but his chest was bare except for dark curls that spread to where his hard muscles tapered into a lean vee that disappeared to where he *did* have britches on. She didn't trust that gleam in his green eyes, and why the rogue picked now to smile she never knew, but when she lowered her own, they saw—Oh, dear, this wasn't a good idea at all.

"It's not what you think, Merry," she hurried to say. "I am not here to compromise you like Niles. Not that *I* meant to compromise Niles, of course, for you know I did not."

His smile broadened. "If you are not here to cry

foul on me, my dear, I am completely and devotedly at your service."

"I am not here for *that* either, you gamecock." If her cheeks were any warmer, they'd surely burst into flame.

He pressed his hand to his heart, reminding her that he had no shirt on, as if she needed a reminder, and said, "You wound me, Junco. I thought my last Christmas wish was coming true."

"Why . . . why you are foxed, my lord!"

"Either that or I must be fast asleep and dreaming, for the oh-so-proper niece of the redoubtable Lady Stanton could not be standing in my bedroom in her night rail. No, I must be jug-bitten because in my dreams you aren't wearing any heavy flannel wrapper. In fact, you aren't wearing—"

"Merry! I came to tell you about the secret passageway. I found the trick to opening the doors in the wardrobes."

"Did you? I always knew you were a clever girl." He had her hand and was leading her toward an enormous canopied bed in the center of the room.

"Merry, you don't understand. We have to go find Uncle George." She tugged to get her hand back.

"Oh yes, Uncle George." The name seemed to sober him, for he released her, but he sank down on the bench at the foot of the bed. He did not seem eager to go search for his missing relative. "Good old Uncle George, the pride of the Jordans."

Juneclaire sat beside him. "Merry, maybe the situation isn't so bad. Lady St. Cloud thinks he can fix things. He promised her."

"And Aunt Florrie thinks King George is going through a stage, like teething." He brushed her long braid back off her shoulder and put his arm there. "I'm sorry, Junco, truly I am. I wish things were different. I wish I could have made your wishes come true. You almost made mine, you know. You helped get the Wilmotts off my hands, and you showed me how happy this old pile could be." He pulled her closer.

"And I felt welcome here, as if I truly did belong, so my wish almost came true, too."

They were quiet for a moment, thinking of what might have been. Then they both started to say, "I wish . . ." at the same time. "You first," Juneclaire told him, nestling at his side.

"I wish there was a way, that's all, without dragging you through a scandalbroth. You?"

"I wish you weren't quite so honorable, my lord, because none of it matters to me." She turned her face up for his kiss, and not even the earl was noble enough to turn down what she was so sweetly offering. He did groan once, but that may not have been his conscience complaining.

Some while later, Juneclaire was half out of her nightgown and more than half out of her mind with wonder at the strange new feelings throbbing through her. Somehow she and Merry were no longer on the bench but were in the middle of his wide, soft mattress. If Merry was whispering her name and nonsense in her ear—and he was, for she could feel the tickle of his breath—then someone else was in the room with them.

"Well, Pansy girl, looks like history repeats itself, all right. If this isn't the way the whole argle-bargle started, my name ain't Giorgio Giordanelli."

Juneclaire looked up. There was a Romany Gypsy at the foot of the bed, complete with flowing shirt, scarlet sash, and colorful scarf tied at his neck. He also had a thick gray beard, a fat belly, and a peg leg. She giggled. "It isn't."

He tossed her a blanket. "But it has been, puss, it has been."

The earl had been struggling to regain his composure if not his buttons. He sat up and made sure

Juneclaire was decently covered before turning to the apparition. "Uncle George, I presume?"

"In the flesh. Or should I say in the nick of time?" He met the earl's hard, green-eyed stare with one of his own. "Are you going to make an honest woman out of her, or am I going to have to run you through?"

"That depends, *Uncle*. Do I have any honor? Are you going to leave me with a name I'd be proud to offer a woman?"

Uncle George sat on the bench and lifted the pig up next to him. "Are you proud of Satan St. Cloud?" he asked, and Juneclaire was astonished to see Merry flush. She was also amazed to see where the color started. Catching her glance, Uncle George snorted and threw the earl his paisley robe from the bottom of the bed. Merry's muffled curses did nothing to ease Juneclaire's embarrassment.

"Don't tease, Uncle George," she begged. "Just tell him what happened."

The earl crossed his arms over his chest and sat back against his pillow, like a pasha holding court. "Hold, Junco. I am not even convinced this ... Gypsy is my uncle. He could be a horse thief or a fortune-teller."

George shook his head. "You know, Merry, I think I liked you a lot better when you were a curly-haired tyke."

"And I think I liked you a lot better when you were dead. Do you have papers? Proof?"

"I have friends working on the paper stuff. But proof?" He scratched the pig's ears while he thought. "You were just a wee lad; I'm not sure how much you remember. Then again, you weren't as young as I thought. Let's see. I found my lead knights for you in the nursery and we repainted them, but there was no red paint, so we stole one of your grandmother's rouge pots. Your pony's

224

name was Thimble, but any of the old grooms would know that. They wouldn't know about the day you tried taking him over a hurdle without a saddle, a groom, or permission, because I promised I wouldn't tell, after I found you, picked you up, and brushed you off. Fanny'd have kept you off a horse till you were twenty if she knew you'd been thrown."

"And you brushed off the back of my pants a trifle more vigorously than necessary, if my memory holds."

"You didn't try that stunt again, did you?"

"No, Uncle George, I didn't. Do you still have the crescent scar from the wound that sent you home that time?"

"Still testing? You know it was shaped like a seven. Lucky seven, we called it. Want to see?" He reached for his sash.

Juneclaire hid her face against St. Cloud's robe. He laughed and she could hear the rumble in his chest. Then St. Cloud sighed.

"God, how I missed you when you died. No one would say why, just that you were too evil to talk about. What the hell happened?"

George got up and poured himself a glass from the decanter on an end table. "Two hotheaded fools, that's what happened. You know about the party?" They both nodded. "I was beside myself and dragged Robbie outside until he agreed to meet me at the old quarry. We went, with no surgeon, no seconds, no witnesses, only my man Hawkins to hold the horses. I cooled down along the way. He always loved Fanny, too, you know, and I hadn't been there when she needed me. He was. So I was going to delope, I swear it. But he shot first, got me in the leg. As I fell, my gun discharged and the shot hit Robbie. It looked bad. He begged me to take what money he had and run away so I wasn't charged with murder, because all of the guests heard me threaten to kill him, and only Hawkins, my own batman, could say nay. I was scared, I was bleeding, I didn't know what to do. So we decided that Hawkins would ride for help and I'd head for Portsmouth and wait for Hawkins to come for me with news." He poured another drink and downed it in a swallow. "He never came. I was in no frame to do anything, delirious, sick, my leg turning uglier and uglier until some butcher amputated the thing and saved my life, I suppose. I cursed him enough at the time. I knew Robbie was dead or he'd have sent for me, even if something had happened to Hawkins. I couldn't face Fanny or my mother, not with one leg and a murder charge against me, so I signed on as junior purser with a cargo ship bound for Bermuda. After that I never wanted to ask about the St. Clouds because I never wanted to hurt more. We went aground, but that's another story. Just know I never meant to kill your father, Merry."

"I believe you, but why did you come home now, after all these years?"

"Not to steal your inheritance, boy, or cause trouble. Robbie called you his son, and you're the earl. I never wanted the title or the Priory either. I'm getting on, Merry, and I just wanted to see Fanny one more time. But she ain't happy, and it fair breaks my heart all over again. I mean to have her this time, if she'll forgive me and if I can straighten up a few loose ends."

"Like a price on your head?"

"I have some friends working on that." He poured another glass but let Pansy slurp this one.

St. Cloud raised his brows. "What are you going to do, if you clear the minor detail of being a criminal, set Mother up in London for the gabblegrinders to picnic on, or take her on the high seas?"

"I'll take her to Town if she wants to go; there's

226

nothing to be ashamed of. And I'm retired, boy, so you don't have to fear seeing her face on a reward poster. I thought she'd be happiest on my island in the Caribbean. You know, flowers and warm weather, beaches."

"You have your own island?" Juneclaire asked.

"I was a *very* good pirate, puss. As I see it, if I get those confounded papers, then I can try convincing Fanny. I daresay I've changed in the twenty years." He ignored Merry's rude noise and Juneclaire's giggle. "I should know by tomorrow. That ought to answer your questions about the family honor, Merry." He nodded toward Juneclaire. "You mind answering mine?"

Juneclaire blushed again, but Merry threw his uncle's words back at him: "I should know by tomorrow."

George laughed hard enough to shake the bed. "None of my business, right? In that case I think I better escort Miss Beaumont back to her room, Merry, since *you* ain't so clear about your intentions." He ignored the earl's furious scowl and turned to Juneclaire. "I'd wager you were the clever one to find the trick panels. This mutton-head must have looked for years. But you were lucky. There's another mechanism in the passageways, a trapdoor that drops trespassers right down to the cellars, unless you know the key." He winked at her. "I'll tell the bacon-brain *that* secret on your wedding night."

Chapter Twenty-five

Juneclaire went to bed without worrying she'd have nightmares about falling through trapdoors. She had no more fear of being dragged back to Stanton Hall in disgrace; she'd stay here in disgrace if she had to. But she was not really worried. Juneclaire was not going to let Merry's pride, or hers, come between them, and no pitfalls either, no matter what Uncle George said.

She woke up smiling and eager. Today was Three Kings Day, Epiphany, Twelfth Night, when Christmas wishes came true. She crossed her fingers, rolled over in bed three times, and said, "Rabbit, rabbit, rabbit," before her feet touched the ground, although that was supposed to be for May Day. She hugged Shamrock for luck and Pansy for good measure.

St. Cloud was showing Uncle Avery the home farm, and the boys were in the stables, most likely losing their allowances to Foley and the other grooms in dice games. The dowager and Lady Fanny were still abed, and Aunt Florrie was helping in the kitchen. Juneclaire took Pansy to visit the Penningtons and Ned rather than sit with Aunt Marta in the morning room listening to lectures. She still had too much bridled excitement after her visit, so she took Flame out for a walk to burn up some energy and minutes.

For dessert after lunch Talbot carried in the traditional Twelfth Night cake, which was supposed to have a pea and a bean hidden in the middle, denoting the king and queen for the day's festivities. Aunt Marta declared it a pagan ritual from pre-Christian days and refused to have anything to do with such rigmarole. Aunt Florrie looked near to crying, so St. Cloud ordered the footman to cut the cake quickly and pass the servings around. Florrie had been toiling all morning, helping make the batter, she told them in a reedy voice. She worked very hard, she said, making sure no one would be left out when the cake was cut. Why, she'd put in a cherry pit saved from last summer and a bit of a colored egg from Easter. A button, a pencil stub, a pussy willow catkin, one of her dear nephew's baby teeth, one of those pretty red mushrooms . . . Eight forks hit eight plates at once.

Late that afternoon they traveled in two carriages to the village of Ayn-Jerome for the local celebration. Aunt Marta went, she said, sniffing in Mr. Hilloughby's direction, only to see a proper church. In truth she did not like being alone in the hulking Priory with no one but servants.

There was a candlelight parade down the main street, headed by three boys dressed in loose robes and paper crowns, followed by the other local children, some dressed as shepherds. They led the adults into St. Jerome's Church for the service and a reenactment of the arrival of the three kings bearing gifts for the Holy Child. Afterward, there were trinkets and pennies, sweets and fruits given to all the children, and mummers, acrobats, and jugglers performing in the torch-lit street. Food stalls were set up, ale was passed round with servings of roast venison or beef, St. Cloud's contribution. The villagers toasted him, his house, and one another.

Root and Newt got a trifle above par, Lady Stanton sat rigid as a rail in her carriage, Juneclaire searched every face for Uncle George, and Aunt Florrie brought home some holy water, since Pansy had never been baptized.

The evening lasted forever, it seemed to Juneclaire, sitting on tenterhooks next to the dowager in the gold parlor. Lady St. Cloud obviously knew something was in the offing, too, for she patted Juneclaire's hand and urged her to keep reading, when Juneclaire's eyes kept straying to the door. The earl was as stone-faced and serious as ever, except for the dancing light in his eyes when he glanced Miss Beaumont's way.

Finally Talbot walked into the room with his stately tread, his head held high. "My lord, my ladies," he pronounced, "there are callers." He paused and gulped audibly. "Lords Caspar, Melchior, and Balthasar." Then he turned and fled.

Aunt Marta's jaw hung open and Aunt Florrie clapped. The three wise men had indeed come, not in rough costumes, but in velvet and ermine and satin, with gold crowns and jewel-laden pendants, each bearing a silver casket on a pillow.

The youngest, Caspar, coughed and stepped forward. "We come from Lon—ah, the East, where, ah, great tidings are heard."

The oldest, Melchior, adjusted his spectacles and pulled down his fake beard so he could speak his piece. "We come bearing gifts."

Balthasar, his clean-shaven face blackened with cork, opened the chest he held to reveal a king's ransom in jewels and gold. Juneclaire squeezed the dowager's hand, quietly describing the scene. Then Balthasar hopped forward on his peg leg and laid the casket in the younger countess's lap. "For you, Fanny, all for you. And don't you dare swoon, because it took me long enough to coach my players and you have to pay attention."

Lady Fanny's lip trembled and she was shredding her handkerchief, but she did not go off in a faint. St. Cloud came to stand behind her, his hand on her shoulder.

Uncle George peered at her, then nodded. "Always knew you were stronger than you let on. Anyway, didn't know what you'd do with frankincense or myrrh. Buy you all you want, if you say so, of course. Thought you'd be happier with this." He directed Caspar forward.

Mr. Langbridge, the solicitor, bowed at Fanny's feet and lifted the lid of his chest. "A royal pardon, my lady."

"And a pretty penny it cost me too, Fanny. Half my island, the sugar plantations, and two of my ships. Don't worry, though, puss, there's plenty left. Oh, and Prinny might throw in a knighthood if I pay a few more of his debts." He beckoned to Melchior.

Melchior stepped forward with twinkling eyes and opened his offering. Then he started to sneeze so hard from the cat in the room that Uncle George had to take over Vicar Broome's lines.

"It's a special license, Fanny. Will you do it? Will you marry me at last?" He wasn't fool enough to get down on one knee, not when the other was a piece of ivory, but he sat next to her, reaching for her hand.

Tears were falling from Lady Fanny's eyes—and a few others in the room—but she raised her handkerchief to wipe the blackening from George's face, leaving him an older, heavier, gray-haired, and sun-weathered version of the boy in the portrait, but with the same straight nose and cleft chin, and the same love for her shining in laughing eyes. "Can you forgive me for not waiting, George? I tried, but I did not know where you were, and the baby . . ."

"Can you forgive me for doubting you? For staying away so long?" He suddenly recalled the avid audience, family, guests, servants crowded in the entry, and pulled Fanny to her feet. When they were near the door, he turned back and took another paper from one of the silver chests. George tossed it to the earl, saying, "I brought you a gift, too, my lord. It's another special license. Merry Christmas, Merry."

St. Cloud took two glasses, one of the champagne bottles opened in celebration, and Juneclaire's hand. "Come, my love." He frowned down Lady Stanton's incipient protests and smiled to Aunt Florrie, decking Pansy with the pirate's treasure like a porcine Christmas tree.

When they reached the library, he quickly looked around. "We never did find the secret panel for this door. I can only hope Mother keeps the old scoundrel busy for a while." He poured the wine and held a filled glass to Juneclaire. He raised his and toasted: "To happiness and laughter, and joy ever after, and you by my side. I cannot be as dramatic as Uncle George, but will you be my wife, Juneclaire? Will you make me the happiest of men?"

"To satisfy your sense of honor?" Juneclaire knew the answer, but she wanted to hear him say it.

"Honor be damned."

That was not good enough. "Because Uncle George gave you no choice?"

"Because my heart gave me no choice, Juneclaire."

He put the glass down and reached into his coat for a small box. "A gift for you."

Juneclaire waited while he opened the box. A ring rested on a satin bed, a square diamond crowned with an emerald, a ruby, and a sapphire. "It's the St. Cloud engagement ring. Will you accept it, my love?" He was putting it on her finger before she could answer. That was good enough.

"But I have no gift for you," Juneclaire protested.

"You have already given me so much, my family, my home. That's more than any man deserves. Yet I ask for the greatest gift of all. Will you give me your love, too, Juneclaire?"

"You don't have to ask, Merry. It's already yours and always has been."

He lifted his glass again but brought it to her lips. "To us." After she sipped, he turned the glass so his lips touched where hers had been. "Now all my wishes have come true." Then he shook his head, put the glass down, and went to lock the library door. He came back and took her in his arms. "On second thought, I still have one wish. . . ."

BURN OUT

Tuesday

✦

OCTOBER 23

I sat on the bluff's edge, facing southeast, where a newly risen full moon cast a shimmery path over the waters of Tufa Lake. To my right, the towering peaks of Yosemite had disappeared into purple darkness. Here in the high desert the evening cooled quickly this time of year, but I'd prepared for it, appropriating a shearling jacket several sizes too big for me from the closet at the ranch house. As I'd appropriated it every night since I'd come up here from the city ten days ago.

Behind me, my husband Hy's twenty-year-old horse, Lear Jet—an ironic name for the red dun gelding, which had never willingly picked up the pace in its life—whickered. I hadn't ridden a horse in more than a decade. Pretty much disliked the creatures, in fact. Lear Jet was big— about fifteen hands and twelve hundred pounds—with a white star on his forehead and a white snip on his nose. He didn't like me any more than I liked him. Every chance he

got he'd lean hard on me, try to stomp my feet, bare his yellow teeth and snort.

I wasn't riding the creature for pleasure but in response to a challenge from Hy's ranch manager, Ramon Perez, who lived on the property and tended Lear Jet and the small herd of sheep Hy kept.

I sat watching the water as the moon rose higher. No longer visible by night or day were the brownish-white towers of calcified vegetation—tufa—that gave the lake its name. Years ago, the siphoning off of feeder streams for drought-stricken southern California had caused the lake's level gradually to sink and reveal the underwater towers; the brine shrimp that inhabited it and the water-fowl that fed on them had seemed doomed. But they were saved by the efforts of a coalition of conservationists, headed by Hy, and now the streams flowed freely, the lake teemed with life.

I wished I were so alive, but all I felt was burned out and hollow inside.

Last February I'd escaped death by mere seconds when a building where Hy and I had been temporarily living blew up—one of a series of bombings directed at the security company in which he was a partner. I'd solved the case of the Ever-Running Man, as the bomber had been called, but the fear and nightmares lingered; the grind-ing day-to-day effort of managing a growing investigative agency had sucked my spirit dry. Throughout spring and summer depression dragged me down. I'd tried coping with it myself, eventually resorted to antidepressants, and, when the pills hadn't worked, consulted a therapist. Ther-apy didn't work, either; I'm a private person, and I found myself lying to the doctor whenever she probed too close to the root causes of my condition.

Severe depression is like being at the bottom of a deep, dark pit: you want to put your feet and your hands against the walls and, squirming like an overturned spider, crawl up into the sunlight. Only when you try you find you can't move your limbs. I dreamed of being in that pit night after night. Finally, at Hy's urging, I'd come to the ranch for a change of pace—rather than the more familiar environs at Touchstone, our place on the Mendocino Coast. I'd planned to rest, regain my perspective, and rethink my future.

Well, everything but the rest part had so far eluded me. *That* I managed just fine, sometimes sleeping twelve to fourteen hours at a stretch. It wasn't good, and I knew it.

I also knew the choice of this spot on the bluff that I returned to night after night wasn't good, but here I sat again. It was the place Hy had come the night his first wife, Julie Spaulding, died of a long, debilitating illness. He'd told me how the sunset had flared above the Sierras, then died on the water. . . .

You're not coming here tomorrow, McCone. It just depresses you more. Get on with figuring out your life.

Behind me, Lear Jet snorted impatiently. He wanted his alfalfa.

"Okay, you smelly old thing," I called and got to my feet. "I'm coming."

The horse, of course, was obstinate. He turned his back on me and tried to pull the reins loose from where I'd tied them to a tree root. I took the reins myself, but when I tried to mount him he sidestepped. I hung on, got my left foot in the stirrup, and threw my right leg over his back. Before I could locate the other stirrup, he began walking; I clung to the pommel until my foot was secure. Then he stopped.

I clicked my heels authoritatively against his sides.

He snorted and put his head down.

"Look, you miserable bag of bones, I'm not in the mood for your antics!" I clicked my heels harder.

Lear Jet took off at a sudden wild run across the mesa.

I lost both stirrups, yanking hard on the reins. "Slow down, dammit!"

And he did—jerking to a dead stop. I flew from the saddle over his lowered head and landed on my butt in an area of soft dried grass.

As the horse turned away and trotted toward the stables, I could have sworn I heard him snicker.

I wasn't hurt, although I'd probably be sore in the morning, but I stayed where I was for a while, lying on my back, my knees bent upward, cursing Lear Jet and watching the emerging stars.

What *else* could go wrong today? That morning I'd nicked myself with a kitchen knife; been snappish for no reason with my office manager, Ted Smalley, who was holding down the fort back in the city; been even more snappish when my sister Charlene, who lived in the LA area, called to see how I was doing.

That afternoon Citibank's fraud division called to tell me someone was using my MasterCard to make Internet purchases; they'd frozen the account and a new card would have to be issued. I should have been grateful to them for spotting the problem within hours, but instead I grumbled at the representative about the inconvenience of having to change the number on all my automatic payments. Then I called my nephew and agency computer expert, Mick Savage, and asked him to find out who'd made the charges; he could work faster than Citibank, who were bound to have more important cases on their hands than mine. When he

said he was swamped, and why not let the bank handle it, I yelled at him and hung up. Then I slept the rest of the afternoon.

Now I'd been thrown by a horrible, hateful horse.

Well, at least you're not having a bad hair day, my inner voice said.

"Shut up," I said. "It's not funny."

Now I was losing my sense of humor! I'd always depended on it to get me through the rough patches, but it was fading along with everything else.

I got up, brushing dried grass from my pants and hair, and started toward the house. The moon and starlight showed me the way, and eventually I found a familiar well-traveled path.

A bobbing light was coming toward me, I saw then. "Sharon?" Ramon Perez's voice called.

"I'm here."

"Lear came back to the stable without you. I thought I'd better mount a search."

"The son of a bitch threw me."

"Are you all right?" I'd come into the circle of Ramon's flashlight, and he frowned as he looked me up and down.

"I'll live."

Ramon Perez was a Northern Paiute, a tribe closely associated and often confused with my own forebears, the Shoshone. A stocky, weathered man in his late forties who spoke little but always had gentle hands for animals and a kind smile for humans. He'd opened up some to me since I told him I'd discovered I was adopted and a full-blooded Indian; since then we'd spent a good bit of time discussing his and my tribes' commonalities and differences.

Which was what had started this horse thing.

We'd been sitting on bales of hay in the stable two

nights ago when Ramon said, "You really should learn to ride."

"Why would I want to do that?"

"Your people are good with horses. They acquired them, I think from the Apaches, in the seventeen-hundreds. Earlier than my people."

"Well then, I'm a piss-poor Shoshone. I took riding lessons in my mid-twenties and did okay, but I quit because I discovered I hate the critters."

Ramon shook his head. "You just don't understand them, is all. What you need to do is show them that you're in control, and that you respect them. Then comes the love."

I eyed him skeptically.

"Take Lear out tomorrow morning."

I shrugged.

"Dare you."

"Oh, Ramon, come on. . . ."

"Double-dare you."

Ah, the games of our childhood . . .

"Double-dog-dare you."

"You're on."

The next morning I'd shown up at nine for my ride. Lear raised his lip in a sneer while Ramon helped me adjust the saddle, bridle, and stirrups, but otherwise he'd walked peaceably enough around the nearby meadow. When I unsaddled him he twitched his tail impatiently.

"Ride him tonight," Ramon suggested. "Let him get used to you. I've seen you walking on the mesa; let him take you there."

I sighed, "Okay. But isn't it dangerous to ride at twilight?"

He laughed. "Horse knows every inch of this ranch.

He'll get you there and back just fine. Bring him a piece of carrot as a reward."

Lear had given me a disdainful look and tried to nip my fingers when he took the carrot, but otherwise the ride had gone well. And then tonight . . .

I took Ramon's arm as we started walking back toward the cluster of ranch buildings. "Lear's not getting the carrot I brought for him."

"No, he shouldn't. He knows he acted out."

"And I'm not riding him again."

Ramon was silent for a moment, and then he said softly, "We'll see."

Ten minutes later I let myself into the house through the door to the mudroom, hung the jacket on a peg, and went into the kitchen. It felt like stepping back into the fifties: black-and-white linoleum floor, yellow Formica countertops, old fridge and stove, porcelain sink, enameled cabinets with scalloped bottoms. A chrome-and-Formica table—yellow, with chairs upholstered in red vinyl—stood in a breakfast nook. I liked the kitchen and the fact that neither Hy nor Julie had attempted to remodel it. It spoke to me of continuity and an acceptance of the past.

And now if I can only learn to accept certain things in my past . . .

No philosophizing, I told myself. I was hungry.

I went to the fridge and peered inside. Bag of salad greens—wilted. Tomato—wrinkling. No eggs—I'd fried the last one for my lunchtime sandwich. Milk, but when I picked up the carton and sniffed it, it smelled bad. Ditto the sandwich meat. I'd used the last edible pieces of bread for lunch; the rest of it had turned hard as stone. And in the ice-clogged freezer—they didn't self-defrost when

this one was made, and I hadn't bothered to do anything about it—I spotted a submerged package of lima beans that had perhaps been there since 2002.

This was what else could go wrong today.

Good God, what was wrong with me? Why hadn't I noticed this lack of food earlier? I hadn't come here to starve myself!

I investigated the pantry. Badly stocked, unless I wanted anchovies and garbanzo beans for dinner. No more wine, either.

That did it. In a minute I was back in the shearling jacket and out the door to Hy's Land Rover.

The town of Vernon, on the shore of Tufa Lake, had changed little over the years since I'd first come there. The red-and-gold neon sign atop Zelda's—a rustic tavern and restaurant where you could dance on the weekends to country-and-western bands—flashed far out at the end of the long point extending into the lake. The liquor store had a new name, and one of the off-brand gas stations was now a Union 76, but otherwise the small businesses in the strip malls along the main street remained: an insurance broker, real-estate agents, a pizza parlor, a bank, the post office, a haircutting salon, a florist, two bars, and various other establishments that provided the necessities of everyday life. The shabby motel on the lakeshore showed a NO VACANCY sign, which never would have been the case in the old days; but the marginally better and more scenic Willow Grove Lodge was closed and up for sale, following the death of its owner, Rose Whittington. I'd stayed there on my first visits to Vernon, and remembered Mrs. Whittington as a pleasant innkeeper with a passion for gardening and trucker movies.

As always, the Food Mart was doing a turn-away business.

I pulled into the lot, parked the Land Rover, and started for the supermarket. Its windows were brightly lighted, and through them I saw busy checkers, stacks of specials, and shoppers pushing carts along the aisles. The lot and the building's plain white facade were well lighted too, but there was a pocket of darkness beyond where a soft-drink machine and some newspaper vending racks stood. With a city dweller's conditioning, I glanced over there.

A young woman—a girl, really, she couldn't have been more than fourteen or fifteen—stood alone; from the way her gaze darted around the parking lot, I assumed she was waiting for a ride. She wore a thin cotton blouse and jeans and hugged herself against the cold. Her hunched posture reminded me of the victims of sexual and domestic violence to whom I'd taught a self-defense course at San Francisco City College last year. When she swung her head around, her long black hair flared out in the chill breeze; her features, I saw, were Indian. Probably Paiute.

The girl projected such an air of loneliness that I paused. The lights of a car pulling into the lot and waiting for a space focused on her, and she blinked at the glare, then looked away in my direction. Her eyes locked on mine, and I was close enough, the lights bright enough that I saw something besides loneliness: fear.

I wondered if I should go over to her, ask if she was all right. But then she began scanning the other side of the lot. I watched her for a few more seconds before I went inside. As I passed along the aisles, buying enough food to last a week, the Indian girl's image stayed with me. When I left the store I looked for her, but she was gone.

Wednesday

✦

OCTOBER 24

to

Monday

✦

OCTOBER 29

For the greater part of the week after my outing to the Food Mart, I stayed on the ranch—reading, watching old movies on TV, sleeping, and steadfastly avoiding any thought of the future. And every evening, in spite of my vow, I returned to the same place on the bluff to watch the moon rise.

I didn't ride Lear Jet again, but after a day I did go to the stables at the time that Ramon returned from exercising him. I'd watch while he groomed and fed the horse, sitting on a bale of hay in amicable silence.

Ramon, I knew, had made overtures to Hy about buying the ranch, but out of sentiment Hy didn't want to sell. He'd grown up there, and it had been willed to him by his mother and stepfather. He'd returned there after a tumultuous stint as a charter pilot in southeast Asia. He'd lived there with Julie and eventually watched her waste away. He'd grieved there, and recovered there. And we'd first slept together

there. While we didn't visit often now, the moments we shared in the high desert were precious. Ramon had understood: sentiment ran thick in his veins too.

Sometimes when he was done with the horse, he'd join me and talk about our heritages. "You know, our tribes generally had good relationships," he said one afternoon. "Maybe that's why we get along so well, huh?"

"Maybe it's got more to do with the fact we're both quiet."

"Well, that *is* a virtue." He took out a cigarette, lit it, and doused the match thoroughly. With Ramon, I never worried about accidental fires; he was too mindful a man.

"Sara, God love her, she chatters," he added. Sara was his wife of thirty-some years. "Of course, when I married a Mexican, I knew she would. And chattering's not such a bad thing; how else would I know what's going on in the world? Now, that man of yours doesn't talk much."

"He's getting better at conversation."

"Since he met you. When I first came to work here for him, about a year after his first wife died, he barely spoke at all. A more depressed man I'd never met."

We sat in silence for a while, Ramon smoking his cigarette, then grinding it out on the floor and putting the butt in his shirt pocket.

"You're damn depressed yourself," he said.

I shrugged.

"You want to talk about it?"

". . . I don't think so. Not now, anyway."

"You change your mind, I'm here."

The next day I brought Ramon a book on Shoshone tribal customs that my birth father, Elwood Farmer, had given me. Lear Jet glowered at me from his stall. Did he think I should've brought *him* something? No way, not after he'd thrown me.

Throughout the week I had contact with the outside world, of course. Daily calls came from my operative Patrick Neilan, to whom I'd turned over administrative matters at the agency, as well as my office manager, Ted Smalley. Just general reports: everything's okay here, we wrapped up the so-and-so case, three new jobs came in today. It was all I cared to know about a business I'd nurtured lovingly for years. And that unnerved me.

Mick had relented and located the person who'd been using my credit card: a deliveryman employed by a Chinese restaurant in our neighborhood who frequently delivered takeout to us. Citibank and the police were dealing with him.

There was also a daily call from Hy, who was restructuring the corporate security firm—formerly RKI, now Ripinsky International—of which he'd become sole owner after the death of one partner and the decampment of another. He'd moved their world headquarters to San Francisco, turned over marginal accounts to other firms, and closed unnecessary branch offices, and was busy creating a corporate culture that—unlike the old RKI's—was free of corruption. His calls further depressed me, although I did my best to hide it. I'd never heard Hy so vibrant and optimistic, but could only briefly get caught up in his enthusiasm. His feelings about his work were so opposite to how I felt about mine that once the calls were over, I wanted to crawl into bed and bury my head under the pillows.

Which I did most nights, falling into a restless sleep that was repeatedly visited by the dream of the pit, as well as an odd new one: an Indian girl standing in the cold shadows outside a large white building. She looked at me in the glare of passing headlights, eyes afraid, and then the earth at her feet cracked open and swallowed her up.

Tuesday

✦

OCTOBER 30

I awoke with the dreams heavy upon me, like a hangover. My hands shook as I fixed coffee and my head throbbed dully, even though I'd had nothing alcoholic to drink the night before.

I took my coffee to the living room and curled up under a woven throw in one of the deeply cushioned chairs by the stone fireplace. Unlike the kitchen, this room was pure Hy: Indian rugs on the pegged-pine floor, antique rifles over the fireplace, and in the bookcases flanking it to either side, his collection of Western novels from the thirties and forties and nonfiction accounts of the Old West. Over the time I'd been staying here, I'd read some of the novels, paged through a few of the nonfiction volumes. But this morning my mind was not on history—at least not anything going back more than five months.

This stay in the high desert wasn't working out as I'd thought it would. I'd managed to fill up empty hours with

useless activity, while avoiding the larger issues: Did I really want to go on sitting behind a desk hour after hour, reviewing client reports, okaying invoices and expense logs, interviewing new clients, assigning jobs, and mediating employee disputes? Did I really want to continue taking on the larger, more complex cases that required me to be on the move a lot and that—too often in the past year—had ended in danger and near death?

Over the course of my career I'd been stabbed, nearly drowned, beaten up, falsely imprisoned, held at gunpoint, and once, ignominiously, shot in the ass. I'd killed two people and nearly succumbed to violent urges against others. Last winter I'd come close to being killed in the explosion. Enough, already.

But taking on a strictly administrative role wasn't an option for me; I'd go crazy confined to my desk. How could I continue activities that had lost their appeal, where I was just going through the motions?

The agency was profitable and well respected. I could sell it for big bucks to another firm looking to grow, negotiate a deal where my present employees would remain on staff. Take the money and . . . then what?

I wasn't cut out for everyday leisure. I didn't play golf or tennis or bridge, take classes, have hobbies, or enjoy most of the activities retired people do.

Retired people.

My God, I was in my early forties! Given the life expectancy of my birth family—relatives on both sides had lived into their nineties—that was a lot of time to fill up. And that's all I'd be doing—just filling it up.

Okay, begin a second career. Lots of people did that. But what? My college degree was in sociology, and that hadn't gotten me anywhere even when my diploma was

freshly minted. Consult? That would only put me back in the thick of things. Write a book on investigative techniques, as I'd recently been asked to? No. I'd rather become a neurosurgeon, train as a master chef, or apply to NASA and fly to Mars. None of which was going to happen either.

Investigation was what I knew how to do—and do well—but I didn't want to work at it any more. At least not now. Maybe not ever.

Hy had suggested I come in as a partner with him, but that wouldn't work. We'd take our business home with us, and ultimately it would consume our marriage. Besides, an executive position in corporate security wasn't to my liking; it didn't provide much involvement with the clients, one aspect that I used to enjoy.

I went to get some more coffee. My headache had faded, and my hands were steady. Back in my chair by the fireplace, I told myself that at least I'd seriously considered the issues I was facing, even if it hadn't solved anything.

Didn't have to be done quickly anyway. The business was in good hands, and I had all the time in the world. A solution would come to me eventually. In the meantime, why not fill up the rest of today with pleasurable activity?

I would have liked to go flying, but Hy had needed our Cessna 270B, so he'd dropped me off at Tufa Tower Airport and flown back to the Bay Area. The airport had a couple of clunker planes I could rent for a nominal fee, but Hy had told me they were untrustworthy, and from a cursory inspection I'd concluded he was correct.

Maybe a picnic. Pack a good book, pick up a sandwich from the Food Mart deli, and go—where? Well, the old Willow Grove Lodge had nice grounds and a dock overlooking the lake. It was closed and isolated. The only

people likely to show up there would be real-estate agents with prospective buyers, and I doubted that would happen. If it did, I'd concoct some story to explain my presence and leave.

The main lodge and six cabins that were scattered over several cottonwood- and willow-shaded acres looked shabby. True, the cabins had never been in great condition, but their nineteen-fifties-vintage furnishings, smoke-stained woodstoves, primitive kitchens, and underlying odor of dry rot reminded me of the resorts where my financially strapped family had stayed on summer vacations during my childhood. And even after the death of her husband, Rose Whittington had worked hard to keep the place up. Now the cabins' green trim was blistered and faded, dark brown wood splintered and cracked, composition roofs sagging. Graffiti decorated their walls. Rose's garden had long gone to the weeds. A developer's dream: bulldoze it and put up condos or a luxury hotel. The hell with the love and care that the Whittingtons had put into this place over their fifty-year marriage, let alone the happy memories of all the people who'd stayed here.

Of course, it was hard to argue with a would-be buyer's logic; these buildings were not salvageable. I only hoped that whoever bought the acreage would leave the trees.

I parked behind the lodge where the Land Rover couldn't be seen from the highway, carried my deli lunch down the rocky slope to the rickety dock, and spread an old blanket on its planks. Sat down, feeling the pale autumn sunshine on my face. The lake rippled on the stones below, and in the distance I could see plovers doing touch-and-goes on the massive central island. The lake is a major stop on the Pacific Flyway, along which approxi-

mately a hundred thousand migratory birds travel, and over the years I've seen most every kind there. If the lake had not been saved through the efforts of dedicated environmentalists like Hy, the birds would have had a long journey to their next stop.

A natural wonder restored, a man-made resort dying.

Suddenly I didn't feel as sad about the Willow Grove Lodge's demise. Long after whatever replaced it was gone, the lake would endure.

The book I'd brought along wasn't very engaging—a long-winded narrative about a former alcoholic holed up in the woods to contemplate what he claimed wasn't a midlife crisis, but that damned well sounded like one, as I should know. After I finished my lunch, I dozed off while reading and woke to a chill wind gusting off the lake. The shadows of the trees had moved over me.

I sat up, disoriented. In my peripheral vision, something moved through the dark grove to the right. I turned my head, narrowed my eyes. Nothing there. Then I saw it again—a figure that darted from trunk to trunk, creating a ripple effect.

An animal? A person? Either way, I was the interloper here. Time to get going.

I folded the blanket, grabbed the book and the sack of leavings from my picnic. At the Land Rover I looked back at the grove. No more motion, but a prickly sensation arose at the base of my spine, spread up to the back of my neck. Something colder than the wind washed over me.

My old woolen peacoat was in the Land Rover and before I drove out I put it on. As I stopped at the top of the drive, I saw the yellow-leafed aspens in the declivities of the hills to the far side of the highway swaying softly in

the breeze; the late afternoon sunlight made them gleam like a river of molten gold.

There had been gold in these hills long ago and some poor veins remained. Normally the beauty of this view would have entranced me, but now its glow was dimmed by the aura of what I'd felt at the lodge. I thought of the ravages that cyanide—which the big mining companies had used to extract gold from the waste dumps and tailings of played-out claims—had wreaked upon the land.

The thought took me back to the case I'd been working here when I met Hy, investigating a conglomerate that planned to start up a large-scale and environmentally unsound mining operation above a semi-ghost town called Promiseville. I remembered us fleeing hand in hand from a dynamite blast that took out a part of a mountain. And Hy saying, as we lay on the ground gasping and panting from our flight, ". . . You've got even more of a death wish than I do."

Not any more.

I waited for a logging truck to pass, then turned left toward town. The highway topped a rise, then began a gradual descent into Vernon. Halfway down I saw an old brown pickup truck, its paint spotted gray like a piebald horse. It was pulled onto the opposite shoulder and, as I approached, its passenger-side door flew open and the figure of a woman hurtled out into the ditch. The truck's driver—bearded, with a knit cap pulled low on his brow— got out and stood on the edge of the ditch, yelling down at her.

Reflexively I U-turned across the highway and pulled onto the shoulder. As I jumped out of the Rover the man turned, his features mostly obscured by his hat and turned-up collar.

"Just a family fight, lady," he said in a rough voice. "No need to get involved."

"The hell you say!" I started forward just as the woman clawed her way up the incline. It was the Indian girl whose face had been haunting my dreams. Now her long hair was tangled, and she looked dazed.

The man made a menacing gesture toward me. I braced for an attack, feet spread wide, arms flexed. He stood still, studying me, then muttered something that sounded like "Ah, fuck it!" He whirled and got into the pickup, revved its engine, and sped off, spraying gravel.

I went over and helped the girl to her feet. I couldn't tell if she recognized me or not; her expression was blank.

"Are you all right?" I asked.

". . . Yes, I'm okay. No big deal." She brushed at her clothing, smoothed down her hair. She was dressed more warmly than she had been the last time I saw her, in a quilted jacket, jeans, and hiking boots.

"What happened here?"

She shrugged. "I said it was no big deal."

"Do you need a ride someplace? I can—"

"Look," she said, "it's none of your business. Okay? I take care of myself, nobody else does." Then she turned and began walking the way the truck had gone.

I watched until she disappeared over the rise, berating myself for trying to intervene in a private matter. It was as if I had a compulsion to get involved in things that didn't concern me—just as I'd often involved myself too deeply in cases I'd handled. Dammit, why couldn't I leave people alone? That was what I wanted to do, wasn't it? It was what I'd been telling myself.

I got back into the Land Rover. A fight with a relative or her boyfriend, I thought. They live someplace

up the highway and by the time she gets there he'll be sorry.

But the way she shot out of that truck, it looked like he pushed her. He's an abuser and all abusers feel sorry— until they do it again.

As she said, it was none of my business. She didn't want my help.

I could ask around in Vernon. . . .

No, I couldn't. Or, more correctly, wouldn't. That kind of uninvited snooping had no place in the new life I was hoping to create.

I stopped by the Food Mart because I was getting low on milk. And only for that reason.

But as the tired-looking woman at the checkstand was ringing up my purchases—I can never go into a grocery store and buy just one item—I said, "There was an Indian girl waiting for a ride outside here last Tuesday night. I wonder if you know her?" I described her and what she was wearing.

The checker nodded and began bagging my groceries. "That's Amy Perez. She stocks shelves here a couple days a week. What d'you want with her?"

Don't go on with this, McCone. Don't.

"She . . . dropped something, and I'd like to return it." God, the lies that rippled off my tongue after so many years in my business! It had gotten to the point that I didn't need to think them up ahead of time.

"You can give it to me, I'll see she gets it."

"Actually, I'd like to return it in person. It's a bracelet, and I want to ask her where she got it, so I can buy one for myself."

The checker shrugged. "Well, I don't know where she's

living these days. She moves around a lot, you know what I mean?"

I asked, "Is she any relation to Ramon Perez up at the Ripinsky place?"

"A niece maybe, I'm not sure. There're Perezes all over Mono County, some related, some not. But, yeah, I think Ramon's her uncle."

I thanked her, paid, and left.

It wouldn't hurt, I thought, to ask Ramon about Amy, tell him what I had witnessed that afternoon. If she was in trouble, maybe her uncle could help.

"Yeah, Amy's my niece." Ramon was sitting on the bale of hay inside the stable door.

Lear Jet was already in his stall. I glared at him, and he glared back.

I said, "Tell me about her."

His gaze shifted to the darkness gathering in the empty stalls beyond Lear Jet's. "My sister-in-law's youngest. She was such a beautiful little girl, and she loved her Uncle Ramon."

"And now?"

"She's still beautiful. You saw that."

"And she still loves you?"

He sighed heavily. "Who knows? Who knows anything these days?"

I couldn't debate the latter question. "She's in trouble, Ramon." I told him what I'd seen that afternoon, and Amy's reaction to my offer of help. "The clerk at Food Mart said she 'moves around a lot.'"

"One boyfriend, another boyfriend, sometimes she crashes at my sister-in-law's house."

"How old is she?"

"Eighteen in three months. She looks a lot younger."

"Still underage, then. Can't her mother rein her in?"

He looked at me, eyes sad. "Look, Sharon, it's not that simple. Her mother has her own problems."

"There's no father in the picture?"

"My son-of-a-bitch brother Jimmy took off when Amy was a year old. Miri—that's his wife—did her best by all five kids, but it wasn't good enough. Her older girl left town nine years ago, before she finished high school. We don't know where she is. Last I heard was a postcard from Las Vegas, and that was over a year ago. The two older boys're in prison. The younger boy was killed in a car wreck—his fault, he'd been drinking."

"And now Miri's in danger of losing Amy, too."

He looked down at where his thick-fingered hands were spread on his denim-covered thighs. "I don't think she'd even notice if Amy was gone."

"Drugs? Booze? Men?"

"You got it. When Vic—the youngest boy—died, Miri totally fell apart."

"What about the kids' Uncle Ramon? Where do you fit into the picture?"

"I don't. Miri and I had a big fight, four, maybe five years ago. The times I came around to apologize, she ran me off with a shotgun."

"D'you think Amy might listen to you, let you help her?"

"Like I said, I don't know how she feels about me these days." He paused, and in the silence Lear Jet whickered. "You say this guy pushed her out of a pickup?"

"Yes. Brown, probably a Ford, with a lot of Bondo on it."

"You see him?"

"Yes. He has a dark brown beard; I couldn't really tell about his features. After he threw Amy out of the truck he went to the edge of the shoulder and was shouting at her. When I intervened, he thought about attacking me, then took off."

"Boz Sheppard. That asshole. If she's hooked up with him, it's statutory rape."

"How old is this Boz?"

"Late twenties, maybe thirty. Hard to tell. Too damn old to be messing with a young girl like Amy."

"Who is he?"

"Local lowlife—not that we haven't got plenty of them. Claims to be a carpenter, but he's usually so stoned he couldn't drive a nail in straight if his life depended on it."

"He from around here?"

"No. Showed up in Vernon one day, took a trailer at that crappy park up the highway. Does odd jobs, but I hear mostly he deals drugs. Rumor is he's got a record."

If he did, I could get Derek Ford, Mick's assistant at the agency, to access it. "Definitely not good company for your niece," I said.

"Yeah. Which way you say she was going when she walked off?"

"North from town."

"Toward that trailer park." Ramon stood. "Think I'll take a run out there, pay a visit. Want to ride along?"

"Ramon, it's a family matter—"

"One that could use a woman's touch."

Well, why not? I had nothing else to do that evening.

The park extended from the edge of the highway to the hillside—two dozen or so old-model trailers up on cement blocks. No amenities such as a rec center,

plantings, or even paved parking areas. No trees. Only a sagging barbed-wire fence between it and the outside world.

Personally, I'd rather have lived in a cave.

Ramon stopped the truck in front of a one-windowed shack with a sign saying OFFICE. Got out, but came right back. "Nobody there."

I looked around, pointed out a woman walking a dog. Ramon nodded and approached her. When he slid into the truck he said, "Last trailer, last row in back. From the look the lady gave me, I'd say Boz's dealing, all right."

We drove back there in silence, gravel crunching under the truck's wheels. The rows were dimly lighted—minimum county requirement—and most of the trailers were dark. Boz Sheppard's was by far the worst of them all—ancient, small, humpbacked, its formerly white paint peeling off to reveal gunmetal gray and rust. There was a glow in its rear window.

Ramon took a deep breath. "I don't know what to say to her."

"Tell her you love her and want to help."

"What if she doesn't think she needs it?"

I pictured the look of defiance in Amy's eyes before she'd turned her back on me that afternoon. Underneath there had been fear—and not of me.

"She does, whether she knows it or not," I said. "This Boz—he'll try to intervene. We should separate them."

"How?"

"Leave that to me." I didn't have a plan, but once we confronted Boz, my instincts would tell me what to do.

We got out of the truck and went up to the door. Ramon knocked.

No answer.

He knocked again, rattling the flimsy door in its frame.

Nothing.

"See if it's unlocked," I said.

"That's not legal—"

"You have probable cause to be concerned for your niece."

"Damn right I do!" He turned the knob and pushed the door inward so hard it smacked into the wall behind it. Moved up the two low steps and inside.

A growl. At first I thought it came from a watchdog, then realized that Ramon himself had made the sound. I pushed around him. And stopped.

The room was tidy, the pullout bed made up into a couch. A woman lay collapsed beside it, her arms outflung on the bloodstained carpet, long dark hair covering most of her face. Freshly spilled blood. It pooled beneath her, and the front of her black silk dress was torn and scorched where a bullet—or bullets—had entered. The scent of cordite was strong on the air.

Before I could stop him, Ramon went to the woman and brushed her hair from her face. Gasped and recoiled.

I went over and pulled on his arm. "Go outside. This is a crime scene. We can't disturb anything more than we already have."

He hesitated, then went, shaking his head.

I looked down at the woman's face. Not Amy, but someone older who closely resembled her. The dress looked expensive, her costume jewelry gaudy. One red spike-heeled shoe had come off her foot and lay on the carpet. I glanced at the breakfast bar on the counter: a half-full shaker of martinis and two glasses, one lying on its side, broken, liquid pooling beside it.

I backed up, left the trailer without touching anything. Ramon was leaning against his truck, trying to light a cigarette with shaking hands.

"You know her?" I asked.

He nodded.

"Who is she?"

He took a deep drag on the cigarette and exhaled. "Hayley."

"And Hayley is . . . ?"

"Amy's older sister. The one I told you sent me a postcard from Las Vegas."

How the hell did I get myself into this? I came up here to make plans to leave this kind of thing behind me—the stench of death, the flashing lights, the paramedics, the radios and official voices droning on and on and on . . .

I should've told Ramon to bring Sara along with him if he felt the situation required a woman's touch. I should've stayed home, waited for the agency calls, phoned Hy. I should've jumped into the Rover and gotten the hell out of Mono County.

Well, you're involved now, McCone, whether you like it or not. At least you're an outsider, an observer with professional judgment, rather than a torn-up family member like Ramon. . . .

He was in one of the sheriff's department cars now, giving his statement to a deputy, but before they'd arrived he'd been crying in my arms. Later he'd be embarrassed by that, I knew, but at the time he'd needed comfort. I'd never mention his tears, and neither would he, but eventually they'd either put up a wall or forge a stronger bond between us.

Another deputy approached me. "Ms. McCone, I'm Deputy Drew Warnell. Can we talk?"

He was young, so smooth-faced that I'd bet he didn't shave but every other day, and he turned his hat in his hands as he spoke, his dark hair falling in a thick shock over his forehead. I suggested we go sit in Ramon's truck.

When we were settled, Deputy Warnell took out a notepad. "I understand you were with Mr. Perez when he discovered the deceased?"

I explained how I'd encountered Amy under disturbing circumstances that afternoon and told Ramon about them. "The man who rented the trailer, Boz Sheppard, was the one who threw her out of his truck. Ramon decided to come here and talk with him. He asked me to come along."

"Why?"

"He said the situation needed a woman's touch."

"It wasn't because you're a private investigator?"

"No, I came as a friend."

"So Mr. Perez entered the trailer and found the victim?"

"Yes."

"Why didn't you take steps to ensure that he didn't disturb the crime scene?"

"Because he moved too fast. I'd only seen the body seconds before he touched it. I did get him outside as quickly as I could."

"Mr. Perez has identified the young woman as his other niece, Hayley Perez, last known address Las Vegas."

"Yes."

"Did you know Hayley Perez?"

"I don't know any of the family, except for Ramon and his wife, Sara. He's foreman at my husband's and my ranch."

"The Ripinsky place?"

"Yes."

For a moment his official facade slipped and Drew

Warnell seemed even younger. "I used to ride horses up there. My mom and dad were friends of Hy's and Julie's."

"There's only one horse left now—Lear Jet."

He shook his head. "Must've come after my time. And I don't think Mr. Perez was working there then." He paused, seeming at a loss for further questions.

I asked, "D'you have any idea how long Hayley Perez has been dead?"

"Not long. The ME said within the last hour."

Shortly before Ramon and I had arrived, then. "Shot at close range. How many times?"

"Once, straight into her heart—" He broke off, then said, "Ms. McCone, I'm sorry, but I shouldn't be giving you these details."

"And I shouldn't've asked—professional habit."

"You work for what agency?"

"I own McCone Investigations, in San Francisco."

Something flickered in his eyes as he put it together. There had been huge publicity earlier in the year on the serial bomber case.

"Sorry," he said. "I must be slow tonight. I didn't make the connection until just now."

"No worries."

"I should've—"

I held up my hand to forestall yet another apology. "As I indicated earlier, I'm not here in a professional capacity. I see your colleague's done with Ramon, and I really should be getting back to him. If you need to ask any further questions, you can reach me at the ranch."

Ramon wasn't fit to drive yet, so I took the wheel of his truck. As I turned onto the highway, he said, "I told the cops I'd break the news to Miri."

"Where does she live?"

"You don't want to go with me."

"Remember what you said before? A woman's touch?"

He was silent for a moment. Then he said, "Make a right turn on the first street this side of the Food Mart."

After I'd driven into town and turned off, he said, "This won't be pretty."

"It never is."

But the small gray clapboard house in the middle of the block was dark, and no one answered when Ramon knocked.

He said, "Miri's probably at one of the bars or the motel—or passed out inside."

"You have a key?"

"Nope." He tried the knob, but unlike at the trailer where we'd found his niece's body, the door was locked. "I better check the bars. Something like this, news gets around fast. A deputy goes off duty, he starts talking. That's no way for Miri to find out."

"Okay, where do we start?"

He looked away from me. "Not we—me. I'm okay now. You take the truck back to the ranch, get some rest. It's almost midnight."

I felt a flash of relief, but still felt compelled to say, "I don't mind—"

"Sharon, I appreciate all you've done tonight. But Miri—I've got to handle her myself."

"How'll you get home?"

"I'll call Sara when I'm done, ask her to come and get me."

"Okay, then. Good luck with Miri."

Wednesday

◆

OCTOBER 31

The phone was ringing when I let myself into the ranch house. As I went to pick up, I noticed the time on the old-fashioned kitchen clock: 12:23.

"Happy Halloween, McCone." Hy.

"And the same to you." I'd completely forgotten what the date was.

"Where've you been all this time? I've left messages on the machine, and on your cell."

"Sorry I haven't checked either. Where I've been is an awfully sad story."

His voice sharpened when he asked, "What's wrong?"

I went over the events of the evening.

"Jesus," he said when I'd finished. "Poor Ramon. How're you?"

"I'm handling it."

"And?"

"That's all. I was there for Ramon when he needed me. Now the county sheriff can deal with it."

". . . Right."

"What does that mean?"

"Nothing, really."

"You think this is going to suck me in, don't you? You think that next thing I'll be prowling around, trying to find out who killed that woman."

"Not necessarily."

"Well, good, because it's not going to happen. That part of my life is over. *Over*."

"I hear you. Have you made any decisions yet? About your future?"

"No, not yet."

We went on to discuss his day, our cats, and his coming up here on the weekend. After we ended the conversation, I took a hot shower and crawled into bed.

All I wanted was to blot out the events of a long, horrible day. Maybe if I could do that, even for a few hours, I'd be able to distance myself from Ramon's trouble.

Maybe.

Distance—sure.

At around ten-thirty that morning I was washing out my coffee cup at the kitchen sink when Sara Perez's SUV drove in and parked next to Ramon's truck. She got out, looked inside the truck. Then she spotted me through the window, waved, and moved toward the house.

Sara was a short, heavy woman with gray hair in a long braid that hung nearly to her waist. In spite of her girth, she moved gracefully. A native of Oaxaca, Mexico, she was a midwife and concocter of herbal medicines, assisting at births and dispensing natural panaceas in remote

towns all over the county, as well as a writer of children's books aimed at the state's soon-to-be-dominant Latino population.

When I met her at the mudroom door, I saw that her eyes were worried, her full lips cracked and raw as if she'd been nibbling at them.

"Ramon didn't come home last night," she said. "I heard about Hayley. The radio said he found her body and that you were with him."

Damn! Why did they have to give out that information? No privacy—

I motioned her in from the cold. "Ramon asked me to drop him off in town, and that he'd call you for a ride home. He had to break the news to Miri."

"He go to her house?"

"Yes, he had me drive him there, but—"

"She was off someplace, or passed out drunk."

"That's what he thought."

"Well, I've tried calling Miri's. No answer there."

"Last I saw him, he was going to look for her in the bars."

"May I use your phone?"

"Sure." I motioned toward it, went to pour her a cup of coffee.

"Bob?" she said into the phone. "Sara. Did my man come in there last night looking for his miserable sister? . . . Yeah . . . Right, about what time? . . . Thanks, Bob, I appreciate it."

To me she said, "He went to Zelda's, Miri hadn't been in." Sara dialed again and left a message on a machine. Made another call. "Jenny, it's Sara. Did Ramon . . . ? Right. She wasn't . . . I see . . . Will you call me if . . . Thanks."

She turned to me, took the cup of coffee I held out.

"Those're the only bars in Vernon," she said, "and the one where I got the machine has eighty-sixed Miri so many times she'd never go there. Ramon was at the other two a little after midnight, asking for her. She hadn't been in."

"Maybe he went back to Miri's and found her there."

"And now nobody's answering the phone?"

"That *is* strange. You should go down there."

Sara shook her head, her braid switching from side to side. "I can't. The last time I tried to reach out to Miri, she threatened me with her shotgun, said she'd kill me if I ever came near the place again. Now, with Hayley dead, she'll be ready to take on the world. Will you go for me?"

No, a thousand times no.

Sara's dark eyes pleaded with me.

Please don't suck me into this. . . .

"I don't have anybody else to ask," she said. "None of our other friends want anything to do with Miri."

She looked so alone. If I could bring Ramon back to her . . .

"I'll go," I said, "and call to tell you what I find out."

Before I left the ranch house, Ted phoned. After he gave me his daily report he asked, "Any idea when you're coming back to the city?"

"No. Why?"

"We miss you. The place isn't the same without you."

And I wasn't the same without it. But I wasn't the same when I was there, either.

"Shar?"

"I'm here."

"Look, we're doing what we can to hold this agency together, but we need you."

"The agency seems to be doing fine without me."

Long pause. "You sound so . . . cold."

I supposed I did. A frozen shell around my emotions was the best way to distance myself from the people I'd known and cared for all these years.

"I'm sorry, Ted. I'm . . . preoccupied this morning, that's all."

"Shar, this is me you're talking to. Ted, from the old days at All Souls."

The poverty law cooperative where we used to work, he as secretary and me as staff investigator. When I'd first met him he'd been sitting with his bare feet propped on his desk, working a *New York Times* crossword puzzle in ink. Those had been good years: filled with camaraderie, poker and Monopoly games in the off hours, and long soul-baring discussions late into the night as we sat around the big oak table in the kitchen of All Souls' Bernal Heights Victorian. Since the co-op had been dissolved and I'd formed my own agency—taking Ted and Mick with me—the camaraderie had continued and enlarged to embrace new people. But these days we were so caught up with a huge caseload and an upscale image—to say nothing of large earning power—that much of the excitement and closeness had bled away.

I said, "I know who I'm talking to, Ted."

"Then really talk. Tell me what's going on with you. Maybe I can help."

Tears stung my eyes, as they had all too often over the past months.

"I can't do that now," I said. "There's someplace I have to be."

Hy's comment about it being Halloween had made me wonder how the locals celebrated. As I drove into town

I noticed jack-o'-lanterns on nearly every doorstep. Several bales of hay had been trucked into the Food Mart's parking lot, and beside them stood a scarecrow. Big deal in a small town. The decorations must've been there days before, but I hadn't been attuned to the holiday.

As I hadn't been attuned to so many things.

I turned onto Miri Perez's street and drove along, bouncing in and out of potholes, to her small gray house. The yard was fenced with chain link, its browned grass littered with takeout containers, soda and beer bottles; an old rusted bicycle that was missing its front wheel lay on its side under a juniper bush. No vehicles out front or in the driveway. As I went up the walk to the concrete stoop, I heard nothing.

I knocked on the door, waited. Knocked again, called out to Mrs. Perez and Ramon. No response.

The windows to either side of the door had their blinds drawn. I went along the driveway, noting that the windows there were too high to see through without a ladder. The backyard was the same as the front: browned grass, dead plants, more litter. A decrepit swing set sat near the rear fence.

The windows here were also covered by blinds. Another concrete stoop led to a back door. I climbed it, looked through the single pane. Straight ahead were an old refrigerator and a counter, to the right an archway.

I reached for the doorknob, pulled my hand away.

Don't do it, McCone.

But Ramon and Miri have gone missing, and Sara asked me—

Don't do it!

Holding fast to my new resolve, I didn't.

*   *   *

It was noon, time for the watering holes to open their doors. I decided to stop in at the bar on whose answering machine Sara had left a message. Hobo's was your typical tavern, the kind I'd visited over and over in the course of my investigations. At night it would be dimly lighted and its scars wouldn't show; by day the shabby booths and chairs and tables and banged-up walls were more obvious. Three old men hunched at the long bar, staring up at a TV that was broadcasting a replay of last weekend's Forty-Niners game. The bartender—white-haired, with a thick beard and a large gut—was setting out bowls of popcorn.

As I took a stool at the bar, I thought of all the hours I'd wasted seeking information in such establishments.

"Help you, ma'am?"

"Maybe. Sara Perez sent me."

"Oh, yeah, I haven't got around to returning her call." The man picked up a rag and began wiping the surface in front of me.

He added, "Reason I've been putting it off is that I had an ugly scene with Miri Perez in here last night, and then this morning I heard the news about Hayley from one of my delivery drivers."

"Did you know her?"

"Hayley? Not really. She was just one of the kids who would come in to drag their drunken parents home. She ran away before she even finished high school."

"What kind of ugly scene did you have with Miri?"

He frowned at me. "You a friend of the Perez family?"

"Ramon's the manager on my husband's and my ranch."

"You're Hy Ripinsky's wife."

"Right."

"Well, then." He leaned forward on the bar, lowering his voice and glancing at the patrons. They were absorbed

in watching a 'Niners pass completion. "Miri came in last night about nine-thirty. I'd permanently eighty-sixed her a year ago, on account of she's a problem drunk. But she was sober and behaving herself so I let her stay. My mistake."

"What happened?"

"She was alone when she came in, but Miri's never alone for long. Not because she's particularly attractive—not any more, anyway—but because she has this reputation." He stopped, probably abashed at having said that much to a friend of Ramon and Sara.

"I know about Miri's problems," I said. "Go on."

"Well, there was a bunch of guys down from Bridgeport. Not bad guys, but they get kinda rowdy when the wives aren't around. One of them started buying Miri shots and she got rowdy too. Started making nasty remarks to the people at the next table, lobbed some popcorn at them, then threw a drink in one woman's face. Was cussing me out and swinging at me when I cut her off. I had to escort her out. The guy went with her."

"What time was this?"

"After eleven, but not much. Ramon came in looking for Miri around midnight."

"You know the name of the guy she left with?"

"His friends called him Dino. Like Dean Martin, the singer."

"What about his friends? You have a full name for any of them?"

"Only Cullen Bradley. Owns a hardware store in Bridgeport."

"Any idea where this Dino and Miri might've been heading?"

"Her place? The motel? That's the usual deal with Miri. No, wait a minute." He touched his fingers to his

brow. "Before I escorted them out the guy said something to her about the Outhouse."

"The *what*?"

He smiled. "It's a tavern, up the highway about fifteen miles. Used to be a gas station. They've got the best fried chicken in the county."

Somehow I doubted Dino and Miri were headed there for the food. "Did you mention this to Ramon?"

"Yeah, I did. He wasn't happy about it."

"You say this place is fifteen miles up the highway?"

"Give or take."

"Ramon couldn't have followed them—he didn't have a vehicle."

"Miri did. I saw her old van in the lot when I showed them the door. But they didn't take it; they got into a red Jeep Cherokee. And the van was gone when I closed up."

"You notice the license plate number of the Cherokee?"

"My eyesight hasn't been that good since 1992."

"So you think Ramon might've taken the van?"

"Maybe."

"It's unlikely he had a key; he and Miri haven't been on speaking terms for years."

"Ramon wouldn't've needed a key. Not old Magic Fingers."

"What does that mean?"

"Ramon's been hot-wiring cars since he was a kid. Made the mistake of getting caught after he was eighteen, did a stretch in prison for it."

As I drove up the highway toward the Outhouse, I thought about the assumptions we make about people and how sometimes they're totally wrong. Hardworking,

upwardly mobile Ramon Perez—a car thief? An ex-con? Did Hy know about his past? Most likely: Vernon was a small town, and Hy had grown up there.

Why hadn't he mentioned it to me? Probably because Ramon had turned his life around and his misdeeds weren't relevant any more. Hy was big on giving people second chances; God knew he'd received more than his fair share of them.

It was a beautiful day, and I tried to enjoy the drive. The lake spread below me as I negotiated the road's switch-backs, its placid surface reflecting the clear blue of the sky. In the distance I could glimpse the dark, glassy mound of Obsidian Dome, one of the many distinctive formations created by the volcanic activity that shaped this land. In 1982 the U.S. Geological Survey issued a hazard warning that an eruption the size of the 1980 Mount Saint Helens disaster could occur here at any time. The warning is in effect to this day.

After I reached the ten-mile mark, the road—still climbing—veered to the east and cut between rocky slopes to which scrub pine clung. Five miles more, and the Outhouse appeared on my left. It was a typical old-fashioned gas station with a roof over the pumps, but the main structure had been considerably enlarged; the pumps were antiques—Socony before it became Mobil Oil—and lighted beer signs hung in the front windows. I parked in the gravel lot and went inside.

In spite of being far from any town, the place was doing a good business: most of the tables and booths were taken. I found one of the last empty seats at the bar. The air was heavy with the smell of frying; my stomach rumbled in response. The best fried chicken in the county, huh? I hadn't had really good fried chicken in ages.

The bartender was working hard; I waited, looking around at the decor: old automobile license plates from various states; signed celebrity photos from the forties and fifties; mildly amusing signs such as IN GOD WE TRUST. ALL OTHERS MUST PAY CASH; mounted animal heads wearing party hats. I'd been in other supposedly vintage places and knew decorations of this kind could be purchased new as a package from restaurant-equipment firms, but the Outhouse's seemed to be the real thing.

When the bartender finally got to me, I ordered a Sierra Nevada and a basket of chicken and fries. The beer came quickly, the chicken much later. "Sorry about the wait," he said as he set it down.

"No problem. You're busy."

"Swamped and shorthanded." Someone down the bar called out to him, and he hurried away.

I ate slowly. The chicken was some of the best I'd ever tasted. The seats around me gradually emptied, as did the booths and tables. I was toying with a french fry when the last customer left.

The bartender—a youngish guy with long hair pulled back in a ponytail—went to the door and turned the sign to CLOSED. Came back around the bar to me and said, "Anything else, ma'am?" Clearly he hoped I'd say no.

"Some information, if you don't mind. You hear about Hayley Perez being killed last night?"

"Yeah." He shook his head. "Tough break, but Hayley always lived dangerously. One wild child."

"You knew her well?"

"No. We went to high school together, but she was older and we didn't run with the same crowd."

"Who did she run with?"

"The wrong people. Druggies, dropouts, you know."

"Any names?"

"Why the interest?"

"I'm a friend of the family. I'm helping them get a list together for the memorial service."

That satisfied him. "Well, let's see. She was tight with a girl named Loni . . . something, but I haven't seen her around in a long time. Her boyfriend was Tom Mathers; he's married now, runs a wilderness supply and guide service. And then there was Rich Three Wings; they had a thing going too, was what broke Hayley and Tom up. You can forget about him, he'd never come to a service."

"Why not?"

"Because him and Hayley left town together and he came back alone three years later. Wouldn't ever talk about what happened. Now he lives alone in a cabin on Elk Lake. I hear he's got a girlfriend who lives in Vernon, spends weekends at the lake with him."

"You know her name?"

He shook his head.

"I take it Three Wings is Indian."

"Paiute." He studied my features. "You're . . . ?"

"Shoshone."

"Well then, maybe you can get through to Rich. You people have a way of communicating, even if you're from different tribes."

You people.

I'd been hearing that all my life, even back before I found out I was adopted, when I'd thought I was seven-eighths Scotch-Irish and my looks a throwback to my Shoshone great-grandmother. I counted to ten—well, seven, actually—and said, "I understand Hayley's mother may have come in here last night. Were you working then?"

"Yeah. I'm doing a triple shift. Like I said, we're shorthanded."

"And Miri . . . ?"

"She didn't come in. I'd've noticed, because she's on our watch list. Terrible, mean drunk."

"What about her brother-in-law, Ramon?"

"He was here. Asked me about her."

"When was this?"

"Around one. I told him I'd call if she turned up, and then he left."

"He say where he was going?"

"Nope. He seemed kind of . . . I don't know. Angry, but keeping a lid on it. Now I understand. If my niece had been murdered, I don't know what I'd do."

I paid for my lunch, including a substantial tip, and left.

Bridgeport, the county seat and the town where the man who had left Hobo's with Miri lived, was some thirty miles northwest on Highway 395. I knew of a cutoff that would take me there from this road. It was early yet, and I didn't feel like going back to the ranch—there would surely be a call from Ted pleading for me to open up to him—so I decided to drive up north and see if I could find the hardware store owner, Cullen Bradley.

Bridgeport is a charming town, with its stately eighteen-eighties courthouse, old homes, and steepled churches. Once known as Big Meadows because of the vast grazing land around it, it's also an outdoor person's paradise, surrounded by pristine lakes and streams for fishing or boating. Its greatest claim to fame is that it was used as the location for many of the scenes in the classic 1947 film

noir *Out of the Past.* Hy disputes that; he says its claim to fame is being the only place that a drunken young man succeeded in lassoing and pulling down a street lamp from the bed of a moving pickup. The young man, of course, was Hy—whose reward for his feat was having to perform community service and pay for a new light pole. Every now and then when we're there we visit it, and he says someday he's going to mount a plaque on it.

I found Bradley's Hardware on a side street two blocks from the courthouse. It had a graveled parking lot in back; I pulled in, left the Land Rover there, and entered through the rear door. I love hardware stores and this smelled like a good one: not the sanitized, filtered odor of a Home Depot, but a mixture of wood and metal and paint and other unidentifiable but appropriate items. The bare floors were warped, the shelves sagging under their wares. I had to weave my way through a warren of aisles to get to the front. Immediately a friendly young clerk appeared and asked if he could help me find anything.

"Is Mr. Bradley in?"

"He's in his office, but . . . If you're selling something, I wouldn't bother him today."

"How come?"

He leaned forward and said in a whisper, "Bad night. He had me bring him some of what he calls 'hair of the dog' a while ago."

"Well, this is a personal matter. I'll take my chances."

"Back that way." He jerked his thumb toward a door behind the sales counter. "Good luck."

The door was slightly ajar. I knocked and called out to Bradley.

"What?" A shade irritable, but not too bad. The dog's hair must have been working.

"May I come in?"

"If you must." As I moved through the door, he added, "Who the hell are you?" He was a red-faced, fortyish man with a shock of gray-blond hair, and his skin had that flaccid look that a night of hard drinking will produce.

I introduced myself, said I was looking for a friend of his who had been with him at Hobo's in Vernon the night before. "The bartender said you called him Dino."

"Dino Martin. His parents named him for the singer. Funny thing is, he can't hold a note. Sounds like my old hound dog when he tries."

"Where can I reach him?"

"Why do you want to?"

"A friend of mine left the bar with him. She hasn't come home, and I'm worried."

"You must mean Miri Perez."

"Yes."

"Well, she's probably shacked up with him someplace. It's kind of what she does."

"Still, I'd like to talk with him."

He hesitated. "Okay. Try Martin Realty, a block west."

I thanked him and left him to his hangover.

Martin's Realty was a small storefront whose windows were plastered with fliers featuring their listings. There were two desks arranged in the front room, but no one was seated at them. A pair of doors opened to the rear, one of which bore a placard saying DINO MARTIN. I knocked and a gravelly voice said to come in.

Martin could not have less resembled the famed singer after whom he'd been named. He was bald except for a badly dyed fringe of black hair and a short, sparse beard. His eyes were red and puffy; purple veins stood out on his large nose. I judged him to be on the far side of fifty. As I

stepped into the office, he picked up a coffee mug with a shaking hand and gulped its contents.

More dog hair?

I introduced myself, said I was a friend of the Perez family.

"And who the hell're they?"

"Miri Perez's relatives. You were with her last night in Hobo's—"

"Oh, that crazy bitch."

"You left with her, said something about going to the Outhouse."

"Yeah. I figured it was the only bar between Vernon and Bridgeport she hadn't been thrown out of yet."

"But you didn't go there."

He put a hand over his eyes like a visor, as if it hurt to look up, and motioned for me to sit down on the chair across from him. "No, we didn't. I was reasonably sober when we left Hobo's, but after what happened, I tied one on when I got back to town. The wife's ready to kill me."

"What happened?"

"Wait a minute. Why're you so interested in Miri?"

"She hasn't been seen since you two left the bar together."

"Hey, I don't know where she is."

"No? Why'd you tie one on after you got back here?"

"... I ... She ... Oh, dammit!"

"Why don't you just tell me?"

"Why should I?"

I took out one of my cards and slid it across the desk to him. "Legally I'm bound to report what I know to the sheriff's department. The deputies will get around to you soon."

"Oh, God. Okay, okay. We were a ways out of town.

She was getting cozy, putting her hands on me, you know what I mean? I thought I was gonna get lucky, take her to a friend's cabin near there that I've got a key to. But all of a sudden she's screaming for me to pull over. I did, right quick—thought she was gonna puke."

"And?"

"Across the highway there's this rundown trailer park. Cop cars all over the place, and an ambulance was pulling out. Miri went nuts. Jumped out of my Jeep and ran across the highway without even looking. Lucky there wasn't anybody coming."

"Did you follow her?"

"Shit, no. I don't mess with cops if I can help it. I've already had two DUIs. And if what was going on was as bad as it looked, I sure didn't want to get involved. The wife—"

"So you just left Miri there."

"Damn right. I didn't owe her a thing. She was just this bitch I picked up in a bar." He took a vodka bottle from the shelf behind his desk, poured into the mug, and drank, flashing me a childishly defiant look. "How much would it cost me to keep you from telling the sheriff?"

"No sale, Mr. Martin. It doesn't work that way."

For some reason my cellular was out of range in Bridgeport, so I found a phone booth—one of the few of that endangered species—and called Drew Warnell, the sheriff's deputy I'd talked with last night at the crime scene. He confirmed that Miri Perez had run across the highway as the ambulance containing her daughter's body was pulling away.

"She went into a total meltdown when I told her what had happened. Assaulted me and another deputy." He

sounded as if he were still shaken by the incident. "We had to restrain her, and now she's up here in the Bridgeport psych ward on a seventy-two-hour hold."

I took down the information about Miri, then called the Perez house. Sara answered and said Ramon had come home shortly after I'd left.

"The fool went all the way to Bridgeport and checked out some bars and a few off-hours places he knows about, but Miri hadn't been to any of them. Then he started back, but was too tired to drive all the way and fell asleep in Miri's van at a rest stop."

That was a relief. Now Ramon could deal with the mess I'd uncovered.

I said, "Well, he can stop worrying about Miri. I'm in Bridgeport, and the sheriff's department tells me she's in the psych ward up here." I explained what Drew Warnell had told me. "She wouldn't give them any information about next of kin, so they couldn't contact you."

Sara sighed deeply. "Maybe now she'll get the help she needs."

"Yes." But I doubted that, knowing how our broken health-care system works—especially for the poor.

"I'll let Ramon know," Sara said. "Thank you so much, Sharon."

"I'm happy to help."

But as I hung up, I realized the words were false. The day had cost me, a reminder of too many years of visiting sleazy bars and talking to sleazy characters. Now I had a long ride home, and nothing but an empty evening to look forward to.

The lights were out in the Perez house when I arrived at the ranch; probably they were up in Bridgeport dealing

with Miri. Damn! Amy missing, Hayley murdered, Miri out of control—how could so much bad happen to good people like Ramon and Sara?

I glanced at the stable, wondering if Ramon had had time to feed Lear Jet. Probably not. I might as well do it.

The horse was in his stall. When he saw me he snorted and looked away.

I said, "Look, you damn creature, I'm here to do you a favor."

I went to the bin where Ramon kept the alfalfa, measured out the amount I'd seen him give the horse, and started back toward the stall.

Lear Jet moved restlessly, snorted.

I tensed and stopped. "Hey, there. Take it easy."

The horse reared and let out a high-pitched whinny. His hooves smacked the stall door, splintering its brittle old wood.

I dropped the food and backed toward the outer door.

What you need to do is show them that you're in control.

Ramon's words.

Move away slowly.

Something I'd read in an article about how to behave in an encounter with a mountain lion.

Get the hell out of here.

My philosophy.

Before I could turn tail, Lear Jet kicked free from the stall and charged at me.

I sidestepped, then scrambled backward toward the outer door. The horse came on. I feinted the other way, momentarily confusing him. As he passed I felt a sharp blow on the back of my head. My eyes lost focus. The last thing I remembered was grasping the wall and sliding down. . . .

*   *   *

"Sharon." Sara's voice, commanding. "Wake up."

"Unh." I could hear, but not see, her.

A sharp, unfamiliar scent in my nostrils. One of her native remedies? But why couldn't she let me sleep?

"Wake up." Insistent.

I opened my eyes. Her round face came into focus.

She held up her hand. "How many fingers do you see?"

Stupid question. "Two."

"Good. Do you know where you are?"

"Mmm." I felt the ground around me. Wooden floor with scattering of straw. Now I remembered. That damn horse! "Stables."

"Very good. Let's sit you up now."

She took hold of me under my armpits, eased me up till my back was against the wall.

"Ramon and I saw the horse running free. I thought I'd better check in here."

"What time is it?" I asked.

"Eight fifty-five."

I'd come out here at about 8:45. I couldn't've been out more than a few minutes.

"Let me look at your head."

It was already bowed forward. I felt her fingers probing, winced when they touched a tender spot.

"Not so bad," she said. "No cuts or abrasions, but you could have a mild concussion. I'll take you back to the house in a few minutes and stay with you tonight. If there are any complications, we'll go to the emergency clinic in the morning."

Hooves clopping. I jerked my head up, wrenching my neck. Ramon, leading Lear Jet into the stable.

"Get him away from me!" I said. "He tried to kill me."

Ramon frowned and looked at Sara. She shook her head.

He said, "The horse was spooked—"

"Damn right he was!"

"But not by you," Sara added.

"What d'you mean?"

"The bump on your head isn't anything he could have inflicted. I'd say someone else was here, possibly antagonizing him. When Lear Jet bolted, whoever it was hit you."

"But why . . . ?"

"I don't know," Ramon said.

I thought—fuzzily—of the people whom I'd come in contact with the whole day. Of others who might have felt they had reason to harm me. Of the rippling shadow at Willow Grove Lodge.

No. Not again. That part of my life was supposed to be over!

Thursday

◆

NOVEMBER 1

When I awoke, Sara was sitting in the rocking chair in the corner of Hy's and my bedroom, her hands manipulating knitting needles and red yarn. She looked up when I stirred.

"Good morning, Sharon. How're you feeling?"

I took inventory, touching my head. There was a fair-sized lump behind my right ear, but strangely it didn't hurt much. "Not bad."

"I put some ointment on your scalp last night. It must have helped."

Vaguely I remembered the earthy smell and oily feel of it. "It did. One of your concoctions?"

"Of course. Are you seeing all right?"

"Yes."

"No headache, or sickness in your stomach?"

"None."

"Then I prescribe twenty-four hours bed rest, and

you'll be fit as ever." She finished a row of knitting and began putting the needles and yarn away in a brightly colored tote bag.

"Thank God you were there last night, Sara. When I didn't see any lights at your place I thought you and Ramon had gone to Bridgeport. That's why I was trying to feed Lear Jet."

"We'd planned to go up there, but when we called the sheriff's department they said Miri couldn't have any visitors until this afternoon. And Ramon made the . . . arrangements for Hayley by phone, and then we went out for dinner at Zelda's. We thought we owed ourselves a nice meal—"

A knock at the bedroom door, and Ramon entered, eyes downcast as if he was afraid I might be scantily clad. No chance of that—Sara had enveloped me in a big terry cloth bathrobe of Hy's. She'd seemed somewhat scandalized that I didn't possess a proper nightgown.

"How are you?" he asked.

"Fine. Sara's given me a clean bill of health."

"Only if you stay in bed today," she said.

I raised my hands in a gesture of surrender.

Ramon said, "I've been thinking about what happened last night. I've been around horses all my life. I can feel what they're feeling. Lear's been testing you, but he would never attack—especially when you were bringing food to him. Somebody else had to be there. Somebody he *would* attack."

"Who?"

"One person comes to mind: Boz Sheppard. He did some work up here a while back, rebuilding part of the pasture fence. He deviled the horse, and when I told him to stop, I suspect he kept on doing it behind my back. Lear

landed him a good kick on the shoulder the last day he worked here."

"But what would Sheppard be doing here last night? And why would he hit me?"

Didn't add up, any of it.

I kept my promise to stay in bed until noon. Then restlessness got the better of me. I got up, showered, and dressed. Had some toast and coffee. Sara's remedies had worked their magic, and I decided to do something nice for her and Ramon: I'd spend the afternoon making a casserole for them for when they returned, stressed and tired, from Bridgeport.

Trouble was, I have a limited repertoire of specialties that runs along the lines of garlic bread, spaghetti, stuffed sourdough loaves, and dressing for the holiday turkey. Hy cooks more than I do; we eat out frequently; I'm the expert on prepackaged foods and the microwave.

When I got back to the ranch house I located an old cookbook—*The Woman's Home Companion*—that I recognized as being one of my mother's bibles, my grandmother's before her. There were a couple of simple recipes for noodle casseroles that I decided to combine, but I didn't have the ingredients; I made a list and set out for town.

Day after Halloween: smashed pumpkins in the streets, trees draped with toilet paper; some windows soaped; candy wrappers on the sidewalk. Simple, old-fashioned mischief, the kind we haven't had in the city in some years. For safety reasons, trick-or-treating doesn't happen in most neighborhoods there, and pranks are usually on the vandalous side. Many times Halloween parties end in injuries and fatalities.

Of course, the day before Halloween here had been fatal for Hayley Perez. A reminder that no matter where you are, the world is a dangerous place.

The scarecrow in the Food Mart's parking lot had been dismembered: its head lay on top of the bales of hay, its clothes strewn around. Black spray paint on the white wall said THE DEVEL MADE ME DO IT! No one ever said graffiti artists can spell.

I went inside, made my selections, and took them to the same checker I'd spoken with last Tuesday night. While she was ringing the order up she asked, "Did you find Amy Perez?"

"No, I haven't."

"You hear about her sister, Hayley?"

"The woman who was murdered? Yes."

"I'm wondering: Amy didn't come in to work today, and nobody's seen her. Maybe she and that scumbag Boz Sheppard killed her sister and took off. Nobody's seen him, either."

"Why would they do such a thing?"

"Money. I hear Hayley had a big life-insurance policy."

"Oh, yeah? How much?"

"Not sure, but they say Amy was the beneficiary."

"Who says this?"

"Well, everybody." She swung out her arm to include the whole store, maybe the whole town.

Small-town gossip. One misleading remark, and everybody thinks it's gospel.

Still, I asked, "D'you know what company insured her?"

"There's only one broker in town—Bud Smith. He represents a lot of companies."

"But Hayley had been gone a long time; she must've taken out the policy somewhere else."

"She's been back long enough. Was staying with Boz Sheppard out in that trailer where she was killed. Didn't show her face in town much, though."

"Why not?"

The clerk shrugged. "Ashamed because she ran off and came back with nothing to show for it? Didn't want to run into her mother? I mean, who *does* want to run into Miri? You should ask Bud Smith."

Bud Smith was in his mid-forties and losing his blond hair; a short military-style cut couldn't disguise it. He was lean and wiry, dressed in a loud plaid polyester jacket that was decades out of date and a shirt and tie of the same era. Obviously a fan of vintage clothing. He was on the phone when I entered his office in a lakeside strip mall, but greeted me with a smile and waved me toward a chair.

The smile faded as he said into the phone, "No, stay there. Stay right there. I'll come as soon as I can."

For a moment after he hung up he stared down at the desk. Then he looked at me and said, "What can I do for you?"

When I said I was helping the Perez family deal with the details of Hayley's death, his face grew even more somber: he reminded me of an eccentrically attired funeral director.

"Such a tragedy," he said, "such a waste." His sorrowful expression looked genuine.

"We understand Hayley had taken out a life-insurance policy with you. And that the beneficiary was her younger sister, Amy."

"Uh, yes, she did." He began fiddling with a stack of papers on his desk, tapping them into a neat pile. "Are you putting in a claim? If so, Amy should be the one—"

"Amy's out of town and we haven't been able to reach her. Basically, all we want to know is if the policy exists and what its terms are."

"Hayley should have had the policy in her possession. She picked it up"—he flipped backward through his desk calendar—"on September twenty-sixth."

So she'd been in town for quite a while. Why, as the clerk at the Food Mart had said, hadn't she "shown her face"?

I said, "Perhaps she put it in a safe place. The trailer where she was staying wasn't very secure."

"Apparently not, since she was murdered there." Smith hesitated, running his hand over his clean-shaven chin. "I'm not sure I should be discussing the policy with you. Are you a relative?"

"A good friend. Ramon Perez is manager at my husband's and my ranch."

"Oh, you're Hy Ripinsky's new wife. I heard he got married again. Forgive me. I'll be glad to tell you anything you need to know."

I love to ask questions in small towns where I'm an insider. Hate it when I'm an outsider and they raise the bar against me.

Bud Smith went to a file cabinet and came back to his desk with a slim manila folder. "She came in on September seventh. Said her mother was unreliable—which is true—and that her other siblings, except for Amy, were either dead or in prison. She wanted to provide for Amy should something happen to her. We agreed on a fifty-thousand-dollar whole-life policy, which would accumulate a cash value that could be withdrawn at any time if Hayley, as owner of the policy, needed money."

"Why fifty thousand?"

"The premiums were affordable, and Hayley felt it was enough to give Amy a new start in life."

"She explain what she meant by that?"

"No. And I didn't ask. I don't pry into my clients' personal affairs."

"Did Hayley have to undergo a medical exam to get the coverage?"

"Not at twenty-five. She filled out the usual health disclosure form; that was enough."

"And what address did she give you?"

He consulted the file. "Her mother's, but she asked the policy not be sent there, which is why she picked it up."

"This type of policy—is there a double indemnity clause, in case of accidental death or murder?"

The right corner of Smith's mouth twitched. "Yes. Of course. Unless she was killed by the beneficiary . . . Not that Amy would've done such a thing. The girl's a little wayward, but not bad."

"How d'you know?"

"My avocation is volunteering as a life-skills coach. Helping kids who are at risk. My friend Dana Ivins, who runs the organization, had several sessions with her. She—Dana—thought Amy had great potential."

"This organization is called . . . ?"

"Friends Helping Friends. The name is designed to let troubled teens know we coaches don't consider ourselves superior, but just people who've undergone and overcome the same obstacles they're facing."

"Sounds like a good program."

Bud Smith's smile was a shade melancholy. "We try. That's all we can do—try."

*   *   *

Friends Helping Friends operated out of a dilapidated cottage on an unpaved side street at the west end of town, across the highway from the point where Zelda's was situated. A sign on the door said COME RIGHT IN, so I did. A short hallway opened in front of me. To my left was a parlor full of shabby but comfortable-looking furnishings; in the room to my right, a thin woman with short gray hair and round glasses that gave her face an owlish look sat at a desk. She saw me and smiled.

"What can I do for you?"

I introduced myself. "I'm interested in speaking with one of your coaches, Dana Ivins."

"You are in luck." She got up and extended her hand across the desk to me. "I'm Dana."

"Bud Smith told me you've been working with a girl named Amy Perez."

She frowned. "Sit down, please. I'm afraid Bud shouldn't have revealed that. Part of our success is that we keep our clients' names confidential."

"Would you explain to me how the organization works?"

"Well, the name describes it. We pair young people who are at risk with coaches who have had similar problems earlier in life. They can meet here in our parlor if the clients' homes aren't a supportive environment—which in most cases they're not—or if they aren't comfortable being seen with their coaches in public. Or they can pick another meeting place—so long as it isn't the coach's home; that's inviting trouble from parents who resent our intrusion. We listen to the clients' stories and tell them ours and what we've learned from them. It's strictly a volunteer program with very little overhead, and what there is is funded by donations from local businesses. This is my house, so we don't have to pay for offices."

"Are you licensed therapists?"

"No, just amateurs who've learned from our past mistakes."

So they couldn't legally claim therapist-client confidentiality.

"Ms. McCone," Dana Ivins said, "what is your interest in Amy Perez?"

I told her the same story I'd told Bud Smith, explaining my relationship to the Perez family.

"I see." She pushed away from her desk and swiveled slightly to her left, toward the front window that overlooked the street. "Are you sure Amy is missing?"

I wasn't. Right at this moment she could be with Ramon and Sara, but some instinct made me doubt that. I'd formed a tentative connection with the young woman the first time I looked into her eyes in the Food Mart parking lot, and it had been strengthened by the fear and defiance I saw in them after Boz Sheppard threw her out of his truck.

I said, "She didn't contact her family about Hayley or go to work today." Then I described my encounter with Amy alongside the highway.

Dana Ivins took off her glasses and chewed thoughtfully on one earpiece, still looking toward the window. "I knew your husband's first wife. Julie was a wonderful person; in spite of her health problems, she did a lot for the community. After she died, I was sure Hy was done for—the environmental protesting with a nasty edge, being thrown into one jail after another. Then, because of another special woman, he settled down. That, apparently, was you."

"Yes."

"Then I'm inclined to trust you. And I will tell you about Amy Perez."

Amy, Dana Ivins said, was highly intelligent but struggled with low self-esteem. "Her home life is chaotic—it's not easy being the daughter of the town slut. I know, because that's what my own mother was. Amy's response was the same as mine: she dropped out of school and set about creating the kind of life she thought she deserved, which included alcohol, drugs, and bad choices when it came to boyfriends. She was arrested once for underage drinking and put in an alcohol education program, which did no good whatsoever. There was another arrest for possession of marijuana, but the charges were dismissed because the quantity was so small and Amy claimed it must have been her mother's."

"Great family dynamics working there."

"I'm inclined to think she was telling the truth: the jacket she was wearing belonged to Miri. Anyway, the home situation became intolerable. Amy stopped living there, began moving from one boyfriend's place to another's. She had two abortions in as many years. The boyfriends invariably abused her and then threw her out. When she came to us, she was squatting in one of the cabins at Willow Grove Lodge."

"And how did she come to you?"

Dana Ivins smiled. "Very directly, if unintentionally. I went to my car one morning and found her passed out in the backseat. If there was ever a candidate for Friends Helping Friends, Amy was the prototype. I woke her and took her into the house. Got her cleaned up—she'd thrown up on herself—and loaned her a pair of my sweats. We talked."

"And then . . . ?"

"I found her a place to stay with a friend who rents out rooms. Talked the manager of Food Mart into taking her on part time as a shelf stocker. And she began to work on

getting her GED. She stayed clean and sober and didn't see any of her old boyfriends. But then she started to backslide."

"When?"

"It's difficult to pinpoint, because it was subtle at first. A month ago? Maybe even six weeks. At first she'd miss scheduled appointments, but she always had a good excuse. Then she slacked off on her work for the GED. She kept working at Food Mart, but the manager told me her attitude wasn't good. And finally she moved out of her room at my friend's house without giving any notice."

"To go where?"

Ivins shook her head. "My friend didn't know. When I asked Amy, she said she'd moved home because her mother needed her. But she never would have done that; she hates Miri."

"People like Miri are good at emotional blackmail. Maybe—"

"No. Amy had come too far for that. I know; I've been there. Besides, I could tell she was lying. When she lies she gives it away by letting her eyes slide away from yours so they're looking at your left earlobe."

Everybody, except for the most accomplished sociopath, has some mannerism that gives him or her away in a lie. Not every lie, but if the stress level is high enough, it'll manifest itself. I've seen it thousands of times: eye movement, facial tics, changes in vocal pitch, tapping fingers, crossing and recrossing of legs—you name it. Once you pinpoint it, you have a better tool than a lie detector.

"When was the last time you saw Amy?" I asked.

"At least a week ago."

"And how did she seem?"

"I didn't really speak with her. She was stocking the

bins in the produce area at Food Mart, and I was in the checkout line."

"This was someone you'd been counseling and had cause to be concerned about, and you—"

"One of the philosophies of our organization is that the clients must be motivated to come to *us*; otherwise the process doesn't work."

I wasn't so sure that was such a good approach, but then, I had no real background in their brand of therapy. Look at how miserably my own recent attempt had failed. "Okay, the time before that . . . ?"

"Weeks before. Amy came here, and we talked in the parlor. She was having trouble with one of her GED courses—algebra—and it was frustrating her. I'm no whiz at math myself, so I advised her to reread the materials and go slowly. I told her if she was still having trouble, I'd locate someone who could tutor her."

"And did you?"

"Yes. I referred her to Bud Smith. Anyone who can figure out insurance-rate tables should be able to explain algebra."

But Smith hadn't mentioned that to me when he spoke of Amy.

"Did she contact him?"

"I don't know. I never heard from her again."

Bud Smith's office was closed. A sign on the inside of the door said he wouldn't return till two. I considered my options, then headed for Zelda's for a burger and a beer, where the owner, Bob Zelda, and I caught up on our personal current events. Afterward I went back to Smith's office. The sign still said back at two, but he wasn't there.

The provisions I'd bought for the Perezes' casserole had

been sitting in the Land Rover too long; I drove back to the
ranch and cooked. The process of grating cheese, slicing
ham and mushrooms, and blending a sauce soothed me. I
put the casserole in the oven along with a smaller one for
my own dinner, set the timer, and went to the living room
to read. After a few pages I dozed off in the comfy over-
sized chair. It was almost time for the casserole to come
out when the phone woke me.

Sara. "Sharon, how are you?"

"Doing splendidly, thanks to you. How's Miri?"

"Going through the d.t.'s. The seventy-two-hour hold
is still on; they want to evaluate her and recommend
treatment."

"Well, that's good, isn't it?"

"It's happened before, and nothing's worked." She
paused. "Ramon wants to talk to you."

Ramon sounded weary. "You're all right?"

"Yes. Did you talk with the sheriff's deputy about Hayley while you were up there?"

"Yeah. There's somebody new in charge of the case—
Kristen Lark."

"So she's still with the department. How come I didn't
see her at the scene the other night?"

"You know her?"

"From a long time ago."

"Well, she was on vacation. Got handed the case this
morning."

"If you like, I can contact her and try to find out more
about the investigation."

"Sharon, you're up here for a vacation—"

"It's no problem. I just fell asleep reading. I think I'm
getting bored."

"Well, then . . ."

"Ramon, have you heard from Amy?"

"Uh-uh. Don't know where she's gone off to and, frankly, I'm worried. Her sister's murder has been all over the news; she should've called us by now."

"Did Lark ask you about her?"

"No. Why?"

"She probably will." I explained about the life-insurance policy.

Ramon groaned. "Little Amy. She couldn't've—"

"No, I don't think so. But I'm worried about her, too." To change the subject, I told him about the casserole I'd made and said I'd bring it over.

"Sharon, thank you. Sara's in the kitchen trying to defrost some chicken in the microwave, but it's not going so good. But don't bother to bring the casserole over; I'll come get it when I feed Lear Jet."

"No, let me feed him and then bring the food over." As soon as the words were out of my mouth, I regretted them.

"You sure you want to?"

I couldn't back down now. "Yes."

"Okay. But take him a couple of pieces of carrot if you have any. Treats are the best way to make friends with a horse."

The horse was in his stall, looking dejected. I approached cautiously, and he whickered. When I offered the first piece of carrot, he looked at it for a moment, then reached forward and gently took it from my fingers. I waited, then offered one more. Again he was gentle.

"I'll feed you in a minute," I told him. "I suppose I should clean your stall, but I'd better leave that to Ramon. Tell the truth, I'm afraid of you."

The horse regarded me solemnly.

"Who spooked you?"

Lear shifted his feet, thrust his head forward. And then he nuzzled my hand. After a moment's hesitation, I stroked his nose. He nuzzled some more. Probably hungry, I thought.

I fed him and left to deliver the casserole to Ramon and Sara.

This dozing off is dreadful.

It was the first thought that came to me when I woke an hour after I'd eaten and sat down to read the book I'd been trying to get through for over a week. I'd dreamed. . . .

Not of the pit or Amy this time—something else, a line of poetry over and over again. It still reverberated in my mind. . . .

I tossed the paperback on the floor. To hell with the former alcoholic and his non-midlife crisis!

In the kitchen I grabbed the keys to the Land Rover from the counter, took down the shearling jacket from its peg in the mudroom. Then, heeding an instinct I'd many times before recognized to be sound, I went to the bedroom, where we kept a .45 automatic—Hy's weapon of choice—in a locked cabinet. Checked its clip. Put it in the jacket's deep pocket, and set out for Willow Grove Lodge.

Home is the place where . . .

The line from Robert Frost's "Death of the Hired Man" was what had echoed in my dream and now filled my mind as I drove.

Amy hadn't had a real home in years—maybe ever—but Willow Grove Lodge, where Dana Ivins had said she'd

been squatting in one of the cabins, was the place she'd be most likely to return to after giving up her rented room. And it was only a short way up the highway from where Boz Sheppard had pushed her out of his truck.

I pulled into the driveway there, coasted down the slope, and cut off the headlights as I tucked the Land Rover out of sight behind the main building. Dark and silent there, no lights showing in any of the cabins, not even exterior security spots. I leaned over to take a powerful flashlight from the pocket behind the seat.

The outside air was chill. The moon had waned, but when I looked up I saw a thick cluster of stars that were part of the Milky Way. The wind rustled the leaves of the cottonwoods and willows. I began walking upslope to the lodge's entrance.

It was solidly padlocked, the windows secured by shutters. I walked around the main building, shining my light, then went to the first of the cabins, the one where I'd stayed years ago. Also padlocked and shuttered. Silver phosphorescent letters were sprayed on the wall next to the door: APRIL & KEITH 4 EVER.

I wished the couple luck, whoever they were.

I shone my light around, picking out the shapes of the other cabins. If I were going to squat here, I'd choose one far from the road, but not too near the lake, where passing boaters might spot evidence of my presence. A tiny one-room cabin surrounded by trees stood right over there, not thirty yards away. There was no outward sign of habitation, but that didn't mean anything. Amy would hardly make a fire in the woodstove or open the shutters if she didn't want to be detected.

Slowly I moved toward the cabin, flashlight in my left hand, right hand on the .45. I doubted Amy would be any

threat to me, but if someone, say Boz Sheppard, was with
her—

Screech!

I started, heard the flapping of wings. An owl speeding
away with its prey.

Laughing softly at my edginess, thinking of how such
a sound wouldn't begin to penetrate my consciousness in
the city, I went ahead toward the cabin.

The shutters were secure, and there was a hasp and
padlock on the door, but when I touched the lock, it swiveled open. I removed it quietly, slid back the hasp, eased
open the door—

A dark figure rushed at me. I tried to dodge, but the
person came on too fast, hunched over, head slamming
into my chest so hard that I expelled my breath with a
grunt and reeled backward. My feet skidded on the layer
of slippery fallen leaves. And down I went on my ass.

Stunned, I took a few seconds to realize that my assailant had run off, was thrashing around in the dark grove.
I pushed up, and—holding the gun in both hands—ran
toward the source of the sounds. My breath tore at my
lungs and sharp pains spread out from my tailbone.

Suddenly the sounds stopped.

I stopped, too, looking around. Nothing moved. The
only thing I could hear was my own panting.

*Whoever it is, they're hiding. That's all right; I can
wait them out.*

I crept over to a thick tree trunk, leaned against it, getting my breathing under control. My lower back throbbed,
and so did my head. What if I really had sustained a concussion last night, and my heavy fall to the ground had
made it worse?

It was frigid under the trees: I could see my breath.

Staying still was an invitation to frostbite. After a few minutes I moved in the direction where I'd last heard the thrashing sounds, placing my feet carefully, as silently as possible. I'd dropped my flashlight back at the cabin, but that didn't matter; using it would have given away my position.

The woods are lovely, dark and deep. . . .

Frost again. But these woods weren't lovely. They were silent, full of potential hazards.

The hell with it.

I retraced my steps to the cabin, where I located the flash and shone it through the open door.

What I saw made me raise the .45.

More wreckage like that at Boz Sheppard's trailer: overturned furniture, broken glass, linens pulled from the bed, pillows and mattress slashed, drawers in the tiny galley kitchen emptied. A door to the bathroom stood partway open.

I slipped inside and across the room. In the bath I found more broken glass and a torn shower curtain, its pole slanting down into the tub. The lid of the toilet had been removed and smashed on the floor. Otherwise the cubicle was as empty as the main room.

No one here, dead or alive.

I tried the light switch beside the bathroom door. No power, of course. My flash's beam was strong, but it wouldn't allow me to examine the place thoroughly. Besides, that was a matter for the sheriff's department.

I moved back into the other room. Stepped on something soft. When I looked closely I saw it was the quilted jacket Amy had been wearing the day Sheppard had thrown her out of the truck. My light illuminated other objects that had been strewn around: T-shirts, costume

jewelry, makeup, jeans, underwear, other teenage-girl attire.

And on the wall above them, a blood spatter.

I leaned against the Land Rover, bundled in the shearling coat, watching Lark's team examining what she'd termed a "possible crime scene." For a remote county that was probably operating on an insufficient salary budget, the deputies seemed well coordinated and knowledgeable. I'd seen less thorough initial investigations in the city. Not that that was any surprise: the SFPD has been through up-and-down cycles as long as I've lived there.

Lark finally approached me—a slender woman in her mid-thirties with blonde curls, worn long now, and freckles on her upturned nose. We'd spoken only briefly when she arrived and entered the cabin, not at all since her backup showed minutes later.

Now she said, "McCone, this scene looks bad. The place was tossed, there's blood in the main room, the girl's gone, and you say she's Hayley Perez's sister. How come you came here?"

"Someone told me—"

A man called out to Lark, and she held up a finger. "My forensics guy wants me. When I'm done with him, I'm going off duty. Let's meet at Zelda's, knock back a couple, and you can tell me what I need to know."

The cavernous interior of Zelda's was strangely quiet for a Thursday night. A couple of late diners lingered over coffee in the room to the left, and only a few drinkers gathered at the bar. Bob Zelda was absent—he'd told me he'd turned over the weekday-evening shifts to his son

Jamie; Bob worked the weekends because he liked to listen to the country-music bands he employed.

I took one of the tables by the lakeside windows in the bar area and waited for Kristen Lark to arrive. After ten minutes I went to the bar and got a glass of white wine. Sipping it, I realized why I usually ordered beer at Zelda's. Five minutes later Lark came through the door.

She pointed questioningly to my half-full glass. I shook my head, and she went to the bar; a minute later she was seated across from me with her own drink—a double bourbon.

"So, McCone, I hear you married Ripinsky."

"I did."

"I'm married, too." She held out her left hand; a wide gold wedding ring circled her third finger.

"Who's the lucky guy?"

"Fellow officer—Denny Rabbitt."

"You look good," I said. "Marriage agrees with you."

"Marriage to another deputy, yes. Anybody else couldn't've put up with the crazy schedule. Hy up here with you?"

"No. I'm taking some time off, but he's busy with a corporate reorganization."

She nodded, clearly having asked only for politeness' sake, placed a tape recorder on the table, and asked, "So what were you doing at the lodge tonight?"

I outlined everything that had happened since I spotted Amy Perez outside the Food Mart, while Lark taped the conversation. "I didn't mean to get involved in a police matter," I finished. "It just occurred to me that Amy might be squatting at Willow Grove, and I thought I might be able to persuade her to go to her aunt and uncle's."

Lark shrugged. "Seems we're having a regular crime

wave this week. You want to help me on an official basis? You did before, remember."

I solved your case for you and nearly lost my life in the process, you ingrate.

Lark waited for my answer.

I didn't want to help out. I didn't even want to be here talking with an officer of the law. But maybe I could find out some inside information about Hayley's murder that I could pass on to Ramon and Sara.

"Okay, but I told you everything I know; it's got to be a two-way street."

"Deal."

Lark turned off the tape, got up and went to the bar for another drink. When her back was turned I switched on the sensitive voice-activated recorder in my purse. The deputy hadn't asked if I minded being taped, and I wasn't going to ask her, either. She was fair, and a good law officer, but I was aware that our arrangement could backfire if I didn't have documentation.

"Okay," she said as she sat down again. "We didn't have the info on the sister having taken out the life-insurance policy. Hadn't really looked at Amy yet because we were concentrating on the Boz Sheppard angle. So far we haven't located him."

"You have any background on Hayley?"

Lark smiled. "Now *that* is where it really gets interesting."

Friday

✦

NOVEMBER 2

On my drive back to the ranch, I didn't dwell on the facts that Lark had confided to me. She'd insisted on buying another round before we'd left Zelda's at twelve-thirty, and even though I'd left most of my wine in the glass and was under the legal limit, I needed to pay close attention to my driving. High-desert people are generally hard-living folks, but it seemed to me that Lark, a law-enforcement officer and supposedly happy woman, had been pushing the envelope with her three double shots of bourbon.

The country around Tufa Lake is largely devoid of traffic at that time of night, and no wildlife sprang into my headlights, so I arrived home unscathed. There was a message on the machine from Hy: "Just wanted to let you know my ETA tomorrow—four p.m. See you then." Pause. "Does your absence indicate you've been 'sucked in' by the Perez murder?"

Damn! He knew me all too well.

But sucked in I was—and with official sanction. I curled up in the armchair in the living room and listened to the tape I'd made of Kristen Lark's confidences.

Haley and Rich Three Wings ran off nine years ago, ended up in Reno. He dealt blackjack at Harrah's, she worked someplace as a waitress, but pretty quick she started turning tricks on the side. . . .

Around three years after they got to Reno, this high roller came to the casino. Hayley was waitressing there by then, and next thing she ran off with the guy, leaving Rich with only his old car and the clothes on his back. . . .

No, we haven't found out who the high roller was. Rich claims he doesn't know. We've got an inquiry in to the casino, though. . . .

That's another thing we don't know—where she was during the period between when she left Reno and three years ago when she turned up in Vegas. Living off the high roller, no doubt, but it didn't last. . . .

In Vegas, she worked cocktails in a casino—the Lucky Sevens. Kind of downscale and dingy, LVPD says. So she went out on the streets again, got busted a few times, but always brought in a high-powered attorney who got the charges dropped. . . .

How could she afford the lawyer? Damned if we know. . . .

Name's Brower. Frank Brower. With a big firm that's rumored to be connected—Brower, Price and Coleman. Of course, everybody in Vegas is rumored to be connected. . . .

No, we haven't been able to get hold of him. He's on a cruise, or some damn thing. . . .

Yeah, we checked out the address on Hayley's driver's

license. A mail drop. We've got no idea where she was liv-ing in Vegas. . . .

Apparently nobody here knew she was back in town, except for that insurance agent you told me about. And Boz Sheppard. And maybe Amy. We've questioned every-body, including Rich Three Wings and her high-school boyfriend, Tom Mathers. . . .

Here's something: you might take another crack at Three Wings. I mean, he might open up more to you. . . .

I turned off the recorder. When, I wondered, would people stop assuming that because you're Indian, other Indians will feel a natural connection with you? There are hundreds of tribes in this country; historically some have been mortal enemies, and today they're squabbling over gaming rights. It's like saying any American ethnic group—be it blacks, Chinese, Italians, Irish, Japanese, or Germans—is drawn together because of its background. Ridiculous. The Scotch-Irish family who adopted me at birth frequently fought like they were out to kill each other. Still do, sometimes.

But what the hell, in the morning I'd take a crack at Rich Three Wings. Tom Mathers, too.

It was the least I could do for the sake of the Perez fam-ily, I told myself.

Well, yes, for their sake, but also for my own. Cases change both the investigated and the investigator. Maybe one last effort would show me the way to the new life I was reaching for. It wouldn't be any worse than dreaming of trying to climb out of a deep, dark pit.

Elk Lake was a small, placid body of water surrounded by forest, some twenty miles southwest of Vernon. Dirt roads led into clearings where rustic cabins stood. Many

of them had cutesy names: Gone Fishin', Bide a Wee Longer, My Lady and the Lake. Rich Three Wings' had no such sign and was one of the shabbier: warped shingles, sagging roofbeam, rusted stovepipe. A large prefab garage sat next to it, and an old International Harvester truck was pulled close to its side. From the rear I could hear the sound of someone chopping wood.

I rounded the cabin, and a spectacular view of the lake opened up: close to shore waterfowl swam and dove for food, far out two fishermen floated in their rowboat, the opposite shore was rimmed by tall pines. The scene was so peaceful that it stood out in sharp contrast to the man wielding the axe.

Wide-shouldered and narrow-waisted, he was without a shirt on this chilly day, and the muscles in his back were strong and sculpted. He attacked the log as if it were an enemy, with hard, rhythmic strokes and frequent animal-like grunts. He didn't hear me approach until I was half-way to him, and then he whirled, axe upheld. I stopped, braced to run.

"Rich Three Wings?" I asked.

"Yeah. Who're you?" His face was beaded with sweat, his long black hair trapped in a damp red bandana.

I introduced myself, taking out one of my business cards. He lowered the axe and leaned it against a larger log. At that I covered the rest of the distance between us and handed the card to him.

"I'm working in cooperation with the sheriff's department on the Hayley Perez case," I added.

He looked at the card, then crushed it in his large fist. His face twitched, as if he felt a sudden pain.

He asked, "They send you on account of you're Indian too?"

"That was the general idea."

"And you don't like it."

"I hate it. And so do you."

He studied me for a moment, then nodded, having made a judgment. "Come inside, we'll drink some coffee." When I hesitated, he added, "I'm harmless. I didn't kill Hayley and I'm sure as hell not gonna do anything to you."

No, he wasn't. That much I sensed. As to whether he'd killed his ex-wife I couldn't hazard a guess yet.

I followed him to the cabin and into a spotlessly neat room with beautifully hewn wooden furnishings and woven rugs like the ones we had at the ranch. Rich Three Wings noticed my surprise and said, "Appearances can be deceiving, huh?"

"I'll say. This is beautiful."

"Thanks. Have a seat." He motioned at a small table that gleamed with polish and shrugged into a sweatshirt that was draped on a chair. "How do you like your coffee?"

"Black."

"Me too." He went through a doorway, returned with two pottery mugs. "This place, I inherited it from my grandfather, who was a real traditional guy. Material possessions didn't mean a thing to him."

"Sounds like my . . . father." I still couldn't call Elwood Farmer my father without hesitation. "He's an artist and lives very simply on the Flathead rez in Montana."

"You born there?"

"No. It's complicated. This furniture . . ." I motioned around us.

"I made it. I've got a shop in the garage. And the rugs—my girlfriend weaves them. Between the two of us we do

pretty well, sell on the Internet and a few shops down in Sacramento and the city."

"It's lovely."

"But that's not what you came here to talk about. Your card says investigative services, and the county sent you."

"I'm a friend of the Perez family, but the deputy in charge of the case said it was okay to talk with you."

"How're you their friend? I haven't seen you around."

I explained my relationship with Ramon and Sara.

"Ripinsky's wife. I'll be damned. He was my hero, back when I was in high school. Real rabble-rouser, but the good kind. If it hadn't been for him, Tufa Lake'd be nothing but mud and crumbling towers by now." He paused. "So what d'you want to know about Hayley?"

"Why don't you give me a chronology of your relationship with her."

"Okay. She was in high school. Dating this asshole, Tom Mathers. I'd come back from a stint in the army; I'm six years older than her. I'd seen her around while I was growing up, but didn't pay her much notice. Then we met at a party. Mathers passed out in the bathroom, so I took her home. She told me how much she hated it here, one thing led to another, and a few weeks later we were on the road to Reno to get married."

"Did you?"

"Yeah. Crappy little wedding chapel, plastic flowers, JP and his wife were both weird. That kind of start, it's natural the wedding vows didn't take. Plus we didn't have much money and fought about it all the time. Three years later she split and I decided to come home. I couldn't take the crap I had to deal with at the casino and this place was waiting for me."

"Kristen Lark told me Hayley was hooking."

"Yeah, she was. I should've realized it, but I didn't—not till it was too late."

"I understand she took off with a high roller, but you don't know his name."

"I just told Lark that to keep the guy from getting in trouble. I mean, he couldn't've cared enough about Hayley to follow her here and kill her. His name was Jack Buckle. From someplace in the Pacific Northwest. I should've guessed what was going on with them, but I never thought . . . well, Hayley was not in this guy's class at all."

"How so?"

"He was rich, smart, and seemed educated. Hayley was just a small-town slut. I know that now, but at the time I was blind in love with her. But a lot of these rich guys, they either don't care or don't look farther than the end of their dicks."

"Did you hear from her again?"

"Only through the divorce papers six months later. By then I'd come back here, started woodworking. After that I never gave a thought to Hayley." He paused. "Well, that's not true. I thought about her some, sure. I hated her for what she did to me, but when I met Cammie—my weaver girlfriend—and things started working out with us, I cooled down."

"You didn't look so cooled down when I got here earlier."

He clasped his hands around the coffee mug, looked into its depths. "Yeah, well, when somebody you once loved is murdered—no matter how much bad they did to you—you get angry. I take my anger out on logs, not people."

"And you didn't know Hayley was back in Vernon?"

"No way. I'm pretty isolated out here. I make a point of

going to town only when I need to. Maybe Cammie knew; she lives in Vernon, spends the weekends here, working on her loom in the shop. But if she did, she didn't tell me."

"I'd like to talk to Cammie."

"I'm sure she won't mind. She works part time at the flower shop in town. In fact, she should be there this morning."

There was only one flower shop in Vernon—Petals, on the main street two doors down from Hobo's. When I walked in I breathed deeply of the fresh and fragrant scents; although a bell rang as I passed through the door, no one appeared, so I studied the simple arrangements in the cold case. Roses, carnations, the usual types. Not much variety, but they probably had little call for anything out of the ordinary.

As I was examining a shelf of houseplants, a woman came through a curtained doorway. She was around thirty, blonde, wearing red-rimmed glasses and a sweater to match. Dimples flashed when she smiled.

"Help you?"

"Are you Cammie?"

"That's right. Cammie Charles. And you are?"

I gave my name, handed her my card, and said, "I just had coffee with Rich Three Wings. He said you might be able to help me out."

"Sure. What d'you need?"

"Information. I'm cooperating with the sheriff's department on the Hayley Perez case."

A shadow crept into her gray eyes. "Poor woman. Rich was really upset when he heard she'd been murdered. I mean, they'd had some bad times, but she was his first love."

"He didn't know she was in town. Did you?"

Her gaze slid away from mine, down to an open book of FTD offerings. "Yeah, I did. Bud Smith mentioned it to me when we ran into each other on the street. I figured it was best not to tell Richie."

"Why?"

"Selfishness, mainly. I didn't want him to see her and maybe get involved again. She was so pretty. . . ."

"You knew her, then?"

"No. I'm not from around here. I came up from the Bay Area for a vacation, met Richie, and never left. But Hayley came into the shop a couple of weeks ago—the day after Bud was here—to order a funeral arrangement to be sent FTD. I recognized her name from her credit card. She's not as pretty as the picture of her I found in a box at Richie's place, but still . . ."

"You have a record of that sale?"

"Somewhere. Is it important?"

"Might be."

"Okay." She rummaged in a drawer under the counter for an order book and paged through it. "Here it is—Jack Buckle, address in Olympia, Washington."

Jack Buckle sounded very much alive when I called the phone number from the flower shop's order form. Amused, too.

"Hayley's idea of a joke," he told me. "She's sent me a funeral arrangement each year on the anniversary of the death of our relationship. I pass them on to the local cemetery."

"So you broke up on October . . . ?"

"October nineteenth, three years and some months after she came up here with me."

"And you've received an arrangement every year since?"

"The first arrived five days after the split. But why does your flower shop need that kind of information?"

I hadn't told him I was a flower shop employee, had just given him my name. Now I explained myself.

"Hayley's *dead*? *Murdered*?" He sounded genuinely shocked.

"Yes, Mr. Buckle. I'm sorry."

". . . Poor kid. She was a whore, and greedy like they all are, but she didn't deserve that."

"Tell me more about her."

"Let's see. . . . I was in Reno for an annual high-stakes poker game at a friend's home. Hayley was serving catered food from the casino to us. Pretty little thing, and afterwards I asked her to come back to my hotel with me. In the course of things she told me that she was with this guy who abused her, that she hated Reno and wanted to get out. So I said, why didn't she come along home with me? When I took her to their apartment she packed her stuff in fifteen minutes. I brought her back here to Olympia and we had fun till the fun ended."

"And why did it end?"

"Like I said, whores are greedy. She behaved for a couple of years, acted like a lady even, but I caught her sneaking cash from my wallet. As if I wasn't footing the bill for everything and also generous with an allowance. Finally, my maid told me Hayley'd been going through my home office, probably looking for the combination to the safe, and practicing signing my signature so she could forge checks."

"So you threw her out."

"No, ma'am. I politely told her to leave and asked her

where she wanted to go. To tell the truth, I felt sorry for the kid; she'd had a miserable upbringing. I didn't want to throw her onto the streets with nothing. She said she guessed she'd go to Vegas. So I bought her a plane ticket and gave her a little money to tide her over till she found a job—or another man. She must've done all right on one front or the other, because this year's funeral arrangement was an expensive one."

"Do you know an attorney in Vegas, Frank Brower, of Brower, Price and Coleman?"

"I've heard of him, but I've never made his acquaintance."

"He got Hayley off on a few charges of prostitution."

"Hard to imagine how she could afford that firm. They're corporate lawyers for some of the bigger casinos."

"One other question, Mr. Buckle, and then I won't take up more of your time: what is it you do for a living?"

"I'm chief counsel for the Northwest Council of God."

"The . . . ?"

"Northwest Council of God."

". . . Oh."

He laughed. "I said chief counsel, Ms. McCone. I'm not a member, and I don't abide by their beliefs, nor do they expect me to. They simply want good legal representation and they pay me a significant retainer."

"I see." The pragmatic approach to faith, or lack thereof. "The Mono County Sheriff's Department will be in touch with you shortly."

"I'll cooperate in any way I can."

Immediately after I ended my call to Jack Buckle, my phone rang. Lark.

"We've designated the cabin at Willow Grove as a possible homicide scene," she said. "We're asking local pilots

to help us out with an air search for a body tomorrow. Would you be willing to join in?"

I wanted to tell her she'd do better with cadaver dogs. It was unlikely a killer would have placed Amy's body out in the open where anyone could see it, and to a pilot flying at legal altitude over that thickly wooded terrain, a concealed corpse would be damned near impossible to spot.

But to keep on her good side I said, "Sure. Hy's coming up this afternoon: we'll both join in. One more thing: this Tom Mathers—I'd like to talk with him."

"No problem. He's at Tom's Wilderness Supplies and Vacations, about five miles out on the Rattlesnake Ranch Cutoff."

The terrain off Rattlesnake Ranch Cutoff was barren, like Mineral County over in Nevada. A few volcanically created formations stood out in the distance, but otherwise the land was flat and covered by coarse grass and sagebrush. Tom's Wilderness Supplies and Vacations, an orange-and-purple-trimmed stucco building with racks of rowboats and canoes at the back of the parking lot, was a bright, if gaudy, spot in the surrounding bleakness. A pair of dune buggies were pulled close to the building on the other side from the parking lot.

The building's interior was fairly large and crammed with all sorts of outdoors gear: backpacks, tents, stoves and lanterns, life jackets, fishing equipment, heavy-duty clothing—if you needed it, it was there. Tom Mathers was also a weapons dealer: guns gleamed in locked cases, in others knives glittered evilly under the fluorescent lights.

Guns I know, understand, and respect for their lethal potential. Knives scare the hell out of me.

The man behind the counter was in his mid-to-late

twenties: sandy-haired, sun-freckled and -tanned, with wide shoulders and biceps that bulged beneath his T-shirt. A bodybuilder, I guessed, as well as an outdoorsman. A cheerful one, too: he smiled as if his best friend had just walked in.

"What can I do you for?"

"Are you Tom Mathers?"

"The one and only."

I went through my friend-of-the-Perez-family, cooperating-with-the-sheriff's-department routine. Mathers' smile faded and he shook his head.

"Hayley. What a shame."

"Do you have any idea who might have killed her?"

Something moved deep in his eyes. He looked down at the knives in the case between us. "No idea at all. Everybody loved Hayley."

Bad body language; I didn't believe him. "Tell me about you and her."

"We went together all through high school. She never even looked at another guy. I thought we'd get married, have kids. Then this older guy shows up at a party, and a week later she's gone."

"I understand she left the party with him because you were passed out in the bathroom."

He shrugged. "That was no reason to run off with him. We partied pretty hard in those days. But she knew I would've straightened up. I mean, I've got a great business here, I'm married, own a house on the property." He jerked his thumb, indicating the house was behind the building. "No complaints from the wife, either—"

"A wife who was second choice and you're never going to let me forget it," a voice said from behind me.

I turned. A woman with long reddish-blonde hair

had come inside. She was trim and well muscled, wearing only a short-sleeved T-shirt and running shorts. Not pretty, as Hayley Perez had been, but strong-featured. Her mouth was bracketed with lines of disappointment—and she must have been all of twenty-five.

No complaints from the wife. Right.

"T.C.," her husband said, "this is a private conversation."

"Not if you're talking about me." She came over and extended her hand to me. "T.C. Mathers."

"Sharon McCone."

Tom Mathers said, "Ms. McCone's cooperating with the sheriff on Hayley Perez's murder."

T.C. rolled her eyes. "The sainted Hayley Perez. What I wonder is why somebody didn't shoot her years ago."

Tom's face reddened. "Theresa!"

She winked at me. "When he gets mad, he always calls me by my given name. Knows I hate it. When he's really mad, he calls me Theresa Christina. Gets to me because it reminds me of my goddamn reactionary Christian parents who saddled me with it."

I was not at all pleased that I'd walked into this situation. I looked at my watch. Nearing two-thirty, I hadn't had a bite to eat all day, and Hy's ETA was four.

I said, "I'd like to talk with both of you again, but there's someplace I have to be soon. May I call you here or at home?"

"We're in the book. Call or drop in. Just keep following the driveway to the house." Tom Mathers was trying to regain his former composure, but his stance radiated fury at his wife.

"I'll be in touch," I said, and walked away from their domestic conflict.

* * *

In town I bought a sandwich and a Coke before I made the drive to Tufa Tower Airport at the northwest end of the lake. It wasn't much: a single runway, a dozen or so planes in tie-downs, a hangar that hadn't housed a resident mechanic in years, and a shack where the manager—a garrulous septuagenarian named Amos Hinsdale—monitored the UNICOM and hoped that some fool would come in and rent one of his two dreadful planes. Normally I tolerated Amos, but today I wasn't in the mood for one of his monologues about the good old days when flying took a real *man's* skill. Forget Amelia Earhart; forget the Powder Puff Derby participants and the women who ferried planes for the military during World War II. Forget the fact that many women, including myself, frequently flew into Tufa Tower. In Amos' mind, aviation was a man's world—although he also thought that the current crop of male pilots, who used up-to-date computerized equipment, were "a bunch of sissies."

I parked behind the hangar where I couldn't be seen from the shack and ate my late lunch. Thought about the case—my absolute last one—and where it was going, where it might lead me. I came to no conclusions about either.

After half an hour I began watching the hills to the north. Hy's and my beautiful red-and-blue Cessna 270B appeared above them; soon I heard the drone of its engine. The wings dipped from side to side, then he executed a barrel roll—showing off, knowing I was waiting for him. Afterward he angled into the pattern, took the downwind leg, and turned for final. I was at our designated tie-down when he taxied over.

He shut down the engine and got out. As always, I felt a rush of pleasure.

This man is my husband; we'll be together the rest of our lives.

Silly thought, because we'd already spent years together before we impulsively flew to Nevada and were married by a judge in Carson City. But those years hadn't been easy. Neither had the past one. I'd had many moments of doubt, and a recent serious crisis that I wasn't sure the union could survive. But through it all, he'd been steady and true and honest. No more doubts. Not now, not ever.

I ran over, threw my arms around him. Kissed him and held on tight. When I stepped back he smiled, even white teeth showing under his swooping mustache. He wasn't classically handsome, with a hawk-like nose and strong, rough-hewn features. His unruly dark-blond hair was now laced with gray. But his loose stride and long, lean body drew the attention of women as he walked through a room. And he possessed one of the finest asses I'd ever seen.

He raised an eyebrow at me and said, "Jesus, McCone, you must've missed me."

"Let's tie down this plane and I'll take you home and show you how much."

"Now, that'll be pure heaven."

That night I did not dream of being trapped in a pit.

Saturday

✦

NOVEMBER 3

Numerous official choppers and private planes from surrounding counties were available for the air search. Hy and I flew together in our Cessna. The morning was crisp and clear, and we'd bundled up in down jackets, jeans, and fleece-lined boots. Hy had brewed an extra pot of coffee, and we took it along in a thermos. I piloted, since he'd had that pleasure on the trip up here.

It had been a while since I'd flown, and on liftoff I'd felt a tremendous rush. It made me realize how important not being earthbound was to me. My depression—these days always a background to whatever I was doing—slipped away, and I settled happily into what felt like a cocoon that only Hy and I could inhabit.

"You realize," I said through our linked headsets as we lifted off, "that this is an exercise in futility."

"Yeah, but you can't tell that to the sheriff's department. And it makes people feel like they're doing something to

help. Besides, maybe somebody in one of the choppers'll spot something." Helicopters are authorized by the FAA to fly at lower altitudes than fixed-wing aircraft, and thus are better for searches.

Hy removed a pair of binoculars from their leather case, and I set course toward the area we'd been assigned to search—a barren plain southeast of Rattlesnake Ranch, some ten miles from where Tom Mathers had his wilderness-guide business. The thousand-plus acres, Hy had told me, used to be a working cattle ranch, but had been sold off a decade or more before to a family from the East Coast, who tore down the existing buildings and put up a luxurious vacation home.

As we flew over the ranch, I saw a sprawling house—had to be a minimum of twenty thousand square feet—with a tile roof, various outbuildings, an airstrip, a tennis court, and a swimming pool.

"Who the hell *are* those people?" I asked.

"Don't know their name or much about them. The property sale was handled by a law firm, and the local real-estate agent who represented the sellers is mum on the subject. They fly in on a private jet, don't come to town at all, hire local staff who're sworn to secrecy about what goes on there. It's rumored that they're anything from exiled royalty to Mafia. I say they're just rich people who value their privacy."

"*Very* rich people."

"Well, sure." Hy was scanning the place with the binoculars. "Nobody in residence today—too chilly for them. They're probably off at a similar retreat on St. Bart's or Tahiti this time of year."

"By the way, that trip to Tahiti my travel agent wants to book us—"

"Will happen as soon as I get RI up and running properly. And after you decide what to do about your future."

We'd talked late into the last night about both subjects. Hy was committed to seeing Ripinsky International through the reorganization and then remaining at the helm. I'd told him I still didn't know what to do about my life or McCone Investigations. Maybe wouldn't know for quite some time. He'd reassured me: as long as the agency was running properly in my absence I had no problem.

"You know," he said after a moment of scanning the land beyond Rattlesnake Ranch, "a killer would have to be an idiot to abandon a body out here in the open."

"Exactly what I've been thinking." I switched the radio to the frequency designated for the search. Negative reports on all fronts.

I let the plane glide to a lower altitude, following a southeasterly course, to an area where snow-like volcanic ash covered the ground, peppered with small obsidian outcroppings and Jeffrey pines. Ash and glass, relics of an ancient conflagration; stubborn pines, reminders of nature's life force. Hy and I had often flown over here—

"Take it lower," he suddenly said.

I pulled back on the throttle, raised the nose to slow the plane. "You see something?"

"I'm not sure. Bank left."

I dipped the wing to a medium angle.

"Over there." He gestured, handed me the binoculars.

I peered through them, made out a brownish mass. "Dead pine. Or maybe a large animal."

"Pines and animals aren't shaped like that. Besides, look over there, behind that outcropping. It's a white truck."

I studied the terrain some more. "Right."

"Can you put down someplace nearby?"

"Not too far from the truck, yes. It'll be a rough landing, but—"

"We've made them before."

It *was* a rough landing, the wheels bumping over rocks and uneven ground—the kind that makes your heart race and your adrenaline surge, knowing that you've got whatever it takes to be a good pilot. As I braked to a stop, I thought, So aviation's a man's world, Amos? Hah!

We got our bearings and started off, boots crunching on the ashy, pebbled ground. The watery fall sunlight bore down, but the day hadn't warmed much; I wished I'd brought along some gloves. We topped a slight rise, where Hy raised the binoculars and looked around. "Over that way."

At first all I recognized was a sleeping bag. Olive drab—which had looked more like brown from the air. Then I made out the shape inside it. A large one.

I said, "It's not Amy. She's much smaller than whoever that is."

Hy moved toward it, and I followed. The bag was zipped to the top. I squatted and pulled the zipper down.

Sandy hair, a freckled face—formerly tanned, but now bluish white in death. No marks marred his features; he looked as if he'd crawled into the bag, zipped it up, and gone to sleep.

Tom Mathers, Hayley Perez's former boyfriend.

The man who, the last time I'd seen him, had been engaged in bitter conflict with his wife, T.C.

Hy stayed with the body while I went to the plane and contacted the search team's headquarters. They said they'd have a chopper there in ten minutes.

"When was it you last saw Mathers?" Hy asked when I returned.

"Around two-thirty yesterday afternoon."

"Well, he must've been here since last night or early this morning. There's no odor; the cold's pretty much preserved the body."

"Rigor?"

"I don't know. I don't want to disturb the scene any more than we already have."

I looked around at the ground: faint tire tracks, no drag marks near the body. Of course, the ash had either drifted in the persistent winds or was hardened by thousands of years of exposure to the elements.

Hy said, "I'll check out that truck. Why don't you wait for the sheriff's people?"

"Okay." As he walked away, I stared down at the shrouded body. Tom Mathers had been a big man; in death he would have been hard to move.

I pictured T.C. Mathers. She'd appeared very strong. And then there were all those guns and knives gleaming in their cases at the wilderness supply. What if the argument I'd triggered by asking about Hayley Perez had spun out of control . . . ?

The drone and flapping of a chopper came from the north. It hovered, then set down nearby. Kristen Lark got out and, ducking her head, ran toward us.

It was after six when we finished giving statements to Lark at her office in Bridgeport, nearly seven when we got back to Vernon. We'd had no lunch, so we headed to Zelda's, where a country band whose members must've been tone deaf were playing. Bob Zelda, who had heard about our discovery via the small-town grapevine, gave

us a table in the bar area, as far from the noise as possible, brought us complimentary glasses of white wine, and took our orders.

"They turn up any traces of the Perez girl?" he asked.

"No," Hy said, "the search was called off at dusk."

"Bad enough what you found. Tom Mathers was a good kid."

"Somebody didn't think so. He was shot in the back."

"God." He turned toward the kitchen.

Hy swirled the wine in his glass, breathed in its aroma, sipped, and made a face. "I'd rather have paid for a really good vintage," he muttered.

Being one who had spent much of her life opening screwtop bottles, I shrugged.

"Come on, McCone. You've got a better palate than that."

I sipped, and my lips puckered. "You're right. Any potted plants we can pour this into?"

"We'll have a bottle of Deer Hill with dinner."

Deer Hill—my favorite chardonnay, which would go perfectly with the golden trout we'd both ordered. Then my mind flashed back to the night last February when RKI's building on Green Street in the city had been bombed; I'd walked out with a bottle of that particular wine to take to a dinner at my half-sister's place in Berkeley just seconds before the former warehouse blew up, killing three people.

Hy studied my face, accustomed by now to my sudden shifts in mood. He put his hand on mine. "It's over, McCone."

"That threat, yes. But what about the next? I still have nightmares—"

"About that and lots of other things, I know. I have

them too. Things like that leave scars, but if you don't have scars, you haven't really lived. Someone like you needs to put herself out on the line."

"I'm not sure that's true any more." I picked up my water glass, drank half, and dumped the sour white wine into it. "You order us a bottle of Deer Hill, and let's forget about crime for tonight."

Sunday

✦

NOVEMBER 4

In the morning Hy slept in and I went to visit Lear Jet, a few carrot pieces in my pocket. Ramon apparently hadn't been there, and the horse was hungry: he took the first carrot eagerly. I offered another, then gave him his morning's ration of mixed hay. While he ate, I watched him. This gentle creature bore no resemblance to the one that had charged me Wednesday night.

I said, "You haven't been getting your exercise, have you, guy?"

A whinny.

"We could go for a short ride, if you cooperate. But if you play games, there'll be no alfalfa tonight."

As if he could actually understand me, he bobbed his head.

It was probably a mistake. No one knew I was taking the horse out, and if he threw me again, I'd have to limp my own way back to the house.

So why're you doing it, McCone? To prove some unimportant point?

No. This one feels important.

Lear Jet allowed me to saddle and mount him with no problem. He trotted sedately toward the mesa overlooking the lake, and by the time we got there I felt as if we'd tentatively formed a rapport.

"You know what?" I said, stroking his mane. "You need a new name. Lear Jet—even if that's what Hy called you—is undignified. How about King Lear? Now that's strong, speaks of a horse with self-esteem."

Also speaks of insanity, but it's not likely he knows his Shakespeare.

The horse bobbed his head again.

"It's settled, then. I'll call you King for short."

When we got back to the stables, King only stepped on my foot once while I was grooming him. And I was pretty sure that was an accident.

When Hy came out of the ranch house, King was in his fenced pasture and I was cleaning out his stall. Hy stared in astonishment, shook his head, and said, "Never thought I'd see you tending to Lear Jet—or any other horse."

"His name," I said, "is now King Lear. King for short. We're almost friends. In fact, I think he likes me better than you. At least I come to the stable bearing carrots."

"Fickle animal. Since the two of you are on your way to becoming buddies, I just may have to buy myself another nag."

"King is not a *nag*."

"Oh yeah, the two of you have bonded big-time. If I

ever get to ride again, I'm definitely going to have to spring for a new nag—I mean, horse."

"King could use some company."

"Do we have onions?" Hy asked.

"Yes, in that wire basket." I sat at the table, thumbing through a report Kristen Lark had faxed me.

"How fresh are these eggs?"

"Check the sell-by date."

"Fresh enough. What's Lark got to say?"

"Not much. Nothing on Boz Sheppard. The sleeping bag Tom Mathers was wrapped in belongs to him; his wife says he kept it in the truck. She's got an alibi for the time of the killing: she slammed out of the wilderness supply a short while after I left; a customer saw her leave, and spent at least an hour afterwards with Tom, talking about a fishing trip he wanted to line up. T.C. went directly to Zelda's, drank and danced for hours, then spent the night with a good old boy at the motel."

"Canned mushrooms all right?"

"They'll have to be; we don't have fresh. The good old boy is Cullen Bradley. I interviewed him at the hardware store he owns in Bridgeport. Glad-handing small-town guy with a serious hangover. Those Bridgeport men really get around. I wonder if— What?"

"Oregano?"

"In an *omelet*? Are you insane?"

"Just trying to get your attention, McCone."

"I'm paying attention."

"No you're not. And that's a sign you're getting better."

Monday

♦

NOVEMBER 5

I spent a good deal of Monday morning on the phone to the agency, going over the week's schedule with Patrick Neilan. Two new clients had set initial appointments with him for the afternoon: one was a deadbeat-dad case, which he'd probably assign to Julia Rafael; the other concerned identity theft. In the past Patrick himself would have taken it on, or it would have ended up on the desk of Charlotte Keim, my chief financial investigator.

But Keim, once my nephew Mick's live-in love, now worked for Hy; after the acrimonious breakup of their relationship, I'd asked Hy to hire her in order to preserve peace within the agency. Her replacement, Thelia Chen, a former analyst for Bank of America, was working out splendidly. She ought to be able to handle the case.

The agency was practically running itself in my absence. Patrick was working out well as a partial stand-in for me. Ted and his assistant, Kendra Williams, were a

superefficient pair. Mick and Derek made short work of the increasing number of computer forensic jobs that came in, and weren't averse to doing mundane searches when nothing complex was on the table. Julia Rafael was bilingual and could deal well with Latino clients with limited English; former FBI agent Craig Morland had wide-ranging contacts with government agencies. And for a good all-around operative I could always call on the freelance talents of Rae Kelleher, who was now writing novels with a strong crime element and welcomed keeping her hand in the detective business.

Once this state of affairs would have made me feel distanced, left out. Now I merely felt relieved. I'd created a great team and, if I accomplished nothing else in my career, it had been worth the effort.

Still I felt restless, the empty day ahead weighing heavily upon me. No leads, no new information. Unless . . .

I dialed Glenn Solomon, a high-powered San Francisco attorney for whom I'd done a great deal of work—and who was also a good friend.

"Glenn, d'you know a Las Vegas firm—Brower, Price and Coleman?"

"Sure. They handle the legal work for at least three major casinos."

"What about Frank Brower?"

"Lousy golfer, but a nice guy."

"So you know him well?"

"We get together down there two, three times a year."

I explained what I needed to know and asked, "Can you get him to tell you who was footing the bill for Hayley Perez's legal work?"

"If I go about it the right way."

"Will you do it for me—as a favor?"

"Yes, my friend. But I thought you were taking a long vacation at that ranch you and Hy have."

"I was. Severe case of burn-out."

"And you're over it now?"

"No, I'm just helping out some friends."

I booted up my laptop and Googled Bud Smith. Good luck, with a name like that. I narrowed the search down to insurance brokers, Mono County, California. No Bud, but there was a Herbert in Vernon. His record was clean—no complaints to the state department of consumer affairs. I then searched for more information on Herbert Smith of Vernon, California. Nothing. Apparently he wasn't important enough to the gods of Google. Finally I logged on to one of the search engines that the agency subscribes to—even though I'm averse to availing myself of company resources for personal reasons—and came up with some revealing information.

Herbert Smith of Vernon, California, was a registered sex offender.

To confirm the information I visited a site that posted the whereabouts of registered sex offenders. He was on it.

How, I wondered, had a community of not more than four hundred people failed to pick up on his status? How could Dana Ivins have arranged for him to mentor young men and women?

I dialed Ivins's number. She picked up, sounding crisp and professional. I told her what I'd found out and asked, "How could you put your clients at risk like that?"

Calmly she replied, "Bud's case was unusual. He never confirmed it to me, but even the prosecutor over in Mineral County thought he was covering for someone else."

"So this happened in Nevada."

"Yes, twenty-six years ago. A girl of thirteen was raped, sodomized, and abandoned in the countryside near the munitions storage site outside of Hawthorne. She managed to crawl to the road and flag down a passing car. There was evidence pointing to Bud—tire tracks from his truck in the sand, a piece of cloth she'd ripped from a shirt belonging to him. Unfortunately, the girl was extremely traumatized. She couldn't even speak, much less identify her attacker."

And over a quarter of a century ago, there wouldn't have been any DNA evidence. DNA testing was in its infancy then.

"So why did the prosecutor think Smith was covering for someone?"

"Bud had a younger brother, Davey. He was sixteen, something of a child prodigy—math, I think—but considered strange by his teachers and peers. Bud raised him after their parents died and was overly protective of him. Originally the police focused on Davey because he'd been seen in town talking with the girl, but then Bud confessed. And stuck to it."

"So Bud did his time and . . . ?"

"And moved back here to Vernon, where he was born and raised till the family moved to Hawthorne during his teens."

I was a little surprised that Smith could have gotten a California insurance broker's license. Many types of licenses are unavailable to sex offenders—such as real estate, because the agents have access to keys. But then with insurance, if the person is registered and up-front about doing time, the state is more lenient. And Bud had apparently been honest about his record.

"Is Bud's status common knowledge around here?" I asked Ivins.

"Not really. I suppose some people may have stumbled across it on the Internet. But Bud's very civic-minded and well liked, so if they have they've kept it to themselves. I know only because he confided his past to me when he applied to become a mentor. Then I did some research on his case."

"What happened to the brother, Davey?"

"I don't know that, either. All I'm really sure of is that Bud has been good at mentoring our clients."

"Does he tell them he was in prison, and why?"

"Whatever goes on between friends who help friends is strictly confidential."

It seemed to me she didn't know a hell of a lot of things she should know about what went on between her organization's clients and their mentors.

"Is Bud aware you told me he might have been tutoring Amy Perez in math?"

". . . I mentioned it to him. He called shortly after you left me that day."

"Why did he call?"

She frowned. "I don't really know. I told him about your visit, but then someone called on his other line. He said he'd get back to me, but he never did."

"Is he still living on Aspen Lane?" It was the address listed for him on the registered sex offenders site.

". . . Yes."

"Do you have a phone number for him?"

"I can't give out—"

"Never mind. I'll get hold of him."

Irresponsibility, I thought. Sheer irresponsibility. I'm all for giving sex offenders a second chance, but given the high rate of recidivism, that chance shouldn't be in a

sensitive area involving young people. And I wasn't sure I bought the rumors of Bud Smith's false confession—even if the Mineral County prosecutor had had his or her doubts.

I called Smith's office, got a machine. Thumbed through the slim local directory; his home number wasn't listed, under either Bud or Herbert. Better to speak with him in person anyway. I'd drive out to Aspen Lane and—

The phone rang. Glenn Solomon.

"I talked with Frank Brower. His instructions to represent Hayley Perez came from a Mount Kisco, New York, law firm—Carpenter and Bates."

"You know anyone there?"

"No, but Frank was on the *Harvard Law Review* with Bates. He'll get back to me later."

"Thanks so much, Glenn. I'm leaving now and my cellular might not work where I'm going. If it doesn't, please leave a message on the machine here at the ranch."

"Certainly." He paused, the silence full of meaning.

"What?" I asked.

"What I always tell you when you embark on one of your quests, my friend: be clever and careful."

Aspen Lane was three miles out the road to Stone Valley—a place I hadn't visited for years and didn't even like to think about. The horrific events that had happened in the valley back then had ultimately brought Hy and me together, but I didn't want to relive them, even in my head. The vision of the mountain exploding, our frantic flight—

So stop reliving them, all right?

The lane was well named: golden-leafed aspen spread out to either side and clustered around the small, mostly

prefab homes. Bud Smith's was at the very end, where the pavement stopped—a double-wide trailer with attractive plantings and a deck with an awning over it. A fishing boat was up on davits, ready to be prepped and tarped for the winter. Usually I think of child molesters as unsavory types who live in squalor and lurk in dark places seeking their prey, but I couldn't reconcile either the man I'd met or his tidy home with such an image.

No one answered the doorbell. I walked around the structure calling out to Smith. No response, but I sensed a presence nearby. Finally I went back to the deck and saw what I hadn't noticed before: the door was slightly ajar.

Not breaking and entering, just trespassing. And trespassing for a good reason: now I'm worried about the man.

The excuses I use to justify my actions . . .

I eased the door open, listening. Silence. Strong smell there, but it wasn't sinister—cooked garlic and onions. Still, I drew Hy's .45 from my bag before I went inside. The living room and galley kitchen were empty. The meal must have been cooked yesterday, since the stove and all the counter surfaces were clean.

I moved along the hallway. Three bedrooms and a bath opened off it, all of them deserted. In one of the smaller rooms, the bed had been left unmade. Otherwise everything was neat.

Why didn't Bud Smith sleep in the larger room with the queen-sized bed? Perhaps he shared the trailer with someone who was tidier than he?

Well, that information could be had online. But while I was here . . .

The master bedroom's closet contained a man's clothing—mostly vintage and odd, as I'd seen Bud wear. So it

was his room after all. The bathroom didn't tell me much.
A Water Pik and two electric toothbrushes, some first-aid
supplies, aspirin, and sinus headache pills. No prescription
drugs. A razor and shaving cream on a shelf below a mirror in the shower stall. Third bedroom, mostly empty—a
guest room that hadn't been used in quite a while, judging
from the layer of dust.

Back to the room with the unmade bed. The closet held
some newish-looking woman's jeans. A couple of sweat-
ers were draped across a chair, and there were a few tops
hanging in the closet. Woman's underwear in the bureau,
and a flannel nightgown tossed on the bed. Makeup items
and a pair of earrings on the bureau.

So Smith had a female roommate. She was probably at
work.

I moved back to the living area, looking in drawers and
cupboards, gave the whole trailer another once-over, then
left and started back to the ranch.

I sat at my laptop, thinking about Bud Smith—a convicted child molester who may have been covering for his
younger brother. Smith, who had told me he knew Amy
Perez and, if Amy had followed Dana Ivins' advice, may
have tutored her in algebra. Who had sold a life-insurance
policy to Hayley, with Amy as beneficiary. Had he known
Hayley before she bought the policy? Probably not, given
their age difference.

I logged on to Mono County property records and
learned the land and the double-wide had belonged to
Smith for seven years. When I went to the state insurance
brokers' registry, I found that he'd received his license the
same year he'd purchased the land. The California Registry of Sex Offenders showed he'd contacted them within

a day of his arrival in the state, and reregistered when required.

Which proved . . . ? Not much.

The *Mineral County Independent News* in Hawthorne didn't have online issues going back twenty-six years. I could drive over there and check their archives, but it was getting on toward five o'clock. Better to wait till morning.

Well, what about the paper in Reno? A controversial rape case would have warranted mention. I checked, found their online archives didn't go back twenty-six years, either. Tomorrow I'd have to visit Mineral County.

But now I'd take a ride on King, who was probably waiting for me. Tonight I'd cut a path across open land where our small herd of sheep grazed. Hy had told me the sheep had something to do with a subsidy or lower taxes—I forget which—but I suspected he kept them out of sentiment. His stepfather, to whom he'd been considerably closer than to his birth father, had been a lifelong sheep rancher.

The ride was without event, and I felt a growing kinship with the horse. I'd been traumatized by the events of the night when he'd charged me, but so had he. Animals are essentially innocent, until we humans treat them badly and give them cause to fear. King needed my reassurance.

As we retraced our steps, I wondered if this caring for the horse indicated a caring for other things in my life.

Ramon was at the stable when King and I got back, cleaning out the stall. He said hello and went on with what he was doing, allowing me to tend to King on my own.

When I finished rubbing King down and led him into the clean stall, I noticed Ramon's dark eyes were shad-

owed and puffy. He attempted a smile, but it didn't quite come off.

"How're you doing?" I asked.

He made a wobbly gesture with his hand. "We buried Hayley up in Bridgeport today."

"Oh, I wish you'd told me. I would've—"

"Not necessary; you didn't know her. It was a nice turn-out, though. Even that wild man she ran off with and his girlfriend came. The girlfriend brought beautiful flowers. She works at Petals."

So Rich Three Wings and Cammie Charles had paid their respects to Hayley. Rich, because he still loved her, and Cammie, probably because she felt guilty that her imagined rival was dead.

I asked, "Did Miri attend?"

Ramon's eyes narrowed, the lines around them deepening. "No."

"Why not? She was only on seventy-two-hour hold at the psychiatric ward."

"Yeah. And then she checked herself into a rehab facility they recommended. By this morning she was gone. She's probably in Reno or Vegas, helling around or selling herself. I've washed my hands of her. Sara's real broken up about this, but she'll get over it. You gotta go on."

"And what about Amy? Anything from her?"

"Not a word." He leaned in the doorway, and for a moment I thought he'd sag to the ground. "I loved that little girl, Sharon. I should've never let Miri run me off. I should've stayed and fought for the last of my nieces and nephews."

I went to him, took his hand, and drew him over to the nearest bales of hay. As we sat, I said, "You couldn't have known what would happen."

"Anybody could've read the signs that she was headed for bad trouble. But not me, I was too offended at Miri, too dug down into my own unhappiness. Sara and I had two boys, you know—Peter and Raymond."

"I didn't know. Neither of you has ever mentioned them."

"They've been gone a long time. Peter died in a gang shootout over in Santa Rosa. Raymond died of a drug overdose. I didn't do so good by them, either."

Sadness welled up inside me—guilt, too. "I'm sorry," I said, "and I understand how you feel. I had a brother, Joey. Always was a rebel and a loner. After he graduated high school, he took off and very seldom came home. Ma—my adoptive mother—got postcards occasionally, but that was it. And then he died all alone of a drug and alcohol overdose in a shack up near Eureka. Ever since then I've wished I'd done more. That any of us had done more. But we just . . . let him go."

"I'm sorry, Sharon. Us people, we're all so careless. I don't want to let go of Amy."

"Neither do I. I promise I'll find her."

That night I dreamed of the pit again—only this time it was bigger. Impossible to place both my hands and feet on its sides and climb into the sunshine like a spider. I woke in a near panic, sat up, collapsed back on the pillows.

Told myself, *I will not allow this to get the better of me*.

Tomorrow I'd keep my promise to Ramon. Start an intensive search for Bud Smith who, my instincts said, was at the center of Amy's disappearance.

Maybe that would keep my nightmares at bay.

Tuesday

✦

NOVEMBER 6

The Nevada sky was cloudless as I coasted past the red-and-white sign welcoming me to Hawthorne, population 3,311. Larger than Vernon by far, and the county seat, but still a small town. Laid out on a grid, so I had no difficulty locating the *Independent News* building on D Street.

The man I talked to was pleasant and friendly. Back issues on microfilm? No problem. They were going to put everything online someday, but who knew when that would be? Soon I was seated in a dusty room fitting reels onto a machine with fumbling fingers. How could I be clumsy at the act I'd performed so many times before I'd become computer literate? Another symptom of burnout?

I returned the films an hour or so later, having learned too few new details to justify such a long drive, except that Smith's rape victim had remained too traumatized to identify her assailant.

It was after two in the afternoon, so I asked about someplace to eat lunch. McDonald's; everyplace else had stopped serving. I hadn't had a Mickey D's burger in years, and it was a strange experience: not what I now think of as a burger, but a different substance entirely. I blocked out thoughts of what that substance might be and ate it anyway.

Back in the car, I checked my cell to see if it worked here—which it did—and consulted my notes. Got the number for the prosecutor in the Smith case from Information. Warren Mills, now retired, was home and willing to see me once I assured him that I was an investigator, not someone planning to write a book on the case. "Too damn much of that sensational crap going around these days," he told me.

Mills lived only a few blocks away on East Eighth Street. The house was a low-slung rancher, one of a number on that block that were probably built in the late forties before developers realized that the wartime boom in the Hawthorne economy—due to activity at the nearby munitions depot—was dropping off. I parked out front and went up a concrete walk bordered on either side by cacti and polished rock. Westernized, I believe it's called, for yards that don't require much water or maintenance.

Warren Mills answered the door—a tall, erect man with thick gray hair and black-rimmed glasses who, according to the newspaper accounts, must now be in his late seventies but could have passed for mid-sixties. He led me inside to a den with a big-screen TV. The furnishings were overstuffed and looked comfortable; framed photos hung on the walls—color shots of Walker Lake to the north, he told me.

"Coffee, Ms. McCone? A soda?" He had a deep, rich voice that must have resonated in the courtroom.

"Nothing, thanks. I've just come from McDonald's."

"I should have offered you an Alka-Seltzer. Please, sit down."

I sank into a brown chair that enveloped me in an embrace that made it hard to sit up straight.

Warren Mills settled on the couch, propped his moccasin-shod feet on a scarred coffee table in front of it. "You said on the phone that you're a private investigator and interested in the Herbert Smith case. Why?"

"He may have recently been involved in the abduction of a young woman over in Mono County. I've read all the newspaper accounts of his case, but there's so much that seems . . . unsaid. And a friend of Smith's claims that you yourself were uncertain Smith was guilty."

Mills nodded. "His confession was as false as I've ever heard."

"Then why did you accept his plea bargain and send him to prison?"

"It was as if Smith was trying to talk his way behind bars. He insisted on his guilt, refused a lie-detector test when his public defender wanted to order one. I didn't need to build a case against him; he built it for me. And of course the district attorney was hot for a quick trial and conviction. The rape and sodomy of a thirteen-year-old . . . small towns like this need to put crimes like that behind them and move on."

"The victim—"

"I can't tell you her name. But she was a nice girl from a decent, hardworking family. Too friendly and trusting, that's all."

"What happened to her?"

"The family moved away. She was severely damaged by the assault. And as you must know, you can keep the victim's name out of the newspapers and court records but word gets out anyway and then it's blame-the-victim time."

"Smith's friend claims he was covering for his younger brother, Davey."

"The friend's likely right. Davey Smith was a genius, had just graduated high school at fifteen, with a full scholarship to some college back East. My thinking is that Herbert—Bud, everybody called him—didn't want to see Davey's promising future disrupted, even if it meant going to prison for something he didn't do."

"Why? If Davey was a rapist—"

"You have to understand the way it was with the two of them. The mother died young. Father raised them well, but he had a fatal heart attack when Bud was sixteen. A young man, just starting out in life, and he could have put his little brother in a foster home, but he didn't. Instead he quit school, picked up where the father left off, took whatever jobs paid best to support the two of them. That's sometimes the way some family members are. Bud loved Davey, and I think he saw his brother's promising future as a kind of a way of ensuring the family would go on."

"And where is this genius today?"

Mills shrugged, shook his head.

I said, "Bud Smith is working as an insurance broker in Vernon, on Tufa Lake. He lives in a double-wide trailer in the country—nice property, but nothing fancy. And he's a registered sex offender. I guess his brother—wherever he is—didn't have the same sense of family."

"He could be dead. Or incarcerated somewhere else."

"True."

Mills was silent for a long moment. Then: "I imagine in your profession, Ms. McCone, you've had reason to regret certain of your actions."

Oh, haven't I. Mr. Mills, you'll never know how much I regret them.

"Of course."

"So have I." His eyes, behind their black-framed glasses, grew pained. "I regret not pushing harder to prove Bud Smith's confession was false. I regret not looking more closely at Davey Smith. Whatever's happened over in Mono County is not Bud's fault."

"And Davey . . . ?"

"My biggest regret: that I may have let a monster walk free."

He paused, seemed to listen to his words. "Talk with an attorney named John Pearl in Carson City." He reached for a pad and pencil on the scarred coffee table and scribbled. "This is his office address and phone number. I'll call ahead to say you'll contact him. He may be able to tell you what I can't."

I took the paper. John Pearl: Bud Smith's former public defender.

The munitions depot occupied a vast expanse of land on the outskirts of Hawthorne. Standard military buildings and cracked and weed-choked pavement were visible from the road, although I'd read on the Net that its golf course and officers' clubhouse had now been turned into a public country club. Storage bunkers covered the land to the east like Indian mounds, and the landscape was stark and uninviting. I passed through the town of Babbitt, which had once been a bedroom community for base workers, and eventually came to Walker Lake.

I drove north along the shore of the elongated body of water that was rimmed by sand-colored hills to the east. It was currently in ecological crisis, as Tufa and Mono Lakes in California had once been, primarily because the waters of its feeder stream, the Walker River, had been overallocated for agricultural use. Hy had done some work with the organization trying to preserve Walker, one of only five deepwater lakes in the world that are able to sustain a good-sized fishery, and had told me that if the water levels continued to drop, increased salinity would destroy its fish population.

Today there were few boats on the lake, and its surface was flat and glassy. The weather had changed: dark clouds hovered over the distant hills—storm clouds that looked to be coming this way. Depression stole over me again, reminding me of all the things I didn't like about my business: the long solo drives and flights; the empty nights in hotel and motel rooms in strange cities; the waiting. Particularly waiting for facts to surface that would allow other facts to materialize and establish the final connection. When that happened, the rush was unbelievable—better, even, than the first time my former flight instructor had put the plane into a controlled spin and the earth had seemed to rush up at us as we plummeted down. . . .

It was an addiction, plain and simple. And addiction, unless it's treated, inevitably ends up in self-destruction.

I wasn't going to become victim to mine. Never again.

So what the hell am I doing here in Nevada?

You promised Ramon you'd find out what happened to Amy.

Carson City: the state capital, and a pleasant town. Not much of a gambling mecca; its big casino, the Ormsby

House, had closed down well over a decade ago and since then cast a derelict shadow over the downtown. Renovation by new owners had seemingly been under way forever, as the project hit delays and snags of all kinds. If it hadn't been so late in the afternoon I'd have driven by to see how much progress had been made, but I was more concerned with locating the law firm of John Pearl, on Fairview Drive, a couple of blocks from the state office building where Hy and I had said our vows before a judge.

At first, when I stepped inside John Pearl's office in a two-story stucco house that had been converted into suites for attorneys, I thought no one was there. But when I called out, a high-pitched, nasal voice that reminded me of a cartoon character—I couldn't place which one—answered. With a voice like that, Pearl couldn't have been too successful at trial work.

He emerged from his inner sanctum: a short, chubby man in a rumpled blue suit. His face was round, his hair a grayish-brown mop that flopped over his forehead; his eyes were too soft and kind for a criminal defense attorney.

"Ms. McCone," he said, pumping my hand heartily, "Warren Mills said you'd be stopping by, so I stayed to catch up on some paperwork. Come in, sit down, please."

I followed him into his office. It was in minor disarray, like his clothing.

"I'd offer you coffee but my secretary drank the last cup and forgot to turn the machine off. The carafe's scorched. You can probably smell it."

Now that he mentioned it, I did. "That's okay," I said. "I had lunch at McDonald's and I'm still recovering. Coffee could cause a serious relapse."

"McDonald's." His eyes—so help me—became nostal-

gic. "I haven't had one of their burgers in years. When they first opened up in the town where I was born, I was in my teens. My friends and I used to go there and order two or three each, and before we'd eat them we'd splat the pickles."

"Do what?"

"You know, splat. Take the pickles—they were terrible—out of the burgers and try to drop them out the car window so they'd land flat on the pavement. You never did that?"

"Uh, not that I recall."

"Oh, well." Pearl leaned back in his chair. "It was pretty stupid, but so were we at the time. Amazing, though: one of the splatters is now a state supreme court justice; another invented some gizmo that allowed him to retire at thirty-five; a third is a big financial planner in Reno. Then there's me: I was the best pickle splatter, but I'm just a small-time lawyer."

It was a set and well-practiced speech, but I couldn't figure what it was designed to accomplish.

"I doubt that," I said. "You have your own practice; you're your own boss. What type of litigation do you do?"

"Whatever comes my way. Family law, mainly." He paused. "No criminal law. I quit the public defender's office down in Mineral County after the Herbert Smith case. Which, Warren Mills told me, is why you're here."

"Yes." I explained why I was interested in speaking with those who were involved in it.

When I finished, Pearl said, "The opinions of Herbert's friend and Warren Mills are essentially the same as mine. Herbert—Bud, as he was called—struck me on first impression as a badly frightened but innocent young man;

he stood by his confession with the tenacity of a bulldog. He resisted all my efforts to help him. Tried twice to fire me."

"And this confession came how long after the rape?"

"About three days, after the investigative officers identified the tire tracks at the scene as having been made by his truck. When they took him in for questioning, he gave them a plausible explanation: he'd been out there taking photographs of the munitions bunkers for an article a friend was writing on the history of the depot. But no one could locate the friend—if he ever existed—and when the sheriff obtained a search warrant for Bud's home, there was only one camera, in a closet, covered in dust and containing no film. And in the trash was a bloody shirt with a piece ripped from it that matched the fabric the girl had torn from her rapist's clothing."

"So they arrested him—"

"Not immediately. The shirt was a size smaller than most of Bud's, and his brother, Davey, had been seen talking to the girl in town that day. The investigators began to focus on Davey and that's when Bud confessed. He didn't ask for an attorney, so the public defender's office assigned him to me. From the beginning he was stubborn and uncooperative. I voiced my doubts to the DA and Warren; Warren was willing to listen, but the DA at that time—he's deceased now—was a real hardnose. I arranged for the best plea bargain I could, but it was still too much prison time for an innocent man."

Like Warren Mills' eyes when he spoke of his regrets, John Pearl's were bleak. "That was the end of my illustrious career as a crusading defender of the poor and powerless. I couldn't stomach the hypocrisy. So here I am." He spread his arms out at his disheveled office.

"Is there anything else you can tell me about the case?"

He considered. "Not really. Except that Davey Smith acted the wide-eyed innocent throughout, and as soon as his brother went to prison, he took off for some college where he'd been given a full scholarship. One thing I do know: if he ever shows his face around here again, I myself may be in need of a public defender."

The rain broke as I was passing the munitions depot. There were a number of motels in Hawthorne, and the man in the newspaper office had recommended a casino that served a great chicken-fried steak—a favorite of mine—as well as an old-time saloon. I'd stowed a small travel bag in the Land Rover, in the event I'd have to stay over.

Well, why not? First the motel, next a good meal, and then a chance to elicit some gossip from the townspeople.

Slim's Tavern, across the street from the casino where I ate, was definitely old-time—decorated with genuine mining, railroad, and military artifacts from the town's colorful past. At ten o'clock it was reasonably crowded and noisy from both the patrons' voices and the clank and whir of the small bank of slot machines. I chose a seat at the bar between two lone men in cowboy hats who looked to be in their mid-forties, and ordered a beer. You don't drink wine in a place like that, not if you want any of the locals to talk with you.

The man to my left stared straight ahead, hunched over his glass of whiskey. Not a talker, I thought, and probably brooding about something. The man to my right gave me a friendly glance, then threw a few dollars on the bar and left.

Well, hell.

I nursed the beer, trying not to breathe too deeply of the smoky air—one of the drawbacks of Nevada casinos and drinking establishments—and checking out the place in the backbar mirror. It was mostly an older crowd, forties on up—my target age group. The brooder ordered another whiskey and continued to stare. A leather-faced, strong-jawed man in a baseball cap squeezed onto the vacated stool to my right and ordered a beer and a shot, calling the bartender by name. Then he looked at me and asked, "You new here, or just passing through?"

"Passing through. How can you tell?"

"I know all the locals who come to Slim's. You want another beer?" He motioned to my empty glass.

"Sure. Thanks. Sierra Nevada."

He waved at the bartender and pointed at my glass, turned to me and, after giving me a long, slow look, said, "I'm Cal McKenzie."

"Sharon McCone." We shook hands as our drinks arrived.

"Where you from, Sharon?"

"I've been staying over at Tufa Lake, trying to figure out where to go next."

He knocked back his shot. "Kind of a wanderer, are you?"

"Kind of. I came up here to Hawthorne looking for an old friend, but I can't find a trace of him."

"Well, I've lived here all my life. Maybe I can help you."

"His name is Herbert Smith, but everybody calls him Bud."

Cal McKenzie's expression became guarded. "How long since you've seen your friend, Sharon?"

"I hate to admit how many years. We lost touch, but I thought since I was in the area . . ."

"Well, Bud's long gone. How close a friend of his were you?"

"Oh, it was just one of those summer things. You know."

"You're lucky that's all it was. Your friend Bud's a criminal. Raped and sodomized the little Darkmoon girl and left her for dead out by the munitions bunkers. She survived and they put him away for a good long time. He hasn't been back here since."

"My God!" I feigned shock, gulping some beer. "When was this?"

"Twenty-six years ago."

"Hard to believe Bud was capable of something like that, even as a kid."

"Some folks around here don't believe it to this day. Nice guy, never in trouble before, everybody liked him. But the evidence was all there, and he confessed."

"This Darkmoon girl—does she still live here?"

"Family moved away right after. Paiutes." He looked more closely at me. "You Paiute, too?"

"Shoshone."

"Well, the Darkmoons were really a nice family. Very religious, too. One of those strict, small sects—I forget which one. Shame what happened to their little girl."

"How old was she?"

"Thirteen."

"D'you recall her first name?"

He thought, shrugged. "No, I don't. They had a bunch of kids, I can't remember what any of them were called." He gestured at my glass. "Another beer?"

"No, thanks. This has been . . . quite a shock, and I think I'd better be getting back to my motel now."

"The evening's young—"

"Maybe I'll see you tomorrow night, Cal. It was good to meet you." I slid off the stool before he could protest and made my exit.

A Paiute family named Darkmoon who'd lived in Hawthorne twenty-six years ago couldn't be too difficult to find. If the Internet couldn't lead me to them, I'd use the moccasin telegraph.

Wednesday

✦

NOVEMBER 7

The moccasin telegraph beat out the Internet.

After I drove home from Hawthorne that morning, I found plenty of listings on Google in the name of Dark-moon—a magazine, a design company, a publisher, even a Wiccan temple—but none of them individuals. There were three on the search engines the agency subscribed to, two in Washington State and one, coincidentally, on the Flathead reservation in Montana, where my birth father, Elwood Farmer, lived.

I could have run more sophisticated searches, but on the moccasin telegraph I could access far more detail. The listings for the three Darkmoons hadn't revealed much about them, other than their whereabouts, and that wasn't surprising: a great many Indians are out of the mainstream and don't own property, have credit ratings, or hold real jobs.

My friend Will Camphouse, creative director at an ad agency in Tucson whom I'd met while searching for my

birth parents, had explained the moccasin telegraph as a coast-to-coast Indian gossip network that worked with amazing speed. It was an accurate description. I'd gotten a lead to Elwood from a Shoshone man in Wyoming, and by the time I reached the Flathead Reservation everyone, including my birth father, knew not only that I was on my way, but also the basic facts about me. Phone calls, inter-familial connections, accidental meetings in such places as the grocery store, and a background check on the Inter-net had told them a private investigator from San Fran-cisco was coming to town.

For this investigation, George Darkmoon in Arlee, a town near St. Ignatius, where my birth father lived, would be the obvious person to start with. The problem was, I would have to call Elwood.

Elwood was not an easy man to deal with on the phone—or in person. The first two times I'd tried to talk with him he'd rebuffed me—telling me to come back to his house when I'd had time to "assemble my thoughts." Then he'd grudgingly allowed me into his simple log home and acknowledged that I was his daughter. Since then we'd established a tentative relationship, but it had its rough edges: on my part because he'd suspected all along he had a child, but had made no effort to locate me; on his part because I'd disrupted his quiet, traditional life as an artist who volunteered to fund and teach art workshops in the schools at various area reservations.

I steeled myself and dialed his number.

"Elwood, it's Sharon."

"Yes."

"How are you?"

"Doing well. How are you?"

"Doing well."

Long silence. I asked, "How are the workshops going?"

"Excellently." Excitement lightened his voice. "Those young people are amazing. Their enthusiasm . . . it makes me feel young again."

And where were you, when my enthusiasm could have made you feel young?

Not fair, McCone. At the time he wasn't even certain that you existed.

"I haven't heard from you in a while," he added. "Are you sure everything's all right? Those bombings . . ."

Did he really want to know? I decided to lay it on him; talked about my burn-out and my flight to the ranch, my doubts about my professional future.

He didn't speak immediately. I heard puffing sounds—he was lighting a cigarette.

"It may be a time for change, Daughter. That kind of empty feeling is a signal that we need to use our gifts in different ways. Me, when I was making all that money from my art in New York City and living high, I felt the kinds of pressures you were feeling. When I met Leila and we came here, I could let go of the things I thought were important back there, and get on with what really counted."

"Your art, and giving to others."

"Yes, exactly."

"Well, I've taken on one last case, as a favor to friends, and I have a problem. D'you know a man in Arlee named George Darkmoon?"

"No. These days, I stay apart from the community more than I used to. But I can put you in touch with him."

"Moccasin telegraph."

"Moccasin telegraph. I'll find someone to relay the information to George. He'll probably have to call you collect."

"If he calls my cellular, it'll be charged to me anyway."
I gave him the number.

"Good. As you know, most of our people can't afford
long distance in the middle of the day. And Daughter, be
in touch with me more often."

When I hung up, my eyes were brimming. Elwood had
called me "Daughter" twice in one conversation.

"Is this Sharon McCone?"

"Yes."

"I'm George Darkmoon, in Arlee, Montana. Donna
Ferguson in St. Ignatius had a call from your father, say-
ing you wanted to get in touch with me. She talked to Jane
Nomee here in Arlee, and Jane called me."

It had been ten minutes since I'd spoken with Elwood.
The telegraph was working at higher speed than my computer ever had.

"Yes, thank you for calling. Mr. Darkmoon, did you
ever live in Hawthorne, Nevada?"

"Never even been there."

"Do you have any relatives who did? Say, twenty-five
years ago?"

"Well . . . the Darkmoons have kind of scattered. Family is Paiute, mostly from northern California, but now
we're all over the map. Me, I married a Flathead woman,
moved here thirty-five years ago. You want I should put it
out on the wire?"

"If you wouldn't mind."

"No problem. Don't know your dad personally, but I
hear about what he's doing for the kids. Happy to help his
daughter."

There was that word again. . . .

*   *   *

"Sharon McCone? This is Phyllis Darkmoon, in Vancouver, B.C. My husband's cousin George says you're looking for a branch of the family who lived in Hawthorne, Nevada, twenty-five years ago."

"That's right. Thanks for calling."

"No problem. My husband wanted me to tell you that he has a second cousin in New Mexico who may have known them. He asked me to put you in touch with him."

"Let me check with some Darkmoon family members in Portland. What number can they reach you at?"

"This is Essie Wilson, in Portland. I'm related to the Darkmoon family. My brother-in-law remembers the Darkmoons of Hawthorne, Nevada. In fact, we visited them once. There was some kind of tragedy with one of their daughters, and then they lost touch."

"Do you recall their first names?"

"The father was Norm, the mother Dora. The kids, no, I don't recall, but a relative in Tonopah, Nevada, might. I'll give you her number."

"Yes, I knew Norm and Dora Darkmoon—they were shirttail cousins. We visited them once, about fifteen years ago when they were living in Yerington. Kind of a sad couple. Their kids had all left home, and he was sick with some kind of lung thing. After that, we lost touch. There's another shirttail cousin in Yerington who might be able to tell you more."

"After the girl was raped, the family moved here to Yerington and stayed for maybe ten years. The girl ran off

a short time after they got here. I never knew her name. But her sister, Joellen, still lives in town. You should talk to her."

"You're looking for Izzy? God, I haven't heard from her since she ran away from home," Joellen Darkmoon Knight said. "No, that's not right. She sent a postcard saying the baby had been born and they were doing fine."

"She had a child?"

"Well, yeah. From the rape, you know."

"And she kept it?"

"Uh-huh, I guess."

"Where was this postcard from?"

"I don't know. Somewhere in California?"

"What's Izzy's full name?"

"Isabel. She hated it because everybody would abbreviate it to Izzy, and she thought that sounded like some weird kind of lizard."

"Is there anybody else in your family who might have heard from her?"

"Well, my parents are dead. Dad had emphysema, and they went down to Arizona, and I swear that hot, dry climate was what killed them both. My older brother, he took off before we moved down here from Hawthorne. Baby brother's overseas in the army, baby sister too. My other sister I don't have nothing to do with, but I've got a phone number for her in Seattle. She was two years older than Izzy, and they were close."

"I'm surprised Joellen gave you my number," Cheri Darkmoon said.

"She mentioned you didn't have much to do with one another."

A laugh. "Try total estrangement. I'm a lesbian, and she couldn't handle it when I came out."

"That's too bad. Families . . ."

"Are not what they show in the TV ads. Take ours: I haven't heard from Isabel for fifteen, sixteen years, since her last kid was born—and we were the closest of us all."

"So Isabel had more children after . . . ?"

"The child born of the rape. Yes, she did. After she ran away she sent me a postcard from Sacramento saying somebody she knew over in California had found her a nice family to stay with."

"Who was this somebody?"

"I don't know. She was only thirteen and had never been anyplace but Hawthorne, so how she had a friend in California I can't imagine. Or how she got there. She didn't have any money of her own; none of us did."

"What happened to her after that?"

"She stayed on with the people, finished high school, got a job. Met a guy and married him. There were more kids—four, that I know of—and I couldn't even congratulate her or send them presents."

"Why not?"

"She would never give me her address. She was afraid that her rapist would find her and ruin her life all over again."

"But he was in prison—"

Another laugh—harsh, this time. "Bud Smith never touched my sister. But his younger brother, Davey, sure did."

"You know this for sure?"

"She told me the night before she ran off. Davey did it, but for a long time afterwards she was so wrecked she couldn't remember, and then she was afraid to tell the

truth. I mean, that girl was so bad off she didn't even *speak* for months. And by the time she could, Bud was convicted and we'd moved to Yerington. After she ran away, I never heard anything from her but an occasional postcard and those birth announcements."

"Do you remember the postmarks?"

"Someplace in California that I'd never heard of. I forget."

"Did you save any?"

"I did for a while, but when I moved here to Seattle I threw away everything I didn't absolutely need. Sorry."

Me too.

A pregnant thirteen-year-old rape victim who has no money runs away from home in Nevada to a friend in Sacramento, where she's never been before. The friend introduces her to a family who takes her in, and she lives with them until she meets a man who marries her and gives her at least four more children.

Moccasin telegraph wasn't going to answer the questions raised by that scenario.

Who did I know who might have some insight into the problem? Dana Ivins?

I called her and, because our last conversation had been less than harmonious, she hesitated before agreeing to allow me to buy her lunch at Zelda's. She was waiting outside when I arrived in Vernon, her cheeks pink from the chill wind off the lake. The temperatures had cooled in the last few days; it would be an early winter in the high desert.

We took a table beside the large rear windows in the dining room and ordered sandwiches. Like me, she didn't have to consult the menu; since Zelda's was by far the best

restaurant in town, we'd both come there often enough to
have it memorized.

As we waited for the food, I explained the Isabel Darkmoon story. When I finished, Dana stared out the window
at the lake, where birds huddled against the wind on the
offshore islands.

"There's one way she could have managed her escape,"
she finally said.

"How?"

"Let me ask you this first: was her family abusive to
her?"

"I doubt it, but I can't say for sure."

"But they were probably embarrassed by the rape and
pregnancy, as evidenced by them moving away from Hawthorne. And they may have taken it out on her in hurtful
ways."

"The sisters I spoke with didn't say, but that's entirely
possible."

Ivins sighed. "Can you keep this confidential?"

"That depends. I don't have a client; I've simply agreed
to help the sheriff's department and the Perez family. I
don't even know for sure if the Darkmoon girl figures in
the case."

"Well, I don't suppose it matters anyway. The organization's no longer active, and they never kept records. If
the authorities contacted any of its members, they'd claim
ignorance. I know I would."

"You were involved in this . . . organization?"

"*Loose* organization." She paused while the waitress
deposited our plates and withdrew. "About fifty activist
women in California and Nevada. We provided money for
girls to escape abusive family situations and sent them to
homes where they could begin new lives. Many of them,

like Isabel Darkmoon, had been impregnated by rapists, often family members."

"Could she have found out about the organization in Yerington?"

"Yes. We had a member there. This would have been before I joined; I was young and still mired down in confusion about which way my life was going to go."

"Is there any way I could get in touch with this member?"

Ivins hesitated, considering. "If this . . . lead of yours turns out to have something to do with the rash of murders we've been having, her identity would come out in court. As you said, you haven't a client, so confidentiality doesn't apply. She's a highly respected attorney—"

"There you have it. I'll ask her to hire me—for a dollar—to find out what happened to Isabel Darkmoon. Any work I do for her falls under the umbrella of attorney-client privilege."

By four that afternoon I was back in Carson City, this time in the offices of Elizabeth Long, attorney-at-law. The firm was situated only a few blocks from John Pearl's building, but mega-miles away in luxury.

Dana Ivins had called and explained the situation, and Elizabeth Long and I were both prepared. After we sat down in her office, she slid a dollar bill across the desk to me and I presented her with one of the agency's contracts—with the lowest retainer fee we'd ever charged inked in. Once she signed it, we were in business.

Ivins had said Long was a highly respected attorney and she certainly looked the part: beautifully styled blonde hair, expensive black suit, heavy gold jewelry. A face with thin lips, a long nose, and eyes that I was sure

could stare down any judge or jury when she was making her case for her clients. She specialized in criminal law.

"Isabel Darkmoon," she said. "She was thirteen, pregnant, and desperate to get away from her family."

"They were abusive?"

"Psychologically. Everyone except for one sister shunned her. That seems like an old-fashioned word, but they were religious in the extreme and literally would have nothing to do with her. She wasn't allowed to eat at the same table, though she could have scraps from the kitchen. No one spoke a word to her, except the one sister who could only whisper in the night after everyone else had gone to sleep. Isabel had shamed them by being in the wrong place at the wrong time."

"Blame it on the victim."

"Yes." Long leaned back in her chair, eyes narrowed—assessing how much information she could trust me with.

"This is all confidential, Ms. Long."

"Of course." She picked up an oddly coiled paper clip from a shallow container, and began toying with it. Picked up another and linked the two together.

"How did Isabel come to you?" I asked.

"She saw a notice on the bulletin board in the grocery store. We had to be so cryptic in those days: Nevada was not like California. I think it said something like 'In trouble? We can help.' And it gave an unlisted number to call—which was mine. I met her at a drive-in restaurant. Bought her a meal and told her what we could do for her. She needed help badly; she was very undernourished for a pregnant woman and severely depressed. But she wanted the baby."

"Why, if she'd been raped?"

"Because no one loved her and she thought the baby would."

"Bad reasoning, wouldn't you say?"

"Immature reasoning, yes. But by then it was too late for her to abort. And she was very determined for such a young woman. I thought she might be persuaded to put her baby up for adoption, so I sent her to a family in our network who had adopted a number of children."

"And then?"

"I heard nothing. That was the rule of our organization: no further contact, because it might jeopardize the person we'd helped."

Long's eyes had shifted from mine, toward the linked paper clips she was toying with. She was lying, or at least not telling the whole truth.

"No contact ever?" I asked.

She looked at the copy of the contract she'd signed. "No contact until last Monday. She came here, said she'd hitchhiked from Bridgeport and she needed help."

She paused. I waited. It was one of those moments when I sensed a major connection was about to be made.

"I don't know how she found me. Maybe she's been keeping track of me all along. She was drunk, asking for help. Spun a tale about her daughter from the rape being murdered and she thought the killer was after her, too."

"Who did she think this killer was?"

"The rapist. The daughter's father."

"Did you believe her?"

"I believed she was in trouble. I told her I'd get her into a shelter that also provides psychiatric care. But then she ran out of the office, and I haven't seen her since."

Miri . . .

"Ms. Long, did Isabel have a middle name?"

"I believe it was Miriam."

Right.

"Did you read in the papers about the murder of a young woman over by Tufa Lake last week—Hayley Perez?"

"There was a brief item—"

"She was Isabel Darkmoon's daughter from the rape. That's why she—now called Miri Perez—is in trouble. And that's why I need to locate her."

Home is the place where . . .

Once again I contemplated the phrase from Robert Frost's "Death of the Hired Man" while Elizabeth Long looked for the notes she'd taken after Miri Perez's sudden appearance and equally sudden departure on Monday.

Miri's oldest daughter, Hayley, had returned to Vernon after years of disappointment and hardship. Miri's youngest daughter, Amy, had returned to the cabin where she'd been squatting at the Willow Grove Lodge.

Where was the home to which Miri would naturally gravitate?

Long sat down at her desk, put on narrow-rimmed glasses, and stared at the notes. "There's nothing here besides what I told you. You can read them, if you like."

I waved the pages away. "These people in Sacramento to whom you sent Miri—who are they?"

"You know I can't—"

"You signed that contract." I pointed to it where it lay on top of a heap of files.

". . . Dean and Jane Ironwood. I don't have an address for them; as a safety measure, we never knew the whereabouts of the people who assisted us."

"Was there anyone else involved in helping Miri—

Isabel—escape? She told her sister there was a friend in California who had introduced her to a nice family."

"I can't remember—"

"Try, please."

". . . Hillary King. Also in the Sacramento area."

"Well, maybe I can locate her, or the Ironwoods."

"Why, after all this time?"

"Because, home is— Never mind. Thank you for your time, Ms. Long."

Another dreary motel room, but on this trip in Carson City I'd brought my laptop. And I was on a roll.

I went straight to the expensive search agencies the agency subscribed to. Hillary King. None in the Sacramento area. She could have moved, married and changed her name, or died. I'd concentrate on the Ironwoods.

Ironwood, Dean, Sacramento. He'd been a lobbyist. There was a ton of information on him, but he'd died two years ago.

Ironwood, Jane. She was a registered nurse, license still active. Address and phone number in Carmichael, a suburb northeast of Sacramento. I phoned the number, but reached an answering machine. Left a message asking her to call me on my cellular. Then I settled down to the takeout dinner I'd picked up across the street and a bad made-for-TV movie.

I was asleep before the movie ended. For once it was a peaceful sleep, without nightmares.

Thursday

✦

NOVEMBER 8

I woke in the morning to my cellular's ring and, as I reached for it, was shocked to see that it was after ten.

Hy. "Sorry I haven't called, McCone. I'm in Tokyo."

"A crisis?"

"No, major new client who wanted to meet in person. I tried to leave a message on the ranch machine before I went, but I think it malfunctioned. Squawking noises, like an enraged chicken."

"Damn machines. I swear they make them with a chip that tells them to die the day after the warranty expires. I'll pick up another."

"Good. I had to rush to catch my flight and I've been jammed up ever since, so I haven't had time till now to call your cell. What's doing?"

I explained what had happened since we last talked. "I may have to go to Sacramento. Where's the best place around here to rent a plane?"

"El Aero at Carson City Airport. Ask for my buddy Pete. He'll give you a discounted rate."

Hy had "buddies" in airports throughout the country—sometimes I thought throughout the world. "Will do. When will you be back stateside?"

"I don't know how long I'll be here, and when I get back home I'll have to play catch-up. Any idea when you'll be coming to the city?"

"I'm not sure. This case—"

"Uh-huh. Now it's a case. Welcome back to the land of the living."

Hy was right, I thought as I stepped into the shower. Since last winter, I hadn't been living—at least not in the sense that I usually did. Although I wasn't yet sure that I wanted to make the reentry, I turned up the water's heat, washed vigorously, and emerged into a new and better day.

There had been a call on my cell while I was in the shower. Ted, with his daily report. I dealt with him, spoke briefly with Patrick, and got off the phone.

Freedom from the tyranny of the agency.

While I was eating breakfast in the motel's coffee shop, the phone rang again. The number on the screen was Jane Ironwood's. While I don't usually talk on the cell in a public place, there were few other patrons and none seated near me, so I picked up.

The voice that spoke was throaty—what in old movies they called a whiskey voice. "Of course I remember Miri," she said after I explained why I'd called. "She was a pleasure to have in our household, more like family than the other children in trouble we usually took in. And we loved Hayley as if she were our own granddaughter. But

eventually Miri married Jimmy Perez and they moved to Mono County."

"You sound as if you didn't approve of the marriage."

"When Miri met Jimmy, he'd been around our neighborhood for a little more than a year, doing gardening and handyman work. We never used him because I'd heard that he was unreliable. My husband and I questioned whether he'd be able to give Miri, Hayley, and any future children they might have a good life, but he said he had a brother who owned a ranch outside of Vernon and would give him a good job."

The brother: Ramon Perez. The ranch: Hy's and my small spread.

"Did you hear from Miri after she moved away?"

"A few letters at first. Christmas cards. Four birth announcements. Then nothing."

"Jimmy left her right after their fourth child was born."

A sigh. "So we were right after all."

"Unfortunately, yes. The house where you lived in Sacramento—I imagine you've sold it."

"Oh, yes. When my husband was diagnosed with Parkinson's disease, we had to stop taking in troubled children. And when he died . . . well, it was like living alone in a drafty old barn. I had friends here in Carmichael I wanted to be closer to, so five years ago I sold the house to a company that was going to convert it into commercial space. So far as I know, nothing's been done with it."

"Would you give me the address?"

"Certainly. But may I ask why?"

"Miri's running, trying to escape her life. I have a hunch she might have gone to the one place where she was happy."

"I see." She gave the address and asked me to call again if I had any news.

I set off to rent an airplane to fly to Sacramento.

The former Ironwood home was on Twenty-fifth Street in midtown Sacramento, a block off J Street, in an ethnically diverse area of mixed-use buildings—small shops, restaurants, offices, and private residences. Huge old elm trees and shrubbery that had run wild screened it from the sidewalk, but I could make out a white, three-story shape with a big porch and dormer windows. A flimsy-looking chain-link fence surrounded the deep lot, and a rusted sign proclaimed it as being under renovation for commercial space by Four Star Associates and gave a number for leasing inquiries. It didn't look as if any renovations had ever been made, and I doubted anyone had called the number in a long time. All the same, I copied it down.

Next door was a similarly old but better-kept-up house, outside which a law firm had hung its shingle. On the other side, a big light blue clapboard house with multicolored banners hanging on the porch and a bicycle on the neat lawn—a private home. Across the street a second-hand bookshop, a dental clinic, and another private home.

My prospects for getting onto the property now didn't look good, even though the runaway shrubbery screened it to either side. The attorneys next door might go home at five, but then again they might not. The family on the other side would probably be there in the evening. The bookshop and dental clinic would close down, but the home next to them had large windows overlooking the street.

Why was I even bothering with this? If I was doubtful of gaining entry, how could Miri have done so?

Because she knew the property. She'd lived there for five years.

It was now close to four-thirty. It had taken a while to get a plane from Hy's buddy in Carson City, longer to get a rental car at Sacramento Executive Airport. And then the rental clerk had given me the wrong directions. In a way, the delays had worked to my advantage: it wouldn't be long until dark.

I started the car, U-turned, and drove to a coffee shop I'd spotted along the way. Primarily I wanted to use their restroom, but I also bought a large coffee and a sandwich to go. Then I drove back and parked a few spaces down from where I'd been before. And waited as dusk fell.

Across the street the bookshop and dental clinic were already closed. Lights were on in the private home, but they glowed from behind closed curtains. Lights shone in an upper window of the law firm, but once it became fully dark they went out. Shortly after, a figure descended the front steps, got into a nearby car, and drove away. The private home on the other side of the former Ironwood property remained dark. I waited half an hour longer, then took my small flashlight from my purse, got out of the car, and slipped into the shadows on the side of the property that abutted the law firm's.

The fence continued to the back of a deep lot. A breeze had come up, rustling the leaves of the old elms. I stopped at the fence's rear boundary, saw that it backed up onto a paved space between two buildings on the next street—parking lot, probably, and empty. I moved along, muting the flash's light with my cupped hand. Shone it on the fence and finally saw a place shielded from the parking lot by a disposal bin, where the chain link had been pried up to the height a normal-sized person could slide under.

I looked around, then scrambled under the chain link on my back, headfirst.

The ground was covered with fallen leaves; they clung to my hair and my back. A vine on the other side of the fence took a stranglehold on my ankle and I kicked it free. Then I was inside, sitting on the damp leaves and feeling moisture soak through the seat of my jeans; it must have rained here recently.

I scooted away from the fence and under the drooping branches of a huge cypress. Ahead I could make out unidentifiable shapes and then the house itself. The moon hadn't yet risen—or at least it couldn't be seen from my vantage point—so in order to make my way across the yard I'd have to risk using my flashlight. Small risk, I thought as I turned it on and started out.

The trees ended after a few more feet, followed by an area of waist-high grass that once must have been a lawn. Trees shielded the property to either side. My flash picked out a jungle gym—iron piping, not the colorful plastic ones they have now. Halfway to the house I banged hard into something hidden by the tall grass: that was going to leave a nasty bruise on my thigh. I brushed the grass away and found a concrete birdbath, its bowl cracked and crumbling. What else was out here—

"Oof!"

My foot had come down on something round and as it rolled away, I fell on my ass. Jesus, what was *that*? I got up on all fours, felt around, and retrieved the object— croquet ball, the colorful stripe bleached out, covered in cracks and nicks.

Terrific. I'd probably trip over a mallet next, or bugger myself on a wicket.

I straightened and moved more slowly toward the

house, feeling around with my hands and feet for other hazards. Arrived unharmed and started up the wide back steps toward a set of French doors.

One of the boards broke under my weight, and I fell through, trapped up to my ankle.

And this is what you used to live for, McCone? Creeping around in dark, dangerous places in search of someone who's probably heard you flailing about and fled to the next county by now?

I dismissed the questions, extricated my foot from the hole in the boards, and tested each step before I put my weight on it. The French doors proved to be no problem: vandals had broken most of their glass panes, and one side stood slightly ajar. I moved slowly into a large room with a fireplace. The walls were marred by graffiti; beer cans and liquor bottles littered the warped hardwood floors. Used condoms and a pair of woman's lacy panties, too.

Only five years, and all this destruction—courtesy of a company that had bought a handsome, valuable property and allowed it to go to seed. I imagined Miri's distress at finding her former home in this condition. Had she run again—and this time to where? Back to the house in Vernon, where she'd led an unhappy life since Jimmy Perez deserted her—and probably before? I didn't think so.

I moved across the destroyed room and through an archway. This space had not been damaged as much, probably because it faced the street from which lights could be seen by neighbors and passing cars. It was a big, old-fashioned foyer. A staircase ran up either side wall toward the rear, then met in the center and continued.

She'd go up. Up to the bedroom she'd shared with baby Hayley.

I went up, too, along the right-hand branch of the stairs.

Turned down the hallway, where open doors revealed rooms empty of anything but more graffiti and trash. Something scuttled across the floor in front of me—a mouse or a rat. Cobwebs brushed my face and clung to my hair. It was cold, and the scents of mold and dry rot clogged my nostrils. Miri couldn't possibly have stayed here. . . .

My instincts prodded me on.

And then I smelled it—faint, but unmistakable. The odor of death.

I moved quickly along the hall to a closed door. Pushed it open and swept the room beyond with my flash. A bare mattress lay on the floor; on it was what looked like a pile of rags.

Not rags. A body.

I crossed the room, shined my light down onto a round face that bore a strong resemblance to both Hayley and Amy Perez. The woman was covered in ratty and torn blankets. She lay on her back, long gray-streaked hair fanned out around her shoulders. Death had removed the evidence of a hard and unhappy life from her features; she looked like a child, deep in peaceful sleep.

I knelt and felt for a pulse that no longer beat. Her skin was as cold as the air around her. I suspected rigor had come and gone.

A shabby purse, an empty liter of a cheap brand of vodka, and an empty vial of pills lay on the floor beside the mattress. I pulled a pair of disposable plastic gloves from my bag, put them on, and checked the purse: driver's license in the name of Miriam Perez, a rumpled card listing Ramon as next of kin, and three dollars. I examined the pill bottle without touching it: a strong tranquilizer prescribed three weeks ago by a doctor in Bridgeport.

How many had been left when she mixed them with the vodka I couldn't guess.

So what to do about this? Legally, I should report Miri's death to the Sacramento PD and wait here at the scene. Except I was on the scene illegally. Thus putting my license in jeopardy once again.

But I couldn't just abandon Miri to the ravages of rats, or to be discovered by young people who used the place as a party house. For Ramon and Sara's sake, she needed to be identified and laid to rest. Even though Ramon had said he'd washed his hands of her, he hadn't really meant it. And Sara still cared for her.

Advances had been made in tracing calls to cellular units, so I didn't want to use mine. Where could I find a pay phone?

There was one at a gas station near my freeway on-ramp. I called 911 and made my voice sound young, male, and frightened. Told the dispatcher that I'd found a dead lady at the Twenty-fifth Street address. Second floor, last room on the right. When they asked for my name, I hung up.

It was a clear, starlit night. No wind, easy flying weather. By eleven I'd be back at my motel in Carson City. And as early as possible tomorrow I'd be at the ranch, to help Ramon and Sara through this latest tragedy in the lives of their family.

The flight back to Carson City had somewhat eased my depression about Miri's sad end. There's nothing like breaking free of the earth to mitigate its claims on you. But once I got back to my motel, the gloomy mood descended again and I knew I wouldn't be able to sleep, so I checked out and began driving along the mostly deserted highway.

I thought about Miri. Understandable why she'd had a meltdown upon finding out Hayley had been murdered. Understandable, too, why she'd fled the rehab facility: the prospect of sobriety can be damn scary to a drunk or an addict; I knew all too well because of my brother Joey. But why had she bolted from Elizabeth Long's office? Because Long had offered her only more of the same, a shelter that provided psychiatric care. She'd then gotten a ride—or rides—to Sacramento and returned to the one place she'd been happy, only to find it in ruins.

Accident or suicide? She'd brought along enough vodka and pills to concoct a lethal cocktail. Before I'd left I'd searched for a note and found none, yet many people who commit suicide don't feel it necessary to document their reasons. Miri's reasons were written in the lines on her face, in the history her family and friends could recall.

Vernon was dark and still when I rolled through town at around eleven-thirty, the surrounding countryside even more so. I didn't turn in at our ranch house, but continued to the driveway that led to Ramon and Sara's cabin; it was ablaze with light. I pulled the Land Rover up to the shed that housed Ramon's truck, got out, and noticed an unfamiliar SUV. When I knocked on the door and Sara let me in, I came face-to-face with Kristen Lark.

The Sacramento PD was prompt in having the local authorities notify the relatives of people who had died in their jurisdiction.

"What're you doing here, McCone?" Lark asked.

"I saw the lights and was worried that Ramon or Sara might be sick."

"I see."

"What're *you* doing here?" I asked.

"Informing these good people that they've lost yet another family member."

I feigned shock. "Amy?"

Lark shook her head. "Amy's mother, Miri, was found dead in a deserted building in Sacramento this evening. SPD asked that we notify the Perezes in person."

"What happened to Miri?"

"Apparent suicide."

I looked past her, saw Sara had left the room and Ramon wasn't in sight. "How did she do it?"

"Booze and prescription drug overdose. Somebody found her and put in an anonymous call—dispatcher thought it was a kid who had been looking forward to an evening of partying and ended up with a corpse on his hands instead."

"That's a shame. Any idea why Miri was in Sacramento?"

"Ramon thinks she used to live there."

"Thinks?"

"He really doesn't know much about Miri's past. His brother Jimmy showed up here one day with a new wife and her four-year-old baby. Miri didn't want to talk about her previous life or the baby's father."

"That baby would have been Hayley."

"Right."

Lark regarded me with narrowed eyes. "Hayley's murdered, her sister disappears, and their mother commits suicide. And there's this other problem of a dead man in the lava fields. Plus you and I are supposed to be working together, but all I get here at the ranch is a machine that makes screaming noises at me, and your cell's always turned off."

"The answering machine has died and I haven't replaced it yet. I've been flying a lot; you can't have the cell on—FAA rules."

"I left messages on your voice mail."

"The mailbox malfunctions a lot."

Again that slitty-eyed look. "Okay for now, McCone. I'll leave, and you go comfort your friends. But I want to meet with you in the morning."

"Where and when?" I asked, hoping she didn't want me to drive to Bridgeport.

"I'll come to your place, around ten-thirty."

"That's good."

I prefer confronting potential adversaries on my own turf.

Friday

✦

NOVEMBER 9

The phone rang as I stepped out of the shower at around eight-thirty. By the time I got to it, the machine had started: Hy was right—it sounded like an enraged chicken. I picked up, but the squawking went on. Moments later my cell rang.

"McCone, you going to have time to replace that damned machine today?"

"I hope so."

"Good. Try the hardware store. Spare no expense."

"Where are you?"

"Still in Tokyo."

"What time is it there?"

"After midnight, your tomorrow. I'm flying back in the morning."

"Everything go well?"

"Better than well. I'll tell you about it when I get back. How're things with you?"

I didn't want to dwell on yesterday's grim discovery, so I said, "Progressing. I'll fill you in later, too."

We talked a little more, then he told me good morning and I told him good night.

While I was drinking my coffee, the cell rang again. Glenn Solomon.

"Sorry to take so long getting back to you, my friend. Frank Brower had difficulty getting hold of Carl Bates, the attorney back East who asked him to represent Hayley Perez."

"No problem." In truth, I'd forgotten about the inquiry I'd asked Glenn to make.

"The client who asked Bates to contact Brower is Trevor Hanover. He's a major power on Wall Street, owns pieces of Long Island and some of the Bronx, as well as majority shares in several multinational corporations."

"Did this Hanover give any reason for wanting to pay the legal expenses of a hooker in Las Vegas?"

"People like Hanover don't have to give reasons for what they do."

"You know anything else about him?"

"No. I don't follow the Street news much; Bette and I leave handling our finances to someone who does. But Google will tell you anything you need to know."

"What would we do without Google?"

"Probably poke our noses in where they don't belong a lot less often."

Before I began my search I glanced out the window and saw the Perezes' truck drive by. Going to Sacramento to identify Miri's body. Grim task, especially for people as broken up as they'd been last night, but there was no one else to do it. Ramon would shoulder it, though, keep-

ing strict rein on his grief. His responsibility, he'd told me. Even if Amy had been found, he would not have let her do it. He'd already failed to protect her from many of life's harsh realities; if she came back to them—*Dios* willing—he vowed to do better.

Google had plenty of information about Trevor Hanover, although the details of his childhood were sketchy: he'd been born in Erwin, Tennessee, a small town in the northeast portion of the state; his only comments about his upbringing were that it had been "dirt poor" and that he was glad he'd been able to help out his parents in their final years. His rapid rise to the summit of finance was something out of the fabled—and largely false—American dream.

The summer after he turned twenty-one, Hanover was working as a bartender in an East Village club when he broke up a violent confrontation between a drunken young woman and her date, sobered her up, and escorted her home. His demeanor when he delivered her so impressed her father—who was CEO of one of the larger Wall Street firms—that Hanover was invited to come in for a job interview. Again the CEO was impressed, particularly by Hanover's grasp of financial complexities, and hired him as his personal assistant. Later Hanover modestly described his knowledge as "nothing more than anybody could find out from reading the business pages and a few books." From then on his career ran on a fast upward trajectory.

Articles I accessed about Hanover compared him to investment guru Warren Buffett—except Hanover had achieved that status at a much earlier age. Photographs on the sites I visited showed a handsome, brown-haired man with a strong jaw and intense gaze. Hanover was

forty-three but looked nowhere near his age—or else he used old publicity photos. He was a skydiver and a pilot, and enjoyed scuba diving. Fifteen years ago he'd married Betsy Willis, a New York City socialite; the union had produced two children—Alyssa, now fourteen, and Trevor Jr., ten.

And then last May the success story had begun to unravel—

I was about to begin a more detailed search when Kristen Lark knocked at the door and called out. I closed the laptop, went to let her in, and poured coffee, and we sat at the table in the breakfast nook.

"So how about you and I bring each other up to speed on what we know," I said.

Lark nodded. "Okay. Start with Boz Sheppard: he's currently in jail in Independence, Inyo County. Got picked up in a drug sting Thursday night. We sent an officer down to interview him. He claims he left Vernon to swing the deal in Inyo County the day you saw him toss Amy out of his pickup, and hasn't been back to town since."

"Has he got people who will alibi him?"

Lark snorted. "Not hardly. His associates're all criminals who're looking for a way to wiggle out of the mess they're in. We'll let Inyo hold him on the drug charges— saves us feeding and housing him—and keep the pressure on. I'm going down there tomorrow."

"Anything on Amy?"

"We've got BOLOs out all over the state and in Nevada, but I don't have much hope."

"And Tom Mathers?"

"Well, that's interesting. The thirty-two-caliber bullet the coroner took out of him is a match for the one that killed Hayley. And it seems T.C.'s alibi isn't as good as we

thought. We're going to get a search warrant for her house and the wilderness supply store. She certainly has access to firepower, and she's been one hell of an angry woman lately."

"Toward her husband?"

"Among others. She recently had something going with Rich Three Wings, but his girlfriend found out and he broke it off. There was a scene between her and Rich at the Union 76 station when they both pulled in at the same time a couple of weeks ago, and she went to Petals and got into it with Cammie Charles in front of two customers."

"May I see your reports on that?"

"I brought copies." Lark tapped her fingers on a file she'd set on the table. "Next we've got Miri Perez. Troubled lady."

"She had reason to be." I explained about the rape over in Nevada, and Miri's family shunning her until she ran away.

"Who told you this?"

"Confidential sources."

She rolled her eyes. "That's what you private operatives always say. It's interesting, though, because it ties in with a local resident—Bud Smith. For years we've known he's a registered sex offender, but of course the details on the underage victim are sealed. Was he Miri's rapist?"

"He was convicted of the crime. But the general consensus, even of the prosecutor, was that he was covering for his brother."

"I've heard rumors to that effect." Lark paused to sip coffee. "So do you have anything else for me?"

"No." I also wasn't about to own up to finding Miri's body and phoning it in anonymously. And I didn't want to hand Lark the Trevor Hanover lead till I'd checked it out

thoroughly. Once an approach by law-enforcement officials is made to someone that powerful, the avenues of
communication become a traffic jam of gatekeepers and
attorneys.

After Lark left I went back to the computer, read
accounts of the latest chapter in Trevor Hanover's story.
In May several of his investment clients had lodged complaints against him with the Securities and Exchange
Commission. Excessive trading without their permission,
obviously looking to score a big home run and enrich
everybody, especially himself. A criminal indictment
against him in August. Divorce papers served upon him
in early September. Since then he'd become increasingly
reclusive, going to ground in an apartment he owned in
Manhattan. His family and financial empire were falling
apart and, according to an anonymous friend, Hanover
"wasn't too well wrapped" these days.

I went to the agency's search engines to dig deeper into
Hanover's background. A child named Trevor had been
born to Ina and Clay Hanover on the date the bios indicated, in Erwin, Tennessee. But there were no further
public records on him or his parents.

I tried neighboring states. Nothing. Widened the
search. Still nothing. By then my eyes were aching from
staring at the screen, and I realized it was after three and
I hadn't eaten. I also realized why I paid Mick and Derek
such handsome salaries for their expertise.

I shut off the machine and went to make a sandwich.

Agency business intruded with a call from Ted. "You've
been on the phone all day," he said.

"Online. There's only dial-up here. You should've
called my cell."

"Maybe you should check its charge."

"Oh, hell, did it discharge again?"

"Yes."

Ted sounded clipped, irritated. I said, "I'm sorry. I'll charge it up right away."

"That would be helpful."

"Is something wrong?"

"Wrong? Nothing except we got a notice from the Port Commission about a big rent increase. As did all the other tenants. I think they're trying to force us out so they can demolish the pier."

Twenty-four and a half was one of a string of piers along the southern waterfront occupied by businesses; none of them measured up to the glitz of the refurbished Ferry Building and upscale restaurants; the city had plans for the area and they didn't include us.

"When do we have to respond?" I asked.

"Not till after the first of the year."

"That gives us some leeway."

A pronounced sigh. "Shar, can I be frank with you?"

"Of course."

"This is urgent. It's hard to find decent space for an operation of our size in the city. And there're other things here that need your attention."

"Such as?"

"Adah Joslyn is fed up with the SFPD and considering a move to Denver." Adah was an inspector on the department's homicide detail and the live-in love of my operative Craig Morland.

"So if she goes, Craig does, too," I said.

"Right. Also, morale is at an all-time low here. Mick and Derek have put up a sign on their office door saying 'genius room' and it's pissing off everybody else."

"For God's sake, Ted, it's a joke."

"It would be if you were here. You'd put an X through the 'genius' and write 'asshole' instead, and that would be the beginning of a long string of jokes. But without you, everything's kind of edgy. The staff meetings suck; Patrick's so . . . earnest."

They need me.

But do I *need them?*

"Look, Ted, just tough it out a little longer. I'll talk to Mick, tell him to tone down the nonsense."

"You need to talk to him about more than that. He's kind of in a bad place."

"I thought he was over the breakup with Charlotte—"

"No, he's not. And he's engaging in self-destructive behavior."

"Such as?"

"Booze. Long, dangerous motorcycle rides at night."

Shit. "I'll call Rae and Ricky. Maybe they can straighten him out."

"Wouldn't it just be better if you came back and talked with him yourself? I don't know anybody he respects more."

Why me? Why am I always the go-to person in a crisis?

"Okay," I finally said, "I'll come down and talk with him. Attend Monday's staff meeting, too. But I'm working on something up here, and I'll need to get back pretty quick."

"When're you planning on coming down?"

"Well, it's almost the weekend. I could drive there tomorrow, talk with Mick on Sunday, attend the staff meeting on Monday." An idea occurred to me. "Actually, I have a project for Mick which may take his mind off his misery."

"Good. Because he's becoming a major pain in the ass."

After I ate my neglected sandwich, I went for a ride across the meadow on King. In spite of the splendid, clear day, I couldn't keep my mind off the Perezes: Ramon's strength in the face of various tragedies, past and present; Sara's love that enabled him to go on. Amy's disappearance, so long ago now that the sheriff's department had effectively back-burnered it. I'd promised Ramon and Sara I'd try to find her and had run around gathering information, but all that had resulted in was the unearthing of yet another tragedy.

And now things were falling apart in the city, and I'd promised to go down there and try to set things right. . . .

King seemed to sense my melancholy mood. He stopped by some shoots of green grass that were pushing their way through the brown, put his head down, and munched. I stared out across the meadow. Even as winter was closing in, new life was claiming the high desert. After a while I clicked my heels against King's flanks, and he trotted obediently toward the stables.

What was it Ramon had said to me about horses?

What you need to do is show them that you're in control, and that you respect them. Then comes the love.

I was in control, and I respected King.

But love? For a *horse?*

When I returned to the house, the answering machine was still doing its chicken imitation but my cell had recharged. It rang soon after the machine gave a final shriek that sounded—to mix a metaphor—like the chicken's swan song.

"McCone? No new machine yet?" Hy.

"Sorry. Busy day. Where are you?"

"SFO, about to grab a cab for home."

Home. I could sleep next to him in our own bed tomorrow night, see our cats . . .

"I need a favor."

"Anything."

"Will you fly up here tomorrow and take me back?"

"Absolutely."

"Thanks. There're some things I need to take care of in the city. And I really want to see you."

"Me too. Here's a suggestion: why don't I come up tonight?"

"Aren't you tired after that long flight?"

"Not any more."

"Well, if that's the case, just phone with your ETA."

"I'll do that, darlin'."

Saturday

◆

NOVEMBER 10

We lazed in bed till almost noon—it had been another nightmare-free sleep for me—and then Hy went over to see how the Perezes were doing. He came back quickly; no one had been there, but he'd left a note of condolence.

"They're probably still in Sacramento," I said. "This is so much for one couple to bear. I wish I could help more. . . ."

Hy hugged me. "You already have, McCone."

"I feel bad, leaving at a time like this. But the situation in the city—"

"I know. And Ramon and Sara will understand."

"But, Ripinsky, what about King?"

"Who?"

"King Lear."

"Lear Jet?"

"No, King. Who's going to take care of him?"

"One of the sheepherders. They know when Ramon's gone, and they pick up the slack. How d'you think Lear . . . uh, King's survived all these years?"

"Are you sure the herders know Ramon's not home?"

"In territory like this, everybody knows what's going on."

"Not everybody. Not by a long shot."

We arrived in San Francisco at around seven that evening. The cats, Ralph and Allie, were happy to see us, and while Hy was ordering a pizza, Michelle Curley, the teenager next door who tended to them and the house when we were away, came over to give us a report and an arrangement of pyracantha berries from her mother's garden.

'Chelle was an amazing young woman: all-A student; star basketball player; budding entrepreneur. She'd told me only a month before that her dad had volunteered to match the funds she had saved to rehab a wreck of a house in the next block; the purchase had been sealed, and Curley & Curley were in business. I wasn't to be concerned about losing her as a house-and-cat-sitter, she'd reassured me, because projects like this first one always went over budget and she'd need the cash flow.

Real-estate mogul in the making—purple hair, tiger-striped fingernails, multiple piercings and all.

'Chelle's report was good: the cats were eating well, the ficus in our bedroom had responded to the new food she'd been giving it, the chimney sweeper had come out and cleaned both fireplaces. We invited her to share the pizza, but she declined, admitting shyly to having a date.

That night we slept peacefully in the new bedroom suite we'd had constructed on the lower level behind the garage. Just before we drifted off I said to Hy, "I can fix these things with Mick and the agency. With you guarding my back, I can fix anything."

Sunday

✦

NOVEMBER 11

Wrong again, McCone.

The phone woke us before eight that morning. Ricky, saying Mick had been involved in a motorcycle accident and was in critical condition at SF General's trauma center.

I didn't ask for details, simply said we'd be there as soon as possible. As I drove, white-knuckled, to the hospital, Hy said, "This is not your fault. You know that."

"I've been up at the ranch wallowing in me, me, me. If I'd been here it wouldn't've happened."

"Maybe, maybe not. You're not that powerful."

I glared at him, and he shrugged, looked out the side window.

The waiting room at the trauma center was quiet at almost nine; presumably most of the victims of a San Francisco Saturday night had been cared for and released

or admitted, and their loved ones—if any—sent home. Rae and Ricky sat on a sofa, holding hands. Her face was pale beneath its freckles. His eyes were bloodshot, his hair unkempt; given that and the beard he was growing for a film role he'd accepted, you'd have thought him a derelict who had come in to escape the fog, rather than a country-music superstar.

We all hugged, and I sat down on the sofa with them while Hy went outside to use his phone.

"You hear anything yet?" I asked.

"He's still in surgery," Rae said. "Broken bones, ruptured spleen, all sorts of injuries."

"Damn kid," Ricky muttered. "Charlene and I never should have let him talk us into that moped."

Ancient history. When he was in his teens Mick had run away at Christmastime because Ricky and my sister had refused him the scooter; as my luck would have it, he'd come to the city and my Christmas Eve job was to find him. And later, as overly well-off and permissive parents will do, my sister and Ricky granted him his wish. A string of more and more powerful bikes had followed.

"He'd have pursued his passion anyway," I said.

"Yeah, that's what the Savage men do—pursue their passions. I should've set a better example—"

"Stop it, Ricky," Rae said. "You've been a good father to him."

"Have I?"

"Yes." She stood. "I'm going to try Charlene again."

Ricky watched her leave the waiting room, then said to me, "This is about Keim, isn't it?"

Charlotte Keim, the operative I'd lured away from Hy's firm years ago, only to have to ask him to lure her

back when she broke up her relationship with Mick. "Probably."

"A passing driver found him under his bike on the shoulder of Highway 1 at five this morning, reeking of alcohol. What the hell was he doing there?"

Playing with his death wish.

I didn't voice the thought. "Apparently he's been in a pretty self-destructive mode lately."

"You knew this? And you didn't warn us?"

"I only found out yesterday. It was one of the reasons I came down."

He nodded, grasped my hand. I followed his gaze as a doctor in scrubs approached us. The doctor looked too young to be so tired; he smiled reassuringly at Ricky.

"Your son's a lucky man, Mr. Savage. He'll be in casts for a while—left arm and leg—but he's young and he should heal completely. He'll need physical therapy, and I'd also recommend counseling. Has he been drinking heavily for long?"

Ricky looked at me, shrugged. "I haven't seen much of him lately."

I said, "I think his drinking may have been escalating since last winter, when his woman friend broke up with him."

The doctor looked questioningly at me. Ricky introduced me as Mick's aunt and employer.

"Well," he said after we'd exchanged greetings, "he's still in recovery, but you should be able to visit with him soon for a few minutes. One of the nurses will take you to him."

Then he was gone and Rae was back, saying Charlene and her husband Vic were on their way up from Los Angeles. Hy followed her in, asked about Mick's condi-

tion; Ricky reported what the doctor had told us. At that point Charlotte Keim rushed through the entrance.

"What's *she* doing here?" Ricky asked.

"I called her," Hy said.

"Why the hell did you do that?"

"She has a right to know. And he has a right to see her if he wants to. It may even help him."

"Get her out of here."

Hy kept silent, his gaze level with Ricky's. After a moment, Ricky looked away. "Ah, what the hell. Just keep her away from me."

Hy went over to Keim, who was pale, her brown curls disheveled, and guided her to the opposite side of the room.

Rae said to Ricky, "You can't blame Charlotte. Mick did this to himself."

". . . I know that. Like I did a lot of things to myself. And like me, I suppose he'll try to blame it on everybody else."

"I don't think so. Over the past few years you've set a good example for him."

"Whatever. I just want to see him."

I moved away, went over to Hy and Keim. She looked at me, eyes moist. I put my arm around her and said, as Hy had to me earlier, "This is not your fault. It's good of you to come."

"I wouldn't be here if I didn't care for him."

"I know." I looked at Hy. "Why don't you guys get some coffee? I'm going to drive over to the pier for a while."

The pier was always occupied, even on a Sunday. This morning, two cars belonging to the architects in the second-story suite opposite ours were parked in their spaces on

the floor. I went up the stairs to the catwalk, and ripped down the GENIUS ROOM sign from Mick and Derek's door, before I continued to my office. I shuffled through the papers in my inbox till I found the Port Commission's rental-increase notice.

They had to be crazy.

No way we could afford this. And even if that hadn't been the case, I'd feel I was being extorted every time I walked through the door.

But where the hell would we find comparable space?

Maybe it was confirmation that I'd be better off out of this business. But maybe not . . .

I settled down to do some hard thinking.

Mick had been moved to a private room when I returned to the hospital. He was awake, his parents and their spouses beside his bed. His left limbs were in casts, the leg elevated; cuts and bruises marred his features and his nose was taped where it had been broken; both eyes were black. And he was angry—with himself.

"I'm such a stupid shit—" He saw me in the doorway. "Hey, Shar, you didn't have to come down here."

"I was already in town when you pulled your genius act."

He smiled weakly. "I guess I better take the sign down."

"I already did."

Charlene hugged me and said, "I think the four of us should take off, so you can talk with Mick before he gets his next pain shot and falls asleep. Meet us at Rae and Ricky's later."

After they'd all exited, I said, "What did you think you were doing?"

He grimaced. "Jesus, I hurt. I don't know. To tell the truth, I don't remember anything except thinking I could fly on the bike."

"Be glad you couldn't."

". . . Charlotte was here. Dad was pissed, but he let her see me."

"And?"

"She told me we'd talk later. I know that probably doesn't mean much, but at least she came."

"And you got the attention you wanted from her."

He closed his eyes. "Not now, Shar."

"Okay. How long're they going to keep you here?"

"Dad's having me moved to a private hospital ASAP."

"Will you have computer access there?"

"Yeah, I'm sure. Why?"

"I don't want your skills atrophying while you recover." I reached out to take his right hand.

Again he grimaced. "I feel half dead. Only dead people don't hurt this much—I hope."

"They'll give you a shot soon."

"I'm counting the minutes."

"Don't talk any more now."

We sat holding hands till the nurse came with the shot and asked me to leave.

The hard thinking at the pier had paid off. Now I detoured on the way home to the Spanish-style apartment my operative Craig Morland and SFPD homicide detective Adah Joslyn shared in the Marina district.

Adah came to the door wearing blue sweats. God, how did she manage to look elegant even when her armpit area was streaked with perspiration?

"Craig and I just got back from our run on the Green,"

she said, catching with her fingertips a drop of moisture from one of the cornrows she'd recently taken to wearing. Her smooth, honey-tan face creased between her eyebrows. "What's wrong?"

"Nobody called you two about Mick?"

"No. What happened?"

"It's bad, but he'll live. If you'll invite me in and give me a drink, I'll tell you both. And then I have a proposition for you."

It was after five, and Hy and I were relaxing in front of the fireplace in the parlor, a cat in either lap, when Glenn Solomon returned my earlier call.

I cut from pleasantries to my main question: "How much influence do you have at city hall these days?"

"If you mean, do I have something on the mayor? No. But I've got the goods on some very highly placed officials."

"What about the Port Commission?"

"One of those highly placed officials has influence there, yes."

"You willing to call in some markers in exchange for a free pass on the next few cases you bring to the agency?"

"Always willing to call in markers for you, my friend."

"Okay, here's what I need. . . ."

When I replaced the receiver, Hy toasted me and said, "You're back, McCone. All the way."

Monday

✦

NOVEMBER 12

The Monday-morning staff meeting had gone well. In fact, a kind of giddiness had prevailed. The boss was back—even temporarily. But as I soared above Oakland's North Field on my way back to Mono County, following the ATC's instructions, once again I felt remote from the everyday concerns of the agency.

Hy had suggested I take Two-Seven-Tango. He didn't have time to deliver me and was sure he wouldn't need the plane for a while. I was more than glad to do so. As I set my course toward the Sierra Nevada, I fell into that strange state that I sometimes enter when flying: alert on one level, contemplative on another.

Contemplative about the new direction my life was taking. Contemplative about my current case. All other concerns slipped away as I planned what to do when I arrived.

*   *   *

As I passed the shack that served as Tufa Tower's terminal, Amos Hinsdale gave me one of his "Female pilots—bah!" looks through the window. I waved cheerily in response.

I drove to the Ace Hardware in town and looked over their limited selection of answering machines. Hy had said to spare no expense, but I bought the cheapest. It would serve for the length of time I remained here, and before we came up again I could pick up a better one at a lower price at Costco.

When I reached the ranch I checked the old machine to see if it had somehow resurrected itself. Not even a peep out of the thing. I disposed of it in the trash bin, set up the new one, and called Kristen Lark for an update.

"Not much to report," she told me. "My interview with Boz Sheppard went nowhere. I'm sure he knows more than he's saying, but he's stonewalling."

"How about if I take a stab at him?"

"If you want, I can set it up. Tomorrow afternoon?"

"Sure."

Otherwise Lark had nothing else to report. She referred to the cases as "dead ends."

I knew otherwise.

I was checking my e-mail when my cell rang. Mick.

"Thought I'd let you know that I'm in this convalescent place Dad had me moved to. It's posh—gourmet meals and pretty nurses and great therapy facilities."

He'd mentioned them in the order I would've expected. "That was fast."

"SF General likes to free up beds."

"You sound good."

"Well, I'm on these terrific pain meds. You asked

if I'd have computer access here, so I assume you need something."

"I've got a situation to run by you." I told him about my interest in why a man like Trevor Hanover would hire a high-priced attorney to represent a Vegas hooker.

"Let me play with this awhile," he said. "Back to you later."

I felt restless, so I drove into town. Petals was open; the clerk told me Cammie Charles and Rich Three Wings were due home from a camping trip in the Toiyabe National Forest that afternoon. Cammie always let her know where they were going and when they'd be back, in case there was a problem such as their vehicle breaking down. When I asked for Charles' home address, the woman gave it to me without hesitation. Small towns— you gotta love them.

The address was a cinder-block house two blocks down on the same street where Miri Perez had lived. An old Toyota with peeling paint and various dents sat in the driveway. I rang the bell, but no one was home.

It was a long drive to Rich Three Wings' place at Elk Lake. I decided to wait a while, see if Cammie came home.

That left T.C. Mathers. Was I up to tackling her? Sure. I'd dealt with tougher, more hostile women in my day and come out with the upper hand.

The wilderness supply store was closed when I got there. Tom Mathers had told me they lived on the property, so I followed a dirt driveway around the store and across a barren acre till I spotted a prefab house nested in the shade of a grove of cottonwoods. A Ford SUV was pulled up outside.

I knocked on the door. For a moment there was no reply, then T.C.'s voice called, "Go away!"

"It's Sharon McCone, T.C. I met you at the wilderness supply last week. I wanted to check and see how you're doing."

"The hell you say." She slurred the words.

"That's what I say."

The remark seemed to confuse her. There was a silence, and then she opened the door.

Drunk, all right: her long reddish-blonde hair was tangled, her eyes unfocused, and there were stains on her sweatshirt and jeans. She reeked of alcohol and cigarette smoke. She stared at me for a time before motioning me inside. I watched her stumble across the room to a sofa and flop down. She picked up a pewter mug from an end table and raised it to me.

"Welcome," she said. "You here to tear my home apart like those fuckin' deputies did?"

I shut the door and sat in an armchair opposite her. "I only want to talk. Tough time, huh?"

She shrugged. "I've seen tougher."

"I don't know. I was married last year, first time. I can't imagine how I'd deal with having my husband murdered."

"Tom? That asshole. I only married him because all the good guys were already taken."

"Like Rich Three Wings?"

She drank from the mug, replenished it from a vodka bottle tucked beneath the table. "How d'you know about us?"

"In a place like this, everybody knows everything."

"Ain't that the damn truth? That Cammie—little Miss Priss—found out about Rich and me getting it on. Then the shit hit the fan."

"I thought Rich was pretty much committed to her."

"*Pretty* much, yeah. But she was pressuring for marriage, wouldn't even move out to the lake to be with him unless they tied the knot, for Chrissake. He was starting to feel trapped and manipulated when I showed up to buy one of his rocking chairs. I wasn't in any position to trap or manipulate him and he knew it, so he took me to bed. Again and again, till the silly little bitch caught on."

"And so you confronted him and Cammie—"

"Give it a rest. I got a bad temper, but they're both alive, aren't they? And I didn't kill Tom. He had another woman, you know. Maybe you should check her out. Lives in that trailer park where Hayley Perez bought it. Little mouse of a woman. I happen to know he was with her that night, they always got together on Tuesdays."

"That make you angry, T.C.?"

"Annoyed, but I didn't care enough about Tom to kill him over any woman."

"This 'mouse'—you know her name?"

"Judy Perkins. She works as a hair stylist at the Vernon Salon. Little skank, wouldn't hurt anybody. And Tom came home alive and well that Tuesday."

"Any other ideas about who might've killed your husband?"

"I don't know. He was such a nothing. I can't imagine why anyone would bother." Her eyebrows pulled together. "He had something else going, though. Knew something he wasn't telling me."

"For how long?"

"Not very."

"And how do you know this?"

"Tom wasn't subtle. He'd been strutting around acting smug and arrogant, talking about all the money he was going to have, and if I was nice to him he'd share."

"But you have no idea where this money was coming from?"

"Uh-uh." She reached for the bottle, refilled the mug. "It must've been something big. But before he could collect, he went and got himself killed. Stupid bastard. Now what am I gonna do?"

I, I, I . . .
Me, me, me . . .

A prevalent mindset in contemporary society, and God knew I'd recently been guilty of it myself.

So Tom Mathers had had something big going. What, possibly, could that be? He was a wilderness guide; good money in that, and in the supply business, but it wasn't going to make him rich—not unless he'd discovered Bigfoot or a vein of gold during one of those treks.

It sounded to me like blackmail.

There are three kinds of major-crime felons who are too stupid for words: bank robbers, kidnappers, and blackmailers. The first two because they almost always get caught; the last one because they are frequently killed by their own victims.

But who could Tom Mathers' prospective victim be? A wealthy client who had committed some indiscretion on one of his wilderness tours? I'd like to get my hands on Tom's calendar and invoices. Perhaps tomorrow when T.C. would—hopefully—be sober.

But right now, onward to see Judy Perkins.

I drove through the trailer park until I found Perkins' space, one row down from Boz Sheppard's. It was small but well kept-up, with her name painted on a cheerful yel-

low mailbox. I got out of the Rover and started along a path of flagstones.

A woman's voice called out, "If you're looking for Judy, she's not home."

I turned. The speaker was elderly, wearing shorts that exposed well-muscled legs; for some reason, she was watering her graveled yard.

"You know where she is?"

"Out of town. Someplace near LA. Her mother's taken sick. Probably'll have to be put in a home."

"That's too bad. When did Judy leave?"

"Almost two weeks ago, Sunday. I been picking up her mail."

Almost two weeks ago, Sunday. The day after Hy and I had found Tom Mathers' body.

"You have her mother's address or phone number?"

"No. Why—?"

"That's okay. I think I have it in my book at home."

I started back to the Rover, but the woman said, "Sure has been a lot of tragedy in this place lately."

"You mean Hayley Perez?"

"Yes. And now I hear they've arrested Boz Sheppard. Such a nice young man; he used to help me take out my garbage."

Well, everybody has a few good points. "The night Hayley was killed—did you hear the shot?"

". . . Yeah, I heard it. Everybody did."

"But nobody called 911."

"Not that I know of. Or if they did, they're not saying. I didn't; I locked my doors and kept the lights low. I'm old and so're a lot of the other folks here. Not easy to defend ourselves."

"Did Judy hear it?"

"She didn't say. You'll have to ask her yourself." She turned back to watering her gravel lawn.

The old Toyota was still in Cammie Charles' driveway, but its trunk lid was up. I parked behind it, glanced inside on my way to the house's propped-open front door. Boxes and plastic garbage bags. The backseat contained more boxes and a couple of suitcases.

As I reached the door, I came face-to-face with Charles. Her arms were loaded with a comforter and pillows, her pert face flushed with exertion.

"What's happening, Cammie?" I asked.

She stared, not recognizing me.

"Sharon McCone. We met at Petals—".

"Oh, right. Would you mind . . . ?" She motioned with her head that she wanted to get around me.

I took a couple of pillows from the top of the bundle, stepped back, and followed her to the car. "You moving in with Rich—?"

"No. That's over. I'm going back to the Bay Area." She stuffed the comforter into the trunk, took the pillows from me.

"What happened?"

She didn't reply, punching the pillows into place as if they were defying her.

"Does this have to do with Rich's affair with T.C. Mathers?"

She slammed the trunk lid shut and turned to face me. "God, how many more people have to remind me of that? No, it does not."

"What, then?"

"None of your damn business."

"The two of you were on a camping trip. What went wrong?"

"What can go wrong on a camping trip? A bear ate our food? We burned the s'mores? Rich didn't catch any fish? Take your pick!"

"Seriously . . ."

"Seriously, I'm out of here. Go away!"

"Cammie—"

She straightened, balling her fists. "You want to know what's wrong? This place. People talking and prying into your life. People who don't really care about anybody but themselves, and will do anything to avoid responsibility. *Go away!*"

No sense in antagonizing her further. I went.

Rich Three Wings was chopping wood again. The sound of the axe smashing its target rang out over the quiet waters of Elk Lake. Given the sorrow and aggravation he'd suffered recently, he'd soon have enough logs to fill all the fireplaces of Vernon.

He heard me approach and turned, eyes reflecting the fire from the late afternoon light off the lake.

"What do *you* want?" he demanded.

"I saw Cammie—"

"Fuck Cammie!"

"What went wrong, Rich? You were camping in Toiyabe—"

"Who said we were in Toiyabe?"

"The clerk at Petals."

"Verna? Stupid bitch doesn't know one camping place from another. We were over in Yosemite."

But the clerk had been sure that they'd gone to the national forest.

"Whatever," I said. "Something went wrong, though."

"Damn right it did!" He turned away, resumed his chopping.

"You want to talk about it?"

No answer, just the ringing of the axe.

"Rich?"

"No, I *don't* want to talk about it."

"But she's moving back to the Bay Area. It must've been serious."

He pivoted, the axe held high, the sunlight making its metal blade shine as fiery as his eyes. "What part of 'no' don't you understand?"

I began moving away, watching him carefully. "I understand you're hurting. You know where you can find me if you need a friend."

It was nearing dusk and Petals was closed. I walked two doors down to Hobo's and asked the friendly bartender with whom I'd spoken nearly two weeks earlier if he knew where Verna lived.

"This got to do with Miri?" he asked.

"In a way. I want to buy some flowers."

"Poor Miri. But I don't think there'll be a service. Just cremation and her ashes scattered on the lake."

"These are for Sara and Ramon—to try to cheer them up."

"Nice idea. Verna's out at that trailer park where Miri's daughter got herself killed."

"You know which space?"

"Just look for the Airstream with all the rosebushes outside."

*   *   *

The rosebushes were blooming. I could see their huge blossoms even in the dim light. Verna must be some gardener, I thought. Rosebushes could be coaxed to bloom year-round at California's lower levels, but I'd never seen them this late in the fall at such a high altitude. The trailer was one of those streamlined silver ones. Light glowed behind its closed blinds, and music filtered out—something soothing and classical that I didn't recognize. Maybe Verna's choice of music was what made the roses grow so well. More likely it was her green thumb: some people just have the knack. For others, like me, the thumb is black.

She answered my knock after a few moments, wearing a Japanese-style robe, her hair wrapped in a terry cloth turban. I gave her my card, said I had a few questions about Cammie Charles' and Rich Three Wings' camping trip.

"Why?" she asked.

"I spoke with Cammie about an hour ago. She's moving back to the Bay Area."

"I know. She called and asked me to cover for her at the shop tomorrow."

"What happened?"

Verna didn't answer the question, but she let me inside. She turned off the music, motioned me to be seated in one of a pair of armchairs facing a small TV.

"I'm worried about Cammie." She reached for a pack of cigarettes on the table between us. "You mind?" she asked.

"No," I lied. "Were she and Rich camping in Yosemite or Toiyabe?"

She flicked a lighter, inhaled deeply, and blew out a plume of smoke. "Toiyabe. I told you that before."

"You did, and that's what puzzles me. Rich claims they were in Yosemite."

"No way. Cammie's still an urbanite—deathly scared of 'something bad happening'—as if it wasn't more likely to happen in the Bay Area than here." She paused, probably reflecting back on the events of the past weeks. "Well, it *used* to be more likely. Anyway, we were good friends, so she always let me know where they'd be going and when they'd be back. Usually she'd call to tell me they'd gotten there okay."

"Did she call this time?"

"Yeah. They were at a combination gas station and convenience store off of 395."

"Was Rich with her when she made the call?"

"I don't know— No, wait. She said he'd forgotten to bring beer and was inside picking up a couple of six-packs."

"You know where they went in Toiyabe?" From what I remembered of my only visit to the forest, there were a number of places where you could enter: some led to secondary roads, others only to trailheads.

"Devil's Gate, a few miles before Fales Hot Springs. There's no overnight parking or camping there, so they'd pull the car off into the trees and hike in to some favorite place of theirs." She stubbed out her cigarette, which was only halfway smoked. "Trying to quit. Figure if I only smoke part . . . But that's bull and I know it."

"Did Cammie explain what went wrong on the trip?"

"Not really. She said something they saw up there and Rich's reaction to it that told her he wasn't the man she thought he was."

"Something they saw?"

"That was all she said." Verna shrugged. "If you ask me, Cammie's trying to throw a scare into Rich."

"Why?"

"Because he won't marry her. She gave me a phone number where I could reach her in the Bay Area. Probably she thinks I'll pass it on to him and he'll come after her."

"May I have it?"

She read it to me from a scratch pad on the table. Area code 510—East Bay, a lot of territory.

"I'm worried about her," Verna said again. "I know for a fact she's broke—probably doesn't have ten bucks on her."

"Well, she gave you that phone number. It must belong to a friend, somebody who'll help her."

"Hope so."

"If she gets in touch, will you let me know? You can call me on my cell."

She looked at my card, nodded again. "Cammie's a nice woman. She deserves better than Rich Three Wings."

"Why d'you say that?"

"Well, he cheated on her and now he doesn't want to get married. In my book, that makes him pond scum."

I drove directly to Tufa Tower, where I fetched the San Francisco aviation sectional that covered this area from the plane. Then I went to Zelda's, took a table in the bar area, and ordered a burger and a beer. I'd also brought with me the *Thomas Guide* from the Rover. While I waited for my food, I sipped and studied them both.

The guide showed me where the Devil's Gate entrance to the Toiyabe National Forest was. A short way inside, the road stopped in the middle of nowhere. Well, that didn't tell me anything. Next I studied the sectional. It showed that the area where the couple had camped was about three miles from the trailhead, southeast of Mount

Patterson, altitude 8,500 feet. There were some buildings nearby—probably maintenance sheds or other rudimentary facilities.

Well, great. That helps a lot.

My food came. I ate, contemplating the situation. They'd gone up toward Mount Patterson and stumbled across something. Rich had reacted in a way that told Cammie he wasn't the man she thought he was.

People who don't really care about anybody but themselves, and will do anything to avoid responsibility.

What had Rich Three Wings done to avoid responsibility?

After I left the restaurant I called the number in the Bay Area that Verna had given me. A machine told me I'd reached the Clarks. I decided not to leave a message; Cammie couldn't possibly be there yet and wouldn't return my call anyway.

On the new machine at home I found—among others—a message from Kristen Lark: "I've arranged for you to see Boz Sheppard down in Inyo at one o'clock tomorrow."

I returned the call, got her machine, and left my own message about my day's activities. Then I curled up in the old, saggy, spindle-posted double bed and pulled up to my ears the quilts that Hy's mother had made for it. In minutes, I was asleep.

No more dreams about pits for me. Other grotesque and disturbing things might haunt my mind in sleep—and probably always would—but somehow I'd climbed my way into the sunlight like a clever spider should.

Tuesday

✦

NOVEMBER 13

Inyo County is one of the largest in California: ten thousand acres that encompass Mount Whitney, the highest point in the U.S. outside Alaska; Owens Valley, the deepest on the American continents; and one of the most beautiful, forbidding, and awe-inspiring places in the world, Death Valley.

Inyo's size makes it a difficult county for its sheriff's department to patrol: a person on the run can easily hide out there; the remains of victims of violence are frequently not found, if at all, until they're reduced to bone fragments; residents of small, hostile enclaves are clannish, impervious to the law, and outright dangerous. An extreme example is the Manson family, who conducted their murderous forays from an isolated ranch east of Death Valley.

In the interest of saving time, I opted to fly Two-Seven-Tango to the county seat of Independence, then call a

taxi to take me to the jail at the opposite end of town. I'd driven through there on the highway before, but always in a hurry to reach another destination; now, as the cab took me along the main street, I noted motels and small businesses, false-fronted buildings, side streets on which modest homes were tucked. Independence reminded me of Bridgeport: an old-fashioned courthouse, definite Western feel, and at its limits the empty, sage-covered desert stretching toward distant purplish hills. Today was clear but cold; snow dusted faraway peaks, and few people moved along the sidewalks; those who did hunched inside their heavy outerwear for warmth.

The driver dropped me at the starkly functional-looking jail and said he'd probably be there when I came out. "Nothing much happening today. You're my first fare. If I'm not here, call and ask for Troy." He gave me his card.

Lark had paved the way for me and, after the usual security checks, I was ushered into the visitors' room; shortly afterward a guard brought in Boz Sheppard.

Now that I had a close-up look at him, I decided Sheppard looked as if he were descended from rodents—white lab rats, perhaps. His nose came to a sharp point; his teeth were long and yellowed; he sported a scraggly mustache and an even more scraggly beard; his greasy brown hair was drawn back into a ponytail. Under the orange jail jumpsuit there would be tattoos—usually are on men like him.

He smiled at me, showing more of those teeth than I'd've liked to see, and said, "So Mono's sent in reinforcements, huh?"

I studied him until his smile faded and he shifted in his chair.

"I don't know what you mean by 'reinforcements,'" I said, "but if it's any comfort to you, I don't think you killed Hayley Perez."

He cocked one eyebrow—interested.

"I do think you know more than you've told the deputies. You're interested in cutting a deal on the drug charges, so you're holding something back."

He shrugged.

"Okay, listen to this, Boz: I don't give a rat's ass about the drug charges. And I'm not a cop. I'm not even acting in my capacity as a private investigator. I'm here as a friend of the Perez family, Ramon and Sara. They've had a lot of grief lately and I want to give them some closure."

"How?"

"By finding out what happened to Amy and who killed Hayley."

He considered, tapping his fingers on the table. "What's in it for me?"

Nothing, you asshole.

"If you cooperate with me, I could work on your case, find you a way out of here." Silver-tongued devil McCone.

"Yeah?" More interested. "You're from some big agency in San Francisco, right?"

"I'm the owner of the big agency."

"Huh." More finger-tapping. "It's not like I know anything. I mean, *really* know."

"But you suppose something."

"More like it."

"And that is . . . ?"

He shook his head. "I gotta have guarantees, man. I can't do any more hard time—"

"Well, there *aren't* any guarantees. I don't know if I

can help you. But what I can do if you don't cooperate
is go out there"—I motioned at the door through which
I'd entered—"and tell the deputies that you're bluffing.
And then I can go back to Mono and tell the authorities
there that in my opinion you're guilty of both Hayley's
and Amy's murders. There's also your trespassing on
my ranch Halloween night, spooking my horse, and then
knocking me unconscious. To say nothing of your second
visit to Willow Grove the next night."

What I'd said left him speechless, but not for long. "I
didn't kill nobody. Amy was alive and kicking last time I
saw her. Hayley, too. And I haven't been on your goddamn
ranch since I did a fencing job there a while back. Thursday night I was down here getting busted."

"Well, Hayley's dead, and Amy hasn't surfaced since I
saw you throw her out of your truck. I'm the one who can
put both deaths solidly on you."

"Amy ain't dead. She's probably out whoring around
someplace."

"You ever heard of a no body conviction? I can provide
enough evidence against you for one on Amy. Hayley,
that's probably open and shut. The jury wouldn't be out
an hour."

"Shit, you wouldn't—"

"Try me." I folded my hands on the table and waited.

It took seven seconds—something of a record in my
experience.

"Okay," Sheppard said, leaning forward and lowering his
voice, even though no one was listening. "I don't know about
Amy. But I told Hayley I had business down here and was
gonna leave the morning of the thirty-first, Halloween. She
asked me to go on the thirtieth. Said she had an important
meeting with somebody and it was better if I wasn't around."

"And?"

"I drove down early. Next thing I hear, she's dead."

"Any idea who this person was?"

"No, but I think it involved money. She said the meeting could change her life if it worked out, and if it didn't she'd go to the media and get famous."

"Was the person male or female?"

"Male, I think. She said 'he' once."

"Where was she meeting him?"

"Well, at the trailer, where else? That's why she wanted me away. That's where she was killed."

I remembered the dress Hayley had been wearing: black silk, expensive-looking. What else? Ridiculously spiked red sling-back heels. Garish red costume jewelry that was supposed to simulate rubies. The shoes and the jewelry were junk, probably what she'd worn for her johns in Vegas. But that dress was stylish—possibly a leftover from her time with Jack Buckle in Oregon. And there'd been a shaker half full of martinis and two glasses on the breakfast bar. One of the glasses had been broken.

So she'd worn her best clothing and made drinks for an important meeting that could change her life. All dressed up for whoever it was. And the man had put a bullet through her finery and into her heart.

Life-changing meeting. Certainly was.

Boz Sheppard was still holding something back, but he'd given me a few ideas. I could tackle him again if those didn't work out.

I flew north, but instead of landing at Tufa Tower I kept going to the northeast, studying my sectional, until I found the Devil's Gate entrance to Toiyabe National Forest. I spiraled down low and slowed the plane. There was

something unusual—although not alarming—about the way the engine was running, and I remembered the plane was due for its hundred-hour inspection next week. Our mechanic would diagnose the problem then.

The entry road ended in a parking area. No cars on a weekday this late in the year. I glimpsed a trail leading through browned grass to the northeast, but it soon disappeared under a stand of scrub pine. I crested them, found a mountain meadow ringed by sunbaked hills, and flew in a circular pattern, hoping to pick up the trail again. No luck. Only a dark wood structure with a tumbledown roof—not one of the buildings indicated on the sectional.

Something hidden out there, I thought. Something that made Cammie Charles leave her lover.

The sun was waning when I drove up to Sara and Ramon's cabin. Their truck was there; I went to the door and knocked.

Ramon greeted me, his face heavy with sorrow. "Thanks for coming, Sharon," he said. "Did somebody tell you?"

"Tell me . . . ?"

His shoulders slumped. An old man before his time.

"I came to see how you and Sara are doing," I said.

"That's more than anybody else has."

"I don't understand."

"We're scattering Miri's ashes on the lake in half an hour. I put out the word in town, said folks should come here first for a drink or some coffee. You're the only one."

Sad. So sad. "Well, I'd love some of that coffee."

We went into the living room, where a fire blazed on the stone hearth. Sara came out of the kitchen, moving

slowly; the past weeks had aged her, too. She hugged me and then sagged onto the sofa.

"Have you heard from Amy?" I asked.

"No. I doubt we'll ever see that girl again."

"Don't give up; I'm still looking for her."

"Thank you, Sharon." Sara put her hand on my arm.

Ramon looked at his watch. "You really want coffee, Sharon?"

"Not if you'd rather get going. Whose boat are you using?"

"Bob Zelda's. We're casting off from his pier."

"Then let's go."

Ramon and Sara exchanged surprised looks. He said, "You want to go with us?"

"I'd like to, unless you'd rather keep it private."

"No, no . . ." He looked away. "But why?"

Because I don't want you and Sara to be alone out there.

"I didn't know Miri, but I feel as if I had. I want to pay my respects."

Because I was the one who found her and left her body all alone till the police could come. Because I owe her.

Tufa Lake: deserted, its waters catching faint fire from the sun disappearing behind the mountains. Silent, too, once Ramon shut off the outboard motor. The birds were tucked into their nests, or had migrated along the Pacific Flyway to their winter homes. Wavelets rocked the boat gently as the three of us sat there, not speaking.

After a moment Ramon cleared his throat. "I don't know how to do this."

I thought of when my brother John and I had scattered my father's and grandfather's ashes from a rented plane—

my grandfather's also, because our family has an unfortunate tendency to avoid dealing with its dead. I didn't remember if John and I had said any words.

Sara said, "Tell her what's in your heart, Ramon."

"Do I have to say it out loud?"

"No."

He bowed his head for a few moments. Then he took the box that lay on the seat next to him, opened it, and emptied it downwind.

I thought I heard him say, "Goodbye, Miri," before he started the motor and headed for shore.

Wednesday

✦

NOVEMBER 14

I was out of bed before dawn and in the Rover by first light, heading for the Devil's Gate entrance to Toiyabe National Forest.

I'd spoken with Lark the night before, reporting on my interview with Boz Sheppard, and telling her the scenario of Cammie Charles and Rich Three Wings' camping trip. Lark had allowed as it wasn't enough of a lead for their overworked department to pursue, but said I was welcome to go ahead myself. So here I was, off on another fool's errand.

The Toiyabe is a huge forest with eight designated wilderness areas, some of whose ranger stations are as far as five hundred miles apart. It stretches over the Great Basin from the Sierra Nevada to the Wasatch Mountains of Utah, and encompasses snowcapped peaks, prairies, and granite canyons. The changes in elevation are sudden and extreme, making for a tremendous variation in climate,

wildlife, and scenery. The Bridgeport Ranger District, where I was headed, is one of the largest in the forest—an area formed by millions of years of glacial, earthquake, and volcanic activity.

I easily found the turnoff I'd seen from the air and drove to the parking area. No cars today, either. I got out of the Rover, shouldered my backpack. The pack was light—a couple of bottles of water, a sandwich and an apple, and a pair of binoculars. After a moment's hesitation I reached back into the vehicle and took out Hy's .45, which I'd stowed in the side pocket.

Rattlesnakes, I'd told myself at the time.

Snakes of any kind—particularly human, I told myself now.

I tucked the gun into my belt and set off toward the trailhead.

Cold under the trees, piney smell strong. The trail was good, frequently traveled. It was quiet here too: only an occasional birdcall. I looked for evidence of where Cammie and Rich might've camped, but found nothing.

Finally I reached the brushy meadow. At its far side was the tumbledown log building that I'd seen from the air and more trees, beyond which the sand-colored hills rose into the clear blue sky. I crossed the meadow toward the building—once a barn, from its appearance. Probably a leftover from the days when this was private ranchland. The roof had partially caved in, but the near wall was intact. I slipped up to it, feeling foolishly dramatic in the bright light of day, and peered around the side. Boards were missing there; I moved along and did some more peering through the openings.

Nothing but the play of light and shadow inside an empty structure.

I kept going to the other side. Most of the wall there was gone, ravaged by time and the elements. Cautiously I stepped inside.

And stopped, sniffing the air. Something had burned here recently. When I moved forward I located the source of the odor—a doused campfire near the far, mostly intact, wall.

Rich and Cammie had camped at a favorite place. What better than a falling-down barn? Shelter from the night cold, a cozy nest at this time of year. The park service had probably left the barn to collapse rather than demolishing it, not thinking it could serve as a haven for unauthorized campers—and be a potential fire hazard.

Okay, then, whatever Rich and Cammie had found here must be reasonably close by. I headed for the stand of trees along the hill's base.

Cold. Dark. You wouldn't think the pines could grow so thickly at this elevation. I batted back branches, avoided exposed tree roots. No trail, just acres of forest.

Would Rich and Cammie have come here? I doubted it. There was no sign of human visitation. I turned back, went the wrong way, and came to a place where a large section of branches had been broken away, so large that through it I could see the meadow and the barn. There were tire tracks in the damp earth here. I followed them, ducking under the fractured branches.

There it was: an SUV, tucked way back under the trees. Filthy white, with a trailer hitch. As I moved forward, I identified it as a Subaru Forester. It was dusty and stained with pine sap and the right rear tire had gone flat. Branches cascaded over its roof.

Christ, not another body?

I peered through the Forester's dirty rear window.

Empty.

I circled it, peering through the side windows.

Empty.

The passenger door was unlocked. I leaned inside it to open the glove box. Maps and some utensil-and-napkin packages from Kentucky Fried Chicken. A pencil flashlight and a bottle opener. Small pack of Kleenex. And, under it all, the Subaru's registration and insurance card.

Herbert Smith, Vernon, California.

I was standing outside the convenience store by the highway when Lark pulled up in her cruiser. She waved at me and yelled, "Come on, McCone!"

I'd driven to the store where Cammie and Rich had stopped for beer on Friday, to use the pay phone because my cell wouldn't work in the area. While I waited for Lark I asked the clerk if he remembered the couple. Yes, he said, they'd come in around three. The woman had made a call, the man had bought beer and beef jerky.

Now I slid into the cruiser next to Lark. "Are your technicians on the way?" I asked her.

"By chopper. You got some kind of divining rod?"

"What?"

"You know, like what they used to use to find water—only *you* find dead people."

"There was no dead person in the SUV."

"You want to bet that we won't find one within a few hundred yards of it?"

"I'm not a betting woman."

"You're lucky. I am."

I sat in the cruiser after I'd shown Lark where the Forester was hidden and watched her technicians

arrive by a sheriff's department helicopter. Then I got out and went to the far side of the barn, where I sat on the dusty ground and ate my sandwich and apple and sipped bottled water. Contemplated the mountains and the pines.

I was feeling at peace again, taking pleasure in the natural world in spite of my discovery in the forest. I'd taken steps toward my future; I'd taken steps to find out what had happened here, however grim. I thought of Amy. A certainty stole over me: I would find her, dead or alive, and set Ramon's and Sara's minds at rest.

About an hour later, Lark found me there. She sat on the ground too, took out her own water bottle, and drank deeply.

"My people've gone over the vehicle and the surrounding scene. We'll have it towed to the garage so the techs can go over it again. I've got deputies on the way to conduct a search."

I looked at my watch, was surprised to find it was only a little after two. Still, the light couldn't be good under those tall trees, and dusk would fall early in the shadow of the mountains.

Lark sensed what I was thinking. "They'll search as long as they can, then come back tomorrow."

I nodded. "You have time to run me back to the convenience store? There's nothing more I can do for you here."

"Sure." She stood up, dusted off her pants. "Just let me tell them I'm going."

On the drive back to Vernon, I thought some more about Amy.

Waiflike woman, standing outside the Food Mart in

the dark, pulling her flimsy clothing around her against the cold. Big eyes, and somehow I'd sensed her fear.

Tossed-away woman by the roadside, too proud to accept my offer of help.

The derelict cabin at Willow Grove Lodge, her meager possessions scattered around. The blood.

Dana Ivins had been a mentor to her. Bud Smith had tutored her. But somehow she'd fallen through the cracks.

The miles slipped by and soon I was in Vernon. I pulled to the curb across from the Food Mart, intending to walk over there and buy something microwavable for dinner. Sat there instead, my hands on the wheel, listening to what my subconscious had been trying to tell me while I sat on the dusty ground in the mountain meadow. Recalled the phone conversation Bud Smith had been finishing in his office when I went to see him. And got the message—loud and clear.

I'd have to move fast, before the sheriff's deputies found Smith's body.

Aspen Lane was deep in shadow when I reached it. I thought I saw a light shining faintly through the trees from Bud Smith's double-wide, but when I turned into his driveway all was dark. I parked the Rover next to the boat that was up on davits and got out, my feet crunching loudly on the gravel. No other vehicle in the yard, yet I could smell the aroma of cooking food coming from inside the mobile home.

None of which was unexpected.

I moved up onto the deck under the awning. Knocked.

No response, but there was a soft scurrying noise. I sensed someone on the other side of the door, breathing shallowly.

I knocked again. Called out, "Amy, open up!"

The breathing stopped, then resumed at an accelerated pace. I tried the doorknob. Locked.

"Amy, I'm a friend of your Uncle Ramon. Please open the door."

Gasping now; she'd begun hyperventilating.

"Please, Amy!"

A click as the lock turned. When I pushed inside, I found her crouching on the floor to the right of the door, her arms clasped across her breasts. Her shoulders heaved; she looked up at me with wide, frightened eyes.

"It's okay," I said. "Stay there."

In the kitchen I found a drawer full of folded grocery bags, took the smallest back to her. "Breathe into this."

She stared, not understanding. I put the bag over her nose and mouth and repeated, "Breathe."

The bag helped her get herself under control. Then she was able to stand, lean on me as I led her to one of the chairs.

"I know you. . . ."

"Yes. I saw you outside the Food Mart, and then again on the highway when Boz Sheppard threw you out of his truck."

". . . You asked me if you could help."

"And you walked away."

Silence.

"I don't think you want to walk away again." Dusk was gathering outside, so I turned on a lamp. Amy was pale and much too thin; I could see her ribs outlined by her tube top.

A burning smell from the kitchen. I went in there and took a saucepan I hadn't noticed before from the stove. Turned a control knob off. Ravioli, courtesy of Chef Boyardee. The empty can sat on the counter.

When I returned to Amy, she had pulled her legs up onto the chair and was wrapping herself in an afghan that had been slung across its back.

I tucked it around her, sat in the other chair.

"You've been here since whatever happened at Willow Grove Lodge?" I asked.

She nodded.

"Amy, talk to me."

"Okay, I been here since the day after. I was asleep that night when somebody broke in. I fought him, and he stuck me on my forehead with a knife." She touched a bandage above her right eyebrow. "So I kneed him in the balls and got away and hid in the grove. Next day, when I thought it was safe, I used the pay phone and called Bud. He brought me here. That night he went back to get my stuff from the cabin, but before he could pack it all somebody almost walked in on him, and he had to run off."

So it had been Bud Smith, not Boz Sheppard, I'd chased through the grove. But whose presence had I sensed while I was having my picnic there? Not Amy's or Boz's; they'd been in his truck on the highway. Probably some trespasser who saw me and thought I belonged there.

"Where's Bud now?"

Amy shrugged.

"Answer me. We don't have much time."

"Why?"

"I found Bud's Forester this morning in the Toiyabe National Forest. The sheriff's people are searching for his body. When they find it, they'll come here."

"Bud? Bud's not dead."

"Then where is he?"

She shook her head. "He said he'd come back. I been waiting every day. . . ."

"Where did he go?"

"I don't know." She pulled the afghan up to her chin. "He had a phone call and he left in a big hurry, didn't even unhitch the empty boat trailer from his SUV. Said something about a relative. . . . I don't know!"

I considered my options. None of them were good. Finally I said, "You go get whatever stuff you need. Two minutes, no more."

Big dark eyes filling with suspicion. "Where're you taking me?"

"Home, to Ramon's."

Home is the place where . . .

Ramon and Sara fussed over Amy, crying and hugging her and bundling her up in front of their fireplace. Sara fetched homemade soup and the four of us sat around the coffee table to eat it.

After we were finished, I asked Ramon and Sara if we could speak privately. We went into the kitchen.

"She's been living in Bud Smith's mobile home since the day after the attack on her at Willow Grove. It happened the same night her sister was killed. I should've figured it out sooner: I sensed somebody was close by when I first went to the trailer looking for Bud. Amy heard my car and hid in the trees. The door was unlocked, so I went in and found clothing in the guest room—Amy's. At the time I thought it belonged to a roommate."

"Poor kid," Sara said. "Why was she living at the lodge in the first place? She had a perfectly nice room here in town."

"From what she told me on the way here, I gather it had to do with Hayley. Amy used to worship her big sister, even though she hadn't seen her for years. But when Hay-

ley came back to Vernon, Amy found out she was a prostitute. It tore up the fragile new life she'd built for herself. She regressed and, essentially, went home to the lodge."

"But after the attack, why didn't she come to us?"

"Because it was the logical place for whoever attacked her to look. She was scared, though she didn't know Hayley was dead till Bud told her."

Ramon's face darkened. "That pervert had our Amy—"

"Smith's not a pervert, and he didn't do anything to Amy but give her shelter. The problem is, he's likely been murdered up in Toiyabe. When the sheriff's department finds his body, they'll go to his trailer and discover somebody else besides Smith has been living there. After that, it's only a short step to finding out it was Amy."

He glanced helplessly at Sara. "What should we do?"

I said, "Do you have a lawyer?"

"Yeah, but I don't think he's up to handling something like this."

"Well, then, just make sure that she gets a lot of reassurance and a good night's sleep. Chances are they won't find Bud's body till tomorrow—the light in Toiyabe was already bad when the sheriff's people started searching. I'll be back here around eight in the morning, take Amy to talk with the deputy in charge of the case. If she needs a lawyer, I can call one."

Ramon asked, "What was this business with Boz Sheppard throwing her out of his truck?"

"On the way here we passed the spot where it happened. She told me he picked her up in town and came on to her, wanted her to go down to Inyo County with him. She refused, things got ugly, and he threw her out. I'd say there's a good possibility that Sheppard was the one who attacked her in the cabin."

"Did he rape her?"

"No."

"But he cut her—the bastard!"

"If he's the one who attacked her, he won't get away with it."

Two pairs of hopeful eyes looked back at me; Amy was all they had left of their family, and they needed me to sort this out.

Please help me. You can make this horrible thing right.

I don't know what to do. Please help me.

I always wanted to say to clients, "Maybe I can, maybe I can't."

I always said, "I'll give it my full attention. Don't worry."

There were various messages on my machine when I got back to the ranch house: Hy, Ted, Adah Joslyn, Ma, Patrick, Mick. I noted them down and began returning them in order of importance. Mick, since he'd said it was urgent, came first.

"I did a nationwide sweep on this Trevor Hanover, using some really sophisticated software Derek and I have worked up."

"You've been creating sophisticated software on *my* time?"

"No, on *ours*. At night and on the weekends. Derek's between women and, well, you know where I'm at. Anyway, today was the first time I'd put it through its paces and judging by its performance, I'd say he and I are due to make a bundle on the licensing. I'd've gotten back to you sooner, but the nurses keep taking my laptop away and telling me I should rest."

"Well, you should. What have you got on Hanover?"

"I concentrated on the gap between when he was born and when he was rewarded with the cushy job for bringing the investment broker's drunken daughter home. But Trevor Hanover—the one born in Tennessee—never lived in New York City or worked as a bartender. He and his folks died in an apartment house fire in Chicago when Trevor was thirteen."

"The old stolen-identity trick. Our Trevor was in his twenties when he surfaced as a lucky bartender. Back then you could still easily get away with that kind of scam. Any details on the fire or the parents?"

"Typical tenement fire. Too many people, too many appliances, bad wiring. The father worked as a security guard. Mother described as a housewife. Trevor was in eighth grade. There's not much information."

"In short, they weren't anybody, so no one cared." Sad, bad truism of our society: we can cry over a movie star's marital crisis, but we give scant attention when an ordinary family is wiped out in an accident that could have been prevented. "Anything else?" I asked Mick.

"I'm going to run a nationwide search on Hanover's personal life as soon as Kelley here will return my laptop to me." He paused, and then I heard him saying, "Kelley, please. Please, please, *please*. I'm going into withdrawal!" He came back on the line and added, "She's relented, thank God. Talk later."

Next I called Adah back. Only the voice mail at any of her numbers. I hoped her message meant she was seriously considering my proposition.

I decided to call Ma next, reserving Hy—the best—for last. The business calls could wait till tomorrow, after I'd taken Amy to Bridgeport to talk with Lark.

Thursday

✦

NOVEMBER 15

Lark was in her office when I called to say I'd located Amy and was bringing her in.

"I thought you'd be supervising the search in Toiyabe," I added.

"Nope. That's in good hands."

"Anything yet?"

"No. So what's the Perez girl's story?"

"I'll let her tell you in person."

I left the sheriff's department after delivering Amy into Lark's hands, and started back toward Vernon. Halfway there my cell rang. Lark.

"We've located Bud Smith's body," she said. "Few hundred yards from his vehicle, in a ravine. Told you it'd be that close."

"Cause of death?"

"Shot in the back. Same as Tom Mathers."

"Estimated time of death?"

"A week at least, probably longer, the ME says. Body was badly decomposed. We tentatively ID'd it from a backpack that was lying next to it. Thing is, Smith's wallet and a bottle of water were inside, but not his car keys or any of the other stuff you'd take along if you were hiking in such an isolated area."

"I'd say whoever killed him wanted him identified and tried to make it look like an accident. He may have been shot elsewhere, then driven to Toiyabe and dumped."

"How'd the killer get back to wherever he came from?" Lark asked. "It's a long way out of there on foot."

"An accomplice, maybe?"

"Maybe."

Lark switched tacks. "The Perez girl was forthcoming about what happened to her. My guess is that Sheppard waited around till after dark, then broke in thinking she wasn't there."

"And tossed the cabin after she got away?"

"Probably. Before he came on to Amy in his truck, he was asking her about something Hayley might've given her for safekeeping. He didn't know what it might be, but insisted it had to do with her sister asking him to clear out of the trailer that night."

"She have any idea what it was?"

"She said no. That's the only point where I felt she wasn't being candid with me."

"So now what?"

"I'm driving down to Inyo tomorrow morning, and taking my best interrogator along."

"Good-cop bad-cop, huh?"

"Yep. And that interrogator is you."

"Then you're flying down."

"McCone, I hate small planes!"

"As I recall, you appeared at the crime scene in the lava fields in a chopper."

"I keep my eyes closed when I'm in one of those things. Really, we can drive—"

"You want to get this job done soon, or what?"

"All right, I'll keep my eyes closed . . . again."

When I got back to Vernon, I drove to Willow Grove Lodge and sat down at the end of the dock to think.

Remembered a night years ago when Hy and I had drifted there in a rowboat, sipping beer while I confessed to things I'd never told another living soul.

This past year, I almost blew two people away. . . . Each time I really wanted to do it. . . . I wanted to act as an executioner.

Our relationship, then so new and fragile, had saved me from those dark feelings. And given rise to the dedicated resolve to quell any and all such inhuman urges. To maintain control. To let go of the idea I could right every wrong and instead settle for righting only a few. So far I'd been able to keep my promises.

But at this moment there were a large number of wrongs that needed righting.

Hayley, all dressed up, offering a martini to her visitor and being shot in return.

Amy, brutally attacked.

Tom Mathers, left dead in the desert.

Miri, a suicide, as the inquest in Sacramento had determined, but equally a victim of the person who had killed her firstborn.

Bud Smith, decomposing in a ravine in a national forest.

Yes, quite a few wrongs.

Time to go see T.C. Mathers, a woman who had free access to guns.

The parking lot of the wilderness supply looked the same as when I'd first visited it. I was about to take the driveway to the Mathers' residence when I saw that the OPEN sign in the window of the store was lighted. I parked and went inside.

T.C. sat on a stool behind the counter, going over some pages in a thick binder. Her face was haggard, her eyes bloodshot—but she appeared to be sober.

"McCone—just who I've been wanting to see," she said, but without rancor.

"How you doing?" I asked.

"Terrible. I think I know what the d.t.'s feel like."

"And what're you doing?" I motioned at the binder.

"I thought maybe Tom had something on one of his clients that he was using for blackmail. He kept a log on each trip he guided. But there's nothing here."

"Well, he wouldn't necessarily have written it down if he planned to cash in on it."

"True. These logs go back years, so I started reading the most recent ones first. Most of the entries are trips with longtime clients. I know them; a lot had their entire families along. I can't imagine . . ."

"Why don't you let me borrow the log? Look it over from an outsider's perspective."

She sighed, shut the binder, and pushed it toward me. "You're welcome to it."

I set it aside, leaned on the counter. "T.C., I spoke with Kristen Lark. She says your alibi doesn't look so solid."

"Oh, Christ, she's probably been talking with Cullen Bradley. I need a drink."

"No, you don't."

"You're right, I don't. At least that's what I've been telling myself all day. Last night I promised myself I'd stay off the stuff, concentrate on running this business. But it's like people think the plague lives here; nobody's come in." She paused. "I guess *I'm* the plague. Everybody thinks I killed Tom."

"Did you?"

"No."

Her eyes looked candidly into mine; she didn't display any unusual body language. I believed her.

"Tell me about Bradley," I said.

"That night I was furious with Tom. So I stomped out of here and had myself a big evening, went to the motel with Bradley. I must've been insane. But then he passed out, so I left his fat ass in bed and came home."

"Was Tom here?"

"No. Right away when I drove in I saw his truck was gone."

"What did you do then?"

"Took three aspirin and went to bed."

"You weren't worried about Tom?"

"No. We fought a lot. One of us would leave, then come home and act as if nothing had happened. That's the way it was with us. We just never thought one of us would leave and never come back."

After I left T.C. I called the number in the 510 area code that Cammie Charles had left with her friend Verna. On the third ring, a familiar voice picked up.

"Cammie? Sharon McCone, the private investigator—"

"I know who you are. Who gave you this number?"

I ignored the question. "I found Bud Smith's SUV in

Toiyabe yesterday. And today the sheriff's department found his body."

"Oh, God. When we saw the Subaru I recognized it. I told Rich we should report it."

"And he didn't want to get involved."

"No. Rich, there was some problem between him and Bud. He said it looked like Bud had been killed and he didn't want anything to do with the cops. I told him we couldn't just walk away from this . . . thing. But we did."

"Why didn't *you* report it?"

Silence.

"Because Rich said not to?"

". . . Yeah. I didn't want him to get in trouble."

"But you left him."

"I thought if I did, he'd shape up, take responsibility for his life, and then we'd get back together."

Verna had been right about Cammie's motives. "So what was this problem between Rich and Bud?"

"I don't know. You'd better ask Rich."

"I'll do that. Any message you want me to pass along?"

". . . No. Well, yes. Just tell him I love him."

I drove to Elk Lake, but Rich Three Wings wasn't there. Finally I caught up with him at Hobo's around eight o'clock that evening. He was sitting at the bar, the two stools to either side of him vacant, as if the other patrons feared the aura of gloom he exuded might be contagious. I sat down to his right.

"Rich, I spoke with Cammie tonight."

He started, his eyes jerking toward me. "Jesus! You scared me."

"Sorry. As I said—"

"You talked to Cammie. Where is she?"

"Some friends' house in the East Bay."

"That would be Kendall and Dan Clark. They visited up here a couple of times. How'd you get their number?"

"Verna, from the flower shop."

"Is Cammie okay?"

"Yes. She asked me to tell you she loves you. I think she's waiting for you to call and make nice."

"Yeah, that's her style. She knows I've got the phone number."

"Are you going to?"

He considered, turning his glass between his hands. The bartender looked questioningly at me, but I shook my head.

"I don't think so," Rich finally said. "Cammie's better off without me. I'm an asshole."

"Because of what happened in Toiyabe?"

Silence.

"She told me about it."

"Then you know why she's better off. Bud Smith was probably out there struggling to survive, and I didn't want to get involved. What kind of a shit does that make me?"

"It makes you human. And you couldn't've done anything for Bud; he was long dead by then. The sheriff's search party found his body today; he'd been shot in the back, probably somewhere else."

"Jesus, all this killing." He shook his head. "Why would somebody shoot Bud?"

"Well, there was trouble between the two of you. What was that about?"

". . . We got into an argument in here a few years ago. One of those pushing and shoving things. Nothing unusual, but people in this town have long memories."

"What was the argument about?"

"Miri wrote a letter to Hayley and asked Bud to hold it for her, in case she ever came home. Bud said he hadn't read it, was keeping it in his office safe. But I could tell he was lying."

"How did you know about the letter?"

"Miri got drunk in here a lot. When she drank, she couldn't hold her tongue; she talked about the letter, but she never would say what was in it. About that she wouldn't say a word."

"And why would she entrust something that important to Bud?"

"Miri had a small insurance policy with him. When it was going to lapse because she couldn't make the payments, Bud took them over. He was nice to her in other ways. She said he never judged her."

Well, that fit with what I knew about Miri's rape and Bud covering for his brother. Guilt, plain and simple. "So you asked Bud about the letter and that led to this pushing and shoving."

"Yeah. Another example of what an asshole I am. I mean, Hayley wasn't any of my business any more. We were divorced. I'd made a new life for myself. But I couldn't let it rest."

"As far as you know, when Hayley came back to town, did Bud give her Miri's letter?"

"I didn't even know Hayley was here till she was killed."

"She took out an insurance policy with Amy as beneficiary. Do you think Bud would've passed on the letter then?"

"Probably. He knew Hayley would never go see her mother. She hated her. Once told me she wished she'd die."

*   *   *

After eleven. I pushed Tom Mathers' log book aside and rubbed my eyes. I'd come back and answered my business messages, then called Ma, and finally Hy, who was in Chicago "cleaning house." Which meant that, as part of his reorganization plan, he was firing and hiring personnel for RI's most inept and corrupt branch office. He was tired, frustrated, and disappointed that he couldn't get back for the weekend. I told him no worries, my case was coming to a conclusion, and I'd probably be in San Francisco when he arrived next week.

I sounded more confident than I felt.

I microwaved myself some mac and cheese, and then, feeling guilty about my recent poor eating habits, made a small salad. Ate while watching an old episode of *All in the Family* on TV. The show held up, even in this tumultuous first decade of the twenty-first century. Come to think of it, not much had really changed since the nineteen-seventies; technological advances, yes, but not matters of the human conscience and heart.

The rest of the evening I devoted to Mathers' log. T.C. was right: there were no notations to indicate trouble on any of the trips. I jotted down names and addresses of the clients for searches to make after I got back from Inyo County tomorrow.

Now, even as tired as I was, I got some carrots from the fridge and took them out to King Lear. The horse whickered when he heard my footsteps, nuzzled my hand as he took his treats. I stood petting him for a while, then said, "You know what? We've got to get you a companion. Being an only horse is not a good thing."

Friday

◆

NOVEMBER 16

There was frost everywhere when I looked out the kitchen window in the morning. Frost so heavy it mimicked the snowcapped peaks of the mountains. I was glad Lark and I weren't due at the Inyo County jail till two, when the day would have warmed some; cold-weather flying is something I prefer to leave to Hy.

I called the agency. Ted told me he'd taken matters into his own hands and was researching copy machines. He was fed up with calling the repairman for our present one, and had been lobbying for a replacement for months.

"I'm getting to know the repair guy so well, I feel like I should invite him to Thanksgiving dinner," he added. "Speaking of which, are you and Hy gonna make it this year?"

Ted's annual Thanksgiving party. God, I'd forgotten all about it! I glanced at the calendar on the wall by the fridge; I hadn't changed it from October.

"Uh, when is Thanksgiving?"

Ted let out a despairing sigh. "Next week. What planet are you living on?"

"A very strange one. Count us in." Even if I had to fly back for just the one day.

"Good. Is it okay to go ahead with the new copier?"

"Yes. But don't finalize the sale till you okay the price with me. And now let me talk to Patrick, please."

Patrick sounded tense. "Six new clients yesterday, Shar. All corporate. Derek and Thelia and I have split them up among us, but there're other cases that're backlogged. What with Mick in rehab . . ."

"Thelia needs an assistant."

"I know."

"Find her one."

"Me?"

"You. First, call around to the agencies we cooperate with and ask if they have any recommendations. If not, run an ad. You know what kind of person we're looking for. Then interview the most promising ones."

"But I just can't go ahead and hire—"

"By the time you complete the interviews, I'll be back to make the final decision and negotiate salary and benefits."

"Okay," he said, "I can do this."

"Of course you can. If you get really swamped with new cases, call on Rae. She delivered her latest book to her publisher last month."

We discussed a few other matters, and by the time we ended the conversation, Patrick seemed more confident and in control than ever.

Way to delegate, McCone.

Next call: Mick. I hadn't heard from him about his

deep backgrounding on Trevor Hanover since Wednesday. There was no answer at his extension at the rehab center. Probably in therapy, I thought. But it wasn't like him not to keep me posted, so I called Rae.

"Oh, God, I should've let you know!" she said. "Yesterday afternoon he had an episode of internal bleeding and they had to transfer him to UC Med Center to perform more surgery."

"Is he okay?"

"He will be. I'll tell you, this experience has taught him a lot. Us, too. We should've kept in closer touch after his breakup with Charlotte, given him the support he needed."

"I should've, too. I was so mired down in my own situation I didn't realize how bad off he was. When's he going back to the rehab center?"

"This afternoon." She paused. "Oh, I just remembered—before he went into surgery he told Ricky that there was some information on his laptop that ought to be forwarded to you. But Ricky forgot, and he had to go to LA this morning. He only called a while ago to tell me about it. Do you want me to go over to the rehab center and try to access it?"

"No, don't bother. I assume when Mick's back there he'll send it along. Give him my love when you see him."

"Frankly, I'd rather give him a good slap upside the head. God, I'm glad I never had children!"

"Yeah—and instead you became stepmother to six of them."

"Independence traffic, Two-Seven-Tango, turning for final."

"Two-Seven-Tango, Three-Eight-Niner. I'm still behind you. That's a damn pretty plane you've got."

"Thank you, Three-Eight-Niner."

I glanced over at Lark. She had her eyes closed. She'd closed them when we'd taken off from Tufa Tower, then kept them rigidly focused on the instrument panel during most of the trip. She was capable of speech, however, and we'd discussed the scenario for our interrogation of Boz Sheppard.

Lark had spoken with her superiors and the DA in Mono County, and then the sheriff and DA in Inyo. Together they'd worked out a plan that would ensure Sheppard's cooperation without either jurisdiction giving up very much. While we were aware that Sheppard—like any criminal or, for that matter, anyone who watched crime shows on TV—knew the good-cop bad-cop routine, very few of them failed to be rattled by it.

"Are we there yet?" Lark asked.

I leveled off, then set the plane down on the runway without so much as a bump.

"Are we—?"

"We're there."

"What?" She opened her eyes and looked around as I braked and turned off toward the tie-downs. "When did—?"

"That was one of my better landings. And since you had your eyes closed, you couldn't tell where we were at."

"No way! I could feel every motion—"

"I'll demonstrate on the way back."

"The hell you will!"

An Inyo County Sheriff's Department car took us to the jail, and a guard led us to an interrogation room that was much smaller than the visiting area where I'd earlier spoken with Sheppard.

Lark pulled out a chair from the metal table and looked around. "The ambience is perfect. Very claustrophobic."

"And scenic." I nodded at an ugly water stain on the ceiling. "Where do you want me?"

"Stand over there by that big crack in the wall. Fold your arms and look relaxed."

"Yes ma'am."

Seconds later Sheppard was brought in. He looked pretty bad—drug withdrawal, I supposed. His face was pale and pinched, more like a lab rat's than ever.

"Hello, Boz," Lark said. "You remember me? And Ms. McCone?"

Sheppard grunted and sat down across from her.

"I'm going to be taping this session," she said, activating the recorder on the table. "I've been talking with the authorities and DA's offices down here and up in Mono. I can offer you a deal, depending on the information you're willing to give up."

Flicker of interest in his eyes. "Yeah? What kind of deal?"

Lark began ticking off the items on her fingers. "No charges in the Hayley Perez murder. No charges in the attack on Amy Perez—"

"Amy? She didn't know I was the one—"

Snared. Snared and stupid. But Mono wasn't giving up anything, because they had no evidence Boz had killed Hayley, and Amy really couldn't identify him as the perp.

"Yes, she knows," Lark lied. "And she's willing to testify to that effect. On the other hand, McCone is willing to forgive you on the trespass on her ranch and assault charges. You tell us what you were looking for in Amy's cabin, it all goes away."

". . . A letter from Miri Perez. Something Bud Smith

gave Hayley. What this meeting the night she was killed was all about—the one she was gonna profit from. I tore the trailer apart, but it wasn't there. So I figured she'd given it to Amy."

"You have to beat up and cut Amy to search for it?" I asked.

Sheppard started. He'd forgotten I was there. "I didn't know the little skank was in the cabin. She woke up and tried to hit me with a lamp. Real fighter, that one."

"Don't browbeat the man, McCone," Lark said, glaring at me. She turned back to Sheppard. "Tell us about your history with Hayley."

"What about the rest of my deal?"

"This information is to cement the deal with Mono."

"Okay, okay. I met Hayley in Vegas. She was hooking."

"And you were . . . ?"

"Working in a casino."

"Which one?"

"Same one she was."

"The name?"

"I forget."

I said, "He was probably dealing—but not cards. Or pimping. Were you her pimp, Sheppard?"

"Leave him be, McCone," Lark said.

"He wasn't doing anything legitimate in Vegas, that's for sure."

Again Lark glared at me. "Not relevant." She turned her attention back to Sheppard. "Okay, you knew Hayley in Vegas. When?"

"When she was first there, I don't remember how many years ago. Then I did a stretch for possession. I was railroaded."

I said, "That's what they all claim."

"And after you got out?" Lark asked him.

"I decided to go to Vernon. I had connections—"

"Drug connections," I said.

Lark gave an exasperated sigh. "You see Hayley in Vegas beforehand?"

"Yeah. I stayed with her a few days till my parole officer gave me permission to leave the state. She said she had family here and might visit me sometime. And she did—late September, I think. She needed a place to stay. She'd come up HIV-positive, was already feeling sick."

So that was why she'd taken out the insurance policy with Amy as beneficiary. The county's pathology reports hadn't showed any evidence of her illness because they hadn't been looking for it. Which meant the life-insurance policy benefiting Amy would pay off.

"And?" Lark asked.

"I let her stay. Next thing I know, she's talking about cashing in on something, living out the rest of her life in luxury."

"Something that was in the note Miri left for her with Bud Smith."

"I guess."

"Did Hayley own a gun?"

"Hayley? Jesus, no. What would she need a gun for?"

"Violent johns?" I said.

"McCone, I'm warning you!"

"Sorry."

"Okay, Boz, do you own a gun?"

Silence.

"Part of your deal."

". . . Okay, I've got a thirty-two I bought off of a guy in Reno."

"Where was this gun the night Hayley was killed?"

". . . In the trailer."

"So Hayley had access to a weapon of the caliber that killed her."

"Yeah, she did."

All three of us were silent. Then I said, "Don't you want to discuss the deal you've got here in Inyo?"

He shot me a look of pure rage. "Who the hell're you, coming in here and trying to take over from *her*?" He motioned at Lark.

"Somebody who thinks you're pond scum. All right if I tell him about his deal down here, Lark?"

"Sure, be my guest."

"There isn't any."

"But she said—"

"She said that she talked with the authorities and DA in Mono and down here. She said 'I can offer you a deal.' Not we—I."

"You stone bitches!" He started to rise from his chair, but the guard, who had been standing by the door the whole time, stepped in quickly to restrain him.

Lark and I exchanged glances. Then she extracted the tape from the machine on the table, and we left Sheppard in the hands of the Inyo County authorities.

"Amazing!" Lark said. "I thought we were headed straight for Tufa Tower, but that's June Lake down there. I didn't even notice when you turned."

"Because you had your eyes closed again. You didn't notice that it was a steep bank, either."

"No kidding."

"Want to close your eyes one more time?"

"Uh, why?"

"It'd be interesting to know if you could tell when we were upside down."

"No way!"

"Just one little spin."

"Spin! Jesus, like a tailspin—?"

"Then I guess you'll have to keep your eyes open and enjoy the scenery."

Back at the ranch house, I found a message from Mick: "Call me ASAP. I'm at the rehab place and Nurse Ratched has confiscated my laptop. Says I can only speak to you for three minutes."

I dialed, and a woman's voice answered. I almost asked her if she was Nurse Ratched, then realized it was Charlotte Keim.

Well, well . . .

She passed me along to Mick.

"Charlotte's forwarding you the information on Hanover that I accessed—*she's* allowed my laptop—but I thought you'd want to hear this."

"How're you feeling?"

"Okay. But listen, they really mean it about the three minutes. What I found out is that Trevor Hanover owns property in Mono County. A lot of it—one thousand acres." He gave me the parcel number, adding that a map was on the way via e-mail.

I booted up my laptop in preparation for Keim's incoming file, while asking Mick more questions about his health. The nurse wrested the phone from him as the e-mail arrived.

The map showing the location of Hanover's property didn't really surprise me. I guess at some level I'd suspected it all along: Hanover was the owner of Rattlesnake Ranch.

A wealthy man from the East Coast, who flew to his private airstrip in his own jet. A man who had been a New York City bartender who happened to get lucky because of his ingratiating manners and impressive knowledge of finance. A man whose financial empire and private life were now crumbling.

A man who, under his real name, held a degree from a prominent Eastern business school. Who had ceased to exist shortly after attaining that degree because he couldn't risk the future possibility of being named a rapist, if for some reason his brother decided to tell the truth.

A man who used to be called Davey Smith.

Time to proceed slowly and cautiously. Build a case that no high-priced defense attorney could tear apart.

I couldn't confide what I knew to Lark. In spite of her elation at our handling of Boz Sheppard, the woman seemed on the ragged edge. In fact, she'd called earlier from her home to tell me her superior officer had told her to take a day off. Her voice had been slurred, and I'd heard ice tinkling in the background. I didn't want her alcohol-impaired judgment to get in my way.

Ramon was at the stable when I went out there, cleaning King's stall. I asked if Amy was still at his house. Yes, she was. I said I was going over there, I needed to talk with her.

Before I left, I slipped King the carrots I'd brought for him.

Amy was clad in a bathrobe that enveloped her petite frame; I assumed it was Sara's. She sat on the living-room couch, listlessly watching a game show while her aunt bustled around in the kitchen. I turned the TV set off and sat down next to her.

"How're you doing?"

She shrugged.

"I hear everything went well with Kristen Lark."

"Yeah, I like her."

"I understand Hayley gave you a letter for safekeeping."

"More like a big, thick envelope."

"Did you open it?"

"No."

"One thing in the envelope is a letter Boz Sheppard was looking for when he came to your cabin and cut you. I think he was going to look for it here too, when he saw the light on in the stable, spooked the horse, and hit me. He didn't find it either place. Where is it?"

". . . At Mrs. Ivins' house. Dana Ivins, who runs Friends Helping Friends. I knew it wouldn't be safe at Willow Grove or here, so I snuck over there and hid it in her garage."

"Why didn't you entrust it to Dana?"

"She's nosy. I knew she'd read it."

"But you didn't read it."

"I told you no. Hayley asked me not to." Her eyes welled up and tears spilled down her cheeks. "I was upset with Hayley when I found out she'd been hooking all those years, and when I found out she was living with that loser Boz I felt even worse. But I still loved her, I would never pry into her private business. Now I wish I had; maybe she wouldn't've gotten killed."

I didn't tell her that Hayley probably would have died of AIDS anyway since she apparently had forgone treatment. Amy didn't need that kind of memory of her big sister.

Instead I said, "The other thing that's in the envelope is a life-insurance policy Hayley took out on herself, with

you as beneficiary. Since she was murdered, the double indemnity clause goes into effect. Eventually you'll receive a hundred thousand dollars."

Amy stared at me, her mouth opening in a little O.

"It's up to you what you do with the money," I went on. "Blow it on expensive cars and clothes and bad boy-friends. Or use it to give yourself a much better life than your mother and sister had."

For a moment she looked away at the blank TV screen, envisioning any number of scenarios. Then: "I could finish up my GED and go to college."

"Yes."

"I could do something that would've made Mama and Hayley really proud of me."

"That, too."

Amy put her hands over her face and shook her head. "Oh, God!"

"What?"

"Oh, God, I'm all of a sudden so afraid."

"Of what?"

"I'm afraid I'll fuck up like I have over and over again."

I grasped her wrists and pulled her hands from her face, looked into her eyes. "You have Ramon and Sara. You have Hy and me. You can be sure if you start to fuck up, one or the other—or all four of us—will tell you."

Dana Ivins opened the side door to her garage, snapped on an overhead light. I followed her inside.

"There's the storage cabinet," she said, motioning to a hulking white assemble-it-yourself piece of the sort you can buy at Home Depot. Its doors were misaligned: one was at least two inches higher than the other.

I went over and reached behind the cabinet. Wedged against the wall beams exactly where Amy had described to me was a thick nine-by-seven envelope.

When I pulled it out, Ivins said, "Why, for God's sake, did she hide it there, rather than give it to me? I could've put it in my safe."

I shrugged. "She's young and she wasn't thinking too clearly, I suppose. Or maybe she thought your safe was too obvious a place and this envelope's presence might've made you a target."

"Amy always was a considerate girl. I'm so happy she's safe with her uncle. What's in the envelope?"

And she's right, you are *a nosy woman.*

"I don't know. Amy just asked me to retrieve it."

"Maybe, for her sake, we should open it."

"No, it's her private property."

"But it could shed some light on these killings—"

"If it can, Amy will turn the information over to the sheriff's department. She's been talking with them."

"About what?"

"I haven't been in on the conversations."

Ivins looked disappointed. For a person who insisted on her organization's right to confidentiality, she certainly played fast and loose with other people's.

I drove a couple of blocks along the main street before I pulled to the curb and opened the envelope, as Amy had given me permission to do. It contained the insurance policy Hayley had taken out with her sister as beneficiary, and a smaller pink envelope with Hayley's name written on it in erratic, badly formed penmanship. It had previously been opened, then closed with the flap slipped inside. I slid the letter out.

Dear Hayley,

I know you never want to lay eyes on me again and I dont blame you. I been a bad mother and a bad woman but that dont mean I dont love you. Bud Smith has been good to me. So I'm leaveing this with him in case you ever come back home or he hears where you are. What you need to know is Jimmy Perez wasnt your father. I was raped when I was 13 by a bastard named Davey Smith. Thats Bud's little brother. He got off scotch free because he was some kind of genius and Bud took the rap for him so he could go away to school. My family wouldnt let me have an abortion, but they treeted me real bad so I ran away and had you. And I kept you— thats how much I loved you. The other thing you need to know is Davey Smith is a rich man now. Goes by the name of Trevor Hanover and lives back east someplace tho he has a big ranch outside of Vernon. Rattlesnake its called. I found out from the woman who cooks for him when he's there—Linda Jeffrey, she lives on Yosemite Street. You can ask her if you want to. The way she knew he was Bud's brother is that Bud went there to dinner once and she heard them fighting. I guess Davey tried to give him money, but he wouldnt take it. Bud told him to put the money in the bank for you and hire a lawyer to help you out because you were bound to get in trouble in Vegas. I guess you must of kept in touch with Bud because he knew where you were. But baby, Davey owes you more than that. Talk to Bud and have him set up a meeting with Davey. Your his daughter. You have rights, you claim them. I know I'll never see you again baby, but you deserve a good life.

All my love,
Mama

Okay—slowly, cautiously. First I'd talk with this Linda Jeffrey.

Her tidy home was in the center of one-block Yosemite Street. A TV flickered in the front window. I rang the bell. After a moment the porch light came on, and a tall, slender woman in sweats, whose gray hair was pulled back into a ponytail, looked out at me.

"Yes?"

I said my name, gave her my card.

"Oh, you're Hy Ripinsky's wife. You've been helping out the Perezes. Come in, please."

The room she led me to was cluttered, but in a clean, comfortable way. Books and magazines stacked on tables, a hand-knitted afghan thrown carelessly over the large sofa, videotapes and DVDs piled high atop the TV. Jeffrey turned off the program she'd been watching and said, "Sit anywhere, but before you do, look for cats."

The chair I went to did contain a cat—a light-gray shorthair, whose sleepy gaze dared me to move it. I did, picking it up and setting it on my lap; instantly it curled into a ball and started purring.

"They run our lives, don't they?" its owner said, taking a place on the sofa and pulling the afghan around her.

"Yes, they do."

"I figured you for a cat person. And I assume you're here to ask about what goes on at Rattlesnake Ranch."

Her statement surprised me. It showed, because she added, "I know who Trevor Hanover is—or was—and I've been debating whether to go to the sheriff's department about him. Your visit has more or less resolved that issue."

"Why were you only 'debating'?"

"For two reasons. When Mr. Hanover hired me to cook

for the family, he had me sign a contract with a confidentiality clause. I was not to talk about him, his family, or anything that went on at the ranch."

"But you've already broken that agreement by talking to Miri Perez."

"How do you . . . ? Well, that doesn't matter. I did it for Miri's safety; it was only right that she know her real rapist had property so close by."

"And the second reason?"

"I don't really *know* anything—at least not about the times when Hayley, Tom Mathers, or Bud Smith were killed. The way my arrangement with Mr. Hanover worked, someone would call and tell me when the family would be there and what to prepare. But as far as I know, the Hanovers haven't visited the ranch for five or six months."

"Who else works there while they're gone?"

"My neighbor: she did the housekeeping. But Mr. Hanover called her in October and told her her services would no longer be needed. He gave no reason, but did send a large severance check. She used the money to take a trip to Philadelphia to spend Thanksgiving with her daughter. And there was a gardener and handyman, but he recently moved to Arizona."

"How recently?"

"A month ago. Around the time Mr. Hanover fired my neighbor. I don't know who's doing the outdoor work out there now."

The timing was interesting. Another generous severance check?

"Did the Hanovers always arrive by private jet?"

"Always. He's a pilot, you know."

"Did you ever hear anything that would explain why he chose to buy a ranch here?"

"I once heard him tell his daughter Alyssa that he'd grown up in Vernon and had always loved it here, but then his family moved to Nevada and his life was never right again. He said he was happy to come back as an important man to the place where he was born."

"But he bought the ranch in strict secrecy and never showed his face in town."

"Probably afraid somebody would find out who he really was. And he seemed content sitting out on that big old terrace and looking down on Vernon. I guess it was enough for him."

Until his daughter Hayley showed up and wanted him to acknowledge her.

"When did Bud Smith come to the ranch for dinner with Hanover?"

"Two years ago, the last Saturday in July. I remember because it was quite an evening. . . ."

It had started out pleasantly enough, Linda Jeffrey told me. Hanover had been alone on the trip and in an expansive mood, ordering her to serve special hors d'oeuvres and wine on the terrace; the dinner menu was similarly elaborate. Bud Smith, who was Linda's insurance broker, arrived about five o'clock and was given a tour of the property by Hanover. Bud called Hanover Davey, and Jeffrey assumed it was a nickname. The two men seemed reserved but were getting along well enough through drinks and hors d'oeuvres and the soup course of the dinner.

"Then their voices got louder. I was shocked to hear Hanover call Bud his brother. Hanover wanted to pay Bud half a million dollars for what he called 'his trouble.' Bud said he preferred to earn an honest living, that no amount of money could make up for those lost years in prison."

Hanover then began pressuring Smith to take the money, and Smith blew up at him.

"He said he had been in touch with Izzy Darkmoon's and Davey's child from the rape, Hayley Perez. She called Bud periodically to ask him about her little sister, Amy. Bud told Hanover to put the half million in trust for Hayley and also retain a good lawyer for her, because she was a prostitute in Las Vegas and headed for serious trouble."

"What was Hanover's reaction?"

"He said he didn't want anything to do with his trailer-trash bastard. That's when Bud threw a glass of wine in his brother's face. He told him he'd better establish the trust and retain the lawyer as soon as he went back to New York, and provide him with confirmation. Otherwise he'd go straight to the authorities over in Nevada and tell them the truth about the rape. And then he stormed out of the house."

"What did Hanover do?"

"Wiped the wine off and called for me to serve the next course. He asked if I'd heard any of their conversation, and I said no, I'd been listening to my iPod. He believed me because there's a light in the kitchen that flashes when somebody presses a button in the dining room, and a lot of times I do have my iPod on while I work. So I served him the roast. He didn't eat much or ask for the dessert course. Afterward he gave me a hundred percent tip on top of my usual fee, which is fairly generous to begin with."

"To ensure your silence, in case you *hadn't* been listening to music."

"Yeah." Linda Jeffrey smiled wryly. "But me, I'm like Bud: I prefer to make an honest living. I wrote a check next morning to Friends Helping Friends for the amount of the tip, and then I went to see Miri Perez."

* * *

So Linda Jeffrey hadn't been summoned to Rattlesnake Ranch in five to six months. And the housekeeper
had been let go and the handyman and gardener had suddenly moved to Arizona.

I had nothing if I couldn't somehow prove Hanover was
at the ranch on the date Hayley died.

Who would have the information I needed?

Amos Hinsdale. He practically lived in that shack at
Tufa Tower. Monitored the UNICOM constantly. No one
in a private jet could land in this territory without Amos
knowing about it—even if the pilot didn't broadcast to
other traffic.

Now, if I could only get the old coot to talk with
me . . .

"Canada Dry ginger ale," the bartender at Hobo's said.
"Amos hasn't had a drink of alcohol in his life that I know
of. But he comes in here every Saturday night and always
has three or four Canada Drys. Likes company and conversation that one day of the week. I keep a supply of the
stuff on hand for him."

"Would you sell me a cold six-pack?"

"Sure. You planning on seducing him?" He winked.

"If only what I have in mind were that simple."

Hinsdale gave me a suspicious look when he opened
the door of the shack at the airport. "We're closed, lady
pilot."

What on earth could be closed? There were no avgas or
mechanic's services here, just the UNICOM and a rudimentary landing-light system that had ceased to work
reliably years ago.

I held up the six-pack of Canada Dry. "I thought we might share a couple. It's my favorite, and I hear it's yours, too."

Now he scowled. "I'd think a woman like you, married to Ripinsky, would prefer beer."

"I like a brew sometimes, but not tonight."

"So you decided to visit an old man and sip some ginger ale. Hard to believe."

"Hell, Amos, you've nailed me. I need help."

"Something wrong with that plane of Ripinsky's? What did you do to it?"

"Nothing's wrong with the plane. But something's very wrong in this town."

His eyes narrowed, wrinkles deepening around them. "What d'you mean—wrong?" But his downturned mouth told me he already knew the answer.

"Hayley Perez, her sister Amy, and her mother Miri. Tom Mathers and Bud Smith. And a private jet that landed at Rattlesnake Ranch around the day Hayley was murdered."

His features seemed to fold inward, and his eyes grew bleak.

"Please, Mr. Hinsdale . . ."

He opened the door wider, motioned me in. "I'll take that Canada Dry, thank you."

Surprisingly, the shack was comfortably furnished, with two overstuffed chairs beside the table that held the UNICOM. Yellowing rental forms for Amos' clunker planes, scribbled slips of paper, old newspapers and magazines, and even older aviation sectionals were scattered beside the unit.

I sat in the chair he indicated, opened two cans of ginger

ale and handed him one. He sipped and stared silently at the opposite wall, where a framed photograph of a young man in a U.S. Navy flight suit was hung; he stood beside a fighter plane, his gaze stern, jaw thrust out aggressively.

Amos caught me looking at it and said, "Me. Down at Miramar before we shipped out for 'Nam on the *Enterprise*. December second, 1965."

"You fly a lot of missions?"

"Yeah. I was one of the lucky ones: I lived to tell about them. A lot of my buddies didn't."

"My father was a Navy man—NCO. In fact, we lived in San Diego and could hear the planes out of Miramar." The sonic boom from one had cracked our swimming pool so badly that my parents had filled it with dirt and turned it into a vegetable garden.

Amos nodded absently, sipped more ginger ale. "Wasn't a private jet."

"What . . . ? Oh, you mean at Rattlesnake Ranch."

"That's what you're asking about, isn't it? That jet, I don't even have to see it approach the ranch; I can hear it. You wouldn't think my hearing could be so keen after all these years around aircraft, but it is. No, that day I was standing in the door trying to work myself up to cutting the grass alongside the runway when this Cessna 152 flew right over the field. Damned low, and the pilot didn't even announce himself to traffic. UNICOM was dead silent. I watched the plane make its descent at the ranch."

"You get the plane's number?"

"I did. Was going to report it to the FAA, but"—he shrugged—"things get away from me these days." His eyes strayed to the photograph on the opposite wall. "It's hard to admit that you're not as energetic or clearheaded as you used to be. But it's a fact, you can't challenge it."

"It was clearheaded to take down the Cessna's number. You still have it?"

"Somewhere." He sifted through the items scattered on the table, came up with a blue Post-it note. He was more clearheaded than he gave himself credit for; I was willing to bet he knew where every item in that clutter was. "Yours," he said, handing it to me. "How about we have another ginger ale?"

"Sure," I said, surprised at how mellow he'd become toward me. I popped two more tabs, passed a can over to him.

"How'd you get interested in flying?" he asked.

"Ripinsky. I'd been at the controls of a plane a few times, years before I met him, when I was dating a Navy pilot stationed at Alameda, but I didn't enjoy it all that much. He was a hotdog pilot and liked to scare people."

"Guy was an asshole then. Ripinsky breaks a lot of rules, but never at the expense of a novice passenger."

"That's true. And he's a terrific pilot. Once I got comfortable flying with him, I asked him to teach me—he's got his CFI, you know. But he didn't think it would be good for the relationship, so he found me an instructor near San Francisco. And I've been happily flying ever since."

Amos pursed his lips; I suspected he was trying not to say something. But the desire to speak won out: "You been flying happily and beautifully. Nobody around here—male or female—makes the kind of landings and takeoffs you do."

I was genuinely touched, but I said lightly, "Not even Ripinsky?"

"Not even him. And I'm not bad-mouthing your husband, because he admits you're the better pilot."

Somehow I—and Canada Dry—had won grouchy
Amos Hinsdale over. I'd been promoted from "lady pilot"
to just plain "pilot"!

From the FAA's Internet site, I found the Cessna whose
number Hinsdale had noted down belonged to a flight service in Fresno. I called the service, got a machine. By then
it was nearly eleven. Hy hadn't called today. No one had,
except for Patrick and Ted with terse reports they'd left on
the machine. Hy's silence didn't bother me; I could sense
him urging me on.

I flipped the TV on to the national news. The recent
happenings in Mono County had become a major story.
Apparently they had been for nearly two days, when the
media smelled links between the murders. Come to think
of it, I'd seen a CBS van in town the previous afternoon,
but had been too distracted to take much notice. Tonight's
follow-up said the sheriff's department was searching for
both Bud Smith's boat trailer and the keys to his Forester,
so far with little success.

After watching the weather report—more snow—I
poured myself a glass of wine and sat down to think.

Trevor Hanover—wherever he was—would be moni-
toring the news. He'd be aware of the interest the cases
had generated. But would he suspect someone had also
linked the events to him?

Maybe, maybe not.

I began to construct my view of what had happened.

Hanover had been intimidated by his brother Bud's
threat to tell the truth about Miri's rape to the Nevada
authorities. He'd retained the attorney for Hayley and
probably put the half million dollars he'd offered Bud
in trust. When Hayley returned to Vernon and took out

the life-insurance policy, Bud gave her her mother's letter. After reading it, she asked Bud to set up a meeting with her father; again the threat hanging over Hanover had worked, and he'd agreed. Perhaps he'd expected some kind of trouble, since he'd flown his jet to Fresno and rented a small plane that wouldn't be recognized as belonging to him.

Still, I couldn't believe even as cold and calculating a man as Hanover was reputed to be would have planned his own daughter's murder.

An accident, then. Hanover refusing Hayley's demands for money and recognition as his child. Hayley taking out Boz's .32. A struggle, and the gun going off and killing Hayley. Happens all the time when irresponsible people untrained in the use of firearms have access to them.

Hanover left the scene, taking the gun with him. And someone saw him leaving. . . .

Tom Mathers. T.C. had told me her husband had a woman friend in that trailer park—a woman friend who'd left to care for her supposedly ailing mother shortly after Hy and I found Tom's body. Mathers could have heard the shot and followed Hanover. After that, he did some checking and made a phone call to the ranch, thinking he had a big deal going.

Blackmail—the fool's crime.

From this point on, my thinking became more speculative.

Bud Smith knew as soon as he heard the news of Hayley's death that his brother had killed her, but for some reason he didn't go to the authorities. Lack of proof? Shock? The habit of lifelong loyalty and protectiveness? The hope he could persuade Davey to turn himself in? Family ties

could be that strong: I'd seen it over and over again, in my own life and those of others.

Did Bud try to talk with his brother, but found himself unable to because Hanover had forted himself up at the ranch?

No way to tell.

On November second, a meeting between Hanover and Mathers at the lava fields. More demands on Hanover. His financial empire is crumbling, his wife has left him, he's killed his daughter, and now this. He snaps, and when Mathers turns away from him, he shoots him in the back with Sheppard's .32.

Premeditated? Yes. Maybe he wasn't expecting the meeting to turn out that way, but the possibility must have been in the back of his mind, or he wouldn't have brought along the gun.

Now he's panicked. He's in the lava fields with a dead man and two vehicles. He doesn't want to leave the body there—the proximity to his ranch. He can put the body in its owner's truck, drive it to some remote place, and dispose of it, but then how the hell does he get back?

The answer is the same as it always has been with the former Davey Smith: he calls on his big brother Bud for help.

Bud comes to the ranch in response to Davey's plea, not even taking time to unhitch his boat trailer from the Forester. But when Davey tells him what he wants done, Bud flat-out refuses. Davey's killed his own daughter as well as Tom Mathers, and Bud confronts him with the facts, threatens to call the sheriff's department. Maybe he even goes to the phone.

It's the first time Bud has ever refused Davey a way out. Davey snaps again, shoots his brother in the back.

Now he's got two bodies on his hands. The one in the desert—which he's zipped into a sleeping bag from the victim's own truck—doesn't matter, he decides, since the only other people who knew he was at his ranch are also dead. And the boat trailer provides a perfect solution for hiding his brother's corpse: put Bud's body into his—Hanover's—own car, the car onto the trailer, drive the Forester up to a remote spot in Toiyabe National Forest, dispose of both. Hitch the trailer to his car—because a vehicle with a boat trailer and no boat would attract a lot more attention when found in the forest than the SUV of a hiker who apparently went astray—and return to the ranch. Then get the hell out of there.

If that was what happened, the trailer might still be at the ranch. Maybe the keys to Bud Smith's Forester, too. Since Hanover had driven it into the woods, he might have pocketed them.

And the ranch house was a probable crime scene. There could be material evidence—blood, fibers, fingerprints . . .

So?

Check out the property from the air, make sure it was deserted. And then get onto it and into the house. Look for something that would give Lark probable cause to obtain a search warrant.

Of course, those actions were totally illegal. Trespassing, breaking and entering. I could lose my private investigator's license, go to jail. And I didn't want to hinder the authorities in building a case against Hanover. While Lark was willing to bend the law when circumstances merited it, no way she'd be able to get a warrant based on information gleaned during an illegal search.

Well, what if my plane's engine went out, and I had to

make an emergency landing on the ranch? Wasn't able to make radio contact with anyone? Was forced to hike to the house to ask to use the phone? Found no one there, but looked through the windows and saw something suspicious? Left and reported it to Lark?

Lark didn't know enough about planes to realize that when you had an engine out, it didn't suddenly start up again. She'd assume it was like a car's flooded motor. And the roughness of the landing could explain the loss of radio contact.

Thin, but Lark wouldn't be inclined to ask too many questions if a multiple murderer was brought to justice as a result.

Okay. I'd sleep on it. But first I'd run a search for the license plate number of Bud Smith's boat trailer.

Saturday

◆

NOVEMBER 17

The morning air was crisp, the sky clear. The projected snowstorm had blown past in the night and was currently blanketing parts of Tuolomne County.

Amos Hinsdale arrived at the UNICOM shack as I was preflighting Two-Seven-Tango. "You leaving?" he asked, genuine disappointment in his voice.

"No, just going out to take a look around."

"At that ranch, you mean."

I hesitated. Could I trust him? Yes, I could: in Amos' world there was a brotherhood of pilots, and last night he'd allowed me to join it.

"That's my approximate destination."

The lines around his eyes crinkled. "Be careful. You got plenty of fuel?"

"Yes. I filled up at Independence yesterday."

"Stop in when you get back. I've still got a couple of Canada Drys on ice."

"Will do."

"And keep tuned to the UNICOM. If there's any unannounced incoming traffic, I'll contact you. Code word Reptile."

We smiled at our little intrigue and shook hands before I climbed into the plane.

I turned the key in the ignition. The engine coughed and then a warning light flickered. Electrical system failure. There was a backup battery, but I didn't know how much charge was left on it; recalling the way the engine had sounded when I'd returned here after my overflight of Toiyabe, I realized I might have been flying on battery for some time. Would I have missed the warning light then and also on the flights to and from Independence? Doubtful, but lately I never knew. . . .

Well, I couldn't take Two-Seven-Tango up without a certified mechanic's okay. And I was no mechanic; neither was Amos.

I removed the key from the ignition, got out, and said to Amos, "Which of those rental planes of yours is the better?"

It was a thirty-seven-year-old Cessna 150—the type of plane I'd trained on—with a banged-up exterior, ripped-up interior, and crazing—small fractures—on the windshield. It preflighted well, though, and started strongly. The gauges were all functioning, and no warning lights flashed. I gave Amos a thumbs-up sign and taxied toward the runway.

A thousand acres of ranch land is a lot of territory to explore, even from the air, but I'd devised a plan. First I checked the house and outbuildings, putting the plane into slow flight, scanning for signs of habitation. None visible. Then I flew over the long airstrip—well paved and equipped with all the bells and whistles of a small municipal airport,

including a large hangar. The hangar's doors were closed; a faded orange windsock at midfield drooped limply. Easy landing day, no strong crosswinds. But I wasn't planning on using this runway.

I kept flying to the southeast, looking for a landing place that was far enough away from the house that I wouldn't attract attention in case someone actually was in residence, but also within a reasonable hiking distance. A long ridge crossed the terrain, rough-surfaced and dotted with small obsidian outcroppings. On the other side of it I found a flat, open area that once must have been cattle graze. I could put down and take off easily there. It would be a fair hike to the house, but I was wearing sturdy boots and had bottled water in my backpack.

Bottled water, binoculars, and Hy's .45.

I didn't want to land just yet, though. Instead I headed back toward the airstrip and house, thinking a second slow overflight might scare up anybody who hadn't been curious enough to come outside the first time.

No one.

Okay, back toward my selected landing place. I spoke into the radio's microphone. "Tufa Tower traffic, Reptile. Anything?"

"Negative, Reptile."

Midway between the ranch compound and the jagged, rocky ridge, something strange caught my eye. I glanced forward at the engine cowling. Nothing. Maybe I'd glimpsed a black bird narrowly missing the plane.

A few seconds later I saw it again: a smoky curl drifting from the edge of the cowling. The paint there looked bubbled. Suddenly bright orange flames flickered upward.

Engine fire!

Fuel-fed, not oil-fed—had to be from the color of those flames.

Panic made my limbs rigid, fused my gaze to the flames. I'd been in a serious emergency situation once before, but long ago—

Time telescoped as fear turned to rage. My life was back on track: I'd made my decisions and was set to enjoy the future. And now maybe I was going to die because Amos Hinsdale hadn't properly maintained his crappy airplane.

Focus. Do what you were trained to do.

Stubborn determination gripped me as I looked at the instrument panel. I was *not* going to die—not now, not like this. Emergency procedures from my old training manual flashed through my mind.

Forced landing, engine fire: Shut off the fuel supply. Keep the ignition switch on to clear the fuel lines. Lower the nose to maintain your airspeed.

My hands moved mechanically through the actions I'd practiced many times in simulated situations.

Now look for a place to bring this piece of shit down.

My altitude and airspeed were not enough to crest the ridge ahead to level ground or return to the airstrip. And that ridge was the worst possible place to try to land.

"Okay," I said aloud, "I don't care about saving the plane. What I need to do is keep the cockpit—and me—intact. Screw the wings, tail section, and landing gear."

The terrain was treacherous, but I could use it to my advantage. Rock was an energy-absorbing medium; even the scrub pines would help stop the plane once it was down. *If* I landed correctly, allowing only the outer parts of the Cessna to be mangled . . .

But what if the plane exploded on impact? I'd never see Hy again. Never see the other people I loved, never—

Focus, dammit!

Lower flaps. That increases mobility. Bank a little here, not too much. More right rudder. Lift the nose slightly. Now hold it level.

I was almost to the ridge now, its black, glassy rocks seeming to jump up at me.

Hold it level.

Slow it down.

Slower . . .

There was a stand of scrub pines near the ridgetop. Perfect. The right wing would hit them, slow the plane before it hit rock.

Brace yourself!

Jarring impact. A shearing sound. Metal screaming. The plane slewed violently to the left.

My seat belt tore loose and I slammed against the door, then forward onto the yoke. Pain shot through my chest, but I clung to the yoke as if it were a life preserver, my eyes squeezed shut, steeled for the *whoosh* of igniting fuel.

The plane dropped downward, its landing gear crushed. Then, with a sound like a great sigh, it settled. Stones rattled, metal groaned, the windshield rained down.

The silence that followed was almost as deafening as the crash.

I raised my head and looked around. The right wing was gone, the plane's nose buried into the ground, facing downhill. But the cockpit and I were intact.

You did it, McCone. You brought it down.

The voice in my mind sounded like Hy's. As if he'd been there all along, urging me on.

Exit and get clear of the aircraft promptly, in case of explosion.

I grabbed my backpack from the passenger seat and

pushed through the half-sprung door. Tumbled to the ground, pushed myself up, and took off running and skidding down the ridge.

At its bottom I looked back at the twisted wreckage of the Cessna. The elevators on the tail section had also been sheared off, the tail itself bent. The slope above it was littered with metal. There was still no fire or explosion, but I wasn't going to wait around for either. As I moved away, I took out my phone: no reception.

Behind me I heard popping and crackling sounds. Then a loud bang. In a few seconds the wreckage was engulfed in flames.

Exit and get clear of the aircraft promptly. . . .

Yeah.

Quickly I turned away. I'd walk to the ranch house and ask for help, playing out my cover scenario for real.

I set out for the ranch compound. In spite of the cold, the sun beat down and soon I began to sweat inside my heavy parka. I unzipped it and went on.

The pain in my chest was becoming more bearable, but every now and then a sudden, vicious stab would make me stop and catch my breath. I wondered if I had a cracked rib or sternum.

The hiking boots weren't ones I frequently wore. My toes and heels began to chafe against them. I promised myself a pedicure when I got back to the city.

As I approached the compound, my backpack tugged uncomfortably at my shoulders. I stopped, took it off, and removed Hy's .45 to reduce the load. Time to have the gun at hand, anyway. I stuck it in the waistband of my jeans, had a drink of bottled water, put the pack back on, and kept going.

When I got to a small stand of Jeffrey pines, I dropped down onto my knees and took out the binoculars. Surveyed the bleak land that stretched in front of me, the cluster of simulated adobe buildings with red tile roofs. No motion, no life.

The sun was glaring down now. Sweat oozed along my rib cage. I shed the parka and left it on the ground. Began to creep along—alert for the presence of other slithering creatures. After all, Rattlesnake Ranch had been aptly named. This was the predators' natural habitat.

House, hangar, and outbuildings clearly in sight now. Drained swimming pool showing through a long, tall hedge of hardy-looking evergreens. I picked up the pace.

Halfway there I paused to raise the binoculars. Empty landscape.

Last hundred yards or so. Parched, but unwilling to stop for water. Hand on gun. If someone had heard the crash, he could be lying in wait.

Emptiness.

I reached the hedge that screened the house and pool.

A hissing sound.

Snake!

I drew the .45, tensing—and then saw droplets clinging to the plants and realized the hiss came from an automatic sprinkler system.

Come on, McCone—after what you've just been through, an encounter with a rattler is nothing.

I slipped up to the hedge. The spray from the sprinklers felt cool on my face and bare arms. I moved through the prickly branches till I could see the house.

Patio on the other side of the pool, furniture covered. French doors, with blinds closed. Other windows, also covered from within.

No one here, but that was what I'd hoped for. I needed to get inside and call for help, so I might as well carry through with my original purpose.

Where was the garage? Not on this side. Try the other.

I followed the line of the shrubbery. More covered windows. Other small patios. A garden, mostly turned earth and weeds, with a border of dried-out sunflowers. Finally a garage, large enough to hold at least three cars. There was a window in the rear, blocked by what looked to be cardboard.

The dead sunflower border of the garden provided shelter. I went to the garage window.

Cardboard, yes. A flattened carton with the words WOLF SUB-ZERO REFRIGERATOR printed on it. A box the appliance had been delivered in, not yet discarded. It didn't quite fit the window; I peered through the crack to its side.

A wall of shelving. A gray SUV; I couldn't make out what kind.

Chances were Hanover had a security system on the house. What would be the responding agency? The sheriff's department? Not likely; they were too shorthanded to provide emergency services every time the system malfunctioned and set off the alarm, as sensitive ones are inclined to do. And none of the big outfits like ADT operated in this area; I knew because Hy and I had considered security for the ranch, then dismissed the idea. The ranch buildings hadn't been subject to a break-in in all the time Hy had owned the property. If Hanover had any kind of security, it would probably be a loud alarm to repel intruders. Or a private patrol that came by once or twice a day.

Take a chance, McCone. If that boat trailer of Bud Smith's is in this garage, you've got Hanover nailed.

Still, I hesitated, thinking of the damage I could do myself and the legal case against him if I was caught.

I felt around the window frame. Flimsy aluminum. Billionaires will spend a fortune on the most ridiculous things, such as toilets that wash and dry your butt, but when it comes to the basics, like a garage window . . .

I tugged at the frame. And the window slid open.

No clanging alarm. Nothing but silence.

I pushed the cardboard aside, peered into the garage.

Door leading into the house. The SUV I'd partially seen earlier—a Saab. Gardening supplies and tools. Hot-water heater and furnace.

And an empty boat trailer.

First piece of evidence.

I pushed the window open wider and climbed—wincing at the pain in my chest—into the garage.

First I looked around to see if there were any junction boxes to indicate I was wrong about a silent alarm. None, and the circuit breakers were all on and clearly labeled. I turned my attention to the trailer. The dusty license plate secured to it was Smith's, all right.

Next I checked out the Saab. It too was dusty but nearly new, its interior clean and smelling of good leather. In the glove box I found a registration card in the name of Trevor Hanover. There was a trailer hitch, also nearly new, but with scratches that showed it had been used to tow something.

Gingerly I got down on my hands and knees and examined the tires. Well-defined tread. I ducked to look at the undercarriage. Pine needles caught there, similar to those in the grove where I'd found Smith's Forester.

That was hard evidence.

It's a little-known fact that, like humans, trees possess

distinctive DNA. I'd once been involved in a murder case in the White Mountains, where a cone from one of the ancient pines that grow there was the star witness that ultimately convicted the killer.

Now for the house.

I tried the knob on the door leading to the interior. It turned smoothly and silently. Beyond was a large laundry room, with tile counters and top-of-the-line appliances. Through a connecting door I stepped into a kitchen that would have been the envy of any celebrity chef.

Another pain in my chest. I braced myself against a counter till it subsided. Even though the house's interior was cool, I was sweating profusely. For a moment I felt disoriented, my sight blurring.

I'd covered a lot of terrain in bad shape. I was dehydrated and could have internal injuries.

There was a wall phone; I should pick up the receiver and call—

A sound came from somewhere deep in the house.

I shook my head, thinking I'd imagined it. The sound came again. I drew the gun, haltingly crossed the kitchen to a swinging door, and pushed it open. Beyond was a huge formal dining room. I stood in the doorway, steadying myself and listening.

The sound continued, a kind of faraway drone. And now I could identify it: someone talking—in spite of the deserted appearance of the house. Hanover? He could have flown in again, stashed the plane in the hangar.

I waited till my equilibrium returned. Then, gripping Hy's .45, I went through the gloomy dining room full of heavy, antique furnishings that might have come from one of the state's original land-grant haciendas, and paused at an archway on the far side. The voice had stopped.

Several seconds of silence. Then I heard a thump and a cry of frustration. It sounded as if it had come from the other side of the hallway I was facing.

I checked out the room opposite: a formal parlor, full of the usual uncomfortable furnishings and a grand piano. Empty.

The hallway was long and tiled, running from a large foyer by the front door, with many arches opening to either side; at its end, a wide staircase swept up to the second story.

I moved along the tiles, back against the wall, both hands steadying the weapon.

First archway: a den. Real he-man's room, with stuffed animal heads, a TV that took up a whole wall, and a pool table. No one there.

Second archway: kids' room. Toys, games, another big TV, jukebox—contemporary replica of those from the fifties—and comfortable furnishings.

Third archway: crafts room. Sewing machine, easel, paints. Canvases stacked against the wall. Supplies arranged in plastic storage boxes on shelving. The topmost painting was a good, though bleak, portrait of the surrounding high desert. It was signed "B. Hanover." Betsy, the soon-to-be ex-wife.

I heard the voice again—subdued, more a mumbling now. Coming from behind the wide staircase. I glanced briefly into the rooms beyond the other archways as I moved ahead.

At first I saw nothing but the high backs of a leather couch and chairs and a wall whose French doors were covered with blinds; probably they were the ones I'd seen overlooking the pool area.

The mumbling continued. I moved into the room, slipped along the wall to the right. The furnishings were arranged in a U, with a handsome distressed wood coffee table in the center. Magazines were fanned out on it, next to a cordless phone unit whose handset was nowhere in sight. Beneath the table was a white, intricately woven area rug.

And on the other side of the coffee table, a man was down on all fours.

A bucket lay on its side next to him; water pooled on the hardwood floor between the rug and the French doors. The man was rubbing at a rust-colored stain on the rug. Back and forth, back and forth, pressing hard. Like a male version of Lady Macbeth.

"Buddy, Buddy, Buddy . . ."

I brought the gun up but didn't speak.

"Why'd you say no to me, Buddy?"

He kept rubbing.

"Why, Buddy?"

I thought he sensed my presence then, because he looked up. But it was just reflex. The handsome face I'd seen in his publicity photos was crumpled and his mouth worked spasmodically. His eyes were dark, bottomless pits. I'd seen that look on people in shock, but never so extreme as this.

This was a man whose interior had been totally shattered.

Slowly I relaxed, lowering the gun. Neither Trevor Hanover nor Davey Smith was a danger to me or anyone else. Wherever this man had gone, he wasn't coming back.

His mouth worked some more, and then he lowered his head and continued scrubbing.

"Buddy, Buddy, Buddy . . ."

Thursday

✦

NOVEMBER 22

The crowd of Thanksgiving Day revelers overflowed Ted and Neal's spacious third-floor apartment on Telegraph Hill's Plum Alley. They filled the living room and dining area, standing beside or sitting on the nineteen-thirties-style sofas, salon chairs, and ottomans, or hovering over the wine bottles and hors d'oeuvres spread on the long table. They sat on the spiral staircase or leaned against the chrome-railed catwalk that connected the apartment's front and rear bedrooms above the dining area. They congregated on the deck, where a sweeping view of Alcatraz and the Bay provided a dramatic backdrop. The only room we'd all been banished from was the kitchen that was tucked under the staircase, where Ted and his life partner, Neal Osborne, were putting together another of their famous Thanksgiving feasts. Wonderful aromas drifted out: roasting turkey, tangy cranberry sauce, sweet apple-cider yams, and stuffing

that I knew contained a powerful combination of spices and sausages.

Hy was on the deck, talking with Ricky. From my vantage point in the living room I watched the glint of sunlight on his dark blond hair and thick mustache. Felt a rush of pleasure at covertly observing the man who held my world together and supported me in everything I did.

I made my way through the crowd and rejoined Rae, balancing my wineglass on a plate laden with Neal's traditional stuffed mushrooms, tiny cheese-filled tarts, shrimp, and crispy cheddar puffs. God, if I kept snacking this way I wouldn't be able to eat any dinner.

Oh yeah? This was the first time I'd enjoyed food in weeks—maybe months.

Rae picked up the thread of our earlier conversation, which I'd interrupted to go to the trough. "So you phoned the guy at Tufa Tower from the ranch and . . . ?"

"He—Amos Hinsdale—made an anonymous call to the sheriff's department. Asked that they send a car to make a welfare check at Rattlesnake Ranch. I walked out and he picked me up before the car arrived and an ambulance followed."

"You ream this Amos out about lending you a plane that nearly caused you to die?"

"I didn't have to; he felt terrible about putting me in so much danger. In fact, he drove me straight to a clinic in Bridgeport to have me checked out for injuries. Badly bruised ribs and sternum, was all, and he insisted on paying for everything, as well as telling the FAA that he was piloting the plane when it crashed. Now he's decided to scrap his other plane, which is even worse than the one I crashed."

"And Smith—what was he doing till the sheriff's people got there?"

"Still scrubbing. Lark said he'd damn near worn a hole in the rug."

"And then?"

"He went quietly. Looked puzzled when the paramedics lifted him up, then dropped his rag and . . . just went."

"It could've been an act, you know. He could be building an insanity defense."

"God, you've gotten cynical! It wasn't an act; I saw his eyes."

"So what tipped him over the edge? Did he come back to destroy the evidence?"

"Probably. But I think there was a more important reason: it was the only home he's ever cared about."

"Why do you suppose he went off and left the evidence in the first place?"

"After he killed Bud and disposed of his body, he had to get back to New York to try to hold his business together— time for the conglomerate's annual stockholders' meeting. But the board of directors scheduled a closed meeting and excluded him on a technicality.

"So then, I guess, to keep his mind off what was happening in New York, he flew his jet back to the ranch and stashed it in the hangar. He must've come in late Thursday night or early Friday morning, because Amos Hinsdale says he was at home asleep then and didn't hear the plane. On Friday at around noon Hanover called New York and was told his board had given him a vote of no confidence and ousted him. Then . . . I don't know. He must've just disintegrated."

"And now?"

I bit into the little cheese-filled tart. It was delicious.

"Mono County will file homicide charges—they have enough evidence for that—but the case'll never come to trial. Trevor Hanover and Davey Smith have ceased to exist. An empty shell will inhabit a facility for the criminally insane until it dries up and dies."

Rae once again looked skeptical. "These rich guys . . . I don't know."

"You're married to one."

"He's different. He has me to keep him honest."

I looked across the room. Adah and Craig had just arrived. "Excuse me," I said. "I need a few minutes alone with Adah."

Rae nodded and headed for the buffet.

Adah smiled at me as I approached, gave me a hug. When we separated, Craig had disappeared in Rae's wake.

"He's starving," she said. "As always." Then her expression sobered. "I guess you want my answer to your proposition."

"If you've decided."

"As far as I'm concerned, it's a done deal."

"Great!"

"An administrative position with your firm is perfect for me. No more getting called out in the middle of the night to look at decomposing bodies. No more SFPD politics. And best of all, I don't have to leave the city and move to Denver. My mom and dad, they're getting up there. Still feisty as hell, but . . ."

"Besides, this is home."

"Sure is. Born and raised on Red Hill." By Red Hill, she meant Bernal Heights, which used to be a hotbed of self-styled communists, socialists, and the occasional anarchist. Her Jewish mother and black father had been

socialists with Marxist leanings, and now called themselves "wild-eyed liberals."

It was the perfect solution for me: I wouldn't have to sell the agency; it was a vital entity, the culmination of everything I'd hoped to accomplish in life—and then some. But I did want to cut out the administrative work and take on only cases that truly interested me, and Adah was the chief component in my scheme. Now that she'd accepted the position I'd offered her almost two weeks ago, I could move forward. And move forward without worrying about the rent increase from the Port Commission; Glenn Solomon's influence had staved that off for at least a year.

We shook on our deal, and she said, "Shouldn't we tell Patrick that I'll be usurping some of his duties?"

"I don't think he'll mind." I looked around the room, spotted Patrick, and motioned him over.

When he joined us, I told him I'd hired Adah as the agency's new executive administrator, meaning she'd handle approving reports and expenditures, plus interview new clients and assign them to the proper operatives. Patrick would continue to coordinate all investigations. Both would report directly to me. I would attend some staff meetings and, when I didn't, they would cochair them.

"Shar, that's good news!" he exclaimed. "I hate all the paperwork, and the staff meetings—I'm just not cut out for them. If you wouldn't mind"—he looked at Adah—"I'd prefer you chair them in Shar's absence."

"I can do that." She smiled at him. They'd work together just fine.

"So Adah's coming on board two weeks from Monday," I said to Ted as we were relaxing on the deck after the crowd had begun to thin.

"It's a damn good thing. We're swamped. Are you coming back in the meantime?"

"Monday. Hy and I are flying to the ranch tomorrow. We're having a delayed Thanksgiving with Sara, Ramon, and Amy tomorrow night. They're all pulling together, doing better, but today's got to be gloomy for them, and they'll need cheering up. And Saturday afternoon we have to greet the next member of our family. We're having a palomino delivered. To keep my horse, King, company."

"*Your* horse? You hate horses!"

"Let's say I hate horses as a breed, but love them on an individual basis."

"I don't believe this: you're backing off on the business, and you're in love with a horse?"

My cell rang. I checked to see who the caller was. Kristen Lark. I excused myself and went inside. There were still enough people there to make talking impossible, so I went down the hall to where the glass-block elevator—a classic from the thirties—stood, its doors open. Inside I sat down on the floor before I called Lark back.

"It's Sharon," I said.

"Happy Turkey Day."

"Thanks. Same to you. What's happening?"

"Nothing bad. Our perp is comfortably residing in the psych ward."

"The case will never to go trial."

"No. Save the county a lot of money. Philadelphia—where Davey Smith went to Wharton for his BA in finance—is looking at him concerning a series of rapes in the area when he was a student, and New York State is also interested. Recidivism of sex offenders . . ."

"Yeah. And how're you doing?"

". . . Better."

"Meaning?"

"All that drinking—which I'm sure you noticed? It was partly because of the pressure of the case, but mostly because the Rabbitt was being strange and distant, so I figured he was having an affair."

"And?"

"He wasn't. He'd been brooding and trying to decide how to tell me he wants to leave the department and go to law school."

"How d'you feel about that?"

"Happy. He's got the GPA to get him into a lot of good schools on at least a partial scholarship. And I can get a job I'll enjoy almost anywhere."

"So this is a happy Thanksgiving for both of you."

"The best yet."

We chatted for a moment or two about her turkey that had turned out well and her pumpkin pie that had burned. Then we promised to keep in touch and broke the connection.

I sat there for a while, savoring the peace and happiness of one perfect holiday. The elevator doors closed, and the car began its slow downward descent. When they opened Hank Zahn, Anne-Marie Altman, and their daughter, Habiba Hamid, stepped in. They hadn't been able to make dinner because of a previous family obligation, but had promised to stop by later.

I looked at them and smiled. They were the perfect blended family: Hank, wire-haired and Jewish; Anne-Marie, blonde and WASPish; Habiba, with the beautiful dark-skinned features of her Arab forebears.

It was all about family, really—and I had such a huge one that seemed to be expanding all the time. A few years ago I'd embraced—albeit tentatively—both branches of

my birth family. This fall I'd added the Perezes and, of all things, a horse.

But the family that was closest and dearest were all assembled in this building. I closed my eyes and sighed, grateful that I'd decided to come home to them.

Hank asked, "You all right, kiddo?"

"Better than I've been in a long time."

A typical July night in San Francisco. Mist swirling off the bay, a foghorn bellowing every thirty seconds out at the Golden Gate. Lights along the Embarcadero dimmed, and the sidewalks and the streets mostly empty at a few minutes after nine. Sounds of traffic on the Bay Bridge curiously muted. In contrast, my boot heels tapped loudly on the pavement.

Ahead of me lay Pier 24 1/2. Three long blocks behind me my vintage MG sat in a No Parking zone, out of gas.

Way to go, McCone. When you fly, you're meticulous about fueling. But with the car, you resist stopping at a station till the damn thing's running on fumes.

Just my luck—the fumes had given out short of my destination tonight.

Pilot error—on the ground.

A sudden blast of wind came off the water, and I gripped my woolen hat, pulled it lower on my forehead.

Something to my right was banging, metal-on-metal; I glanced over and saw a No Trespassing sign loosely attached to a chain-link fence barring access to one of the old piers scheduled for demolition.

This is my workday neighborhood. I walk this lovely, palm-lined boulevard all the time. I shouldn't allow sounds to spook me.

Another moan from the foghorn. Why did it sometimes seem melancholy, at other times strident, and at still others like the scream of a victim in pain?

Now I was passing a derelict shed on the far side of the doomed pier. A heap of rags lay on its loading dock. No, not rags—a human being seeking shelter from the inclement weather. Another member of San Francisco's homeless population.

One of many things wrong with this damned city—too few resources, too little compassion.

I had a love-hate relationship with the town I'd made my home. But I knew, no matter how bad the urban situation became, I'd never leave.

Ahead the security lights of Pier 24 1/2 glowed through the mist. I quickened my steps.

The city's port commission had tried to raise the tenants' rental rates last fall—a first step toward also demolishing this pier—but an influential attorney friend of mine had prevailed upon them to maintain the status quo. For a while, anyway.

Where, I wondered now, would I find a comparable rate and space for an agency that was growing quickly? Profits were up, yes, but salaries and the cost of employee benefits were also escalating. Maybe . . .

I put my worries aside and concentrated on my original purpose: retrieve the cell phone that I'd accidentally

left on my desk before going out to dinner with my friend and operative, Julia Rafael. The phone whose absence had prevented me from calling Triple A when the car ran out of gas. If I contacted them from the office, they'd be there by the time I walked back to the MG—

A hand touched my forearm. I jerked away, moving into a defensive stance. A dark figure had loomed out of the mist.

"Lady, can you spare a dollar?"

Jesus, he was panhandling in a nearly deserted area in *this* weather? Better to fort up in the shelter of one of the sheds, like the person I'd glimpsed earlier.

He waited, arms loose at his sides, shoulders slumped. I couldn't see his features, but the wind whipped at his jacket and I saw it was thin and had a ragged tear.

I reached into the pocket of my pea coat and found some bills that I'd left there whenever I last wore it. Held them out to him. He hesitated before taking them, as if he couldn't believe his good fortune.

"Thank you, lady. God bless."

He disappeared into the fog as swiftly as he'd appeared.

I pulled the collar of my coat more tightly around my neck and went on toward the pier.

The powers-that-be say you shouldn't give money to the homeless; they'll only spend it on drugs and liquor. What was that slogan they made up? *Care, not cash.* All shiny and idealistic, but the truth is, some people slip through the cracks in the care department, and cash for a bottle or a fix is what they need to get themselves through a cold, damp night like this one.

I thrust my hands deeper into my pockets, but a chill had invaded me that couldn't be touched by the warmth of wool and lining.

The fog seemed thicker now. It played tricks on my vision. Someone was coming at me from the bayside. . . . No, advancing toward me on the left. . . . No, there was nobody—

A shriek echoed over the boulevard, high-pitched tones bouncing off the surrounding buildings.

I stopped, peered hard through the churning mist.

Laughter, and the sound of running feet over at Hills Brothers Plaza. More laughter, fading into the distance along with the footsteps. People clowning around after leaving one of the restaurants.

The security grille had been pulled down over the yawning, arched entrance to the pier. My opener was back in the MG. I grasped the cold bars and called out to Lewis, the guard we tenants collectively employed.

No answer.

Well, sure. He was probably drinking deep in the recesses of the cavernous structure. Or already passed out. A nice guy, Lewis, but a serious alcoholic. At the last tenants' meeting we'd talked about firing him, but none of us had taken the initiative to find a replacement. I should have—

That's not your bailiwick any more, McCone. You've got Adah to take care of things like that now.

Adah Joslyn, formerly of the SFPD's homicide detail, now my executive administrator. Last winter I'd stepped back from the day-to-day running of the agency so I could concentrate on cases that really interested me. There hadn't been many, and in the meantime I'd started giving self-defense classes at a women's shelter in my neighborhood and working their emergency hotline during the day when most of their volunteers were out earning a living. I'd been able to spend more time at Touchstone, Hy's and

my seaside home in Mendocino County, and at our ranch in the high desert country with our horses, King Lear and Sidekick.

I shouted again for Lewis.

Still no answer.

Damn. I'd have to use my security code to open the door to the right of the pier's entrance. But I'd just changed it, as we did every month, and I wasn't sure . . .

Favorite canned chili. Right. I punched in 6255397—the numerical equivalent on the keypad of Nalley's—and gained entry.

Usually there were cars belonging to tenants parked on the pier's floor at any time of day or night; employees of my agency, the architectural firm and desktop publisher on the opposite catwalk, and the various small businesses running along either side of the downstairs worked long and irregular hours. Tonight I was surprised to find no vehicles and no light leaking around doorways. The desk where Lewis was supposed to be stationed was deserted.

That does it. We're firing your ass tomorrow.

I crossed the floor to the stairs to our catwalk, footsteps echoing off the walls and high corrugated iron roof, then clanging on the metal as I climbed up and went toward my office at the bayside end. God, this place was spooky at night with nobody around.

As I passed the space occupied by my office manager, Ted Smalley, and his assistant, Kendra Williams, I thought I saw a flicker of light.

So somebody was there after all. Maybe Ted had left his car on the street; if so, he could give me a ride back to the MG. Kendra took public transit; she could keep me company while I waited for Triple A, and then I'd drive

her home. I went to the door, calling out to them. No response. I rattled the knob. Locked.

I'd imagined the light. Or it had been a reflection off the high north-facing windows.

I went along to my office, slid the key into its deadbolt lock. When I turned it, the bolt clicked into place. Now that was wrong; I'd locked it when I left the office. We all made a point to do so because we had so many sensitive files in cabinets and on our computers.

I turned the key again and shoved the door open. Stepped inside and reached for the light switch.

Motion in the darkness, more sensed than heard.

My fingertips touched the switch but before I could flip it, a dark figure appeared only a few feet away and then barreled into me, knocked me against the wall. My head bounced off the Sheetrock hard enough to blur my vision. In the next second I reeled backward through the door, spun around, and was down on my knees on the hard iron catwalk. As I tried to scramble away, push up and regain my footing, one of my groping hands brushed over some kind of metal—

Sudden flash, loud pop.

Rush of pain.

Oh my God, I've been shot—

Nothing.

VISIT US ONLINE

@ WWW.HACHETTEBOOKGROUP.COM.

AT THE HACHETTE BOOK GROUP WEB SITE YOU'LL FIND:

CHAPTER EXCERPTS FROM SELECTED NEW RELEASES

•

ORIGINAL AUTHOR AND EDITOR ARTICLES

•

AUDIO EXCERPTS

•

BESTSELLER NEWS

•

ELECTRONIC NEWSLETTERS

•

AUTHOR TOUR INFORMATION

•

CONTESTS, QUIZZES, AND POLLS

•

FUN, QUIRKY RECOMMENDATION CENTER

•

PLUS MUCH MORE!

Bookmark Hachette Book Group
@ www.HachetteBookGroup.com.

Thanks to:
Marcie Galick, good friend to horses—and to me.
Bill, my first editor and best friend.
Les Pockell—your suggestions were right on.
Celia Johnson—yours, too.

For Melissa Meith and Mike White:
Friends through both the good times and the bad.

This book is a work of fiction. Names, characters, places, and incidents are the product of the author's imagination or are used fictitiously. Any resemblance to actual events, locales, or persons, living or dead, is coincidental.

Copyright © 2008 by Pronzini-Muller Family Trust
Excerpt from *Locked In* copyright © 2009 by Pronzini-Muller Family Trust
All rights reserved. Except as permitted under the U.S. Copyright Act of 1976, no part of this publication may be reproduced, distributed, or transmitted in any form or by any means, or stored in a database or retrieval system, without the prior written permission of the publisher.

Grand Central Publishing
Hachette Book Group
237 Park Avenue
New York, NY 10017
Visit our website at www.HachetteBookGroup.com

Grand Central Publishing is a division of Hachette Book Group, Inc.
The Grand Central Publishing name and logo is a trademark of Hachette Book Group, Inc.

Printed in the United States of America

Originally published in hardcover by Hachette Book Group
First mass market edition, October 2009

10 9 8 7 6 5 4 3 2 1

MARCIA MULLER

BURN OUT

GC

GRAND CENTRAL
PUBLISHING

NEW YORK   BOSTON

"One of mystery's best authors . . . very satisfying . . . I wholly appreciated BURN OUT and am just so damn glad Marcia Muller is around."

—ReviewingtheEvidence.com

"BURN OUT is a perfect follow up to the excellent *The Ever-Running Man* . . . a solid whodunit."

—*Midwest Book Review*

"Like all of Muller's best work, BURN OUT is about Sharon's personal growth as much as the mystery to be solved . . . Muller's long-lived series is one of the strongest sustained series in crime fiction."

—*Alfred Hitchcock Mystery Magazine*

Introduction

If there is one word that can be used to describe our lives today, it is fast. We hurry through our days moving from appointment to appointment, responsibility to responsibility, activity to activity. A recent advertisement for high-speed Internet promised the one thing we all want—time. No one is exempt from the fast pace of our lifestyle; everyone from preschool children to older adults is caught on a treadmill set on high.

The thing that suffers most in our hurried lives is relationships: relationships with our families, relationships with friends, relationships within our faith communities, and relationship with God. There just is not time to sit down and talk with one another, to share our stories and concerns, to listen for the whisper of God's voice. Since God made us for relationship—with God, with ourselves, with one another and with the creation—it is counter to God's plan for us not to take care of this basic foundation of our lives. God made us so that in the deepest part of our being, we long to be joined together in community.

The demands of our modern lives separate us from others not only emotionally, but physically. Grandparents live great distances from grandchildren; grown siblings are separated by miles; even spouses spend parts of weeks or months away from each other. Once upon a time generations lived close by and could see one another and support one another. Often in today's world, generations live and work and play with people of the same age. No longer is the wisdom of one generation passed on to the next one through modeling and close contact.

From the first moments of creation God's intention was that we would stop on a regular basis for rest and renewal. St. Augustine said, "We are restless until we find our rest in you." These words from long ago are still true. We long to stop and catch our breath, to pay attention, to find wonder and imagination, to use our creativity in order to see things through a new lens. The Hebrew word that we translate "Sabbath" means to catch our breath and reflects God's longing for us to have rest.

Intergenerational Church Family Retreats

All of these dynamics are also present in our churches. The rushing of our secular lives creeps into our religious ones. Church attendance has often become just one of many choices for Sunday mornings. Volunteers for church responsibilities are hard to find; volunteers who *can* be found are overextended. During Sunday school and worship, church members are separated by age: older adults with older adults, youth with youth, children with children. Children are shuffled off for children's worship; sometimes youth become bored and stay home; babies and toddlers are kept in the nursery where they won't bother adults.

The result of this age group division is that church members only know the names of people of their own age, children don't get to snuggle during worship with the grandmothers of the church, young mothers and fathers don't learn from the insights of those who have parented before them, and older church members don't have the chance to nurture younger members or to enjoy the energy of youth. There are few means for finding common ground and exploring common stories. There are few chances to pass on the faith across the generations.

Retreats for Renewal offers a chance for all people of all ages within a congregation to praise God, find a shared story, learn about one another, and discover those things that bind them together in Christ. Such retreats provide opportunities to stop and listen and rest together as a community of God's people.

Intergenerational defines a group of people from all age groups participating together in study, conversation, play, and worship.

Church identifies the people of God who gather in a shared faith in Jesus Christ and who invite Christ into the midst of everything that is done and experienced.

Family recognizes that in Christ we are all brothers and sisters—bound together by faith and love.

Retreat indicates the movement of participants to a place apart—away from their regular lives and the pace of those lives.

The Designs in This Collection

Five designs for *Retreats for Renewal* can be found in this collection. Each retreat is organized around an element of nature or life that incorporates a familiar biblical theme.

- **Follow the Good Shepherd** focuses on the many references to sheep and shepherds in Scripture and reminds us of our call to follow the lamb who laid down his life for us.

- **Come to the Waters** focuses on the many scriptural events that include water and are a reminder of our entrance into the community of faith through baptism.

- **Shine the Light** reminds us that Jesus proclaimed that he is the light of the world and invites us to hold our light high so all can see it.

- **Sow Seeds of Faith** focuses on Jesus' stories about seeds and reminds us of the way the faith of each of us grows like a seed

- **Claim Your Name** explores the importance of our names and God's love for each of us as unique individuals set apart at baptism and called into relationship.

The purpose of this collection of *Retreats for Renewal* is to deepen and strengthen relationships within the whole congregation through the opportunity to explore the biblical story, to have conversations across generations, and to play and worship together. Bridges will be built that span the different ages, names and stories will become familiar, and a common life of faith will be celebrated.

By carving out a sabbath time, all participants will be able to pause in the midst of their busy lives to rest and to pay attention to their relationships with God and with one another. A sense of being part of the community of God's people will emerge and will continue to affect the lives of all who retreated together. The memory of this time away together will touch the way congregational members relate over the days, months, and years ahead. The faith of each person and of the community as a whole will be enriched.

Assumptions That Guide the Retreat Designs

There are many ways that the schedule, activities, and worship of an intergenerational retreat can be designed. This collection is informed by several educational, theological, and developmental assumptions. They reflect a particular understanding of God, of how people learn their faith, and of the church's call to ministry.

You will want to examine these assumptions in order to determine whether these designs will match your needs and the theological and educational environment of your congregation. These assumptions affect both the flow and form of the retreats. They determine the schedule, type of activities, form of leadership, and style of worship. These designs assume that:

- people of all ages can learn with and from one another;
- people of all ages are partners in ministry;
- people of all ages can participate in worship leadership;
- people of all ages can interpret Scripture;

- worship is the center of all the community does;

- storytelling builds bridges across generations;

- an emotionally and spiritually safe place can be created through the intentional practices of community building and hospitality;

- experiential learning models enrich the opportunities for intergenerational learning.

These assumptions lend a rationale for some particular, specific practices.

- Retreat participants will sit in a circle rather than rows of chairs so that everyone can see the faces of everyone else

- A worship center will be placed in the center of the circle of chairs as a reminder that worship is the center of the community's life

- Music will be easy to sing so that all ages can sing along

- Small groups will be composed of people of all ages so that the voice of each person can be heard

- Children ages 1 month through 5 years will be offered special activities during small group times but will be welcomed in all other activities so that they can experience the love and acceptance of the community

- Small group time will begin with community building activities so that people can learn about one another in a fun and safe way

- Play and fun are an essential aspect of community life

Format of Each Retreat

Each retreat design will include everything you need to plan and lead a retreat, including:

- introductory article on the biblical and theological background of the theme;

- Small Group Sessions with detailed plans for each session;

13

- suggestions for songs;

- additional resources for welcome, crafts and nature activities;

- complete list of supplies;

- orders for worship.

A general chapter provides an overview of planning a retreat, suggestions for room setup, hints for hospitality, and ideas for adapting the session designs for two- or three-day retreats.

How to Use the Retreat Designs

Each retreat design in this book includes everything you need to hold an inter-generational church family retreat. There are instructions for theme study sessions and worship as well as community building activities, crafts, nature study, and music—all related to the theme. The purpose of this chapter is to describe each section of the retreat designs and to make suggestions for how to use the components of the design for your congregation. By becoming more familiar with the retreat design format, you will be able to make decisions about scheduling the sessions and worship at your retreat and be equipped with information about supplies, welcome activities, and room arrangements.

The retreats in this collection all have as their focus a natural or everyday element: sheep (and their shepherds), light, water, seeds, and names. The retreats invite the participants to consider the ways in which these everyday elements have meaning in their lives, biblical insights or stories about these elements, and reflection on what these elements tell us about God and God's call to us.

Each retreat design includes identical elements and is arranged in the same order. You can see the components on page 5 and read more about each one in the following section. You will need to make several decisions about the ways you will use the elements at your retreat.

The first decision has to do with the length of your retreat. Within a two-day retreat (usually lasting from Friday night until Saturday afternoon), theme sessions will be scheduled differently than at a three-day retreat (usually lasting from Friday evening until Sunday noon). Sample schedules for both two- and three-day retreats are provided so you can consider what will work best for your congregation.

The second decision you will want to make is about leadership for the retreat. The retreat designs are written in such a way that they can be led by one person or by a team. One person who is comfortable working with groups and letting the groups make their own discoveries about the theme and meaning for them can lead the theme sessions. The leader needs to be able to introduce the focus of the theme for each session and to direct and facilitate the work of the small and large groups. However, this person does not need to be an "expert" on the theme to be able to lead them. A single person can lead singing and act as worship leader or different members of the team can assume leadership for these components of the retreat. Other members of the team can direct the welcome activities, make announcements and oversee free time choices. At your retreat the leadership can be shared in the way that makes the best use of the gifts and skills of the leadership team.

Sections of the Retreat Designs

BIBLICAL THEOLOGICAL INTRODUCTION

At the beginning of each retreat design is a short introduction to the theme topic, including background information about the theme as well as biblical and theological reflections. The leader charged with introducing the focus on the theme for each session will find this information sufficient for providing the focus on the theme in each session. However, if a retreat leader wants to do additional study, he or she can consult Bible dictionaries on the topic and commentaries on the passages referred to in the retreat design.

What Is Included in Each Retreat Design

Biblical Theological Introduction

Retreat Resources
- Suggested Songs
- Supplies
- Worship Center
- Welcome Activities
    - Nametags
    - Get Acquainted
- Crafts
- Nature Activities

Theme Sessions
- Session One
    - Supplies
    - Preparation
    - Focus on the Theme
    - Small and Large Group Activities
- Session Two
- Session Three
- Session Four

Orders for Worship
- Worship One
- Worship Two
- Worship Three
- Worship Four

RETREAT RESOURCES

A retreat is much more than a series of church school or Bible study sessions. It offers a congregation a unique experience in Christian community that includes time for conversation, fun, crafts, nature walks, and worship. This section in each retreat design provides a variety of resources that will assist the leadership team in their planning. This section includes:

Suggested Songs The songs in this list are related to the retreat theme. The list is not exhaustive and you will probably want to add some of your own favorites. At the end of this chapter you will find the names of songs books that include some of these songs.

Supplies This list will give you a complete look at all the supplies you will need for the whole retreat. Supplies for each activity are also listed within individual session plans.

Worship Center The worship center sits in the center of the community circle of chairs. Suggestions are made for setting that table related to the retreat theme.

Welcome Activities These activities are intended to be done as participants arrive to help them learn one another's names and begin to feel comfortable and welcomed at the retreat.

> **Nametags** Shapes for theme-related nametags are provided with each design. Enlarge/reduce these images as needed for various activities.

> **Get Acquainted** These activities include having each participant make a contribution to a group project such as a community quilt or mosaic.

Crafts Several simple crafts related to the theme are suggested as options for free-time activities. They are in addition to the creative activities included in the theme sessions.

Nature Activities These are also related to the theme and are suggested as options for free-time activities.

THEME SESSIONS

Within each retreat design there are four theme sessions. There is a sequential intent behind them for the development of the theme as they move from welcome and introduction to reflection, creative response, and final challenge. You are encouraged to use all four sessions and to use them in the order they appear.

- Session One gives participants a chance to get to know one another and introduces the theme.

- Session Two explores the biblical foundation for the theme.

- Session Three offers a creative response to the theme through activity centers or large group activities.

- Session Four brings closure to the small groups and challenges participants to action after they leave the retreat.

Within each session are directions for preparation, a list of supplies, suggestions for announcements, a brief focus on the theme, and detailed instructions for small and large group activities. Preparation for the session, introduction of the focus, and direction of the activities can be shared by the leadership team or done by one person.

At a two-day retreat, you can hold Session One on Friday evening with Sessions Two and Three on Saturday morning, and Session Four on Saturday afternoon. At a three-day retreat there is more time for flexibility in the scheduling of the theme sessions. In the Sample Schedules, Session Two is held on Saturday morning and Session Three on Saturday evening. However, both Two and Three could be held on Saturday morning, giving the participants time to enjoy free time and optional activities in the afternoon and a group event such as square dancing or a talent show on Saturday evening.

ORDERS FOR WORSHIP

Four orders for worship are provided in each retreat design—one morning worship, two evening worships, and a closing worship. The suggestions for worship are intended to be just that, and you are encouraged to add your own music and prayers. The worship leader can shape the reflection on the Scripture in a way that is meaningful to your congregation. Holy Communion can be celebrated at the closing worship in a way consistent with your tradition.

Worship One An evening worship for Friday evening

Worship Two A brief morning worship for Saturday

Worship Three An evening worship for Saturday (skip this service in the Two-Day model)

Worship Four An order for closing worship, sometimes planned by the participants.

At a two-day retreat you can use Worship One, Two, and Four; at a longer retreat you can use all four orders for worship.

Sample Schedules

Two-Day Retreat
Friday
    5:00—Registration
    6:30—Dinner
    7:30—Session One
    8:30—Worship One
    9:00—Fellowship
Saturday
    8:30—Breakfast
    9:30—Worship Two

Sample Schedules, continued

    9:45—Session Two

    10:45—Break

    11:00—Session Three

    12:30—Lunch

    1:00—Free Time

    2:00—Small Session Four

    3:30—Worship Four

    4:00—Say Good-bye

Three-Day Retreat

Friday

    5:00—Registration

    6:30—Dinner

    7:30—Session One

    8:30—Worship One

    9:00—Fellowship

Saturday

    8:30—Breakfast

    10:00—Worship Two

    10:30—Session Two

    12:00—Break

    12:30—Lunch

    1:00—Free Time

    6:00—Dinner

    7:00—Session Three

    8:30—Worship Three

    9:00—Fellowship

Sample Schedules, continued

Sunday

    8:30—Breakfast

    10:00—Session Four

    11:00—Worship Four

    Noon—Lunch or Say Good-bye

ROOM SETUP

The room arrangement for all five retreats is identical. Set up a circle of chairs with one chair for each expected participant. In the center of the circle of chairs, set up a worship center on a low table. Suggestions for how to set the Worship Center are given in the Retreat Resources section of each retreat design.

Outside the circle of chairs, arrange small group tables with six to eight chairs, depending upon the number of participants you are expecting. At some retreat centers it is not possible to have the circle of chairs and the small group tables in the same room. In that case, be sure to arrange for smaller breakout space when you make your reservation with the retreat center.

Somewhere in the meeting room, arrange a table to hold the supplies. A list of the supplies needed for the entire retreat can be found in the Retreat Resources section of each retreat design. At the beginning of each session plan, there is a separate list of supplies for that session. Arrange the supplies in the order you will need them so that you can find them quickly and easily. Some of the supplies will be used in more than one session.

AGE GROUPS

These designs are planned in such a way that congregational members of all ages will be able to participate in the retreat experience. All small groups will include participants of all ages—children from six or seven to adults of all ages—since activities and discussions are designed for intergenerational groups. During small group times, you may want to provide alternative activities or care for children younger than five or six so their parents can participate fully in the small groups. The remainder of the activities—including worship—welcome children of all ages.

HOSPITALITY

There are many things you can do as a retreat leader to help the people feel welcome and comfortable. Retreat participants are more apt to enter into small and large group discussions if they feel safe.

1. Set up a hospitality area with water/coffee/tea/sodas and snacks. Find out whether the retreat center can provide this or whether you will need to bring it.

2. Help everyone feel welcome as they arrive through a variety of intentional activities:

    *   Use the suggestions for Nametags and Get Acquainted activities in the Retreat Resources section of each retreat design to help participants gather and meet each other informally as they arrive.

    *   Be sure everyone knows their way around the retreat facility by distributing maps, putting up signs, and giving clear directions to the meeting rooms, sleeping assignments, and bathrooms.

    *   Make copies of the schedule available and post it on the doors of meeting rooms and in the registration area. This will help everyone know when they need to be where.

3. Make frequent announcements throughout the retreat about the next events, mealtimes, checking out, etc. Suggestions for general announcements are included in the retreat designs. However, you can add your own as needed for your group.

4. It is normal that some participants will arrive late or come for only part of the retreat. Be sure that participants who arrive late are welcomed and introduced. Have them make a nametag and complete the Get Acquainted activity. Assign newcomers to a small group and introduce them to the other members of the group. Encourage the group to tell them about any sessions they have missed.

5. On the last day give everyone a chance to pack up and clean sleeping spaces after breakfast. Be clear about what needs to be done and what time retreat participants need to return for Session Four and closing worship.

6. Recognize that everyone is going to have a hard time settling down for the last session, and plan for the time folks need to say good-bye. A suggestion for bringing closure for the small group is provided within each retreat design. This often includes a chance to say what they have liked about the retreat and to pray for one another.

7. Be intentional about doing community building so that you give participants a chance to find out about one another and to set a tone of fun and discovery. Community Building activities are included in the plans for Session One in each retreat design.

8. Make retreat folders including a schedule, orders for worship, and words of the songs. If you don't put names on the folders, then they can be handed out at worship and gathering times without having to find their "owners." Collect them afterward.

Music

Suggested Songs related to the theme are included in the Retreat Resources section of each retreat design. However, there are many short praise songs and fun "camp" songs that can be included as part of any retreat for community gathering and worship. Some of those songs are listed here as well as several songbooks.

A Partial List of Songs

Awesome God

Seek Ye First

They Will Know We Are Christians by Our Love

Lord, Be Glorified

Amazing Grace

Kum Ba Ya

This is the Day the Lord Has Made

Spirit of the Living God

A Place in the Choir

Sanctuary

Father, We Adore You

Allelu, Praise Ye the Lord

A Partial List of Songbooks

Chalice Praise, Chalice Press, St. Louis, 2003

The Faith We Sing, Abingdon Press, Nashville, 2000

Sing the Faith, Geneva Press, Louisville, 2003

Songs, Songs and Creation, San Anselmo—800-227-2188 (This is a large collection of fun, popular, and praise songs, as well as traditional hymns. It is available with just words and with musical settings.)

New Song (Volumes One and Two), Presbyterian Youth Connection, 800-524-2612 (Available with participants' book, musical settings book, and CD.)

Follow the Good Shepherd

Biblical and Theological Introduction

In biblical times, the hills of Galilee were dotted with flocks of sheep accompanied by their shepherds. This was a well-known and familiar sight to all those who listened to the words of the psalmist and of Jesus. No one had to stop for a single moment to wonder about the nature of sheep or the work of those who cared for them.

On the other hand, this sight is much less common in our industrial, technological society. Sheep do not graze within the everyday experience of most people. Shepherds do not wander across our hillsides.

Some people claim that to understand the biblical references to sheep and shepherds we must translate them into modern persons who are like shepherds or into other relationships similar to that between a lamb and the shepherd. However, there really is no relationship quite like this one.

Rather than trying to make a contemporary rendition of the stories, it is more helpful to learn about the nature of sheep and the specific kind of oversight that shepherds provide for these unique little animals. Through learning more about sheep and their caretakers, the images of God as shepherd and humans as sheep become more available to us. We can then celebrate the immanent care God offers us and confess with deeper understanding our nature as willful, foolish creatures who are in deep need of that care.

Sheep are not very smart animals. Left to their own devices they will graze a field down to its roots, run from danger regardless of where it comes from, follow one another without reason, and break down a fence to get to greener grass. It is well known among sheep owners that if a stick is placed in the front of a line of sheep, the first few will jump over it. However, when the stick is moved the rest of the line will continue to mimic each other by jumping over the stick.

Sheep are prone to all kinds of maladies that need treatment. Their feet have a tendency to rot and continually need to be trimmed. They fall victim to maggot and lice infestations in their skin and wool. They are infected by intestinal parasites that threaten their lives.

On the other hand, sheep had great economic value. They formed the foundation of the biblical agrarian society by supplying meat and wool and skins to their owners. Sheep's wool grows constantly, so it needs to be cut or sheared at least once a year. The wool can then be spun into yarn and woven into fabric. It is not unusual for ewes—female sheep—to give birth to two or even three offspring. This means that the flock can double in size within one year. In Middle Eastern culture, sheep milk is drunk and made into cheese.

It is clear, then, why sheep need caretakers who are constantly on the lookout for them. Shepherds live close to their flocks, watching out for straying members, threatening predators, birthing ewes, and hurting lambs. They move sheep from field to field, provide them with still water (sheep don't like to drink from moving water), cut their wool, and care for the young. Unlike those who care for other domesticated animals, shepherds cannot leave their sheep alone for long. Their care has to be constant.

Knowing what we have learned about shepherds enables us to compare the shepherd's care of the sheep to God's care for us. The image reminds us that God's love and presence with us is constant, that God looks out for our needs and provides for them, that God's care is close and personal. This God of ours leads us to still water, rubs oil in our wounds, welcomes us to a feast even when our enemies are nearby. Finally, this God of ours loves us so much that God became a sheep for our sakes and was killed.

Interestingly, in one of his last conversations with his disciples, Jesus charges them to care for his sheep. As followers of the Good Shepherd, we are called not only to be sheep—foolish animals that need constant care—but to become caretakers, providing the same kind of care and love to others.

The image of sheep and shepherds provides the opportunity to explore the nature of God, the nature of humanity and our dependence on God, as well as the charge to tend for others as God cares for us. Through exploration of this image our gratitude for the abundance of God's care will deepen and the understanding of our own nature as foolish creatures wholly dependant on God's grace will grow.

Retreat Resources

Suggested Songs: "His Name Is Wonderful," "His Sheep Am I," "Psalm 100," "Come, Let Us Worship and Bow Down," versions of the 23rd Psalm, "You Are My All in All"

Supplies:

candle

several wooden and/or ceramic sheep, and baskets of raw wool or purchased white yarn

10" x 10" squares of various colored construction paper or fabric

markers or fabric pens

masking tape or pushpins

3" x 5" cards

bags of M & M's

copies of True and False activity

large sheep cutout

markers

(optional) song sheets

Bibles

newsprint

construction or drawing paper

crayons

clay	piano
pieces of 12" x 12" heavy cardboard	guitar
(you can cut from boxes)	watercolors
newsprint	brushes
60" x 36" burlap or white fabric	water
fabric glue	watercolor paper
assorted felt and/or fabric	cotton balls
music staff paper	safety pins

Worship Center: Place a low table in the center of the circle and cover it with a colorful cloth. On it arrange a Bible, candle, several wooden and/or ceramic sheep, and baskets of raw wool or purchased white yarn.

Welcome Activities

Nametags: Make nametags using the sheep shape found in the back of this section. Attach with safety pins or masking tape.

Get Acquainted: As people are gathering at registration, invite them to complete a name square for the "Sheep Quilt." Have each person write his or her name in the center of the square of construction paper or fabric and to decorate it with words or drawings about him or herself. After everyone has arrived, tape or pin the squares together to make a "quilt" and hang it on the wall of the meeting space. If you use fabric, the quilt can be sown together later and become a permanent reminder to the congregation of the retreat.

Supplies: 10" χ 10" squares of various colored construction paper or fabric, markers or fabric pens, masking tape or pushpins

Crafts

Make Cotton Sheep: Make a large sheep cutout on white paper using the shape found at the end of this retreat design. Glue cotton balls over the shape, cut out the shape and glue onto colored paper. Draw in sky, sun, grass, etc. Write "The Lord Is My Shepherd" at the top of the page.

Supplies: White paper, cotton balls, glue, colored paper, markers

Learn about Wool and Spinning: If you have found some raw wool, encourage the participants to handle and smell the wool. They can try twisting the wool to make yarn. Find out about spinning by doing an Internet search for "how to spin wool" or getting books from your public library. If there is a spinners group in your area, invite a spinner to come and demonstrate how to spin.

Supplies: Raw wool

Learn to Knit: One of the most common uses of spun wool is for knitting or crocheting. Find someone to teach knitting or crocheting. Knitting is experiencing a resurgence of popularity. There are several ways knitting projects can be completed for others. See about *Guidepost's* sweater project at: www.dailyguideposts.com/help/knitforkids.asp and making prayer shawls at www.shawlministry.com.

Nature Activities

Hear from a Shepherd: Invite someone who raises sheep to visit and talk about sheep and the requirements of raising them. Ask them to bring a sheep along if possible.

Think about God's Creatures: Take a walk around the retreat center property. Learn about the creatures that live there. Watch for evidence of their homes and food supply. Talk about the ways that these creatures and their habitats can be protected.

Session One

Goal: To explore the nature of sheep

Expected Outcomes:

- Participants will become familiar with the nature of sheep

- Participants will identify with the nature of sheep

- Participants will be able to name some reasons sheep need shepherds

Supplies: 3" χ 5" cards, bags of M & M's, copies of True and False activity, large sheep, markers

1. PREPARATION

Prior to meeting, choose three to five animals that make a distinctive, familiar noise and write the name of that animal on 3" χ 4" cards. Make enough cards of each animal so each person will have one. Before people arrive, place a card on each chair.

Make large sheep cutouts for each small group. You can use the sheep pattern found at the end of this section. To make it larger, project it on a wall and draw around it. The finished sheep can be as large as 18" χ 25".

On each small group table place a bowl of M & M's, the large cutout of a sheep, a copy of the True and False activity, and markers.

2. ANNOUNCEMENTS

After dinner has been finished, gather the group together in a circle of chairs with the open space in the middle. Welcome everyone to the retreat and introduce all the leaders for the weekend. Be sure that everyone knows the schedule for the evening, where the bathrooms are, and what time you will be finished. Take care of any hospitality needs and/or announcements.

3. INTRODUCTION TO THE THEME

Introduce the weekend theme of sheep and shepherds. Remind participants that references to sheep and shepherds appear throughout Scripture and were familiar images to the people of biblical times. However, they are less familiar to us and so we need to learn about the nature of sheep and the work of shepherds to fully understand these frequent references. Explain that during the course of the weekend they will be learning about sheep and those who care for them, as well as looking at some familiar scriptural passages.

4. Singing

Choose several songs from the "Suggested Songs," the "Other Songs" found in the "How-to" chapter, or sing some of your own favorites.

5. Community Building

Join the Circle: Invite participants to learn about one another by playing the game. Explain that you will name a category and everyone who can answer yes will come to the middle of the circle. Read the statements one at a time and let people come to the center of the circle.

- If you drove more than 10 miles to get to the retreat

- If you have jeans on

- If you have sneakers on

- If you have blue eyes

- If you were born after 1990

- If you exercised today

- If you ate a candy bar today

- If you were born before 1955

- If this is your first (give name of church) retreat

- If you are here to have fun

Barnyard Shuffle: Point out the index cards on each chair in the circle. Explain to the participants they are to make the noise of the animal and to find all the other people in the group making the same noise. Once all the same animals have found each other, have the groups take turns making their noise. Have the groups of common animals find a table and sit down together. Caution them not to eat the M & M's until you tell them.

6. SMALL GROUPS

Introductions Game: Once everyone is in a small group sitting around a table, encourage each person to take some M & M's. Once everyone has taken some M & M's, explain that they are to each tell something about himself or herself for each M & M they have taken. Have them go around the table and say one thing about themselves and eat an M & M. Since some will take many M & M, you can call time when most everyone has eaten his or her M & M's.

True and False on Sheep: Call attention to the "True and False" sheet on the table. Ask each group to work together and decide whether each statement is true or false. When all the groups are finished, let the groups call out their answer to the statement.

(Answers for True and False: 1. True; 2. True; 3. False; 4. True; 5. False; 6. True; 7. True; 8. False; 9. True; 10. False.)

Reasons Sheep Need Shepherds: Point out the large sheep form on the tables. Encourage the group to work together to make a list of the ways sheep need the care of shepherds. Give them time to write the lists and then invite them to share what they have written. Thank everyone for participating. Post the sheep form on the wall of the meeting space for the remainder of the retreat.

7. ANNOUNCEMENTS

Explain that it is time for evening worship that they will be returning to the circle of chairs or to another worship area of your choice. Before letting the group move for worship, be sure everyone knows what will happen after worship such as snacks, campfire, games, etc., and what time breakfast will be in the morning. Be sure that youth and children know about lights out expectations for their age group. If the retreat center asks guests to set tables for meals, identify some people to come early in the morning to do that.

Session Two

Goal: To explore the nature of shepherds

Expected Outcomes:

- Participants will become familiar with the work of shepherds
- Participants will examine references to sheep and shepherds in Psalm 23
- Participants will share what they learned about sheep and shepherds

Supplies: Bibles, newsprint, construction or drawing paper, markers and/or crayons

1. PREPARATION

Set up the room in the same manner used in Session One. Put out Bibles, paper, markers and/or crayons on each small group table.

2. ANNOUNCEMENTS

Introduce newcomers. Be sure that participants who arrive for the day on Saturday morning get welcomed and introduced. Have them make a nametag and invite them to add their square to the "Sheep Quilt."

Review the morning schedule and find volunteers for setting tables at lunch, if needed.

3. SMALL GROUPS

As the participants are sitting in the circle of chairs following worship, give them instructions for Session Two activities. Explain that retreat participants will be getting back into their small groups from Session One. In those groups they are to:

Hear the Psalm: Have the small groups begin by reading Psalm 23 again using one of the translations used during worship or their own Bibles. Encourage them to notice the actions of the shepherd. Ask: What does the shepherd in the psalm do? How does he care for the sheep? What needs of the sheep does the shepherd meet?

Make a List: Have them record the actions on newsprint and to compare that list with the one they made on the sheep shape on Friday evening.

Prepare a Response: Explain that each group is to prepare an interpretation of the psalm as a skit, song, dramatic reading, picture, etc.

4. Large Group

After about 30 minutes, gather everyone back to the circle of chairs and invite each group to share their interpretations of Psalm 23. Discuss what they have learned so far about sheep and shepherds. Ask: Why are shepherds necessary to the care of sheep? What did you learn about shepherds today you did not know? What new things did you learn about God's care? Why do you think this is such a wonderful image for humans and God?

5. Announcements

Remind everyone of time for lunch. Remind the table setters when they need to set tables. Review the plans and arrangements for afternoon. If the group will be traveling away from the retreat center, be sure everyone knows when cars/buses will leave and when they will be returning.

Session Three

Goal: To explore the image of Jesus as Good Shepherd
Expected Outcomes:

- Participants will consider the ways in which God's care is like that of shepherds

36

- Participants will identify the promises of the Good Shepherd

- Participants will respond creatively to the image of the Good Shepherd

Supplies:

Clay Center: Clay, pieces of 12" χ 12" heavy cardboard (you can cut from boxes)

Litany or Prayer Center: Newsprint, markers

Banner Center: 60" χ 36" burlap or white fabric, fabric glue, assorted felt and/or fabric, fabric markers

Music Center: Newsprint, markers, staff paper, piano, guitar

Paint Center: Watercolors, brushes, water, watercolor paper

1. PREPARATION

Use the small group tables to set up Activity Centers and put out the art supplies as listed above.

2. INTRODUCTION TO THE CONCEPT OF GOOD SHEPHERD

Read John 10:3-18 and talk about the image of the Good Shepherd. Encourage participants to remember the characteristics of sheep they learned in Session One and those of shepherds they learned about in Session Two. Invite retreat participants to share what it means for Jesus to be their Good Shepherd. Ask questions such as:

How is Jesus like a good shepherd?

How does Jesus care for his sheep? Why do they need care?

When you hear that Jesus is your Good Shepherd what images come to mind?

What does it mean to you that Jesus is your Good Shepherd?

3. ACTIVITY CENTERS

Explain to the retreat participants that they will have a chance to make a creative response using a variety of artistic expressions to the idea of Jesus as Good Shepherd. Tell them that they do not have to stay in their regular small groups. Point out the variety of art supplies on the tables and explain that they can make:

- A litany or prayer of thanksgiving
- A banner
- A song
- Clay shapes/figures
- Watercolor paintings

4. LARGE GROUP

Give group members a chance to work with the art supplies as they choose. After about 30-40 minutes, encourage everyone to display his or her creations. Invite anyone who wishes to share any new insight about the image of Jesus as the Good Shepherd they gained through this activity. Have participants circulate among the tables to see what has been created.

5. ANNOUNCEMENTS

Be sure everyone knows when and where Evening Worship will begin. If you are going to read the Christmas story during Evening Worship, use the break between the activities and worship to invite some retreat participants to act out the parts as you read or tell the story.

Session Four

Goal: To plan worship
Expected Outcomes:

- Participants will work together to develop one element of closing worship

- Participants will remember what they have learned about sheep and shepherds

- Participants will celebrate their time together

Supplies: On small group table put out all the creative expressions—songs, litanies, banners, etc.—created during Session Three, Bibles, hymnals or songbooks, an Order for Worship

1. PREPARATION

Use the same setup as on Friday and Saturday

Write the Order for Worship (see below or adapt from your own tradition) on newsprint or poster board.

> Call to Worship
>
> Music
>
> Confession (if part of your tradition)
>
> Music (hymn or special music)
>
> Scripture
>
> Interpretation of Scripture
>
> Prayers
>
> Offering
>
> Music
>
> Closing

2. ANNOUNCEMENTS

Explain the arrangements for getting out of the sleeping and meeting spaces. Be sure everyone knows what to do with linens, where brooms and/or vacuums are located if groups are required to clean, and where trash and recycling go. Let everyone know what to do with luggage.

Encourage everyone to complete an evaluation form. Be sure they know where they are and what to do with them when they are completed.

3. SMALL GROUPS

Have small groups from Session One and Session Two get together. Explain that each group will choose an element of worship they want to plan and lead during worship. Here are the assignments for worship for groups to plan.

1. Set up of the worship space

2. Music (hymns or special music)

3. Reading or telling of the Scripture (John 21:1-17)

4. Interpretation of the Scripture

5. Prayers (more than one group can work on different prayers)

6. Offering

Show the groups the Order for Worship you have written and let them choose the part of worship for which they want to be responsible. When the groups have chosen, write their names on the order of worship. Tell the groups they have about 30 minutes to work together in their preparation for worship. Remind the groups that they have created a variety of artistic expressions (songs, litanies, banners, etc.) and that they can use these as part of worship.

Be sure everyone knows where worship will be held—within the circle of chairs, in a chapel space, or outdoors somewhere else on the site.

Encourage the groups to take a few minutes during their time together to bring closure to the group. Encourage them to pray together, affirm the gifts of others, or take turns saying what the retreat has meant to them.

Worship One

Call to Worship

L: Let us worship God.

Singing

Sing several of the "Suggested Songs" or use some of your own favorites.

Scripture (Psalm 100)

Read the psalm responsively. Invite one of the participants to read the part of the Leader.

L: Make a joyful noise to the Lord, all the lands!

P: Serve the Lord with gladness! Come into his presence with singing!

L: Know that the Lord is God! It is God who has made us, and we are God's.

P: We are God's people, the sheep of God's pasture.

L: Enter the gates of the Lord with thanksgiving and God's courts with praise

P: For the Lord is good.

L: God's steadfast love endures forever,

P: And God's faithfulness to all generations.

Prayers for the Night

Invite the participants to make their prayers of thanksgiving for the blessings of the day and to make requests for those not at the retreat. Close with the Lord's Prayer.

Singing

Sing several of the "Suggested Songs" or use some of your own favorites.

Dismissal

L: The God of peace be with us.

P: Amen.

L: Bless the Lord.

P: The Lord's name be praised.

Worship Two

Opening Words

    L: Satisfy us with your love in the morning

    P: And we will live this day in joy and praise.

Singing

Sing several of the "Suggested Songs" or use some of your own favorites.

Scripture

Invite several retreat participants to read Psalm 23 from several translations of the Bible. You can also have someone read a children's book on the psalm and arrange for someone to sing a musical version.

Unison Prayer

    All: Be present with us this day, dear Lord. Teach us to be your people, the sheep of your hand, ready to do your will and eager to share your love. Lead us through your Spirit that we may be followers of Jesus Christ, our Good Shepherd. Amen.

Worship Three

Call to Worship

    L: Come away to Bethlehem. Come today.

    P: Come on bended knee and listen for the angel songs.

    L: Come away from the sounds of the world to quiet and peace.

    P: Be filled with wonder and awe.

    L: Sing with joy! Praise God!

    P: Sing the great news of the Good Shepherd!

Scripture (Luke 2:8-20)

Encourage the volunteers to act out the story as you read or tell it.

Christmas Carols

While Shepherds Watched Their Flocks by Night—vs. 1

Angels, from the Realms of Glory—vs. 2

What Child Is This?—vs. 1

The First Noel—vs. 1

Silent Night! Holy Night!—vs. 2

O Sing a Song of Bethlehem—vs. 1

Any other Christmas carols that mention sheep and/or shepherds

Prayer for the Night

Invite the participants to make their prayers of thanksgiving for the blessings of the day and to make requests for those not at the retreat. Close with the Lord's Prayer.

Dismissal

L: The God of peace be with us.

P: Amen.

L: Bless the Lord.

P: The Lord's name be praised.

True and False

1. Sheep will graze a field down to the roots.   True False

2. Sheep butt their heads against fences and through
   fences to get to greener grass.   True False

3. It is unusual for sheep to have twins and triplets. True False

4. Sheep are prone to intestinal parasites, foot rot
   and infestation of maggot and lice in their skin.   True False

5. Sheep like to flock together.   True False

6. When frightened, sheep will run off a cliff to get
   away from the perceived danger.   True False

7. If one or two sheep in a line jump over a stick,
   the remaining sheep will also jump whether the
   stick is present or not.   True False

8. Sheep are shorn twice a year.   True False

9. Cheese is made from sheep milk.   True False

10. Sheep like to drink from moving water.   True False

Sheep for Nametags and Session One

Come to the Waters

Biblical and Theological Introduction

Water is all around us. We drink cool water when we are thirsty; take hot showers when we are dirty; boil, steam, and stew our food when we are hungry; swim in pools and sail on oceans when we play. Listening to the sounds of water falling over rocks calms us, and walking beside a mountain lake renews us. Seventy percent of the earth's surface is covered with water; 70% of our bodies are composed of water. The earth is watered by snow and rain. Too little water falling from the heavens creates deserts and droughts. The raging waters of a tsunami or hurricane spread havoc across everything in their path, changing the lives of everyone it touches.

Contemporary peoples have assumed that water will always be fresh and clean and present in the quantities they require. However, the impact of modern life frequently poisons the fresh water supply. Pesticides, detergents, and factory sewage entering field runoff have polluted many of the rivers and lakes of this land. Dams have diverted the course of water flow restricting it so that it can be used by one group of people, robbing others of it original course. The damage done to ground water has crept into bays and oceans, killing creatures of the deep and depleting their food supply. The misuse of water in one place has had global consequences.

Throughout history and across cultures, water has been used to transform the ordinary into the holy. It is understood as the source of life and valued for its inclusion in religious rituals. Used for purification and understood as a symbol for death and life, water flows across the chasm between our lives and those things that hover beyond our understanding.

As Christians it is impossible to read either the Old or New Testament without encountering stories of water in which God acts and humans respond. In the beginning, God created out of nothing. On the first day, the divine hovered over the waters, separating the dry land from the waters. When the people of God's hand turned away from God and sinned, God sent a flood over the whole creation, saving only two of each kind. When the Hebrews suffered in slavery in Egypt, God rescued them by dividing the waters of a great river; at the end of their wilderness wandering, they crossed another great river into the land of God's promise.

At the beginning of his ministry, Jesus' first act was to be baptized in the river Jordan by his cousin John. Throughout the next three years, time and time again, Jesus sat beside the Sea of Galilee teaching and healing. With his fishermen disciples he rode in boats, slept through storms, and walked on the water. He compared making disciples to fishing. On the eve of his death, Jesus commissioned his followers to baptize in his name. We hear in the second chapter of Acts that the new church began its life as a unique community of believers by baptizing 3,000 people on the day of Pentecost.

So from the beginning of the church, Christians have marked the entry into the community of faith through baptism. The form and practices have changed over the years and across denominations. In the early centuries of the church, those wishing to become part of the church studied for two or three years before they could participate in the celebration of the Lord's Supper. Finally on Easter morning, they put on new, white robes and were baptized by being covered by the water. Afterward they were led into worship and joined with others in the Supper of our Lord.

This practice changed over the years when it became the common practice to baptize infants and confirm adults into membership in the church. At the time of the Reformation, the Anabaptists declared that only those who could make a confession of faith should be baptized, challenging the practice of infant baptism.

The everyday uses of water deepen our understanding of baptism. As water washes dirt and grime from our bodies and cleanses them, so the church has understood that in baptism we are cleansed from our sin. Water has the power to both take life and to give life. Paul explained that in baptism we die with Christ and are raised to new life in him. Whether baptism is through sprinkling, dipping, or immersion, we believe that we are given new life and welcomed into the community of faith. In baptism, God acts on our behalf transforming us into new creatures and calling us to take a part in the ministry of the church. Some faith communities understand baptism as the ordination of each Christian into the ministry of Christ.

Retreat Resources

Suggested Songs: "Put Your Hand in the Hand," "Down by the Riverside," "Michael, Row Your Boat," "Here Comes Jesus," "Fill My Cup," "Wade in the Water," "Row, Row, Row," "Cool Waters," Peace is Flowing Like a River," "Peace Like a River," "As the Deer"

Supplies:

Colorful cloth or quilt
a fresh plant
Bibles
a small towel
a large earthenware bowl filled with
    water
pictures cut from magazines and
    photos of water and water
    scenes
blue paper
scissors

glue or glue sticks
markers
copies of the worship order used in
    your church for baptism
newsprint
music paper
piano
guitar
60" χ 36" burlap or white fabric
fabric glue
assorted felt and/or colored fabric

fabric markers
large white construction paper
crayons
watercolor paints
brushes
finger paints

CD player
CD of soft music
colored 3" χ 5" index cards
tape
butcher paper

Worship Center: In the center of the circle create a worship center on a low table. Place on it a colorful cloth or quilt, a fresh plant, a Bible, a small towel, and a large earthenware bowl filled with water.

Welcome Activities:

Nametag: Use blue paper to create nametags using the wave shape found at the end of this section.

Get Acquainted: Ocean Collage

As people are gathering, invite them to complete a wave for the ocean collage. Have them use the water photo or picture they have brought or one of the ones provided and glue it onto a "wave." Invite them to cut the picture so it fits over the wave in an interesting way. Encourage the participants to write their names on the "wave" and to identify the picture or what he or she likes about the picture. Hang the complete "waves" so they fit together using mounting putty or pushpins.

Supplies: Pictures cut from magazines and photos of water and water scenes, blue paper in assorted hues cut in the wave shape found at the end of this section, scissors, glue or glue sticks, markers

Arts and Crafts

Try out Watercolors: Use a brush to stroke water on watercolor paper. Then use watercolors to paint. Notice the effect the water has spreading the paint.

Supplies: Watercolor paints, water, brushes

Try out Finger Paints: Use finger paints to paint a picture. Try having soft music while you paint.

Supplies: Finger paints, paper, CD and CD player

Nature Activities

Take a Walk: Walk beside a lake, pond, or river at the retreat center. Notice the plants that grow along the shore. Sit quietly and listen to the sounds of the water.

Take a Swamp or Creek Walk: If there is a swampy area or creek at the retreat center, consider talking a walk into the swamp or creek. Notice the feel of the water, rocks, and mud. Pay attention to the plants that grow near or in the water and any evidence of creatures that live here. Be sure to consult with the retreat center staff about any requirements of the center. As a precaution, have everyone wear old shoes.

Do Water Experiments: Do some experiments with water. You can get books with ideas and directions in the juvenile section of the public library.

Find out about the Watershed: Invite a local county extension or 4-H agent to visit and to tell you about your local watersheds. Find out where the watershed is, what the dangers are to the system, and what you can do to protect it.

Session One

Goal: To think about the importance of water in our lives

Expected Outcomes:

- Participants will work together as a group.
- Participants will have fun.
- Participants will think about all the ways they use water.

Supplies: Newsprint and markers for each group

1. PREPARATION

Set up the room with a circle of chair and small group tables with six to eight chairs. Place a piece of newsprint and markers on each small group table.

2. ANNOUNCEMENTS

After dinner is finished, gather the group together into the circle of chairs. Welcome them to the retreat. This is a good chance to introduce all the leaders for the weekend and to take care of any hospitality needs and announcements. Be sure everyone knows the schedule for the evening, where bathrooms are, and what time you will be finished.

3. INTRODUCTION TO THE THEME

Introduce the weekend theme of water and baptism. Explain that during the weekend the focus will be on the uses for water and the Christian tradition of baptism. Time will be spent thinking about the many ways in which we use water, looking at both scriptural understanding of baptism and the church traditions related to baptism.

4. SINGING

Choose several songs from the "Suggested Songs", the "Retreat Songs" found in the Retreat Information chapter or sing some of your own favorites.

5. COMMUNITY BUILDING

> **Play "Have You Ever . . ."**: Stand in the middle of the circle and be sure that there are the same numbers of chairs in the circle as there are people. Remove any extra chairs. Explain that you—or anyone who will stand in the circle during the game—will complete the sentence "Have you ever . . ." with something he or she has done. Everyone in the circle who has done this will get up and try to find another chair in the circle.

The person who is left over without a chair will come to the center of the circle and continue the game. Play five to seven rounds of the game.

Mingle, Mingle, Mingle: Invite the participants to stand up and be ready to move around the room. As they mingle with one another, invite them to roll their hands around (like they're washing their hands) and chant, "Mingle, Mingle, Mingle." Explain that when you call out "stop" (or ring a bell) they are to form small groups of four or five. At that time you will give them a topic to talk to one another about. Make the topics comfortable subjects for people who may not know one another well to talk about such as:

- Favorite food

- Best-loved pet

- House where lived at age seven

- Favorite thing about your church

- Favorite kind of water

Each time, give the groups about five minutes to talk and then call "Mingle, Mingle, Mingle" again. Repeat the process, asking them to talk about another comfortable topic.

After the group has mingled for three or four cycles, have the small groups get into larger groups of six to ten, depending upon how many participants there are, and to find a table where they can all sit down together. Be sure that the groups include participants of all ages.

6. SMALL GROUPS

Play "I am . . .": Have the small groups formed at the end of the "Mingle, Mingle, Mingle" sit together at a table. Invite them to get to know one another by playing, "I am __(name)_____ and I am ____(a descriptive word beginning with the same letter as their first name)____. Then make a motion that also describes you. Go around the table and have each person say name, descriptive word, and motion. The next person will say his or her own name and the name, descriptive word, and action of everyone who has gone before them.

Make a Water List: Explain they are to brainstorm a list of everything for which water is used. Remind them that in brainstorming all ideas are acceptable. Give out newsprint and markers to each group for the group's responses. Encourage them to have fun making the lists, including silly as well as serious uses of water. This is not a competition between the groups about who can make the longest list—although the groups will probably have fun trying to outdo one another!

Share with Others: When all the groups have had a chance to complete their list, invite them to share them one at a time with the whole group. Thank everyone for participating. Post the lists on the wall of the meeting space for the remainder of the retreat.

6. ANNOUNCEMENTS

Before you break up for worship, explain what will happen after worship, such as snacks, campfire, games, etc., and what time breakfast will be in the morning. Be sure that youth and children know about lights out expectations for their age group. If the retreat center asks guests to set tables for meals, identify some people to come early in the morning to do that.

Session Two

Goal: To explore what Scripture has to say about baptism.
Expected Outcomes:

- Participants will become familiar with several biblical passages about baptism

- Participants will think about the biblical understanding for baptism

- Participants will make a symbol for baptism

Supplies: Bibles, newsprint, colored markers, construction paper, scissors, glue

1. PREPARATION

Put out supplies on each small group table. Write the biblical passages on 3" χ 5" cards and place one or two on each small group table.

2. ANNOUNCEMENTS

Be sure to welcome and introduce any participants who arrive for the day on Saturday morning. Assign these people to a small group and introduce them to the other members of the small group. Encourage that group to tell them about Friday evening and show them the list of water uses they made.

3. FOCUS ON THE THEME

Invite the group to look back on the list for uses of water they made in Session One. Ask them to call out some of the uses for water they named. Remind them that water is used for drinking, cooking, play, cleaning, and maintaining life in plants. The New Testament tells about the way water was used for baptism because it cleans and brings life. Explain that this morning they will be looking at some of the different passages about baptism to learn more about it.

4. SMALL GROUPS

Read the Scripture: Invite participants to gather around a table in the same small groups they formed in Session One. Explain that on the table are 3" χ 5" cards with biblical passages about baptism. They will have 30 minutes to look up the passages and discuss what the passages have to say about baptism. What is said about water? What does it say about baptism?

John the Baptist (Mark 1:1-8)

Jesus' Baptism (Matthew 3:13-17)

Acts (Acts 2:37-42)

Philip and the Eunuch (Acts 8:26-40)

Paul on putting on Christ (Galatians 3:27-28)

Paul on death and rising (Romans 5:3-4)

Great Commission (Matthew 28:16-20)

One Baptism (Ephesians 4:5)

Make a Symbol: Invite the small groups to design a symbol or image for baptism based on the biblical passages they read. Have them draw or make the symbol on construction paper. Encourage them to be ready to tell the rest of the community about their symbols and why they chose them.

5. LARGE GROUP

Gather the groups back together. Invite them to share the passages they read and what they found out about baptism. Have them share the symbol they made for baptism. Ask: What new thing did you learn about baptism? What are the images of baptism you made? Why is water a good symbol for baptism?

6. ANNOUNCEMENTS

Remind everyone of time for lunch and the table setters of the time they need to set tables. Review the plans and arrangements for afternoon. If the group will be traveling away from the retreat center, be sure everyone knows when cars/buses will leave and when they will be returning.

Session Three

Goal: To create a visual or spoken resource to be used in baptism.

Expected Outcomes:

- Participants will have a chance to use their creativity

- Participants will have a chance to work together as a group

- Participants will respond creatively to their understanding of baptism

Supplies: Copies of the worship order used in your church for baptism, newsprint, markers, music paper, piano, guitar, 60" x 36" burlap or white fabric, fabric glue, assorted felt and/or colored fabric, fabric markers, large white construction paper, crayons

1. PREPARATION

Set up the Activity Centers as follows and put out the needed supplies.

A Baptism Song (newsprint, markers, music paper, piano, guitar)

Litany for Baptism (newsprint, markers)

A Baptismal Banner (60" x 36" burlap or white fabric, fabric glue, assorted felt and/or colored fabric, fabric markers)

A Story about baptism for children (newsprint or large white construction paper, markers, crayons)

2. FOCUS ON THE THEME

At the end of the break have participants gather back in the large circle of chairs. Invite them to discuss the meaning of baptism. Ask questions such as: What does it mean to be baptized into the community of faith? How does baptism change us? How do we practice baptism in our church? Why? Be ready to discuss your denomination's understanding of baptism and/or to read through the service for baptism used in your tradition. Role-play a baptism using the service of worship used in your church. Invite the community to discuss what happened. What did you notice? What surprised you?

3. ACTIVITY CENTERS

Explain to the participants that they will now have a chance to gather in groups by interest and to make resources they can use in their church for baptisms such as:

- A Baptism Song

- Litany for Baptism

- A Baptismal Banner

- A Story about baptism for children

Put out supplies for their creations and mingle among the groups as they are working. When the time is up invite the groups to share what they have created. Hang the banner, songs, and litanies in the worship area.

4. ANNOUNCEMENTS

Be sure everyone knows when and where Evening Worship will begin.

Session Four

Goal: To understand the meaning of being Christ's baptized people
Expected Outcomes:

- Participants will name place they can go, people they can tell, things they can teach

- Participants will pray for each other.

- Participants will understand about being commissioned to do Christ's ministry.

Supplies: Green, red, and yellow 3" x 5" index cards, mounting putty or tape, pens, butcher paper or brown paper

1. PREPARATION

Set up the room with a circle of chairs and small group tables. Put out green, red, and yellow index cards and pens on each small group table.

Hang a large piece of butcher paper or brown wrapping paper on the wall of the meeting space. Write "Great Commission Board" on the top of the paper.

2. ANNOUNCEMENTS

Explain the arrangements for getting out of the sleeping and meeting spaces. Be sure everyone knows what to do with linens, where brooms and/or vacuums are located if groups are required to clean, and where trash and recycling go. Let everyone know what to do with luggage.

Encourage everyone to complete an evaluation form. Be sure they know where they are and what to do with them when they are completed.

3. FOCUS ON THE THEME

Remind the participants that they have been commissioned to live as disciples at baptism. Read the Great Commission in Matthew 28:19-20. Explain that according to this charge of Jesus, each of us has been commissioned to do three things: to Go, to Teach, and to Make Disciples. Talk about what they think each of those things mean.

4. SMALL GROUPS

Point out the Great Commission board. Have participants return to their original small groups. Give out green, red, and yellow 3" x 5" index cards. Invite each person to write:

- On a green card one place they can go
- On a red card one thing they can teach
- On a yellow card one person they can tell about Jesus

When everyone in the group is finished writing on the cards, encourage them to share what they have written with one another. As a group, have them post their cards on "Great Commission" board. Encourage them to return to the table and to share one thing they have liked about the retreat, and to pray for one another as a group.

Worship One

Call to Worship

L: See what love God has given to us, that we should be called Children of God and so we are.

Singing

Sing several of the "Suggested Songs" or use some of your own favorites.

Scripture (Genesis 1:6-10; Matthew 3:1-17)

Remember Baptism

Invite participants to come forward and to dip their hands in the water and to remember their baptism.

Prayer for the Night

Invite the participants to make their prayers of thanksgiving for the blessings of the day and to make requests for those not at the retreat. Close with the Lord's Prayer.

Singing

Sing several of the "Suggested Songs" or use some of your own favorites.

Blessing

L: The peace of God be with you.

P: And also with you.

L: Go in peace

P: Amen.

Worship Two

Supplies: A Video/DVD player or projector and screen or TV, DVD or Video of Godspell.

Singing

Sing several of the "Suggested Songs" or use some of your own favorites.

Scripture (Mark 1:1-8)

Reflection on the Scripture

Show section of *Godspell* about the baptism of Jesus at the beginning of the film.

Prayers of the People

Invite participants to share their prayers of thanksgiving and intercession.

Singing

Sing several of the "Suggested Songs" or use some of your own favorites.

Worship Three

Call to Worship (Psalm 104)

L: You set the earth on its foundations, so that it shall never be shaken.

P: You cover it with the deep as with a garment; the waters stood above the mountains.

L: You make springs gush forth in the valleys; they flow between the hills,

P: Giving drink to every wild animal.

L: By the streams the birds of the air have their habitation; they sing among the branches.

P: From your lofty abode you water the mountains; the earth is satisfied with the fruit of your work.

Singing

Sing several of the "Suggested Songs" or use some of your own favorites about water.

Scripture

There are many stories involving water in both the Old and New Testaments.

Choose one of these stories to be acted out. Use your own imagination and make the skit as simple or elaborate as you wish. Another option is to give each small group a story and let them each act out the stories.

Noah and the Flood (Genesis 6:11-15; 19-22; 7:17-19, 24; 8:13, 1-19; 9:11-17)

Crossing the Red Sea (Exodus 14:19-30)

Jonah and the Whale (Jonah 1:1-3:10)

Storm on the Lake (Mark 4:35-41)

Jesus Walking on the Water (Matthew 14:22-33)

Evening Prayer

All: God of Water, pour out your blessings on us this night as we rest this night under the blanket of your stars. Be with those who worry or suffer or work this night. Give them your peace and fill them with the hope of your presence. Amen.

Worship Four

Worship Set up/Preparation: Hang the banner where it can be seen and display litanies or songs written earlier by the group.

Call to Worship

L: See what love God has given to us, that we should be called Children of God and so we are.

Singing

Sing several of the "Suggested Songs" or use some of your own favorites.

Prayer

Use the baptismal litany or song the group wrote in the morning.

Scripture (1 Peter 2:9)

Invite retreat participants to share their response to the Scripture and what they have found meaningful about the retreat.

Singing

Sing several of the "Suggested Songs" or use some of your own favorites.

Blessing

L: The peace of God be with you.

P: And also with you.

L: Go in peace

P: Amen.

Waves for Nametags and Wave Collage

Shine the Light

Biblical and Theological Reflection

Think for a moment what would happen if the sun were to burn out. What would happen without the light and warmth and fire from the sun? What would be left? Scientists tells us that without the light of the sun, the earth would be cold—perhaps even frozen—and without life. Plants, animals, and humans are completely dependant on the sun for light and for the energy that that light brings with it. Without it, there would be nothing!

Genesis tells us that before God began to create that is exactly what there was—nothing—a formless void, filled with darkness. Knowing that before there could be any form of life, God create the light first. Interestingly, God did not do away with the darkness but separated it with the light. Before anything else was called into being, God, knowing that the rest of creation depended upon it, made the light.

Once there was light, God went on to create the many forms of life—fish to swim in the waters, animals to creep and walk across the dry land, plants to grow upon the earth. Finally, God made humans in God's own likeness. But first, God made light.

God called the light Day and the darkness Night. In every period of twenty-four hours, the earth spins once on its axis and revolves around the sun, bathing each place on earth with light followed by darkness. Our lives are governed by this rhythm of day and night, light and darkness. During the day, we work and build community and play. In the darkness, we sleep and rest. When we use the night for work or fun, then we must replace God's light with an artificial one such as a candle, lamp, or gaslight.

Light travels in a straight line at a speed of 186,282 miles per second. Nothing in the universe travels faster. Even at that rate it takes eight and a half minutes for light to make the journey from the sun to the earth. We know its speed during a storm when lightning flashes seconds before we hear the thunder.

Light gives us sight as it bounces off of objects and reflects into our eyes where our brains translate the images into information. We are unable to see in the darkness because there is no light to reflect on objects and shapes. Within each ray of light is the whole spectrum of colors—yellow, orange, red, green, blue and violet. We see this spectrum of colors when sunlight shines through raindrops making a rainbow.

Light, broken into different lengths, reacts chemically with silver to make photographs, enables plants to create their own food, brings warmth, and burns—or tans—our skins. Within the electromagnetic spectrum of light are the long, medium, and short waves of radio and TV signals. Light as short rays passes through bone and muscle as X-rays; shorter gamma rays are radioactive and dangerous.

Since light is life, it is not surprising that Scripture would refer to God and God's actions as light. The people of Israel were in captivity in Babylon, far from God's favor and the land of Canaan that God had given to them. Into this time of great darkness comes the promise of God's light. "Arise, shine; for your light has come." (Isaiah 60:1) The promise of this light was the return to their land and a restoration of God's blessings.

When the writer of John's Gospel spoke of Jesus, he called him the Light. John the Baptist was portrayed as the one who declared the coming of the Light. Later in John's Gospel, Jesus says of himself, "I am the light of the world. Whoever follows me will never walk in darkness but will have the light of life." (John 8:12)

In a biblical sense, light is a sign of God's presence and the energy of God's abundant life. The church—as the people of God—is called to carry that light into the world. Jesus reminds the people listening to the Sermon on the Mount that they are the "light of the world." The writers of Ephesians and 1 John remind Christians that they are children of light and called to live in a way that is a pleasing to God.

In the first centuries of the church, new Christians were given a candle as a sign of their new faith as they were led into worship. The light of the candle was a reminder that now they too were the light of the world. Today's church continues to light candles to remember that Christ is the Light of the world and that Christians are called to carry that Christ's light into places of darkness.

Retreat Resources

Suggested Songs: "I Am the Light of the World," "Jesus is the Light," "Shine a Little Light," "Light the Fire," "Into His Marvelous Light," Those Who See Light," "This Little Light of Mine," "Rise and Shine" (chorus), "Shine, Jesus, Shine," "Take My Hand, Precious Lord," "Pass It On"

Supplies:

Colorful cloth or quilt
several candles of different sizes
a circle of florist foam
small candles such as those used
    for Advent
candle shields that come with
    Advent candles or the pattern
    for candle shields found at the
    end of this section
fine tipped markers
scissors
cereal box puzzles
3" χ 5" cards
plastic or wooden building blocks
dice

different kinds of wrapped candy
Bibles
construction or drawing paper
markers and/or crayons
poster board
glue
magazines
yellow paper or index cards
pencils/pens
double boiler
spoon
candle wicks
metal wick tabs
candle wax
dry sand

Worship Center: In the center of the circle create a worship center on a low table. Place on it a colorful cloth or quilt, several candles of different sizes, a circle of florist foam large enough for the candles of each retreat participant. Depending upon the number of people attending the retreat you may need two circles of foam.

Welcome Activities

Nametags: On yellow paper, make nametags using the flame shape found at the end of this section.

Get Acquainted: Decorate a Candle Holder

Supplies: Small candles such as those used for Advent, candle shields that come with Advent candles or the pattern for candle shields found at the end of this section, fine-tipped markers, scissors.

As people are gathering, invite them to decorate a candle shield. If you use the purchased shields, have the retreat participants turn them over to the blank side. If you use the pattern included here, be sure to cut a hole beforehand in the center for candle. Invite everyone to draw a picture of light or a light source on the shield and to sign his or her name. When the shields are complete, give each person a candle and point out the worship center. Encourage them to place their candles into the foam or sand.

Crafts

Make a Candle: Mix enough water with the sand so it is damp and put it into a container about six inches high and six inches wide. Make a hole in the sand. Melt the wax and pour it slowly over a metal spoon into the hole. Continue to add wax until the hole is completely filled. Dip the wicks into the melted wax and set aside to harden. When the wicks are hard, insert the end of each wick into a metal wick tab and place a wick into candle. When the wax has hardened, trim the wicks to $\frac{1}{2}$ inch. Dig out the candle and brush off the loose sand.

Supplies: Double boiler, spoon, scissors, candlewicks, metal wick tabs, candle wax, dry sand. You can find candle-making supplies at a craft store.

Draw with Charcoal: Collect charcoal from the fireplace or fire circle at the retreat center or purchase drawing charcoal at the craft store. Try out drawing a picture on white paper with the charcoal.

Nature Activities

Do Experiments with Light: Do some experiments with light. You can get books with ideas and directions in the juvenile section of the public library.

Learn about Forest Fires: Invite a forest ranger or county extension agent to come and tell about forest fires. How they start, the changes they cause, and how to prevent them.

Go Star Gazing: Lie down on blankets or tarps in a flat open place at the retreat center. Enjoy the stars. Use a book to identify the constellations.

Session One

Goal: To think about the role of light in our lives

Expected Outcomes:

- Participants will get to know one another

- Participants will think about the differences between light and dark

- Participants will work together in small groups

Supplies: Cereal box puzzles, 3" x 5" cards, plastic or wooden building blocks, dice, different kinds of wrapped candy

1. PREPARATION

Set up the room with a circle of chairs and small group tables. Collect six to ten cereal boxes—depending upon how many groups of six to eight participants you will have. Cut off the fronts and then cut the fronts into six to eight puzzle pieces. Put the puzzle pieces in a basket.

Write the following topics on 3" χ 5" cards; make a set for each small group.

- Your favorite music group

- Your favorite recent movie

- A place you would like to visit someday

- Your favorite place to sit in the sun

- Your favorite food

- Your favorite TV show

- Something you like to do in your spare time

- A person you admire

Place a wrapped candy for each participant and one dice on each small group table. Arrange the cards in a circle on the table facedown.

Collect a variety of plastic and wooden building blocks in a box for each table. Do not put them on the table until after the first small group activity.

2. ANNOUNCEMENTS

After dinner has been finished, gather the group together in a circle of chairs with open space in the middle. Welcome everyone to the retreat. This is a good chance to introduce all the leaders for the weekend and to take care of any hospitality needs and announcements. Be sure that everyone knows the schedule for the evening, where the bathrooms are, and what time you will be finished.

3 Introduction to the Theme

Introduce the weekend theme of light. Explain that during the retreat the focus will be on light both as image for God and Jesus and for sharing the good news. Time will be spent thinking about the many ways in which we depend on light, looking at both scriptural understanding of light and the church's commission to be those who hold up Christ's light for all the world to see.

4. Community Building

Singing: Choose several songs from the "Suggested Songs," the "Retreat Songs" found in the How to Use chapter, or sing some of your own favorites.

Line Up: Have the participants line up according to their birthdays. Begin with January 1st on the left side of the meeting space and continue through December 31st on the right side. Participants may not speak while they are lining up, and must figure out how to communicate their birthdates non-verbally. When everyone finds a place, have the group count off beginning on January 1.

Cereal Box Puzzles: Pass out the cereal box puzzles so everyone has a piece. Explain to the participants that they are to circulate until they find all the other pieces of the cereal box puzzles. Then have the groups find a small group table and sit down.

5. Small Group

Play a Game: Point out to the small groups the dice, candy, and cards on their tables. Explain that they are to take turns throwing the dice and answering the questions on the card. Have the person whose birthday is closest to today begin. Tell that person to throw the dice and then use one wrapped candy to count off the cards—left to right. Have the person turn over the card and tell something about him or herself related to the topic on the card. He or she should leave the candy on the card. The next person throws the dice and counts the cards beginning on the next card. Continue the game until everyone has had two or three turns.

Make a Source of Light: Pass out the boxes of building blocks to each table. Explain that the group is to work together to construct a source of light. When the groups are finished, invite each small group one by one to show what they have created to the whole group.

6. ANNOUNCEMENTS

Explain that it is time for evening worship and that they will be returning to the circle of chairs. Before letting the group move for worship, be sure everyone knows what will happen after worship such as snacks, campfire, games, etc., and what time breakfast will be in the morning. Be sure that youth and children know about lights out expectations for their age group. If the retreat center asks guests to set tables for meals, identify some people to come early in the morning to do that.

Session Two

Goal: To reflect on what the Bible says about light

Expected Outcomes:

- Participants will read and study several Bible passages about light
- Participants will plan and share a creative way to explore one of the passages
- Participants will have opportunity to see the creative expression of other groups

Supplies: Bibles, construction or drawing paper, and markers and/or crayons

1. PREPARATION

Use the same set up as Session One.

Write the following biblical passages on the 3" χ 5" cards and distribute among the small group tables so each group has a different passage.

Genesis 1:1-5; 14-19

Isaiah 9:2b-6

Isaiah 60:1-3

John 1:1-5

John 8:12

Ephesians 5:8-14

1 John 1:5-7

Put out Bibles, the 3" χ 5" cards, construction or drawing paper, markers and/or crayons, scissors, and glue on each small group table.

2. ANNOUNCEMENTS

Be sure that participants who arrive for the day on Saturday morning get welcomed and introduced. Assign them to a small group and introduce them to the other members of the group. Encourage the group to tell them about Friday night's discussion and show them the sources of light they made.

3. FOCUS ON THE THEME

Remind the retreat participants that the image of light is used throughout both the Old and New Testaments. God promised to send light to God's people in captivity in Babylon; Jesus declared he was the light of the world. Explain that during Session Two they will be examining some of the passages about light in Scripture and seeing what they can discover about the many ways in which the Bible uses this image.

4. SMALL GROUP

Read the Scripture: Have the participants gather in the same small groups they were in during Session One. Explain that they will find a 3" χ 5" card on their table with a Scripture passage about light. Have the small groups look up and read the passages. Encourage them to talk about what the passage says about light. What is the source of light in the passage? What does the light do? What does the passage say about God? What does the passage say about humans?

Share with Others: Have each small group plan a creative way to share the message of the passage. They can make up a dance or skit, sing a song, write a poem or prayer, draw a picture or cartoon, etc.

5. LARGE GROUP

Gather the small groups back in the circle of chairs after about 30 minutes. Give each small group an opportunity to share what they have created with the whole group. Talk about what they learned about God's gift of light.

6. ANNOUNCEMENTS

Remind everyone of time for lunch. Remind the table setters when they need to set tables. Review the plans and arrangements for afternoon. If the group will be traveling away from the retreat center, be sure everyone knows when cars/buses will leave and when they will be returning.

Session Three

Goal: To think about the ways in which the church shares God's light
Expected Outcomes:

- Participants will be able to identify the five functions of the church from Acts

- Participants will identify specific ways in which the church fulfils these five tasks/functions
- Participants will create a vision of the church at work

Supplies: Magazines, glue, scissors, poster board, signs to identify each Activity Center: Worship, Proclamation, Service, Education, and Fellowship

1. PREPARATION

Set up the five Activity Centers. Put a sign on each Activity Center to mark the church task for that activity (service, proclamation, prayer, teaching, and fellowship). In each Activity Center, put a piece of poster board, markers, scissors, glue and magazines.

2. FOCUS ON THE THEME

Remind the participants that they have affirmed the goodness of light and confessed Jesus as the light of the world. Explain that now it is time to think about ways that the church can bear God's light into the world.

Read Acts 2:45-47. Encourage the participants to identify the things that the early church did. Record their responses. Help them identify five tasks of the church as service, proclamation, prayer, teaching, and fellowship.

3. ACTIVITY CENTERS

Point out the five Activity Centers, one for each task of the church. Invite the participants to choose one task of the church and go to that center; they do not need to stay in the same small groups from Session One and Two. Explain that the group at each activity center will work together to make a collage to show the ways that the church does and can do that task. Explain they can use magazine pictures, words, their own drawings, and passages from Scripture. Tell the groups that they can exchange magazines, pictures, and words with one another if they wish.

4. LARGE GROUP

Gather everyone back into the circle of chairs after about 30 minutes. Invite each activity group to share the collage they have created. Encourage them to talk about the ways they identified ways that the church can shine God's light. At the end of the sharing, hang the collages on the wall of the meeting space.

5. ANNOUNCEMENTS

Be sure everyone knows when and where Evening Worship will begin.

Session Four

Goal: To make a personal commitment to being the light

Expected Outcomes:

- Participants will reflect on their own gifts and decide a way in which to share that gift

- Participants will write down a way to use their gifts and share that with group

- Participants will celebrate the group and reach closure

Supplies: Yellow paper or index cards, pencils/pens

1. PREPARATION

Set up the room with a circle of chairs and small group tables. Gather yellow paper or index cards and pencils.

2. ANNOUNCEMENTS

Explain the arrangements for getting out of the sleeping and meeting spaces. Be sure everyone knows what to do with linens, where brooms and/or vacuums are located if groups are required to clean, and where trash and recycling go. Let everyone know what to do with luggage.

Encourage everyone to complete an evaluation form. Be sure they know where they are and what to do with them when they are completed.

3. Focus on the Theme

Remind the retreat participants that Jesus has declared that they are the light of the world and that they are to put their light on a stand so it will give light to all who see it. Explain that during Session Four they will each have a chance to decide a way they can shine Christ's light into the world.

4. Small Groups

Explain that this is a chance for each person to think of the ways he or she can hold up God's light. Pass out yellow paper or index cards and pencils to everyone. Invite the participants to circulate for about ten minutes and to look at the collages they made in Session Three. Have everyone decide one or two specific ways he or she can share his or her light and to write it on the yellow paper. Have the small groups from Sessions One and Two gather again. Invite the small group members to share what they have written with others in their small group. Encourage them to close the group time by praying for one another. Explain that everyone is to bring his or her yellow paper or index card to the closing worship.

Worship One

Setup for Worship: *Pass out the small candles that participants placed in the florist foam on the worship center and the candle shields that participants decorated when they arrived. They do not need to have their own. Invite some participants to be readers and give them the passages to read. Begin the time of worship with the lights out.*

Call to Worship

L: Jesus Christ is the light of the world, the light that no darkness can put out.

Singing

Sing several of the "Suggested Songs," such as "Sanctuary," or some of your favorite quiet songs that the participants know.

Scripture

Light the candle in the center. Have the readers light their candles as they read the following passages.

Psalm 4:6-8

Psalm 18:28 and 30

Psalm 27:1

Psalm 104:1-2

Psalm 119:105

Psalm 139:11-12

After all the passages have been read, have the readers light the candles of others.

Singing

Sing the verses of "This Little Light of Mine"

Prayer for the Night

L: Stay with us, Lord, for it is evening and the day is almost over. Scatter the darkness and make bright your church. Let us now pray together the prayer Jesus taught us, saying,

All: Our Father . . .

Blessing for the Night

L: The grace and the light of the Lord be with us, now and always.

Worship Two

Call to Worship

    L: Arise, shine, for your light has come.

    P: The new day is here!

    L: Let us rejoice

    P: And be glad in it.

Singing

Sing several of the "Suggested Songs" or use some of your own favorites.

Scripture

Read Ephesians 5:8-10. Invite participants to talk about what they think it means to live as children of the light. What does it mean to be children of the light as you live together in this retreat community today?

Prayer for the Day

    L: Gracious God, we thank you for the new day. We thank you for the light that brings warmth and comfort and life to us. Keep us open to each other and to the movement of your Spirit as we gather together today. Give us the grace to live as children of the light. Amen.

Worship Three

Meet for this worship at an outside campfire, if possible. (If not, meet around an inside fireplace.) Walk to the outdoor campfire area in the dark. Use flashlights as needed. Sit in the campfire area in the dark and listen to the sounds of the night. Look up into the stars. Light the fire and watch the way the light grows, scattering the darkness so it brightens a wider and wider area.

Singing

Sing several of the "Suggested Songs" or use some of your own favorites that participants know.

Scripture

Have different people read the following passages about stars.

- Genesis 1:16
- Genesis 15:5
- Psalm 148:1-6
- Philippians 2:14-15

Singing

Sing several of the "Suggested Songs" or use some of your own favorites that participants know.

Blessing for the Night

L: God of light, give us rest this night. Cover us with the blessings of you heavens. Watch over us and all those we love. Amen.

Follow the time of worship with fellowship. Tell campfire stories and make s'mores.

Worship Four

Preparation: Light the central candle on the worship center.

Call to Worship

L: Jesus Christ is the light of the world, the light that no darkness can put out.

P: Come, let us follow the light of Christ.

Singing

Sing several of the "Suggested Songs" or use some of your own favorites that participants know.

Scripture (1 John 1:1-7)

Proclamation

Invite the participants to share what they have learned about the light during the retreat, how they are going to carry the light after the retreat, and what has been most important to them about the retreat.

Offering

Invite the participants to make an offering of the commitments they made during Session Four to share the light. Place baskets on the worship center and invite them to come one at a time and place in the baskets the yellow paper or index card they completed. As they bring their offerings up have them take a candle and a candle shield— not their own—and light the candle by the central candle. They should then return to the circle of chairs.

Prayer of Dedication

L: God of light, you have called us your children and passed into our hands the light of Christ to share with the whole world. Bless these gifts of commitment we bring to you. Give us the strength and dedication to be faithful to what we have promised. Come with us as we leave this place and this time. Fill us with your grace. Send us out with joy to share your good news and to spread your love into all the earth. Amen.

Dismissal

L: The God of peace be with us.

P: Amen.

L: Bless the Lord.

P: The Lord's name be praised.

Have participants blow out their candles. Encourage them to take home the candle as a reminder that they are the light of Christ and the shield of someone else as a reminder that they are part of this community of light.

Nametags and Candle Shield Pattern

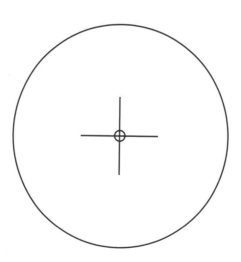

Sow Seeds of Faith

Biblical Theological Reflection

Each seed—large and small—contains everything it needs to grow into a plant identical to the one that produced it. Within each seed is the beginning of sprout and roots, food for its first growth, and a seed coat to protect it. For each seed, no matter the size, the process of growth is the same. Stimulated by warmth and moisture, the roots and sprout break through the seed coat—the roots reaching into the soil and the sprout reaching up for the sun.

As the plant continues to grow it needs the light and warmth provided by the sun, it needs the water of rain (or sprinkler), and the nourishment of soil. Without all of these in the right proportions, it cannot grow, and it will wither or rot or stay dormant.

The seed grows into a plant making its own flowers where the process of seed production is repeated. Within the flower the pollen fertilizes the plant so that new seeds are produced. The wind, birds, and insects assist in this process of moving the pollen from stamen (the male) to stigma (the female). Once the seed is formed, a fruit grows around it to protect it. Some of the fruits, like apple and peaches and grapes, are fleshy and good to each. Some fruits are dry pods like beans, milkweed, and maple, and are eaten by birds, animals, and humans.

Once the fruit is formed, the seeds are ready to be dropped into the ground where they can continue the cycle. However, there is not room under parent plants for all the seeds to grow so nature provides a way for the seeds to spread. Seeds travel on the wind—some equipped with wings to help their flight. Seeds travel in the fur of animals. Fruits eaten by animals and humans scatter their seeds in this way.

We humans also come from seeds, fertilized by males and nurtured in the womb of female. The psalmist reminds us that God formed our "inward parts" and "knit" us together in our mothers' wombs. We can rejoice that we are "fearfully and won-derfully made" and that we were "intricately woven in the depths of the earth." (Psalm 139) These words are a reminder that God knew us and was with us even there. In the Old Testament, descendants of Abraham and others were referred to as the "seed" of that person.

Like seeds in the ground, we humans also need to be nurtured and nourished so that we will grow. It is the church that provides an environment within which we can grow. It is within the company of God's people that we hear the good news of Christ's love and grace, that we learn about this God, and that we give thanks and praise to God. It is within the church that the gifts given to us for service are named and encouraged.

The first account of creation in Genesis tells us that humans were made in the image of God, in God's likeness. While this makes it clear that we are creatures and not God, it also confirms that we share with God some of the same characteristics. God put within us the ability to love, to make choices, and to create. Both versions of the creation story make clear God's intention for humans to care for the earth and its creatures. As God's people, we are to be gardeners, "tilling and keeping" (Genesis 2:15) the earth, watching over the growth of seeds.

The biblical images of seed help us to understand that we are both seeds—peo-ple of God's creation—and gardeners who nurture the growth of others. The image moves back and forth. In Matthew's account of the Parable of the Sower, Jesus says that the seed is the word of God that we humans scatter on the ground. However, it is God who brings the harvest. In Mark, Jesus says that the mustard seed is like the kingdom of God, growing from something difficult to see into a mighty thing.

The image switches in John's Gospel. Jesus says he is the vine and we are branches that bear good fruit. Paul in the letter to the church at Galatia describes our fruit in more detail, saying that the fruits of the Spirit are "love, joy, peace, patience, kindness, generosity, faithfulness, gentleness, and self-control." (Galatians 5:22-23)

Retreat Resources

Suggested Songs: "Fairest Lord Jesus," "For the Beauty of the Earth," "I Sing the Mighty Power of God," "Garden Song," "All Things Bright and Beautiful," "Morning Has Broken," "This Is My Father's World"

Supplies:

Colorful cloth or quilt

several plants

a variety of large and small seeds

one or two baskets

green paper

a variety of colorful fabric

a bowl of mixed beans

ribbon

scissors

fabric pens

a variety of seeds

zipped plastic bags

newsprint and markers

masking tape

index cards

construction and other paper

glue sticks

newsprint

copies of the BINGO game (from the
    back of this chapter) and pencils

markers (that will not bleed
    through the paper onto clothing)

CD of peaceful music

and CD player

variety of larger seeds

bowls

glue

acrylic paints

brushes

water

potting soil

small plants such as marigolds or
    violets, note cards and
    envelopes, basket, pens

Worship Center: In the center of the circle create a worship center on a low table. Place on it a colorful cloth or quilt, several plants, a variety of large and small seeds, and one or two baskets for the prayer pouches

Welcome Activities

Nametags: Use green paper to create nametags using the leaf and flower shapes found at the end of this section.

Get Acquainted: Prayer Pouches Invite each person to make a Prayer Pouch. Point out the squares of fabric, bowls of beans, and ribbon. Have each person first write his or her name on the corner of the fabric. Then have each person put about a tablespoon of seeds in the center of a fabric square and gather up the corners into a bag. Then he or she can tie the bag together using the ribbon. Encourage each person to place his or her prayer pouch in the baskets on the worship center.

Supplies: 8" χ 8" squares out of a variety of colorful fabric, a bowl of mixed beans, ribbon, scissors, fabric pens

Crafts

Seed Pictures: Put out bowls of a variety of seeds and encourage participants to use the seeds to make a mosaic or picture.

Supplies: Variety of larger seeds (dried beans work well for this), bowls, construction paper, white school glue

Paint a Pot: Invite participants to paint a small clay pot. Allow to dry, then let participants plant a small plant in the pot. They can take the plant home or to give them to someone who visits shut-in members.

Supplies: Clay pots, acrylic paints, brushes, water, potting soil, small plants such as marigolds or African violets.

Nature Activities

Go on a Hike: Take a hike on the retreat center property. Look for seeds. Collect a variety of seeds and seed pods that are not actively growing. Bring them back to the meeting space. Try to identify them. Display them on the worship center.

Do a Service Project: Make arrangements with the retreat center ahead of time for the group to do a service project such as planting flowers or a tree, raking leaves, etc. Remind the retreat participants that their fruit of their service will be enjoyed by those who come after them to the retreat center.

Supplies: Flowers, a tree, tools for project as needed.

Session One

Goal: To think about characteristics of seeds

Expected Outcomes:

- Participants will reflect on the many forms of seeds
- Participants will be able to identify a variety of seeds
- Participants will create a definition of seeds

Supplies: Bags with variety of seeds, newsprint and markers, tape

1. PREPARATION

Make bags of a variety of seeds. Use purchased seeds and put ten different kinds of seeds in small zipped plastic bags. Choose both seeds that are easily recognized, such as pumpkin and watermelon, and seeds that may be less familiar. Attach a list of the seeds to each bag. Prepare enough bags so each small group can have one. Put a bag of seeds, list of seeds, newsprint, and markers on each small group table. Make copies of the BINGO game. Place a copy of the game and a pencil on each chair in the circle.

2. ANNOUNCEMENTS

After dinner has been finished, gather the group together in a circle of chairs with open space in the middle. Welcome everyone to the retreat. This is a good chance to introduce all the leaders for the weekend and to take care of any hospitality needs and announcements. Be sure that everyone knows the schedule for the evening, where the bathrooms are, and what time you will be finished.

3. INTRODUCTION TO THE THEME

Introduce the weekend theme of seeds. Remind them that within every seed is a complete plant, exactly like other plants of its kind. God has provided everything that seeds needed to grow and produce fruit—sun, water, and nourishment. God calls each of us to grow into faithful plants and provide what we need to grow. Explain that they will be hearing some stories about seeds in scripture, considering how God nurtures their faith, and how they can nurture the faith of others.

4. COMMUNITY BUILDING

> **Singing:** Choose several songs from the "Fun Songs" list found in the back of the book or sing some of your own favorites.

> **Play BINGO:** Point out the BINGO sheet and pencils that are on their chairs. Explain that retreat participants are to move around and find someone who meets the description in each square. That person then writes his or her name in the square. Encourage them to find out one another's names and one other piece of information about themselves. Tell them to call out "Bingo" when they have filled all the boxes. After about 15 minutes call a halt to the game if no one has called out "Bingo." Ask, "How many have many filled all 25 squares? 20 squares? 15 squares? etc.

Mingle, Mingle, Mingle: Invite the participants to stand up and be ready to move around the room. As they mingle with one another, invite them to roll their hands around (like they're washing their hands) and chant, "Mingle, Mingle, Mingle." Explain that when you call out a number, they are to form groups of that size. Explain that when they are in groups, you will give them a question to talk about with one another.

- Groups of 8: What is your favorite tree/plant/flower?

- Groups of 4: Imagine it is summer. What would you put in a garden-fresh salad?

- Groups of 6: Where is your favorite place to go outdoors and why?

- Groups of 6-8: Describe a beautiful garden you have seen or know. How do you feel when you are in that garden?

Have these last groups of eight find a table and sit down.

5. SMALL GROUP

Introductions: Have each member of the group introduce himself or herself again by saying his or her name, a favorite plant that begins with the same letter, and a reason he or she likes that plant.

Identify Seeds: Explain that each group has a bag of seeds and a list of the seeds in the bag. Tell the groups they need to work together to identify the seeds in the bag. When the groups are finished, call for attention. Invite the group members to identify the seeds for the whole group so small groups can check how well they did.

Write a Definition of Seed: Then have each group write a definition of a "seed" on the newsprint. Invite the groups one by one to share their definitions. Hang the definitions on the wall of the meeting space.

6. ANNOUNCEMENTS

Explain that it is time for evening worship and that they will be returning to the circle of chairs. Before letting the group move for worship, be sure everyone knows what will happen after worship such as snacks, campfire, games, etc., and what time breakfast will be in the morning. Be sure that youth and children know about lights out expectations for their age group. If the retreat center asks guests to set tables for meals, identify some people to come early in the morning to do that.

Session Two

Goal: To reflect on the ways in which seeds grow

Expected Outcomes:

- Participants will remember the story of creation

- Participants will identify the elements in nature that God created

- Participants will demonstrate the way in which seeds are nurtured

Supplies: Index cards, construction and other paper, markers, scissors, glue sticks, newsprint and markers, tape

1. PREPARATION

Use the same setup as on Friday evening. Put Bibles, construction or drawing paper, and markers and/or crayons on each table.

2. ANNOUNCEMENTS

Introduce newcomers. Be sure that participants who arrive for the day on Saturday morning get welcomed and introduced. Have them make a nametag and invite them to make a Prayer Pouch.

Review the morning schedule and find volunteers for setting tables at lunch, if needed.

3. FOCUS ON THE THEME

Explain to the participants that each seed contains within it everything needed to make a new plant exactly like the one it came from. However, to grow the seed needs the elements of sunlight, water, soil nourishment, and cultivation. It is the nurture of these elements that helps seeds grow into plants. Tell them they will be looking at the first creation story in Genesis, thinking about the elements God created, and compare the nurture of seeds to the nurture of the church.

4. SMALL GROUP

Read Scripture: Tell each small group that they have a section of Genesis 1, the first creation story, to read. Explain that particular resources that seeds/plants need to grow are named in each section. Have the groups read their section of the story and identify the natural resource that plants need to grow highlighted in the passage.

- Light and dark (Genesis 1–5)

- Water (Genesis 6–8)

- Dry Land and Vegetation (Genesis 9–13)

- Seasons (Genesis 14–19)

- Creatures (Genesis 20–25; 29)

- Humans (Genesis 26–31; 2:15)

Focus on Each Particular of Seed/Plant Growth: Once the group has identified the element: light and dark, water/rain, soil/food, seasons, connections to creatures, and human cultivation and care, have them talk about what this element adds to seed/plant growth. What contribution to growth does this element make? What happens to the seed/plant if it is robbed of this resource? How is it connected to the other elements? What does the creation and the interconnections tell us about God? What are the ways that God nurtures our faith through the church in ways that are like these natural elements?

Prepare to Tell: Explain to the small groups that they are to prepare a skit, song, or poem about their resource and its role in the growth of seeds. Talk about the ways in which the church nourishes and nurtures our faith.

5. LARGE GROUP

Using the resources in the order they were created, have the small groups share their part of the story of the growth of a seed/plant. After all the groups have share, invite the participants to share any new insights they had about the growth of seeds and plants. Ask, "How does God nurture our faith in the same way that these natural resources nurture seeds?"

6. ANNOUNCEMENTS

Remind everyone of time for lunch. Remind the table setters when they need to set tables. Review the plans and arrangements for afternoon. If the group will be traveling away from the retreat center, be sure everyone knows when cars/buses will leave and when they will be returning.

Session Three

Goal: To reflect on what kind of fruit you are like

Expected Outcomes:

- Participants will be able to identify a plant and fruit that they are like
- Participants will ponder the ways they are like their chosen plant
- Participants will affirm one another's gifts

Supplies: Colored construction paper, markers (that will not bleed through the paper onto clothing), masking tape, CD, and CD player

1. PREPARATION

Put colored construction paper and markers on each of the small group tables.

2. FOCUS ON THE THEME

Read John 15:5, 8. Explain that you are going to help everyone think about what kind of seed/plant they are. Be sure that everyone understands he or she can open his or her eyes anytime. Invite everyone to sit comfortably and close his or her eyes.

Say, "Imagine you are a seed. What do you see, feel? What kind of seed are you? Imagine you are growing, breaking through the soil. What do you see/feel? What is happening to you? Imagine you are growing into a plant. What kind of plant are you? What do you look like now? What do you see/feel? Imagine that you are making flowers. What do they look like? How do you see/feel? Imagine you are making fruit. What kind of fruit are you? How do you look? How do you taste? What is wonderful about you? What do you have to offer to other people? What do you like most about being a fruit? Imagine now the seeds that are part of your flower or fruit. What do they look like? What happened to them? How do you feel when the seeds return to the ground?"

Invite the participants to open their eyes when they are ready.

3. LARGE GROUP

Point out the paper and markers on the tables around the room. Invite the participants to get a piece of paper, to write their name and the name of their fruit and to draw a picture of the fruit. Remind the participants that affirmation and encouragement are one of the ways that we can nurture the faith growth of one another. Have them help one another to hang the pictures on their backs with tape. Invite everyone to move around the meeting space and to write words of encouragement and affirmation on the pictures. Test out the markers ahead of time to be sure they do not bleed onto clothing. As the participants are moving around, play some peaceful music.

After about 20-30 minutes, encourage everyone to take the pictures off their backs and to look at what others have said about them. Hang the pictures on the wall of your meeting space.

Session Four

Goal: To deepen our understanding of God's call to be fruitful
Expected Outcomes:

- Participants will reflect on their own call to service

- Participants will make a commitment to use their gifts in service

- Participants will pray for one another

Supplies: Note cards and envelopes, basket, pens

1. PREPARATION

Provide small, plain note cards with matching envelopes. Place note cards, envelopes, and pens/pencils on each small group table.

2. FOCUS ON THE THEME

Remind the participants that just as each flower and plant has its own gift and place in creation, so each of them has gifts and purpose within creation. Explain that during this session they will be considering their gifts and how they can best use these gifts. Tell them that the fruit they choose in Session Three and the affirmations and comments of others are clues to their individual gifts. In this session they will be considering those gifts and how they can use them in service to God.

3. SMALL GROUPS

Ask participants to get the picture of fruit they made in Session Three off the wall and to gather in their small groups from Session One and Two. Encourage each group member to tell why they chose the fruit they did and what they have discovered about their gifts. When everyone has shared, invite each person to think of a place or way they can share God's love with others. Have them write that place or way on notepaper provided and put it into the envelope. Explain that the envelopes will be placed in the offering during the closing worship. Encourage the group to close the small group time by praying for one another.

4. ANNOUNCEMENTS

Explain the arrangements for getting out of the sleeping and meeting spaces. Be sure everyone knows what to do with linens, where brooms and/or vacuums are located if groups are required to clean, and where trash and recycling go. Let everyone know what to do with luggage.

Encourage everyone to complete an evaluation form. Be sure they know where they are and what to do with them when they are completed.

Worship One

Call to Worship (Psalm 1)

L: "Happy are those who delight in the law of the Lord. . . . They are like trees planted by streams of water which yield their fruit in its season and its leaves do not wither."

Singing

Sing several of the "Suggested Songs" or use some of your own favorites.

Scripture (Psalm 92:1-10, 12-15)

Refrain: "It is good to give thanks to the Lord"

Prayers for the Night

Pass around the baskets of the prayer pouches the participants made at the beginning of the retreat. Have them take one—not necessarily their own—and to hold the pouch during this time of prayer. Invite the participants to make their prayers of thanks-giving for the blessings of the day and to make requests for those not at the retreat. Close with the Lord's Prayer.

Singing

Sing several of the "Suggested Songs" or use some of your own favorites.

Dismissal

L: The God of peace be with us.

P: Amen.

L: Bless the Lord.

P: The Lord's name be praised.

Worship Two

Call to Worship

L: Day is done; evening has come.

P: Let us rejoice for the gifts of this day.

Singing

Sing several of the "Suggested Songs" or use some of your own favorites that praise God for the creation.

Scripture

Read the creation story in Genesis 1:1–2:3. Arrange for different voices to read each day of creation. Have the rest of the participants respond, "And God saw that it was good" after each day of creation is read.

Prayer of Thanksgiving

Invite participants to name their favorite parts of creation. Record their responses on newsprint. Use the list as a litany by reading several things on the list and then invit-ing the participants to respond, "Thank you, God, for all the good gifts of your creation."

Singing

Sing several of the "Suggested Songs" or use some of your own favorites that praise God for the creation.

Worship Three

Call to Worship (Matthew 13:31)

L: "The kingdom of heaven is like a mustard seed that someone took and sowed in his field, it is the smallest of all the seeds but when it has grown it is the greatest of all shrubs and becomes a tree, so that the birds of the air come and make their nests in its branches."

Singing

Sing several of the "Suggested Songs" or use some of your own favorites.

Scripture

Read John 15:1-6

Reflection

Invite the participants to talk about the kind of fruit they chose and why. Encourage them to bring their pictures with them to worship.

Evening Prayer

L: Great and wonderful God, we praise and thank you for the gift of grace in Jesus Christ. Tonight we thank you for the opportunity to rest and enjoy the company of one another, fun and laughter, and the signs of hope and new life that are all around us. Gracious God, we bring to your our concerns for others and name them before you now. Give us peace and rest in our sleep so that we may rise to praise you in the new day. Amen.

Singing

Sing several of the "Suggested Songs" or use some of your own favorites.

Worship Four

Call to Worship (Psalm 1)

L: "Happy are those who delight in the law of the Lord . . . They are like trees planted by streams of water which yield their fruit in its season and its leaves do not wither."

Singing

Sing several of the "Suggested Songs" or use some of your own favorites.

Scripture

Read John 6:7-11.

Reflection

Invite the participants to talk about the ways in which the retreat has been a time of growth for them and how they hope to be fruitful as they leave this place.

Offering

Invite the participants to make an offering of the commitments they made during Session Four to share their gifts. Place baskets on the worship center and invite them to come one at a time and place in the baskets the note cards they completed. As they bring their offerings up have them take a prayer pouch—not their own. Explain that following the retreat they can take home the prayer pouch to use as they pray and as a reminder of their promise to be fruitful.

Prayer of Dedication

L: God of Grace, accept these gifts we bring to you. Use us to sow the seeds of the kingdom so that through your grace the harvest will be filled with much fruit. Go with us as we return to our homes and bless us as we grow in grace. Amen.

Dismissal

L: The God of peace be with us.

P: Amen.

L: Bless the Lord.

P: The Lord's name be praised.

Nametags

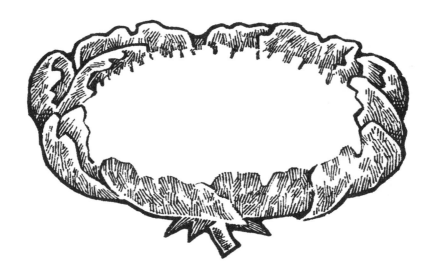

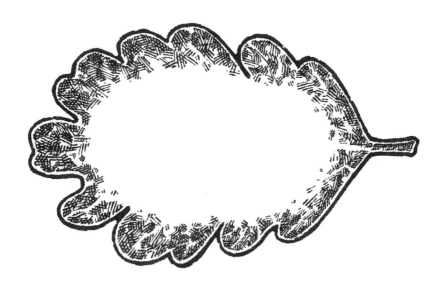

Bingo Game

Find someone who . . .

B	I	N	G	O
Uses the same kind of toothpaste	Was born in the same state	Knows your state's flower	Likes the same music group	The tallest person in the group
Has traveled to another country	Is *not* wearing blue jeans	Has never had a garden	Speaks another language beside English	Planted a vegetable garden last summer
Can name six common flowers	Likes broccoli	Has slept in a tent	Knows the Latin name for a plant	Has more than 5 children
Has seen a redwood tree	Grows flowers	Has the same color eyes as you do	Owns a hoe	Was born outside the United States
Has ordered plants online	Has been to Williamsburg	Is retired	Likes strawberry ice cream	Has the same birthday as you

Each person can only sign one square

Claim Your Name

Biblical and Theological Reflections

We are each known and called by our names. Across all cultures it is a custom to name babies when they are born. Names distinguish us from others. Names are a symbol of who we are. Names define and identify us. Names recognize our placement within a family system. Our name makes us unique from all others.

The Hebrews—of both Old and New Testament—believed that in addition to all of this a name expressed a person's personality. Therefore, if a person's name was changed the person became different. In Scripture, we have many accounts of people to whom God spoke by name—and even in some cases, changed their name. The name of Abram, which means "exalted father," was changed to Abraham, which means "father of the multitudes" [*Harper's Bible Dictionary*, ed. Paul J. Achtemeier (San Francisco: HarperSanFrancisco, 1985), p. 6] and is reflective of his role as the father of the nation of Israel. His son, Jacob (meaning "supplanter" [*Harper's*, p. 443]) was renamed Israel—meaning "may God rule." Later in the New Testament we hear that both Simon and Saul received new names after they decided to follow Jesus. Peter—"the rock"—became one of the organizers of the church after Jesus' resurrection. When we first meet Saul, he is called by the Aramaic version of his name, and later called Paul, the Roman version of his name, perhaps signifying his call to spread the good news of Christ throughout the Roman world.

The most commonly used name for God in the Old Testament is represented by the letters YHWH and is pronounced "Yahweh." However, to recognize the holiness attached to the name, the title "Adonai" ("My Great Lord") was said instead. When written, "Adonai" was combined with YHWH to remind readers to pronounce it "Adonai" in place of Yahweh. When translated into English, the letters YHWH became "Lord." A variety of other names were also used for God in Old Testament writings. (*Harper's*, p. 685)

When Moses met God at the burning bush, he asked God to tell him God's name. God's response to Moses is usually translated, "I am who I am." However, the words in Hebrew have been the source of much discussion among scholars about exactly how to translate them. Of more importance than the correct grammatical construction is what this incident has to tell us about God. Here is a God who wants to enter into a personal relationship with a particular people.

A relationship is created anytime we tell one another our names. Think about being some place where no one knows your name. There is often a feeling of anonymity, of being an outsider, of distance, or of being left out. On the other hand, there is a sense of welcome, of belonging, of inclusion, of vulnerability that goes along with the use of our name. A sense of community is created where we are called by our names.

It is not an accident, therefore, that the church has created traditions by which new members are welcomed into the community of faith. At baptism and infant dedication, a child or adult enters into the community by name. Within this family of faith, we are never anonymous but always persons with a name, "Child of God." During these traditions of welcome, the community accepts the responsibility of integrating the new member and of teaching him or her the meaning of being a member of this community.

As we make ourselves vulnerable when we tell our names to each other, God made the Godself vulnerable when Moses asked for God's name. In the response of

"I am who I am," God was demonstrating a willingness to be in relationship with humans. At the burning bush, God first called Moses by name and then cemented the relationship by revealing the divine name. God's actions in the following days, months, and years showed Moses and all of Israel the meaning of this relationship. God overcame the power of Pharaoh, led the people of Israel out of the slavery of Egypt and into the blessings of a new land.

In the New Testament, Jesus is called by a variety of names: Son of God, Messiah, Teacher, Son of Man, Good Shepherd, etc. The names used by the gospel writers for Jesus reflect their understanding of both his personhood and his ministry.

We continue to recognize the power of using God's name whenever we pray "in Jesus' name", baptize in the "name of the Father, Son, and Holy Spirit," or even when we swear, taking God's name in vain. We recognize the power of names when we gather together and begin the process of introducing ourselves—moving from being an outsider to belonging.

Retreat Resources

Suggested Songs: "His Name Is Wonderful," 'Jesus, Name Above all Names," "He Calls Us Each by Name," "Glorify Your Name," "Lord, I Lift Your Name on High," "In His Name," "His Name is Jesus," "There's Something about That Name," "Here I Am"

Supplies:

A colorful cloth or quilt	2" χ 4" address labels
a book of names	colored dots
candle	yarn
construction paper	basket
markers	Bibles
glitter	markers and/or crayons
tissue paper	3" χ 5" cards
a variety of stickers	pen
book of names for each small group	12" × 12" piece(s) of wood

acrylic paints

brushes

digital or Polaroid camera

printer

photo paper

scissors

a large branch

bucket of sand

fishing line or yarn

brown paper

mounting putty

historical documents about your
    church

photos

old bulletins and/or newsletters

poster board

glue

fabric dye

five-gallon plastic buckets (one for
    each color)

salt (if required)

white t-shirts

rubber bands

rubber gloves

butcher paper

scissors

access to a copy machine

hymnals

music paper

pencils

musical instruments

certificates (see page 122)

Worship Center: In the center of the circle create a worship center on a low table. Place on it a colorful cloth or quilt, Bible, a book of names, and a candle.

Welcome Activities

Nametags: Make nametags using the six-sided shape found at the end of this section

Get Acquainted: Mosaic Use the pattern found at the end of this section to cut six-sided "mosaics" from different colored construction paper. Invite each person to sign his or her name on a hexagon and to decorate in whatever way they he or she would like. Arrange a mosaic as you hang them on the wall of the meeting room with mounting putty or pushpins.

Supplies: Construction paper, markers, glitter, tissue paper, a variety of stickers

Crafts

Try Tie-Dyeing: Follow the manufacturer's directions to prepare the dye. (You may need to add one cup of salt to the dye bath or use a separate bath depending upon the dye you use.) Prepare one or two colors of dye baths. Have participants bunch together plain white t-shirts with rubber bands. Dip the bunches into the dye bath as many times as you wish. Remove the rubber bands and let dry. Remind everyone to wash and dry the shirts to set the dye before wearing them. Each shirt is unique just as each of us is unique.

Supplies: Fabric dye, five-gallon plastic buckets (one for each color), salt (depending on type of dye), white t-shirts, rubber bands, rubber gloves

Autograph a Shirt: Before the retreat ask everyone to bring a plain t-shirt. Using permanent markers, everyone can autograph one another's shirts. If you tie-dyed shirts, use those for autographs.

Draw a Self Portrait: Let retreat participants try their hand at drawing a self-portrait using pastels or chalk. If there is someone familiar with cutting silhouettes, let participants try this form of making a portrait of each other.

Nature Activities

Find It by Name: Find a book with the names and pictures of plants or animals or insects in your area. Take a hike and use the book to locate plants, animals, or insects. Look up their names.

Scavenger Hike: Make the list of the items found around the retreat center. The retreat center staff can help you with this. Divide into teams and have a scavenger hunt. Be sure that everyone knows the boundaries of the game and that the children have adult supervision. See which team can find the most items.

Find Out the History: Invite a staff member or board member of the retreat center to tell about the history of the retreat center. If there are buildings and places with special names, find out about these names and how they got them. Take a hike to visit special places at the retreat center.

Session One

Goal: To explore the idea that God calls us each by name
Expected Outcomes:

- Participants will think about their own names

- Participants will have played community-building games

- Participants will get to know one another by name

Supplies: Construction paper, markers, a book of names for each small group, 2" x 4" address labels, colored dots, yarn, basket

1. PREPARATION

Set up the room with a circle of chairs and small group tables. Cut yarn into 15" lengths and put them into a basket. Put out construction paper, markers, and a book of names on each small group table. Prepare labels for "Who Am I?" Put familiar names from the Bible on labels. Use a different colored marker for every six to eight labels or place dots of different colors on the labels. These will be used for small group assignments. Ask one or two people to put the labels on the backs of participants as they arrive for Session One. Encourage them to mix age groups within the small groups.

2. ANNOUNCEMENTS

After dinner has been finished, gather the group together in a circle of chairs with the open space in the middle. Welcome everyone to the retreat and introduce all the leaders for the weekend. Be sure that everyone knows the schedule for the evening, where the bathrooms are, and what time you will be finished. Take care of any hospitality needs and/or announcements.

3. INTRODUCTION TO THE THEME

Introduce the weekend theme of names. Remind participants that each of us has a name and that our names distinguish us from everyone else. They identify us as unique individuals and tell what family we belong to. Giving a child a name is something parents often spend a lot of time to decide. Explain that during the retreat they will be thinking first about their own names and then about the names of people in the Bible. God called these people and us by name and invites us to follow. During the retreat, participants will be thinking about God's call to them.

4. COMMUNITY BUILDING

Singing: Choose several songs from the "Suggested Songs," the "Retreat Songs" found in the Retreat Information chapter or sing some of your own favorites.

Who Am I?: Explain to the participants that they each have a label on their backs. Each label has the name of a person from the Bible. Have everyone circulate and figure out whose name is on his or her back. They can only ask yes or no questions to find out and can only ask each person one question at a time. When they have guessed the name on their backs have them move the label to the front and continue to answer questions to help others guess. Play until everyone has guessed who he or she is. Be sure to tell the participants not to discard the labels because they will use them for another activity later.

Community Rope: Remind the group that during the time of the retreat they will all be part of one community and will be called by their names within that community. Each person is both an individual and a member of the community. Explain that to symbolize this, the group will be tying together a community rope. Pass around the basket of 15" piece of yarn. Hold your piece of yarn, say your first name and your community last name, "Child of God." Tie your piece of yarn to the piece of the person to your right. That person also says his or her first name and the community last name, "Child of God." That pattern is continued around the circle until the yarn returns to you. Do not tie the two ends of the yarn together. Roll the yarn into a ball and place the ball on the worship center as a sign of the community.

Point out that the name labels used in "Who Am I?" are printed in different colors or have different colored dots on them. Have participants circulate and find others with the same colored nametag or dots. Then have small groups find a table and sit down.

5. SMALL GROUP

Name Anagram: On the construction paper have each person write his or her name down the side of the paper. Explain that beside each letter of his or her name, he or she is to put something about himself or herself beginning with each letter. When everyone in the group has completed the anagram, encourage them to share them with the other members of the small group. Invite them to talk together about where they got their name and what it means. Encourage groups to look up their names in the name book on the table.

Choose a Group Name: Explain that each small group will be together for several sessions during the retreat. Invite them to choose a name for the group and to create a group cheer or rap to tell others about the name they have chosen. When all the groups have chosen a name and created a cheer or rap, give each group a chance to tell their name and to share their cheer or rap.

6. ANNOUNCEMENTS

Explain that it is time for evening worship and explain they will be returning to the circle of chairs. Before letting the group move for worship, be sure everyone knows what will happen after worship such as snacks, campfire, games, etc., and what time breakfast will be in the morning. Be sure that youth and children know about lights out expectations for their age group. If the retreat center asks guests to set tables for meals, identify some people to come early in the morning to do that.

Session Two

Goal: To explore stories of biblical characters

Expected Outcomes:

- Participants will become familiar with the stories of biblical characters God called by name

- Participants will find a creative way to tell that story

- Participants will hear about God's personal call

Supplies: Bibles, markers and/or crayons, 3" x 5" cards, pen,

1. PREPARATION

Use the same setup as Session One. Put Bibles on each small group table. Write the names of the following biblical characters and the passage from the Bible on the 3" x 5" cards and put one on each small group table:

Moses (Exodus 3:1-12)

Jeremiah (Jeremiah 1:1-10)

Samuel (1 Samuel 3:1-10)

Saul/Paul (Acts 9:1-19)

Zechariah about John the Baptist (Luke 1:5-17, 57-63)

Lydia (Acts 16:13-15)

2. ANNOUNCEMENTS

Introduce newcomers. Be sure that participants who arrive for the day on Saturday morning get welcomed and introduced. Have them make a nametag and invite them to add their hexagon to the group mosaic. Review the morning schedule and find volunteers for setting tables at lunch, if needed.

3. FOCUS ON THE THEME

There are many stories in the Bible that tell about God calling a person by name and asking that person to do something for God. Sometimes God even changed the person's name so his or her name would reflect God's call. During this session the participants will explore some of those stories and learn more about the people that God called.

4. SMALL GROUP

> **Read the Scripture:** Explain that each group has been given a biblical character to find out about. Each of the characters was given a name by God and called into relationship with God and the community of God's people. Have the group read about the biblical character.

> **Talk about the biblical character:** Have the group talk about the character. What was he or she like? What did God call him or her to do? What did this character do? If you could meet this character what would you like to ask that person?

> **Develop a Way to Tell the Story:** Explain to the group that they are to prepare a way to tell the story of the biblical character to the other groups. Some of the ways they can tell that story are: first-person storytelling, a newspaper interview, a cartoon, a mural, a song or rap, or a skit.

5. LARGE GROUP

After about 30 minutes, gather everyone back to the circle of chairs and invite each group to introduce its biblical character. Discuss what the characters have in common and what is different about their stories.

6. ANNOUNCEMENTS

Remind everyone of time for lunch and when the tables need to be set. Review the plans and arrangements for afternoon. If the group will be traveling away from the retreat center, be sure everyone knows when cars/buses will leave and when they will be returning.

Session Three

Goal: To express the meaning of being a "Child of God"

Expected Outcomes:

- Participants will reflect on the children of God who have come before them

- Participants will remember those who have come before them

- Participants will use a creative medium to express their membership in community of God's children

Supplies:

Family Plaques: 12" χ 12" piece(s) of wood, acrylic paints, brushes, pencils, paper

Family Tree: Digital or Polaroid camera, printer, photo paper, scissors, a large branch, bucket of sand, fishing line or yarn, brown paper, mounting putty

Your Church's Story: Historical documents, photos, old bulletins and/or newsletters, poster board, glue, scissors, access to a copy machine

Song about Saints: hymnals, music paper, pencils, musical instruments

1. PREPARATION

Use the small group tables to set up activity centers and put out the supplies listed above.

2. Focus on the Theme

In Scripture and in the church, believers are frequently called "Children of God"—both individually and as a community. Being part of God's family—God's community—is an important part of following Jesus. It is within this community that we find out what it means to be God's child. During this session, participants will have the chance to express their understanding of what it means to be part of God's family through a variety of activities.

3. Activity Centers

Point out the four activity centers and describe what participants will do at each center. Explain that they do not need to stay in their small groups from Session One and Two but can select the center in which they would like to work.

> **Make God's Family Plaques:** Have the group design a Family of God emblem and motto. Encourage them to sketch the emblem on paper before they transfer it to the wood and paint. They can include the motto. The family shield can signify all God's family or just your congregation. The group can make one plaque as a group or each participant can make one.
>
> **Create Retreat Family Tree:** There are two parts to this project. First, take digital or Polaroid pictures of everyone at the retreat—either as individuals or family units. If you use a digital camera, you will need to arrange to print the photos. The finished photos should be 3" χ 3" or 3" χ 5". When you have the photos of everyone, then you will need to do the second step, which is to make a tree. There are two ways you can do this. You can find a tree branch that can be put into a tub of sand and placed near the worship center. If you choose this option, hang the photos from the branches using fishing line or yarn. A second way to make a tree is to create a tree shape on a wall of the meeting space using brown paper. Then arrange the photos on the branches.
>
> *Note: In preparation for this activity, you may want to designate someone*

to take pictures throughout the retreat so the photos will be ready for this activity.

Tell the Story of Your Church: Make a poster to tell an "at a glance" history of your church. Look through the gathered photos and documents and lay them out in chronological order. Decide what you want to include and how you want to arrange the history. Make copies of one-of-a-kind or old documents. You may also want to interview some of the older members of the congregation who are at the retreat to add their stories or insights to the poster. Label the documents and photos.

Learn or Write a Song about Saints: Look through the hymnals to identify songs about saints. If you find one that is not familiar to your congregation, plan a way to teach the song. Or you can write a new song. Include the names of some of the saints from church history and from your congregation. Use a familiar tune or write a new tune. Your song can be in any music style such as country, gospel, rap, etc.

5. LARGE GROUP

Give the participants about 30-40 minutes to work in the activity centers. At the end of that time gather everyone together again in the circle of chairs. Invite each group to share what they have created.

6. ANNOUNCEMENTS

Be sure everyone knows when and where Evening Worship will begin.

 ## Session Four

Goal: To hear the call to God's children today
Expected Outcomes:

- Participants will hear the story of God's call to Isaiah

- Participants will identify a place God is sending them

- Participants will pray for one another

Supplies: Certificates, pens/pencils

1. PREPARATION

Set the room with small group tables. Copy the Certificates (p. 122), cut them apart, and place on small group tables along with pens or pencils.

2. FOCUS ON THE THEME

Remind the participants of the stories they heard during Session One about the biblical characters God called by name. Explain that this is another story in which God called someone. Read Isaiah 6:1-8. Point out that Isaiah's response, "Here am I; send me!" provides a model for us. During this session everyone will have a chance to identify a call from God and the way he or she will respond. The Gift Certificates everyone will write will be dedicated during the closing worship.

3. SMALL GROUPS

Have the small groups from Sessions One and Two sit together at the small group tables. Point out the Gift Certificates and markers you have put on the tables. Explain that these are promises of gifts they will give to God. Have each person fill in his or her name and then complete the sentence, "Here Am I, Lord. Send me to _____." Encourage everyone to think of a place or situation that he or she can go for God. When everyone has completed a Gift Certificate invite those who wish to share within the small group where he or she will go for God. Encourage the groups to close this time by praying for each person by name. Ask them to bring the Gift Certificates to worship.

4. ANNOUNCEMENTS

Explain the arrangements for getting out of the sleeping and meeting spaces. Be sure everyone knows what to do with linens, where brooms and/or vacuums are located if groups are required to clean, and where trash and recycling go. Let everyone know what to do with luggage.

Encourage everyone to complete an evaluation form. Be sure they know where they are and what to do with them when they are completed.

Worship One

Call to Worship (Isaiah 43:1 NRSV)

L: "I have called you by name and you are mine."

Singing

Sing several of the "Suggested Songs" or use some of your own favorites.

Scripture

Choose two readers or two groups of readers. Make copies of the verse from Psalm 139:13-15 and Isaiah 43:1-7. Have them read one verse at time so the groups alternate.

Reflection

Invite participants to talk about what it means for God to have known them from the time they were formed in their mothers' wombs and called them by name. After some reflection, read again Isaiah 43:1. Have the participants go around the circle and repeat the verse replacing Jacob and Israel with his or her own name.

Prayer for the Night

L: God who calls us each by name, we thank you for this day. Fill us with your peace so that we may rest. Bring us to the new day filled with praise for you. Amen.

Dismissal

L: The Lord's name be praised.

P: Bless the Lord.

All: Amen.

Worship Two

Call to Worship

L: This is the day the Lord has made

P: Let us rejoice and be glad in it.

Singing

Sing several of the "Suggested Songs" or use some of your own favorites.

Scripture

Read Genesis 12:1-2; 17:1-6, 15-16.

Reflection

Invite participant to think about why God changed Abram and Sarai's names. What was God's call to Abram and Sarai? Why do you think God changed their names? What was important about this change? Can you remember some other people who were called by God and got new names? Who?

Unison Prayer

Be present with us this day, dear Lord. Teach us to be your people, the ones you have called by name. Fill us with love and give us ears ready to hear your call. Lead us through your Spirit that we may be followers of Jesus Christ in whose name we pray. Amen.

Worship Three

Preparation: Hang a large piece of butcher paper on the wall of the meeting space. Have available a lot of markers.

Call to Worship

L: At the name of Jesus, every knee shall bow and confess him Lord.

Singing

Sing several of the "Suggested Songs" or use some of your own favorites.

Scripture

Invite several readers to read the following passages.

Luke 1:26-38; 2:21

Matthew 18:20

John 1:12

John 16:23-24

Acts 3:1-9

Philippians 2:9-11

Reflection

Invite the participants to talk about what it means to call Jesus by name and to pray in Jesus' name.

Evening Prayer for Others

Have everyone gather around the butcher paper you have hung on the wall. Explain that they will make the evening prayer by writing the names of people they want to pray for on the paper. When everyone has had a chance to write, close with the following prayer:

L: Jesus, Lord, Teacher, Shepherd, Christ, we make our prayers for others. Bless and heal those whose names we have written here. We make this prayer in your strong and good name. Amen.

Dismissal

L: The Lord's name be praised.

P: Bless the Lord.

All: Amen.

Worship Four

Preparation: You will need to place basket on the worship center. Have a pair of scissors available.

Call to Worship (Isaiah 43:1)

L: "I have called you by name, you are mine."

Singing

Sing several of the "Suggested Songs" or use some of your own favorites.

Scripture

Read Isaiah 6:1-8 again.

Reflection

Invite participants to share what they have learned about God's call during the retreat.

Offering

Invite participants to bring their certificates to the worship center and place them in baskets. Ask the participants to remain standing in a circle.

Prayer of Dedication

Pick up the Community Rope that was made during Session One. Pass it to the person next to you and begin to unroll it. Cut the yarn right beyond the first knot and say,

"Here, I am, Lord. Send me."

Name a place God is sending you. Continue to pass the Community Rope around the circle until everyone has cut a piece of yarn including a knot. Encourage the participant to take the piece of Community Rope home and to hang in a place they can see it as a reminder that they are part of a community where they are called by name and that they have made a promise to God.

Singing

Sing "Here Am I" or another favorite song of commitment.

Dismissal

    L: The Lord's name be praised.

    P: Bless the Lord.

    All: Amen.

Certificate

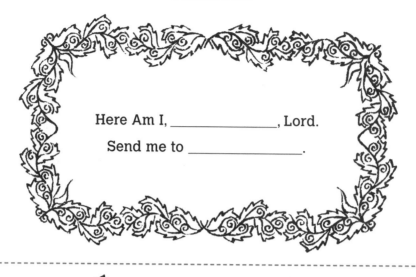

Here Am I, _____, Lord.

Send me to _____.

Here Am I, _____, Lord.

Send me to _____.

Here Am I, _____, Lord.

Send me to _____.

Nametags and Mosaic Piece

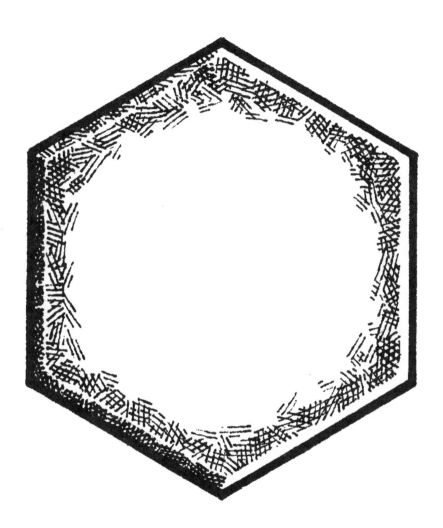